The Edge of All That Lingers

Diana Lockhart

Published by Diana Lockhart, 2024.

THE EDGE OF ALL THAT LINGERS

First edition. October 8, 2024.

ISBN: 979-8227072009

Written by Diana Lockhart.

Chapter 1: Entangled Hearts

The moment I stepped into my best friend's lavish garden party, a strange energy hummed through the air like the buzz of electric anticipation. The sun hung low, casting golden rays that danced through the leaves, illuminating clusters of vibrant blooms as if nature itself were celebrating. Jasmine filled the air with its sweet perfume, mingling with the crisp scent of freshly cut grass. Laughter bubbled around me, creating a symphony of joy that felt almost palpable. Yet, amid the laughter and swirling conversations, my gaze was inexplicably drawn to a figure standing apart from the crowd.

Michael Devereaux loomed at the edge of the festivities, an enigmatic presence that seemed to cast a shadow despite the warm glow of the afternoon. His sharp features were accentuated by the dappled light filtering through the trees, and he surveyed the guests with an expression that danced between amusement and weariness. He wore a tailored navy suit that hugged his broad shoulders, exuding an effortless charm that could have put any celebrity to shame. Yet, there was something in his stance—a hint of solitude, perhaps—that made him stand out even more than the most extravagant guests.

I was usually the type to flit about parties like a carefree butterfly, but today, I found myself tethered to the spot, rooted in curiosity. It was absurd to be so captivated by someone I barely knew, yet there was a magnetic pull about Michael that sent my heart racing in a way that felt utterly forbidden. He was a man of mystery, the kind of person who likely had a thousand stories wrapped in that brooding demeanor. And I was simply Emma—an ordinary girl with a penchant for daydreaming and a rather unfortunate history of falling for the wrong kinds of men.

"Hey, Earth to Emma!" Jess's voice sliced through my reverie, her bright red lips curled in a teasing smile. She wore a pastel sundress that flowed around her like a summer breeze, her eyes sparkling with mischief. "You look like you've seen a ghost. Or worse, you're about to start swooning over the most elusive bachelor in town."

"Very funny." I forced a smile, glancing back at Michael, who now seemed to be engaged in a conversation with a group of guests. "I just—he's interesting, that's all. Who is he, anyway?"

"Michael Devereaux," Jess replied, leaning in as if divulging a great secret. "The king of investment firms and, rumor has it, the biggest heartbreaker. But seriously, if you're going to crush on someone, at least pick someone with a better track record than that."

"Oh, come on," I protested, a hint of defiance creeping into my voice. "Just because he's got a reputation doesn't mean he's a bad guy. Maybe he's just misunderstood." I tried to sound nonchalant, but the flutter in my stomach betrayed me. "What if he's actually a nice person trapped in a world of high expectations?"

"Sure, and I'm the queen of England." Jess rolled her eyes, but her playful smirk was hard to resist. "Just don't let him catch you staring. He's the kind of guy who makes you feel like you're under a microscope when he looks your way."

As if summoned by our conversation, Michael's gaze shifted, locking onto mine with an intensity that sent a shiver down my spine. My breath caught, and for a fleeting moment, the cacophony of the party faded away, leaving just the two of us in a suspended bubble of tension. It was disarming, almost overwhelming, and I could feel my cheeks flushing under the weight of his scrutiny. I quickly averted my gaze, pretending to be deeply interested in a nearby cluster of peonies.

"See?" Jess nudged me with a grin. "He's got that whole brooding billionaire thing down to an art form. You should totally go talk to him. What's the worst that could happen? A heart-stopping moment followed by crushing disappointment?"

"Thanks for the vote of confidence." I shot her a look, my heart pounding like a drum in my chest. What would I even say? "Hey, I noticed you looking gloomy from across the garden. Want to share your life story?"

"Better than you pretending to be fascinated by those flowers." Jess smirked, her playful jab coaxing a reluctant laugh from me.

With a deep breath, I steeled myself. Why not? What did I have to lose aside from my dignity and the last shred of my common sense? Pushing my nerves aside, I smoothed down my sundress and took a step toward Michael, my heart thumping wildly with each passing second.

"Emma," I told myself, "just be yourself." I approached him, each step laden with a mixture of excitement and apprehension, ready to face whatever consequences awaited me.

"Enjoying the party?" I ventured, forcing my voice to remain steady as I drew nearer. The murmur of guests faded into the background, leaving only the sound of my heartbeat echoing in my ears.

Michael turned, his eyes narrowing slightly as he appraised me, the corners of his lips curling into an amused smile. "I suppose. It's a bit overwhelming, though," he admitted, his voice low and smooth, laced with an accent that hinted at sophistication. "Too many people, not enough intrigue."

A laugh escaped me before I could stop it—a sound that surprised even myself. "That's one way to put it. It's a bit like a circus out here, isn't it?"

He chuckled, a warm, rich sound that sent a thrill through me. "Exactly. And I'm not much for the spotlight. Too many clowns."

With every word exchanged, I felt the initial tension begin to ebb away, replaced by something far more exhilarating. Here, amidst the chaos of the party, I had found an unexpected connection, an oasis in a sea of frivolity. And as the afternoon sun dipped lower, casting a warm glow over the garden, I couldn't shake the feeling that this moment might be the beginning of something utterly unpredictable.

The moment I stepped into my best friend's lavish garden party, a strange energy hummed through the air like the buzz of electric anticipation. The sun hung low, casting golden rays that danced through the leaves, illuminating clusters of vibrant blooms as if nature itself were celebrating. Jasmine filled the air with its sweet perfume, mingling with the crisp scent of freshly cut grass. Laughter bubbled around me, creating a symphony of joy that felt almost palpable. Yet, amid the laughter and swirling conversations, my gaze was inexplicably drawn to a figure standing apart from the crowd.

Michael Devereaux loomed at the edge of the festivities, an enigmatic presence that seemed to cast a shadow despite the warm glow of the afternoon. His sharp features were accentuated by the dappled light filtering through the trees, and he surveyed the guests with an expression that danced between amusement and weariness. He wore a tailored navy suit that hugged his broad shoulders, exuding an effortless charm that could have put any celebrity to shame. Yet, there was something in his stance—a hint of solitude, perhaps—that made him stand out even more than the most extravagant guests.

I was usually the type to flit about parties like a carefree butterfly, but today, I found myself tethered to the spot, rooted in curiosity. It was absurd to be so captivated by someone I barely knew, yet there was a magnetic pull about Michael that sent my heart racing in a way that felt utterly forbidden. He was a man of mystery, the kind of person who likely had a thousand stories wrapped in that brooding demeanor. And I was simply Emma—an ordinary girl with a penchant for daydreaming and a rather unfortunate history of falling for the wrong kinds of men.

"Hey, Earth to Emma!" Jess's voice sliced through my reverie, her bright red lips curled in a teasing smile. She wore a pastel sundress that flowed around her like a summer breeze, her eyes sparkling with mischief. "You look like you've seen a ghost. Or worse, you're about to start swooning over the most elusive bachelor in town."

"Very funny." I forced a smile, glancing back at Michael, who now seemed to be engaged in a conversation with a group of guests. "I just—he's interesting, that's all. Who is he, anyway?"

"Michael Devereaux," Jess replied, leaning in as if divulging a great secret. "The king of investment firms and, rumor has it, the biggest heartbreaker. But seriously, if you're going to crush on someone, at least pick someone with a better track record than that."

"Oh, come on," I protested, a hint of defiance creeping into my voice. "Just because he's got a reputation doesn't mean he's a bad guy. Maybe he's just misunderstood." I tried to sound nonchalant, but the flutter in my stomach betrayed me. "What if he's actually a nice person trapped in a world of high expectations?"

"Sure, and I'm the queen of England." Jess rolled her eyes, but her playful smirk was hard to resist. "Just don't let him catch you staring. He's the kind of guy who makes you feel like you're under a microscope when he looks your way."

As if summoned by our conversation, Michael's gaze shifted, locking onto mine with an intensity that sent a shiver down my spine. My breath caught, and for a fleeting moment, the cacophony of the party faded away, leaving just the two of us in a suspended bubble of tension. It was disarming, almost overwhelming, and I could feel my cheeks flushing under the weight of his scrutiny. I quickly averted my gaze, pretending to be deeply interested in a nearby cluster of peonies.

"See?" Jess nudged me with a grin. "He's got that whole brooding billionaire thing down to an art form. You should totally go talk to him. What's the worst that could happen? A heart-stopping moment followed by crushing disappointment?"

"Thanks for the vote of confidence." I shot her a look, my heart pounding like a drum in my chest. What would I even say? "Hey, I noticed you looking gloomy from across the garden. Want to share your life story?"

"Better than you pretending to be fascinated by those flowers." Jess smirked, her playful jab coaxing a reluctant laugh from me.

With a deep breath, I steeled myself. Why not? What did I have to lose aside from my dignity and the last shred of my common sense? Pushing my nerves aside, I smoothed down my sundress and took a step toward Michael, my heart thumping wildly with each passing second.

"Emma," I told myself, "just be yourself." I approached him, each step laden with a mixture of excitement and apprehension, ready to face whatever consequences awaited me.

"Enjoying the party?" I ventured, forcing my voice to remain steady as I drew nearer. The murmur of guests faded into the background, leaving only the sound of my heartbeat echoing in my ears.

Michael turned, his eyes narrowing slightly as he appraised me, the corners of his lips curling into an amused smile. "I suppose. It's a bit overwhelming, though," he admitted, his voice low and smooth, laced with an accent that hinted at sophistication. "Too many people, not enough intrigue."

A laugh escaped me before I could stop it—a sound that surprised even myself. "That's one way to put it. It's a bit like a circus out here, isn't it?"

He chuckled, a warm, rich sound that sent a thrill through me. "Exactly. And I'm not much for the spotlight. Too many clowns."

With every word exchanged, I felt the initial tension begin to ebb away, replaced by something far more exhilarating. Here, amidst the chaos of the party, I had found an unexpected connection, an oasis in a sea of frivolity. And as the afternoon sun dipped lower, casting a warm glow over the garden, I couldn't shake the feeling that this moment might be the beginning of something utterly unpredictable.

Our conversation flowed like a gentle stream, weaving through topics both trivial and profound. Michael spoke with a disarming candor, sharing snippets about his life that hinted at a deeper complexity. I found myself enchanted, hanging onto his every word as he talked about his latest business venture—a bold initiative aimed at transforming sustainable practices within the city's construction industry. "It's all about the balance, you know?" he mused, his dark eyes gleaming with passion. "Building spaces that respect the environment while still serving the needs of the people."

"Sounds noble," I replied, a genuine smile breaking through my initial hesitations. "Though I suspect there are plenty of hurdles involved. Like convincing people to prioritize ethics over profits."

He smirked, a flicker of amusement dancing in his gaze. "Ah, yes, the great conundrum. Many are too wrapped up in the bottom line to notice that sustainability is the future of their business. They'll catch on eventually, or they'll be left behind."

His determination was infectious, and I felt an unexpected urge to support him, to cheer for his cause like a fan at a championship game. "I'd buy a ticket to that show," I said, my tone teasing but sincere. "But tell me, how do you find the time to manage that? You don't strike me as someone who plays by the rules of a typical workweek."

Michael leaned closer, the sunlight catching the planes of his face, casting shadows that made him look almost otherworldly. "You'd be surprised," he said, lowering his voice conspiratorially. "The key is knowing how to delegate. Besides, life is too short for boredom. Don't you agree?"

His proximity sent warmth coursing through me, and I leaned in just a fraction, drawn by the gravity of his presence. "Absolutely. I've always believed in living life to the fullest. It's just... sometimes the mundane creeps in and tries to steal the show."

"That's when you have to be your own hero," he replied, his tone shifting slightly, as if we had crossed into an unspoken territory where vulnerability thrived. "Be the one to rescue yourself from the humdrum."

I chuckled, the sound light and airy. "And here I thought I was just saving myself from another week of laundry and bills."

"Laundry?" He feigned horror. "You have no idea how hard I fought to escape that battle. My washing machine is a relic of the past. I think it might actually be older than my last two relationships combined."

I laughed again, unable to suppress the delight bubbling within me. "And how long is that, exactly?"

"Let's just say my romantic history is a little less than stellar," he admitted, a hint of shadow passing over his features. "Relationships have always been a complex puzzle for me. Sometimes it feels like I'm stuck trying to find the right pieces."

There was something disarming about his honesty, something that stirred a fierce desire within me to know more about the man behind the charming exterior. "Maybe you just haven't found the right puzzle yet," I suggested, a gentle nudge of encouragement. "Or maybe you've been too busy building a fortress around yourself to see what's right in front of you."

The air shifted, thick with unspoken understanding. Michael's expression softened, his guarded demeanor cracking just enough for me to catch a glimpse of the vulnerability beneath. "Maybe you're right," he said, his voice barely above a whisper. "Or maybe I've just been looking in all the wrong places."

Before I could respond, a sudden commotion erupted nearby, the laughter growing louder as a group of guests spilled a tray of drinks all over the pristine grass. The laughter, once a backdrop to our intimate conversation, became an eruption of chaotic energy, pulling

The moment I stepped into my best friend's lavish garden party, a strange energy hummed through the air like the buzz of electric anticipation. The sun hung low, casting golden rays that danced through the leaves, illuminating clusters of vibrant blooms as if nature itself were celebrating. Jasmine filled the air with its sweet perfume, mingling with the crisp scent of freshly cut grass. Laughter bubbled around me, creating a symphony of joy that felt almost palpable. Yet, amid the laughter and swirling conversations, my gaze was inexplicably drawn to a figure standing apart from the crowd.

Michael Devereaux loomed at the edge of the festivities, an enigmatic presence that seemed to cast a shadow despite the warm glow of the afternoon. His sharp features were accentuated by the dappled light filtering through the trees, and he surveyed the guests with an expression that danced between amusement and weariness. He wore a tailored navy suit that hugged his broad shoulders, exuding an effortless charm that could have put any celebrity to shame. Yet, there was something in his stance—a hint of solitude, perhaps—that made him stand out even more than the most extravagant guests.

I was usually the type to flit about parties like a carefree butterfly, but today, I found myself tethered to the spot, rooted in curiosity. It was absurd to be so captivated by someone I barely knew, yet there was a magnetic pull about Michael that sent my heart racing in a way that felt utterly forbidden. He was a man of mystery, the kind of person who likely had a thousand stories wrapped in that brooding demeanor. And I was simply Emma—an ordinary girl with a penchant for daydreaming and a rather unfortunate history of falling for the wrong kinds of men.

"Hey, Earth to Emma!" Jess's voice sliced through my reverie, her bright red lips curled in a teasing smile. She wore a pastel sundress that flowed around her like a summer breeze, her eyes sparkling with mischief. "You look like you've seen a ghost. Or worse, you're about to start swooning over the most elusive bachelor in town."

"Very funny." I forced a smile, glancing back at Michael, who now seemed to be engaged in a conversation with a group of guests. "I just—he's interesting, that's all. Who is he, anyway?"

"Michael Devereaux," Jess replied, leaning in as if divulging a great secret. "The king of investment firms and, rumor has it, the biggest heartbreaker. But seriously, if you're going to crush on someone, at least pick someone with a better track record than that."

"Oh, come on," I protested, a hint of defiance creeping into my voice. "Just because he's got a reputation doesn't mean he's a bad guy. Maybe he's just misunderstood." I tried to sound nonchalant, but the flutter in my stomach betrayed me. "What if he's actually a nice person trapped in a world of high expectations?"

"Sure, and I'm the queen of England." Jess rolled her eyes, but her playful smirk was hard to resist. "Just don't let him catch you staring. He's the kind of guy who makes you feel like you're under a microscope when he looks your way."

As if summoned by our conversation, Michael's gaze shifted, locking onto mine with an intensity that sent a shiver down my spine. My breath caught, and for a fleeting moment, the cacophony of the party faded away, leaving just the two of us in a suspended bubble of tension. It was disarming, almost overwhelming, and I could feel my cheeks flushing under the weight of his scrutiny. I quickly averted my gaze, pretending to be deeply interested in a nearby cluster of peonies.

"See?" Jess nudged me with a grin. "He's got that whole brooding billionaire thing down to an art form. You should totally go talk to him. What's the worst that could happen? A heart-stopping moment followed by crushing disappointment?"

"Thanks for the vote of confidence." I shot her a look, my heart pounding like a drum in my chest. What would I even say? "Hey, I noticed you looking gloomy from across the garden. Want to share your life story?"

"Better than you pretending to be fascinated by those flowers." Jess smirked, her playful jab coaxing a reluctant laugh from me.

With a deep breath, I steeled myself. Why not? What did I have to lose aside from my dignity and the last shred of my common sense? Pushing my nerves aside, I smoothed down my sundress and took a step toward Michael, my heart thumping wildly with each passing second.

"Emma," I told myself, "just be yourself." I approached him, each step laden with a mixture of excitement and apprehension, ready to face whatever consequences awaited me.

"Enjoying the party?" I ventured, forcing my voice to remain steady as I drew nearer. The murmur of guests faded into the background, leaving only the sound of my heartbeat echoing in my ears.

Michael turned, his eyes narrowing slightly as he appraised me, the corners of his lips curling into an amused smile. "I suppose. It's a bit overwhelming, though," he admitted, his voice low and smooth, laced with an accent that hinted at sophistication. "Too many people, not enough intrigue."

A laugh escaped me before I could stop it—a sound that surprised even myself. "That's one way to put it. It's a bit like a circus out here, isn't it?"

He chuckled, a warm, rich sound that sent a thrill through me. "Exactly. And I'm not much for the spotlight. Too many clowns."

With every word exchanged, I felt the initial tension begin to ebb away, replaced by something far more exhilarating. Here, amidst the chaos of the party, I had found an unexpected connection, an oasis in a sea of frivolity. And as the afternoon sun dipped lower, casting a warm glow over the garden, I couldn't shake the feeling that this moment might be the beginning of something utterly unpredictable.

Our conversation flowed like a gentle stream, weaving through topics both trivial and profound. Michael spoke with a disarming candor, sharing snippets about his life that hinted at a deeper complexity. I found myself enchanted, hanging onto his every word as he talked about his latest business venture—a bold initiative aimed at transforming sustainable practices within the city's construction industry. "It's all about the balance, you know?" he mused, his dark eyes gleaming with passion. "Building spaces that respect the environment while still serving the needs of the people."

"Sounds noble," I replied, a genuine smile breaking through my initial hesitations. "Though I suspect there are plenty of hurdles involved. Like convincing people to prioritize ethics over profits."

He smirked, a flicker of amusement dancing in his gaze. "Ah, yes, the great conundrum. Many are too wrapped up in the bottom line to notice that sustainability is the future of their business. They'll catch on eventually, or they'll be left behind."

His determination was infectious, and I felt an unexpected urge to support him, to cheer for his cause like a fan at a championship game. "I'd buy a ticket to that show," I said, my tone teasing but sincere. "But tell me, how do you find the time to manage that? You don't strike me as someone who plays by the rules of a typical workweek."

Michael leaned closer, the sunlight catching the planes of his face, casting shadows that made him look almost otherworldly. "You'd be surprised," he said, lowering his voice conspiratorially. "The key is knowing how to delegate. Besides, life is too short for boredom. Don't you agree?"

"Absolutely. I've always believed in living life to the fullest. It's just... sometimes the mundane creeps in and tries to steal the show."

"That's when you have to be your own hero," he replied, his tone shifting slightly, as if we had crossed into an unspoken territory where vulnerability thrived. "Be the one to rescue yourself from the humdrum."

I chuckled, the sound light and airy. "And here I thought I was just saving myself from another week of laundry and bills."

"Laundry?" He feigned horror. "You have no idea how hard I fought to escape that battle. My washing machine is a relic of the past. I think it might actually be older than my last two relationships combined."

I laughed again, unable to suppress the delight bubbling within me. "And how long is that, exactly?"

"Let's just say my romantic history is a little less than stellar," he admitted, a hint of shadow passing over his features. "Relationships have always been a complex puzzle for me. Sometimes it feels like I'm stuck trying to find the right pieces."

There was something disarming about his honesty, something that stirred a fierce desire within me to know more about the man behind the charming exterior. "Maybe you just haven't found the right puzzle yet," I suggested, a gentle nudge of encouragement. "Or maybe you've been too busy building a fortress around yourself to see what's right in front of you."

The air shifted, thick with unspoken understanding. Michael's expression softened, his guarded demeanor cracking just enough for me to catch a glimpse of the vulnerability beneath. "Maybe you're right," he said, his voice barely above a whisper. "Or maybe I've just been looking in all the wrong places."

Before I could respond, a sudden commotion erupted nearby, the laughter growing louder as a group of guests spilled a tray of drinks all over the pristine grass. The laughter, once a backdrop to our intimate conversation, became an eruption of chaotic energy, pulling me back to the party's frivolous pulse.

"Looks like the circus is back in town," I quipped,

Chapter 2: Glances in the Dark

The party pulsed around us like a heartbeat, a kaleidoscope of laughter, music, and swirling bodies, each person lost in their own world of revelry. But amidst the chaos, there was a stillness where I stood, locked in an unyielding gaze with Michael. He was a vision against the backdrop of twinkling fairy lights and bubbling champagne, the faintest smirk playing at the corners of his mouth. It was as if the vibrant hues of the evening dimmed, focusing all my attention on him. Every laugh that echoed through the room faded into a muffled hum, and I could only hear the pounding of my heart in response to the electric pull between us.

He leaned casually against the bar, the confident ease of his posture drawing the eye, and somehow, my thoughts fell silent. The weight of his gaze felt like a gentle pressure against my skin, warm and inviting. I had known him as Emily's father, a figure who had lingered in the background of my life—an enigmatic man whose absence had always created a strange sort of space. Yet tonight, that absence seemed to flip on its head, morphing into a magnetic presence that captivated my attention. I swallowed hard, my throat suddenly dry, battling with the sudden impulse to walk over and close the distance between us.

"Why do you look like you've just seen a ghost?" Emily's voice broke through my reverie, a teasing note lacing her tone. She materialized at my side, her hair shimmering under the soft light like spun gold, her eyes darting between me and her father.

"It's just... crowded," I replied, forcing a laugh to mask my sudden awareness of how close Michael stood, how he watched me with an intensity that sent shivers down my spine.

"Uh-huh, crowded," Emily echoed, her eyebrow arching skeptically. "You might want to stand a little closer to the bar then, so you don't faint."

A laughter erupted nearby, drawing Emily's attention, and she turned to join the fray, leaving me standing there with a growing sense of vulnerability and confusion. I shifted my weight, pretending to peruse the array of bottles displayed behind the bar. The moment was charged with a tension that felt both exhilarating and unnerving.

I risked another glance at Michael, who was now observing me with a sly smile, as if we shared some private joke. "You're avoiding me, aren't you?" he asked, his voice smooth and teasing, cutting through the din of laughter and music.

"Hardly," I countered, surprising myself with the steadiness of my own voice. "Just contemplating the merits of... um, cranberry juice over soda."

He chuckled softly, a low, rich sound that sent a ripple of warmth through me. "I'd recommend the cranberry. It pairs well with secrets."

The way he said the word "secrets" made my heart race. I shifted uncomfortably, feeling the weight of the moment settle around us like a thick fog. What was this? Flirting? A game we were playing? I had never thought of Michael in that light, always seeing him as Emily's estranged father, a ghost haunting her past. But standing there now, I could almost forget the tangled history that lay between us, just for a heartbeat.

"Your daughter is..." I began, the words stumbling over each other as I tried to keep the conversation light. "She's quite the party planner."

"She has her mother's touch," he replied, his eyes flickering with a hint of nostalgia. "She can create magic out of thin air."

The mention of Emily's mother hung in the air like a ghost of its own, a reminder of the complexities woven into their lives. I sensed a shadow passing over Michael's expression, his smile faltering for just a moment. It was an unguarded glimpse into the pain that lay beneath the surface, and my heart twisted in response.

"Do you miss her?" The question slipped from my lips before I could stop it, a soft intrusion into our playful exchange.

Michael paused, his gaze drifting past me to where Emily was chatting animatedly with a group of friends. The weight of unspoken words loomed large between us. "Every day," he admitted, his voice low and gravelly, laced with a vulnerability I hadn't anticipated. "But it's complicated. There are things... choices that led us here."

Before I could probe further, a sudden commotion erupted near the front of the house. A burst of laughter and the sound of a clattering glass broke the fragile moment. Michael glanced over, his expression shifting as the distraction pulled him away from our intimate exchange.

"Let me go check on that," he said, his tone lightening again. "Don't drown in soda or cranberry juice without me."

With a playful wink, he stepped away, disappearing into the crowd. I watched him go, my mind swirling with a mix of confusion and longing. What had just happened? It felt as if I had skated on the edge of something profound and dangerous, only to watch it slip away into the chaos of the party.

I searched the room for Emily, needing her grounding presence. There she was, laughing with her friends, blissfully unaware of the tension that had just unfolded. The lively atmosphere resumed its hold, and the vibrant energy of the party enveloped me once more. But my heart remained tethered to that moment with Michael, to the way he looked at me, as if I were the only person in the room.

As the evening wore on, I couldn't shake the sensation that something fundamental had shifted. The lines between our past and present blurred, and the possibility of a future I hadn't dared to imagine began to flicker in my mind like the lights around us, bright and yet so very precarious. What if there was more to our story? What if this night was only the beginning of a much deeper narrative waiting to unfold?

The party unfurled around me like a vibrant tapestry woven with laughter and chatter, a cacophony of joy that seemed to drown out my chaotic thoughts. As I struggled to regain my composure, I let myself be swept along by the thrumming energy, yet my mind kept returning to Michael, the magnetic force who had disrupted my evening. Each moment spent in his orbit left me breathless, yet a nagging worry lingered in the back of my mind, whispering that this was a dangerous game.

I ambled toward the refreshment table, my fingers skimming the edge of the cool marble surface. A bowl of brightly colored fruit sat invitingly nearby, and I scooped a handful of berries, letting their sweet and tart juices burst against my tongue, the taste a brief distraction from my racing heart. I needed to calm down. Michael was Emily's father, and flirting with him was like navigating a minefield blindfolded. But my internal reasoning was quickly being overrun by an unexpected thrill that accompanied his every glance.

"Are you secretly plotting world domination, or just trying to eat your feelings?" Emily's voice broke through my reverie as she sidled up beside me, her playful smirk cutting through the tension like a knife. She looked radiant, her eyes sparkling with the kind of mischief that made everyone around her feel a bit lighter.

"Just appreciating the art of berry consumption," I replied with a grin, playing along. "You know, a very serious undertaking."

She laughed, a light, ringing sound that danced in the air. "You do you. But, let's be honest, you're far too focused on that fruit to be plotting anything else. How about you join me for a dance instead?"

"I'm pretty sure I'd just embarrass myself," I admitted, glancing back toward the makeshift dance floor, where a gaggle of partygoers swayed under the twinkling lights. "Besides, I might need to avoid... certain people."

"Ah, you mean Dad?" Her tone was playful, but her expression softened. "You know, it's okay to look at him without turning into a statue. He might be a dork, but he's still my dork."

I laughed, but it felt hollow against the weight of my feelings. "That's the problem. He's not just your dad; he's a whole emotional complex wrapped in charm and mystery. It's disorienting."

Emily rolled her eyes, clearly not understanding the depths of my confusion. "Look, I get it. He has a past, but you're not dating him. You're just enjoying the company of an attractive man who happens to be my father."

"Just enjoying the company? Is that what we call it now?" I shot back, unable to suppress the grin tugging at my lips.

Her laughter was infectious, and for a moment, the cloud of uncertainty that hung over me began to dissipate. But as I glanced over Emily's shoulder, there was Michael again, standing at the edge of the crowd, the way the light caught his hair and the shadows danced across his face igniting a pulse of warmth in my chest. The urge to approach him was overwhelming, yet the warning bells in my head clamored louder.

"Hey, I'm going to go over and... do something," I blurted, my voice lacking the confidence I hoped it would convey.

Emily tilted her head, a knowing smile spreading across her face. "You mean, you're going to go and flirt with my dad? Good luck with that."

I rolled my eyes, feeling both embarrassed and liberated. "Yeah, because that's the goal, right?"

With a playful nudge, she sent me on my way, her laughter fading into the background as I navigated through the throng of people. My heart raced, a mix of excitement and apprehension fueling each step. What was I even doing? Did I really want to engage in this chaotic dance with Michael, or was I merely caught up in the moment?

When I reached him, Michael looked up from a conversation with a group of people, his expression shifting as he spotted me. The atmosphere felt charged, as if the air around us crackled with unspoken words. "I was beginning to think you'd vanished into the berry bowl," he said, his smile widening.

"I almost did. Those berries are surprisingly captivating," I replied, the playful banter slipping off my tongue with ease.

"Good to know my daughter's party has solid snack options," he quipped, taking a step closer. "What's next? You going to critique the punch?"

"I don't want to hurt its feelings, but it could use a little more... pizzazz," I teased, and he laughed, a sound that sent butterflies fluttering through my stomach.

"Pizzazz, huh? I'll pass that along to the bartender." His gaze lingered on me, a flicker of something deeper simmering beneath the surface.

The tension between us tightened, an invisible string tugging us closer. The world around us faded again, sounds melding into an indistinct murmur as I fought to maintain my composure. "So, how do you feel about... parties?" I ventured, desperate to break the spell.

"I feel like they're necessary evils," he replied, a hint of mischief dancing in his eyes. "Great for socializing but even better for observing the absurdity of it all."

I chuckled, grateful for his honesty. "You mean like the guy in the corner trying to impress the girl with his dance moves?"

"Exactly. I'm pretty sure he's trying to invent a new form of dance called 'the awkward crab.'"

We exchanged amused glances, laughter bubbling between us like champagne, and for a moment, the weight of our complex relationship slipped away. But then, in an instant, the humor in his eyes darkened, the smile fading as he glanced past me.

"Hey, I think I need to—" he started, but the moment was interrupted by a sudden loud crash from the other side of the room.

A table laden with snacks had toppled over, scattering chips and pretzels across the floor like confetti. The guests erupted into laughter, a mix of shock and delight, and I couldn't help but giggle at the absurdity of it all.

"See?" Michael said, amusement returning to his voice. "Now that's how you make a memorable impression at a party."

"Who knew snack disasters could be so entertaining?" I grinned, feeling the tension ease back into something lighter, though I couldn't shake the feeling that something had shifted between us.

"Maybe we should try that next time," he suggested, his eyes sparkling with a mixture of humor and intrigue. "It might become our signature move."

"Only if we can come up with a clever name for it. 'The Crunch and Crash,' perhaps?"

We exchanged witty repartee, the lightness in the air enveloping us like a cocoon, but I sensed the undercurrent of complexity still lurking beneath the surface. How much longer could we dance around this chemistry without addressing the elephant in the room?

Before I could dive deeper into my thoughts, a ripple of movement caught my attention as Emily reappeared, her expression shifting from joy to concern as she caught sight of us. I sensed the abrupt end to our playful banter looming ahead, a collision of worlds about to occur.

"Hey, Dad! Can I borrow you for a sec?" she called out, the enthusiasm in her voice carrying a hint of urgency.

Michael's gaze flicked between me and Emily, and just like that, the moment shifted again, the fragile connection we had forged slipping away into the chaos of the party.

The moment Emily called for Michael hung in the air like an unfinished sentence, and as he turned away, a part of me felt the tug of disappointment tightening its grip. He shot me a glance that seemed to say, "Hold that thought," and then he was gone, swept into the current of laughter and voices that surged toward my best friend. I stood there, watching them with a mix of envy and confusion, as if I were an unwilling participant in a play I hadn't auditioned for.

The vibrant atmosphere of the party swirled around me, but I felt strangely detached, like I was observing from behind a glass wall. Emily and Michael engaged in a lively discussion, his earlier warmth replaced by the jovial banter only a father and daughter could share. I couldn't help but admire the way she effortlessly drew him back into her world, igniting an easy camaraderie that felt foreign to me.

A sudden burst of laughter brought my attention back to the crowd. I shifted my gaze to the dance floor, where two friends had taken it upon themselves to demonstrate the latest TikTok dance craze, a whirlwind of flailing arms and exaggerated moves that had everyone in stitches. I wanted to join them, to lose myself in the rhythm of the music, but I found myself hesitating, the shadows of my earlier encounter with Michael lingering in my mind.

"C'mon, are you just going to stand there looking moody?" Jess said, sidling up to me, her voice bright and teasing. "You look like you've just spotted your ex at a wedding."

"I'm just... processing," I replied, forcing a smile to mask my uncertainty. "Processing the overwhelming urge to dance like a complete fool."

Jess raised an eyebrow, a playful grin spreading across her face. "Ah, I see. Your soul yearns for the rhythm, but your brain is telling you to stay put. Let me guess, it's because of the mysterious allure of Emily's dad?"

"Maybe I'm just not ready to become the topic of gossip at the next brunch," I shot back, but I felt the heat creeping up my cheeks despite myself.

"Gossip? Honey, if you two were any more obvious, we'd need to hire a skywriter to announce it!" Jess laughed, throwing an arm around my shoulders. "But seriously, you need to lighten up. Why not embrace the chaos of tonight?"

With a sigh, I let her pull me toward the dance floor, where the crowd moved in a synchronized frenzy of laughter and joy. Music pulsed through the air, vibrant and alive, but my mind drifted back to Michael, his lingering gaze and that elusive connection we had begun to form. I needed to shake off the weight of it all, to not let the evening slip away in regrets and what-ifs.

Jess twirled me into the throng, and I found myself swept up in the rhythm of the moment. I danced with abandon, laughter spilling from my lips as I lost myself in the infectious energy surrounding us. But no matter how hard I tried to immerse myself in the fun, the nagging thoughts of Michael returned like a stubborn itch I couldn't quite scratch.

"See? This is much better!" Jess shouted over the music, her face flushed with excitement. "Who cares about any of that nonsense? You're here to enjoy yourself!"

"Yeah, you're right!" I shouted back, attempting to match her enthusiasm. Just as I started to let go, the music slowed to a gentle rhythm, and I felt a shift in the air. People began to pair off, seeking out those they felt closest to, and I suddenly found myself standing on the outskirts once more.

And then, from the corner of my eye, I saw Michael watching me. The playful banter with Emily had faded, and he stood there, arms crossed, a look of both admiration and contemplation etched on his face. A flutter of nerves ignited in my stomach, and for a moment, it felt like the world around us faded once again, leaving just the two of us suspended in time.

"Do you always steal the spotlight?" he asked, striding over as the last notes of the song faded away.

"Only when the mood strikes," I replied, forcing a lightness into my voice. "And tonight, the mood is very much in favor of ridiculous dance moves."

"I can't tell if that was a compliment or a warning," he shot back, amusement dancing in his eyes.

"Definitely a warning. I'm not responsible for what happens next."

"Good to know. Do you mind if I join you?" He gestured toward the dance floor, and the unexpected thrill that accompanied his invitation sent a rush of heat through me.

"Only if you promise to try your best not to embarrass me," I quipped, stepping back to let him take the lead.

He laughed, and the sound echoed in my ears as he stepped closer, the crowd swirling around us as if creating a protective bubble. The music resumed, a slower, romantic tune filling the air. The world outside faded, leaving only the two of us, caught in a moment that felt charged with possibility.

"Just remember," I said, meeting his gaze with a playful challenge, "you asked for this."

Michael stepped closer, our bodies nearly brushing against each other, the chemistry between us palpable. "I'm always up for a challenge. Especially when it involves a dance-off."

"Dance-off? With you? You might regret that!" I teased, a smile breaking through my earlier uncertainty as we moved together, the rhythm guiding our steps.

He led me through the movements, a graceful blend of humor and skill that left me breathless. Every turn and twirl sparked laughter, and I felt the weight of my inhibitions begin to dissolve. This was what I had been craving: freedom, laughter, and a sense of connection that was both thrilling and terrifying.

As we spun under the warm glow of the lights, my heart raced, and I lost myself in the moment, the world around us disappearing. Until it didn't.

The music suddenly changed again, morphing into a pounding beat that sent the crowd into a frenzy. People began to cheer, their energy ramping up, and the atmosphere shifted dramatically. I found myself laughing, the thrill of the dance urging me to push boundaries and take risks.

"Let's give them a show!" Michael shouted, his eyes sparkling with mischief.

"Are you sure you're ready for this?" I challenged, feeling a rush of adrenaline as the beat intensified.

"Ready as I'll ever be," he grinned, and we dove into the chaos together, moving as one fluid entity amid the rhythm of the music.

But just as I began to lose myself in the exhilaration, the lights flickered ominously, the thrum of the music wavering as a shadow crossed my vision. I turned to see a figure standing at the edge of the dance floor, watching us with an intensity that sent a chill racing down my spine.

My heart skipped, the joyful energy draining from the room as a heavy silence settled like a thick fog. The figure was familiar but unsettling, the face obscured in shadows that twisted the features into something almost sinister. I blinked, trying to shake off the feeling of dread that washed over me.

"Are you okay?" Michael asked, his voice pulling me back from the brink of panic.

"Yeah, just... I think I saw someone I know," I lied, but the unease gnawed at me, making it hard to focus.

Before I could elaborate, the figure stepped closer, the light catching their face, and I froze. It was someone I hadn't seen in years, a ghost from my past that had suddenly resurfaced in a place I least expected. My heart raced, panic clawing at my throat as I realized the implications of their presence.

"Everything alright?" Michael's voice wrapped around me, but my attention was locked on the intruder.

"Not really," I whispered, my breath hitching as the figure moved toward us, determination etched across their features.

Michael turned to see who I was staring at, his expression shifting as realization dawned. The music faded into an eerie silence, the energy in the room collapsing as tension hung thick in the air.

And just like that, the joyful atmosphere shattered, leaving only uncertainty and the heavy weight of secrets that threatened to unravel everything we'd just begun to explore.

Chapter 3: Forbidden Conversations

Our paths crossed frequently in the days that followed, weaving a delicate tapestry of shared moments and lingering glances. I found myself anticipating those chance encounters, each one a whisper of something more than mere friendship. Michael's presence was like a breath of fresh air on a sweltering summer day, and I couldn't help but lean into the warmth of his smile, even as a flicker of anxiety danced in the pit of my stomach.

The coffee shop became our sanctuary, a bustling hub where laughter mingled with the rich aroma of espresso and baked goods. I would watch him from behind my cup, his brows knitting together in concentration as he navigated the endless questions of parenting, work, and life. He spoke in hushed tones, the weight of his burdens evident in the furrow of his brow. I admired how he juggled everything—a job that required both his body and soul, and the fierce love he poured into his son, Danny. Yet, beneath that resilient exterior, I caught glimpses of a vulnerability that stirred something deep within me.

"Can I ask you something?" I ventured one afternoon, as we sat at our usual table near the window, sunlight spilling over us like liquid gold. The chatter of the café felt like a distant hum, a mere backdrop to the electricity that thrummed in the air between us.

"Sure," he replied, leaning back in his chair, his fingers absentmindedly tracing the rim of his mug. "What's on your mind?"

"Why do you always order the same thing? The dark roast with a splash of cream. It's like you've got a set routine." I knew it was a mundane question, yet it felt like a door opening into a deeper conversation.

He chuckled softly, the sound warm and inviting. "It's comforting. Like a favorite song that plays at just the right moment.

Besides, life is chaotic enough. Why not find little moments of consistency?"

"True," I mused, swirling the remnants of my vanilla latte. "But wouldn't it be more exciting to try something new? Adventure is out there, waiting to be discovered."

His gaze met mine, the corners of his lips curling upward in that charming way that sent my heart racing. "Sometimes, adventure is just a change in perspective. You don't have to go far to find it."

His words hung in the air, charged with a meaning that made my pulse quicken. In those moments, I felt as if we were navigating uncharted territory—two souls on the precipice of something profound. The café around us faded, and all I could focus on was the way the sunlight danced in his dark hair, the way his eyes sparkled with hidden depths. Yet, the truth of our situation loomed large, a cloud casting shadows over our burgeoning connection.

As we fell into a comfortable rhythm, Michael began to share more about his life—his struggles as a single father, the late-night juggling act of work and parenting, and the pain that lingered in his eyes like an unwelcome guest. There was a rawness to his stories that resonated within me, a symphony of regret and resilience that left my heart aching for him.

"I thought being a father would come naturally," he confessed one evening, his voice barely above a whisper. "But it's more like walking a tightrope—balancing love and discipline, joy and frustration. And sometimes, I feel like I'm one misstep away from falling."

My heart twisted at his vulnerability. I wanted to reach out, to offer him some semblance of comfort, but the weight of our circumstances felt insurmountable. It was as if we were standing on opposing sides of a chasm, and I was terrified of what would happen if I dared to jump. What would it mean for him, for me? The fear of crossing that line loomed over us like a dark cloud, tainting our laughter with an undercurrent of longing.

As the days melted into each other, the conversations flowed, each word building a bridge between us. He spoke of Danny with such fierce love that it painted a vivid picture of their life together—an adorable whirlwind of mismatched socks, LEGO disasters, and impromptu dance parties in their cramped living room. I could picture them, two adventurers on a quest to conquer bedtime stories and cereal for dinner. But in every tale, I sensed an undertone of solitude, a yearning for companionship that echoed in the silence of his heart.

One rainy afternoon, as the storm pounded against the café windows, I leaned in closer, the warmth of our shared space wrapping around us like a cozy blanket. "Do you ever feel like you're just going through the motions? Like life is a series of tasks to check off?" I asked, the question hanging heavy in the air.

Michael's eyes flickered with surprise before settling into contemplation. "All the time. It's easy to get lost in the routine. But when I see Danny's smile or hear his laughter, it jolts me back to what matters. I want him to grow up feeling alive, to embrace every moment like it's a gift."

I couldn't help but smile at the passion in his voice, his eyes alight with determination. "You're a good dad, you know that?"

He shrugged, but the modesty in his gesture only made me admire him more. "I'm just trying to do my best. But it's hard when you feel like you're doing it alone."

"Maybe you don't have to," I suggested, my heart racing at the thought of offering my support. "I mean, if you ever need a break, I'd love to help out with Danny. I've always had a knack for kids, and who knows? It could be fun."

His expression shifted, a mix of surprise and contemplation. "Are you sure? I wouldn't want to impose."

"No imposition," I assured him, a grin breaking through. "Just a friendly offer from one adventurer to another."

As he studied me, I could almost hear the gears turning in his mind, and I braced myself for the unexpected twist that might come next. But instead of a refusal or a guarded response, he simply nodded, the corners of his lips twitching upward. "Maybe it's time to embrace a little adventure."

The weight of those words settled between us, a promise of possibilities yet to unfold. We both knew the implications of such a step—one that could pull us closer while also threatening the fragile balance we'd struck. But in that moment, as the rain danced against the window and the café buzzed around us, I felt something shift in the air, a subtle acknowledgment of the connection we were building. It was a new beginning, one tinged with both excitement and trepidation, and I was ready to see where it might lead.

As the days unfurled like the delicate petals of a spring flower, our encounters deepened in a way that felt both exhilarating and terrifying. I found myself mesmerized by Michael's stories, his words spinning a tapestry of everyday life laced with unspoken dreams and heartbreak. Each coffee shop rendezvous became a chapter in our own narrative, punctuated by laughter, silence, and the occasional sharp wit that slipped into our conversations like a welcome breeze.

It was during one particularly busy afternoon that I noticed the subtle change in the atmosphere between us. The café buzzed with the familiar sounds of steaming milk and lively chatter, but in our corner, an electric tension hummed just below the surface. I leaned forward, resting my elbows on the table, my chin cupped in my hands, ready to delve deeper into the heart of his world.

"Tell me about the last time you did something just for you," I urged, a playful challenge in my tone. "I mean, something that didn't involve parenting, work, or that ever-present laundry monster lurking in your basement."

He chuckled, the sound rich and warm, before falling into a contemplative silence. I could see the gears turning in his mind, wrestling with the thought of indulging himself in a rare moment of self-care. "It's been a while," he admitted, scratching the stubble on his chin. "Maybe it was the last time I had a weekend to myself—oh wait, I remember! I decided to take a painting class."

"Really? A painter? You must have an inner Van Gogh waiting to burst forth," I teased, tilting my head. "What did you paint? A landscape? A bowl of fruit? Or perhaps a self-portrait with just a hint of melancholy?"

He laughed, the sound rich and warm, and I felt a spark ignite in the space between us. "More like a smattering of colorful chaos that could best be described as a 'What Not to Do' guide for aspiring artists. But it was liberating. For a few hours, I wasn't a dad or an employee. I was just... me."

The sincerity in his voice struck a chord within me. "And what happened to 'you'? Does he ever resurface?" I asked, half-joking but serious enough that my heart raced at the thought of unearthing parts of ourselves long buried under responsibility and routine.

"Not often enough," he sighed, his gaze drifting past the window, where the world outside continued to whirl in a vibrant dance of colors and movement. "But I'm working on it. I want Danny to know that life isn't just about survival; it's about living fully, even in the chaos."

"And how does one find that balance?" I wondered aloud, feeling the pull of his earnestness. "What's the secret ingredient? Is it extra cream in your coffee or a side of adventure?"

"Maybe a bit of both," he quipped, his eyes sparkling with mischief. "But honestly, I think it's about letting yourself be vulnerable. I've spent too much time hiding behind my responsibilities, afraid that stepping outside of them would mean failing."

I wanted to reach across the table, to grasp his hand and assure him that he was not alone in this struggle. Instead, I settled for a smile, one that I hoped conveyed my understanding. "You're doing a great job, Michael. Danny is lucky to have you."

His eyes softened, and for a moment, the weight of our respective circumstances hung between us, heavy and charged. But before the silence could thicken uncomfortably, a small voice broke through the haze. "Mom! Dad! Look at me!" Danny burst into the café, his cheeks flushed and hair wild, a blur of energy that lit up the room. He was a whirlwind of youth, laughter, and pure joy, a living reminder of the beauty that still existed amidst the struggles of adulthood.

"Hey, buddy! Did you have fun at the park?" Michael asked, instantly transforming into the doting father. I watched, enchanted, as Danny regaled us with tales of imaginary dragons and heroic rescues from the playground. The way Michael's eyes sparkled as he listened filled me with a warmth that swelled in my chest, a longing to be a part of this intimate world they had created.

The afternoon melted away, punctuated by laughter and games of pretend, as I became a spectator in their delightful bond. Danny's imagination knew no bounds, weaving stories that included me in the grand adventures of space travel and treasure hunting. I felt honored, almost awed, by the way he effortlessly included me in his imaginative play, as if I belonged in this world of whimsical wonder.

But as the laughter faded into the background, a familiar feeling nagged at the edges of my mind—the reminder that I was still a guest in their lives. The realization hung over me, a dark cloud threatening to unleash its storm. I was falling for both Michael and Danny, yet the path ahead felt fraught with complications.

After our impromptu adventure, Michael and I found ourselves alone again, seated at the same table, the remnants of our shared experience lingering in the air like the aroma of coffee. "You're amazing with him," he said, his voice low and sincere. "I'm grateful you came today."

I shrugged, my cheeks warming at the compliment. "What can I say? Kids love me. I have a natural talent for turning mundane tasks into epic quests."

He chuckled, his eyes dancing with amusement. "And you have a knack for making me feel like I'm not the only one in this chaotic life. You bring a little light to the shadows."

The sincerity in his words sent a thrill racing through me, igniting a spark of hope in the darkness. But just as quickly, a wave of uncertainty washed over me, reminding me of the precariousness of our connection. What if this was a fleeting moment of happiness, a brief interlude in our complicated lives?

"Michael, I..." I hesitated, my heart pounding as I gathered the courage to speak my truth. But before I could finish, his phone buzzed on the table, cutting through the moment like a knife. He glanced at the screen, the warmth in his eyes flickering out as concern replaced it.

"I have to take this," he said, the weight of his responsibilities returning. "It's my mother."

The urgency in his tone pulled me back, and I nodded, feeling the chasm between us widen once more. As he stepped away to take the call, I found myself lost in thought, grappling with the whirlwind of emotions that had taken root in my heart. The walls I had carefully erected around myself felt unsteady, teetering on the brink of collapse. I wanted to reach out, to bridge the gap between us, but the reality of our lives lingered in the air like a heavy fog, clouding my judgment and shrouding our future in uncertainty.

The moments between us felt both fleeting and eternal, a delicate balance of intimacy and distance that kept me on my toes. Each encounter was laced with a nervous energy, a delightful tension that crackled like static in the air. As the days passed, I found myself inextricably drawn to Michael, navigating a labyrinth of emotions that threatened to consume me.

On a particularly drizzly Thursday, the kind of day that makes you want to curl up with a book and a blanket, I arrived at the café to find it unusually quiet. The usual clamor of voices and the hissing of steam seemed muted, as if the world outside had conspired to create an intimate cocoon just for us. I spotted Michael at our usual table, his eyes cast downward, furrowed in concentration. The sight of him, lost in thought, made my heart race, a mixture of excitement and apprehension.

"Hey there, Picasso," I teased as I slid into the seat across from him, unable to resist the urge to lighten the mood. "Plotting your next great masterpiece?"

He looked up, a flicker of surprise followed by a smile. "More like trying to figure out how to get Danny to eat vegetables without resorting to bribery. Any suggestions?"

"Ah, the eternal struggle. You could try disguising them as superheroes," I said, leaning forward with a conspiratorial grin. "Carrots can be Captain Crunch, and broccoli? Broccoli can be the Hulk. Just remember, if he refuses, you can always use the 'they're magic powers' line."

He laughed, the tension in his shoulders easing. "I'll keep that in mind. Maybe I'll even don a cape myself. Super Dad to the rescue!"

I couldn't help but admire the way he transformed mundane parenting challenges into whimsical battles. But beneath that humor lay a deeper layer of complexity, a reminder that the world he navigated was often more serious than he let on. As the café filled with the comforting scent of coffee and pastries, I studied him, intrigued by the depth of his character.

"Do you ever wonder what it would be like to live without any responsibilities?" I asked, the question tumbling out before I could rein it in. "To wake up one day and not have to worry about work or the future? Just pure, unadulterated freedom?"

Michael's expression shifted, his brow furrowing as if he were contemplating a riddle. "It sounds tempting," he replied slowly. "But I think I'd miss the chaos. There's a certain beauty in it, even if it drives me insane sometimes. The moments that make me feel alive are usually wrapped up in the mess."

"Ah, so you're saying that life's like a messy painting? All chaotic strokes but somehow coming together to form something beautiful?" I countered, my playful tone veiling the deeper question lurking behind my words.

"Exactly," he said, nodding thoughtfully. "It's the chaos that teaches us. Every splatter of paint tells a story."

In that moment, I realized we were both weaving our narratives in the colors of our lives, each brushstroke a reflection of our choices. And yet, as much as I craved to explore the canvas of our connection, I was acutely aware of the obstacles before us. I wanted to lean closer, to reach across the invisible line that separated us, but fear held me back.

"Do you ever think about what comes next?" I asked, the weight of the question settling between us. "I mean, after the chaos fades and we're left with the quiet?"

Michael's gaze flickered with a mix of surprise and something deeper—maybe fear. "I try not to. Thinking too far ahead tends to complicate things. I mean, life has a way of throwing curveballs. One minute you're on track, and the next, you're dodging disaster."

"Are you speaking from experience?" I ventured, leaning in closer. "Because you seem to have a lot of wisdom wrapped up in that easy smile."

He fell silent, his expression darkening as if he were wrestling with a shadow that had crept into our conversation. "Let's just say

I've learned that not everything is as simple as it seems," he replied, the weight of his words lingering in the air.

Before I could probe further, Danny bounded into the café again, this time holding a crumpled drawing in his hands, his eyes sparkling with excitement. "Look! I made you a picture!" he exclaimed, holding it out like a trophy, his smile wide and infectious.

I felt my heart swell as I took the paper from his hands. It was a chaotic yet charming representation of what appeared to be a family of stick figures, complete with an abundance of wild colors that bled into one another like a messy watercolor. "This is amazing! I love it!" I said, genuinely impressed.

"Yeah, Dad says it's like a masterpiece," Danny chimed in, his pride evident as he bounced on the balls of his feet. "It's a family adventure! We're going to space!"

"Space, huh?" I said, catching Michael's eye. "What do we need to pack for this epic journey?"

"Pizza! And... and chocolate!" Danny declared, nodding vigorously. "And we need to wear cool helmets, like the ones I saw in the movies!"

"Cool helmets it is," I affirmed, trying to mirror Danny's enthusiasm even as my mind danced with thoughts of reality crashing back in. I could almost see the stars twinkling in Danny's eyes, but the more I played along, the more I felt the boundaries of our worlds pressing in on me, threatening to steal away this moment of joy.

Once again, Michael stepped into the role of the devoted father, his smile widening as he engaged with Danny's vivid imagination. "Okay, let's plan our intergalactic mission. But we have to promise not to let the aliens steal our pizza."

"What if they do?" I interjected, feigning a serious tone. "What do we do then?"

"Then we do battle!" Danny shouted, swinging his imaginary sword dramatically, his energy infectious.

Michael grinned, his laughter ringing like music in the air. "Then we'll have to use our secret weapon—super tickles!"

As the banter continued, a voice in my mind urged me to step back, to retreat into the shadows of my own thoughts. The joy we shared was tinged with a bittersweet awareness that it was ephemeral, a fleeting escape from the realities awaiting us outside the café doors.

Then, just as I started to relax, my phone buzzed, a harsh reminder of the world waiting beyond this bubble. I pulled it from my pocket and glanced at the screen, my heart dropping at the sight of a message from my mother: We need to talk. It's important.

I felt my stomach twist, anxiety flooding my veins like a cold wave. "Excuse me for just a moment," I said, forcing a smile as I stood. "I have to take this."

As I stepped outside, the brisk air greeted me like a slap, each breath feeling heavier than the last. I paced along the sidewalk, my thoughts racing as I hit "call." The conversation I'd been dreading unfolded like a dark cloud rolling in, the weight of her words wrapping around me tighter with each passing moment.

"I know you're getting close to him," my mother's voice crackled through the line, laced with concern. "But you need to be careful. You don't know his past, and it could end badly."

Her warning hung in the air like a thunderstorm about to break. "Mom, I know what I'm doing," I replied, my voice steadier than I felt. "I just want to help him and Danny."

"Help him? Or get yourself hurt?" she shot back, and I could hear the worry crackling in her tone. "Just promise me you'll be cautious. You don't want to dive into something you can't swim out of."

I was about to retort when a figure stepped into my line of sight, cutting through my thoughts. It was Michael, his brows drawn together in concern as he approached, clearly having noticed my sudden departure. My heart raced, a mix of emotions surging as I tried to gauge his expression.

"Everything okay?" he asked, his voice low and steady, grounding me amidst the storm brewing inside my mind.

Before I could answer, the silence shattered. A shout erupted from the café, followed by the sound of chairs scraping against the floor. My heart leaped into my throat as I turned to see a commotion unfolding—a group of people hurriedly rushing toward the exit, their faces painted with panic.

"Stay here," Michael said, his tone shifting to something urgent. But before I could respond, he was already moving toward the chaos, leaving me standing on the sidewalk, rooted in place as fear gripped my heart.

The world around me blurred, and I could only watch as he disappeared into the fray, drawn into the storm I'd tried so hard to navigate. And in that moment, a chilling realization settled over me like a shroud: the chaos we had tried to embrace might just be the very thing that tore us apart.

Chapter 4: Cracks in the Facade

The air in Michael's estate crackled with an energy that was both intoxicating and disorienting. I stood in the grand foyer, my fingers grazing the intricate banister, marveling at the contrast between the elegance surrounding me and the modest charm of my own life. Here, the chandeliers sparkled like constellations trapped within the vaulted ceiling, and the faint scent of cedar and vanilla wafted through the open spaces, enveloping me in a luxurious embrace. Each piece of art that adorned the walls seemed to whisper stories of a world I could only dream of—lush landscapes, refined elegance, and a certain, well-polished mystique.

As I ventured further into the sprawling house, the warmth of laughter echoed from the adjoining sitting room. There, I found Michael, his smile bright against the soft amber glow of the fireplace. He was leaning back in his chair, exuding a relaxed confidence that made my heart race. The way the flames flickered danced upon his features, accentuating the sharp angles of his jaw, the way his dark hair fell across his forehead, an alluring mess that somehow looked deliberate.

"Hey there," he said, his voice warm and inviting, as if I were the only person in the room—no, the universe. "Care for a drink?"

"Only if it comes with a side of your infamous charm," I teased, arching an eyebrow as I settled into the plush chair opposite him. The fabric enveloped me, a stark reminder of how different our lives were. "I have to admit, this place is like stepping into a different world. I keep half-expecting a butler to glide in and offer me a spot of tea."

Michael chuckled, a deep, melodic sound that sent shivers down my spine. "If I had a butler, I'd make sure he had impeccable taste in tea. But alas, it's just me and my collection of whiskey." He gestured to a well-stocked bar, his gaze lingering on me, almost as if he was trying to read the layers of my thoughts.

"What's your poison then?" I asked, leaning forward, intrigued. There was something refreshing about the way he broke the mold of the wealthy elite. Behind his polished exterior, I sensed a longing—a desire to break free from the constraints of his world, just as I yearned to escape mine.

"Depends," he replied, a playful grin spreading across his lips. "Do you prefer something smooth, or do you want a little bite?" His eyes sparkled with mischief, inviting me to step outside the comfortable boundaries we'd each created.

"Surprise me," I challenged, matching his playful tone. "But make it strong. I think I'm going to need it."

With a swift motion, he poured two glasses, the amber liquid glistening under the soft light. "To new experiences," he toasted, lifting his glass, his eyes never leaving mine. I felt a flush creep into my cheeks as I clinked my glass against his, the sound resonating like a promise hanging in the air.

As the night deepened, we shared stories, laughter flowing freely between us like a river swollen with spring rains. I found myself drawn to the layers of his personality—how he wore his wealth like a tailored suit, but beneath it, there was a softness, a vulnerability that made him accessible. He spoke of his childhood, of summers spent exploring the woods surrounding his family's estate, and the joy he found in simple things—like the taste of wild strawberries stolen from the bushes. It was as if he was peeling back the layers of himself, revealing the heart beneath the polished facade.

But just as the atmosphere thickened with unspoken words and the potential for something more, the soft chime of the doorbell cut through our moment like a knife. My stomach dropped, a sense of foreboding settling over me. I watched as Michael's expression shifted, his lighthearted demeanor replaced by a flicker of concern. He glanced toward the door, the playful spark in his eyes dimming.

"Stay here," he said, rising from his seat. There was an urgency in his voice that pulled at my instincts. I nodded, though dread pooled in my gut. I could feel it before the door swung open—an unwelcome presence about to invade the warmth we had cultivated.

Emily stepped into the room, her entrance like a gust of winter wind that extinguished the flickering candle of intimacy between us. Dressed impeccably, she radiated confidence, her eyes sweeping the space before landing on Michael with a practiced ease. "I didn't think you'd mind me dropping by," she said, her voice smooth, as if she were addressing a room full of acquaintances rather than interrupting a moment that had felt so ripe, so full of promise.

I shifted in my seat, the remnants of our laughter hanging in the air like mist. The fragile thread that had begun to weave between Michael and me now felt frayed, hanging by the thinnest of strands. I couldn't help but observe the way Emily's presence shifted the dynamics. She was beautiful in that effortless way that made heads turn, but it was the way she moved—like she owned the space—that unsettled me.

"Hey, Em," Michael replied, his tone light, but I detected a hint of strain in his voice. "What's up?"

"I thought we could talk," she said, her gaze darting between us. I could almost hear the gears turning in her mind, assessing the situation with an unsettling clarity. It was clear that she had walked into something and wasn't about to let it slip through her fingers.

"Now?" he asked, his brow furrowing slightly.

"Is there a better time?" she countered, her tone sharp, laced with an edge that made my heart race. I could feel the tension rising like steam in the air, thickening around us, drowning out the warmth that had just been igniting.

As the words hung between us, I realized that this was more than just an interruption; it was a challenge. I had no intention of retreating to the shadows while she wove her narrative around him. The room pulsed with unspoken words, and I could feel the cracks forming in the facade we had built, ready to spill everything out in a way that would change everything.

The tension in the air thickened, and I could almost hear the echo of a thousand unsaid words. Emily's gaze flitted between us, assessing the situation with the keen eye of someone who thrived on control. I could feel my cheeks warming under the intensity of her scrutiny, while Michael's posture straightened, his relaxed demeanor giving way to something more guarded.

"Sorry to drop in like this," Emily said, her voice smooth as silk, though I could detect a slight tremor beneath the surface. "I just thought you might want some company, Michael."

"Right," he replied, a note of hesitation lingering in his tone. "I was just..." He faltered, glancing at me, then back to her, as if searching for a suitable excuse that wouldn't raise suspicions. "We were catching up."

"Catching up?" she echoed, her eyebrow arching in disbelief. "In a place like this? You know, I always thought you preferred a more... lively atmosphere." The way she emphasized the word "lively" felt like a pointed jab, an undercurrent that prickled at the edge of my awareness.

"I'm more than capable of enjoying quieter moments," he shot back, his voice laced with a challenge. I felt a thrill at his defense, a flicker of hope that perhaps he was willing to stake a claim on our connection.

Emily took a step closer, her heels clicking against the polished wood floor, and I instinctively leaned back in my chair, aware that this was her territory, and I was the uninvited guest. "So, what were you discussing? Secret plans for world domination?" She laughed lightly, but the laughter didn't quite reach her eyes, which gleamed with something predatory.

"Oh, just life and whatnot," I said, injecting a lightness into my voice that belied the storm brewing beneath my surface. "You know how it is. Some of us find solace in the quiet instead of a crowded dance floor."

Michael caught my eye, and I could see a flicker of admiration mixed with surprise at my boldness.

Emily turned to me, a calculated smile playing on her lips. "How charming. It must be nice to escape to a different world, even for just a moment."

I held her gaze, refusing to let her dismissiveness knock me off my feet. "It is nice," I said, my voice steady. "Especially when the company is worth it."

Michael shifted in his seat, and I could sense the weight of the moment pressing in around us. I could almost hear the clock ticking, each second pulling tighter around us like the strings of a bow, ready to snap.

"Why don't you join us, Emily?" Michael suggested, his voice firm, but a hint of uncertainty tinged his words. "We were just having a drink. It's a bit too quiet for a party of two."

A flicker of surprise crossed Emily's face, but she quickly masked it with an expression of feigned delight. "Oh, I wouldn't want to intrude. It's clear you two were deep in conversation."

"Please," I said, eager to defuse the situation. "We'd love to have you. I'm sure there's plenty of room for three."

The corners of Emily's mouth twitched, and for a moment, I thought she might agree. But then she straightened, an imperceptible change in her demeanor. "Well, if you insist," she said, her smile a perfect mask that could easily hide her true feelings. "Just don't blame me when things get chaotic."

The tension in the room shifted, and I could feel Michael's discomfort as we all settled into a fragile truce. I sipped my drink, the whiskey warm against my throat, grounding me as I watched Emily and Michael navigate the delicate dance of conversation.

"So, what have you been up to lately?" Michael asked, trying to steer the conversation into calmer waters.

Emily smiled, a glimmer of mischief dancing in her eyes. "Oh, you know how it is—just charming my way through life, one gala at a time. Last week, I attended a charity event that was nothing short of spectacular. The food was exquisite, and the guests? Well, let's just say they were quite... influential."

"Sounds riveting," I said, my tone dry as the desert. "Nothing like rubbing elbows with the elite to spice up your week."

She turned her gaze toward me, her smile unwavering. "And what about you? I can't imagine your life involves much of that sort of glamour."

I felt the heat of embarrassment creep into my cheeks but forced myself to stand firm. "You'd be surprised. Sometimes, the simplest moments can be the most glamorous—like watching the sunset from a park bench or sharing a laugh over a cup of coffee."

"Ah, the simple life," Emily replied, her tone tinged with condescension. "Charming, in its own way."

Just then, the doorbell chimed again, cutting through the charged atmosphere like a bolt of lightning. I felt a jolt of nerves as I glanced toward the entrance, dreading who might come next.

"I'll get it," Michael said, rising quickly from his chair. I could see his relief in the way he moved, grateful for the distraction.

As he stepped away, I could sense Emily's eyes on me, evaluating, calculating. "You seem to be quite taken with him," she remarked, her voice light but laced with something sharper beneath the surface.

I arched an eyebrow, matching her gaze with defiance. "And you seem to be quite taken with yourself. Is that a surprise?"

She chuckled, the sound smooth but devoid of true humor. "Oh, darling, confidence is key in this world. But I'd be cautious if I were you. Michael can be... elusive."

Before I could respond, Michael returned, and with him came another unexpected guest—Julian, a whirlwind of energy and charm that seemed to illuminate the dimly lit room. "Surprise!" he declared, his smile infectious as he strode in, holding two colorful cocktail glasses, like a magician revealing his latest trick.

"Julian!" Michael exclaimed, his relief evident as he accepted a drink. "What are you doing here?"

"I thought I'd drop by and liven up the place," Julian said, his gaze darting between Emily and me. "I heard this was the party to be at, and I can't resist a good soirée."

"Looks like you arrived just in time," Emily said, her demeanor shifting as she directed her charm toward him. "Michael was just about to engage in a riveting conversation about sunsets and park benches."

"Fascinating! My favorite topic!" Julian interjected, taking a seat next to me, his eyes sparkling with amusement. "But tell me, who needs park benches when you can have a party? Let's talk about real fun."

The energy in the room shifted again, as Julian effortlessly infused a dose of liveliness into the atmosphere. As the conversation turned toward light-hearted banter and playful teasing, I felt a mix of gratitude and annoyance wash over me. For the moment, the storm that Emily had brought with her receded, replaced by Julian's infectious energy.

But beneath it all, the cracks in our fragile facade remained. I couldn't shake the feeling that the night was a precarious balancing act, each interaction an intricate dance around the truth we were all trying to avoid. The tension swirled like the whiskey in my glass, enticing and dangerous, leaving me wondering just how much longer we could maintain our delicate equilibrium.

Julian's arrival sent ripples through the room, and I found myself caught in a delightful storm of wit and charm. He settled into the conversation with a flourish, his animated gestures punctuating every word as if he were conducting a symphony. "So, tell me, what are we discussing? Sunsets, park benches, or perhaps the existential dread that comes with attending yet another lavish gathering?"

Michael shot him a mock glare. "I was hoping for something a little more uplifting, but I see you're set on chaos."

"Chaos is just another name for fun," Julian replied, winking at me as if we shared a secret. I felt a smile break free despite the lingering tension from earlier. In that moment, Julian became the unexpected lifeline that pulled me back from the edge of discomfort, creating a reprieve from the unease that had settled between Emily and me.

"Fun, you say? Then let's indulge in a little chaos," I chimed in, daring to embrace the lightheartedness of the evening. "What's your drink of choice, Julian? I hope it's something as extravagant as your entrance."

"I'd say a fine gin and tonic, but I think we should do something more adventurous—like adding a splash of elderflower liqueur. It's like the party fairy dust." He turned to Michael, who looked torn between amusement and exasperation.

"Fairy dust? Is that what we're calling it now? Should I be worried about being turned into a toad?" Michael quipped, his eyes glimmering with humor.

"Only if you're wearing green," Julian shot back, and the banter continued, weaving a vibrant tapestry of camaraderie that enveloped the room. For a brief moment, it felt as if the undercurrents of rivalry and unspoken feelings had receded, leaving only laughter and warmth.

Emily, however, remained an omnipresent storm cloud, her lips pressed into a tight line. I caught her eye several times, and with each glance, I felt the weight of her unyielding gaze on my back, like a hawk watching its prey. While Julian and Michael reveled in the merriment, I found myself wrestling with a growing sense of unease, a primal instinct whispering that the evening's peace was as fragile as spun sugar.

"Speaking of chaos," I ventured, trying to steer the conversation toward safer waters, "what's the wildest thing you've ever done at one of these parties, Julian?"

"Ah, I remember a gala last summer," he began, his voice rich with nostalgia. "We had a magician perform, and I, in a moment of uncharacteristic bravery, challenged him to turn me into a rabbit. Instead, he managed to make me disappear for a good thirty minutes! When I finally reappeared, everyone thought I'd run off with the silverware."

The room erupted in laughter, and I found myself genuinely enjoying Julian's playful storytelling, but my mind was still half-focused on Emily. Her tension was palpable, like a taut string ready to snap.

"Let's be honest," she interjected suddenly, breaking the wave of laughter. "The real magic trick here is how long Michael can keep pretending everything is just fine."

A hush fell over the room, the lightheartedness evaporating like mist in the morning sun. Julian looked between the two of us, his expression shifting as if he sensed the danger lurking beneath her seemingly casual words.

"What do you mean by that?" he asked, the playful lilt in his tone replaced by curiosity.

Emily leaned back slightly, her gaze locked on Michael with an intensity that felt as suffocating as the weight of an impending storm. "I mean, it's all fun and games until someone gets hurt. Michael might be living in a world of glittering chandeliers and tailored suits, but we both know that's just a facade, isn't it?"

A flush crept up Michael's neck, and I felt an instinctive urge to defend him. "Maybe some of us prefer a little magic in our lives, Emily. We all have our ways of coping."

"Coping? Or hiding?" she challenged, her voice low but sharp enough to cut through the air. "It's not just Michael, after all. There's a reason why you're here, isn't there? Why you were drawn to his world?"

My pulse quickened, and I was aware of how my breath hitched in my throat. I wasn't ready to have this conversation, not here, not now. "I'm here because I like spending time with him," I replied, trying to keep my voice steady. "Is that such a crime?"

"I think we all know it's more complicated than that," she shot back, her smile icy, the facade of friendliness slipping. "But then again, maybe some of us prefer to play at being friends while hiding the real stakes involved."

Julian glanced between us, the tension palpable enough to slice through. "Maybe we should all take a moment to breathe," he suggested, attempting to diffuse the atmosphere. "Perhaps some more elderflower in our drinks would do the trick?"

"Or perhaps a dose of honesty," Emily countered, her eyes narrowing. "Because that's the only way any of us will truly move forward."

The air thickened with unspoken truths, and I could feel my resolve wavering. I turned to Michael, searching his face for answers, for some sign that he wasn't as lost in this intricate web of emotions as I felt. But his expression was carefully guarded, a mask that betrayed nothing, and my heart sank.

"Maybe you should just say it, Michael," Emily pressed, the challenge in her voice unmistakable. "Tell her why you really brought her here."

A silence fell, heavy and oppressive, and I could see Michael's mind racing. I could almost hear the gears grinding behind his cool facade, and I knew he was weighing his options. I leaned in, eager to hear whatever revelation might spill from his lips, desperate for clarity amidst the chaos.

"Emily, I—" he started, but before he could finish, the sound of shattering glass cut through the tension like a knife.

We all turned toward the source of the noise, hearts racing. A figure stood in the doorway, silhouetted against the dim light of the hallway, clutching a broken shard of glass. The room fell eerily silent as recognition dawned— a young woman with wide eyes, panic etched across her face, her breath coming in sharp gasps.

"I'm sorry," she stammered, her voice quaking. "I didn't mean to interrupt, but... you need to see this."

The chill in her words settled over us, the laughter and lightness of the evening evaporating in an instant. I exchanged glances with Michael, and the unease that had hovered in the air transformed into something darker, more foreboding.

"What's going on?" Michael demanded, stepping forward, his protective instinct kicking in.

"It's about... the estate. There's something happening outside. You need to come now."

The world outside, the one that had felt so distant, so perfectly contained within the walls of this opulent home, suddenly loomed large and threatening. The stakes had shifted, and as I looked at the faces surrounding me—Michael's bewilderment, Emily's apprehension, Julian's sudden alertness—I knew that whatever secrets lay outside, they would change everything.

Chapter 5: Whispers of Betrayal

I glanced up from my conversation with Lucas, only to find Emily standing at the entrance of the café, her eyes wide and unblinking, like a deer caught in the headlights of an oncoming train. The world around us faded into a muted blur, as if the universe itself had decided to freeze in that agonizing moment. I could feel the air thicken, pressing against my chest, making it harder to breathe. The laughter and chatter of the bustling café, once a comforting backdrop, became a distant echo, swallowed by the sudden weight of uncertainty.

Emily's cheeks, usually adorned with a soft blush, had drained of color, leaving her looking ghostly pale. I had spent countless afternoons in this café, sipping coffee and sharing laughter with Lucas, but never had I felt the walls closing in so fast. It was just supposed to be a harmless get-together, a break from the chaos of school and looming responsibilities. Yet now, with Emily's gaze piercing through me, it felt as if we were playing a game we had no intention of continuing, only the stakes had somehow escalated without our consent.

"Hey, Em!" Lucas called, his tone light and carefree, oblivious to the charged atmosphere. "We were just—"

"Just what?" Emily cut in, her voice steadier than I expected. She took a step forward, her brows knitting together in a way that made my heart sink. "Just hanging out without me?"

"Come on, don't be like that," Lucas replied, a hint of nervousness creeping into his voice. "It's not what it looks like. We just wanted to—"

I could feel the heat rising in my cheeks as I shifted in my seat, unsure of how to navigate this sudden minefield. Lucas and I hadn't meant to exclude Emily; it had just happened organically, like a gentle tide pulling us further from shore without realizing we were drifting.

"Right," she said, her tone laced with sarcasm. "Because it's totally normal to just hang out and not think about how I might feel." Her words cut like shards of glass, each one a reminder of the unspoken tension we had all felt brewing beneath the surface.

As she stood there, arms crossed, I caught a glimpse of the hurt buried behind her eyes, a flicker of vulnerability that made my heart ache. I had always known Emily was tough, fiercely independent and unyielding like a mountain against a storm, but in that moment, she was also a fragile bird caught in a gale. I hated that we had put her in this position, but I couldn't deny the pull I felt toward Lucas either. It was intoxicating, a dangerous dance that left me dizzy.

"Emily, we're friends," I interjected, desperately seeking the right words. "I didn't mean for you to feel left out. We thought you were busy with Jess."

"Busy, huh?" she retorted, raising an eyebrow. "Busy hiding in my room, crying over how I'm not good enough for either of you?"

"Stop it," Lucas said, his voice firm now. "You know that's not true."

"Do I?" she shot back, the walls of her defenses rapidly building higher. "Because it sure feels like it."

I wanted to reach out, to pull her into a warm embrace and tell her everything would be okay, but the invisible line between us felt thicker than a brick wall. Every instinct urged me to bridge that gap, but my feet remained glued to the floor, held captive by the weight of the moment.

"Let's just sit down and talk," Lucas suggested, motioning toward an empty table in the corner. "No one is saying you're not enough. That's not what this is about."

Emily narrowed her eyes but finally relented, sliding into the chair opposite us. The tension in the air shimmered like heat rising off pavement, and I couldn't shake the feeling that we were teetering on the edge of something irreparable.

"I'm not here to play games," Emily said, her voice low but fierce. "If you two think this is some kind of joke, it's not. You can't just brush me aside like I'm some side character in your story."

Her words hung heavily between us, a storm cloud of unexpressed emotions. I felt a pang of guilt settle deep within me. We had inadvertently sidelined her in a way that felt entirely unfair. My heart raced as I searched for a way to diffuse the situation, to ease the hurt that simmered in her eyes.

"Look, Emily," I began, choosing my words carefully, "I never wanted to make you feel like you weren't important to us. You're not just a side character; you're a huge part of my life. Both of you are."

"I get it, you're in this little bubble now," Emily said, her tone softening just a fraction, "but it feels like I'm the only one outside, looking in."

Before I could respond, a barista bustled by, placing steaming mugs of coffee in front of us. The rich aroma enveloped the table, momentarily distracting us from the weighty conversation. Emily wrapped her hands around her cup, eyes flickering to Lucas and back to me. I could see the tension in her shoulders begin to ease just a bit, though the shadow of betrayal still lingered in her gaze.

"I just don't want to lose you both," she finally admitted, her voice barely above a whisper. "This whole thing is just... confusing."

Lucas nodded, his expression softening as he leaned forward, genuine concern etched across his features. "We're not going anywhere, Emily. We just have to navigate this together. We all care about each other, and that's what matters."

But as I glanced between them, I couldn't shake the feeling that the ground beneath us was shifting. Secrets lingered in the shadows, and the game we thought we were playing might be more perilous than we ever intended. That night, as the vibrant café buzzed around us, I sensed that our tangled emotions had morphed into something more than just friendship—a dangerous game where the stakes had never been so high.

The following days dragged on like molasses in January, the air thick with the kind of tension that made every little interaction feel like walking on a tightrope. Emily avoided eye contact in class, her laughter now a rare bird song, flitting past me but never landing. I caught glimpses of her during lunch, her smile only half-formed, as if the joy had been siphoned away. Meanwhile, Lucas and I attempted to maintain our semblance of normalcy, but every shared joke felt tinged with guilt, like salt on an open wound.

One afternoon, I found myself alone in the library, surrounded by stacks of dusty tomes that promised adventure but failed to distract from the weight pressing down on my chest. I had hoped to escape the drama swirling outside these walls, but the silence only amplified my thoughts. I needed to talk to Emily, to clear the air and unravel the knots that had formed between us. However, the thought of facing her filled me with dread. What could I possibly say to bridge this chasm we'd created?

"Lost in the pages of despair again?" A familiar voice broke through my reverie, and I looked up to find Lucas leaning against the bookshelf, arms crossed, an easy smile dancing on his lips. I rolled my eyes, grateful for his lightheartedness even as I felt the corners of my mouth twitching upward in response.

"I'm doing research on the emotional impacts of awkward love triangles. Fascinating stuff," I shot back, the sarcasm a shield against my unease.

"Do you think they have a section for 'How to Ruin Friendships 101'?" he quipped, pushing off the shelf to join me at the table. "You know, just for us."

"Ha ha, very funny," I replied, attempting to maintain my serious facade but failing miserably. "But seriously, what do I do about Emily?"

Lucas sighed, running a hand through his messy hair, the sunlight catching the golden strands and illuminating the worry lines etched on his forehead. "Just talk to her. I know she's hurting. You saw how she reacted. But the more we avoid her, the worse it'll get."

"Easier said than done," I muttered, my heart racing at the prospect of confronting her again. "She might throw a coffee mug at me or something."

"Then maybe you should take her a new mug as a peace offering," he suggested, his eyes twinkling with mischief. "Or just bring her an entire coffee shop's worth of caffeine. That should win her over."

A reluctant laugh escaped my lips, easing some of the tension coiling within me. "You might be onto something there. A heart-shaped mug filled with frothy caramel macchiato. Very original."

Lucas leaned closer, the playful glint in his eyes fading slightly. "No, seriously. I think she just needs to know that you care. You both do."

His sincerity wrapped around me like a warm blanket, reminding me of the bond we shared, one that felt precarious in the wake of the recent fallout. "Okay," I said, steeling myself. "I'll do it. I'll talk to her."

"Good. But you should probably make it a real coffee date. Set the mood, you know? Maybe somewhere she can't throw mugs. A nice café, or that little park where you used to hang out?"

His suggestion painted a picture in my mind, one filled with sunlight filtering through green leaves and laughter echoing in the air. I nodded, even though a wave of apprehension washed over me.

Later that afternoon, I took a deep breath and sent Emily a text, suggesting we meet at our favorite café—our little sanctuary from the world, where laughter and warmth had once flowed freely. The minutes ticked by agonizingly as I waited for her response, my heart thrumming like a restless bird inside my chest.

Finally, my phone buzzed. "Sure, I'll be there," she replied.

It felt like a small victory, but I couldn't shake the anxiety clawing at my insides. As I made my way to the café later that evening, I mentally rehearsed every possible scenario. Would she be distant? Would she confront me? Or would she throw her arms around me, forgiveness lighting up her face?

When I arrived, the café buzzed with life, the aroma of fresh coffee enveloping me like a comforting embrace. I spotted her at a corner table, her head bent over her phone, the warm glow of the overhead lights highlighting the soft contours of her face. A flicker of hope ignited within me as I approached, but it quickly dimmed as I noticed the way her shoulders hunched slightly, as if trying to make herself smaller, inconspicuous.

"Hey, Em," I said softly, sliding into the chair opposite her.

She looked up, and for a brief moment, her expression was unreadable—a canvas of emotions splashed with uncertainty and hurt. "Hey," she replied, her voice barely above a whisper.

"Thanks for coming," I said, trying to keep my tone light but feeling the heaviness in the air. "I know things have been... awkward."

"Awkward is one word for it," she said, crossing her arms defensively. "I just— I didn't expect to walk in on you and Lucas like that. It felt like a scene from a bad teen drama."

I swallowed hard, the lump in my throat growing. "I didn't mean for you to feel that way. I really care about you, and I'm sorry for how things have been."

Emily's gaze softened, but there was still a flicker of doubt in her eyes. "It's just... hard. I don't want to be a third wheel. I thought we had something special, you know?"

I reached across the table, my hand hovering just above hers, hesitant. "You do. You always will. It's just... complicated."

"Complicated is an understatement." She leaned back in her chair, her defenses slowly crumbling. "I don't want to lose you two. But it feels like I'm just waiting for the inevitable."

Before I could respond, the barista approached with a tray, setting down three steaming mugs in front of us. "On the house, for the lovely ladies," he said with a wink before moving on to the next table.

I chuckled softly, a warmth spreading through me at the gesture, and took a sip from the mug, the rich coffee swirling with caramel dancing on my taste buds. "Maybe it's not all bad, huh?"

Emily raised her mug, a tentative smile creeping across her lips. "To awkward love triangles, then."

"To awkward love triangles," I echoed, clinking my mug against hers, the sound a small spark of hope in the thick fog of uncertainty.

As we sipped our drinks, the conversation began to flow, slowly unraveling the threads of tension that had woven themselves tightly around us. We laughed, reminiscing about our shared memories, the warmth of the café wrapping around us like a familiar blanket. Yet beneath the laughter, I felt the storm still brewing, a reminder that our tangled emotions were only just beginning to surface.

As Emily and I continued to sip our drinks, the conversation gradually shifted from the awkwardness that had marked our reunion to lighter memories. The laughter felt good, but I couldn't shake the lingering tension that danced on the edges of our dialogue. Each chuckle seemed to brush against the truth we were both trying to avoid—a truth that hovered like a specter, waiting for its moment to reveal itself.

"Do you remember the time we decided to sneak into the old movie theater?" Emily asked, a glimmer of mischief lighting up her eyes. "We thought we were being so stealthy, but then we tripped over the broken fence and fell right into the parking lot."

I burst out laughing, picturing the scene vividly. "And you yelled 'CINEMA SINS!' at the top of your lungs, like we were in some ridiculous horror film. I was convinced we were going to be caught by the cops or worse—by our parents."

"Hey, at least we had the best seats in the house," she replied with a smirk. "Front row, right next to the screen. I think we got whiplash from trying to follow the action."

"Totally worth it for those nachos, though," I said, playfully nudging her. The memory was like a balm, easing the tension and stitching together the frayed edges of our friendship. "I'm pretty sure you ate half of them yourself."

"Guilty as charged," she laughed, a lightness settling over her that I hoped was a sign of healing. But even as we joked, I sensed a flicker of something deeper beneath the surface—a current that neither of us wanted to acknowledge.

"Do you think we can go back to how things were?" she asked suddenly, her smile fading as the question hung heavy between us.

The laughter faded, replaced by a weight that settled heavily on my shoulders. "I want to," I admitted, my heart racing. "But I can't promise it'll be easy. We're all a bit different now."

She nodded, her eyes reflecting a mixture of hope and uncertainty. "Different isn't always bad, though. Sometimes, it just means we're evolving."

"Or complicating everything," I murmured, taking another sip from my mug, hoping to drown out the whirlwind of emotions swirling inside me. "You know, the last thing I want is to hurt you."

"Then don't." Her voice was steady, but there was an edge to it that sent a shiver down my spine. "Just be honest. If this—" she gestured between us, "—is going to change everything, I need to know. We all need to know."

The weight of her words settled heavily on my heart. It felt like standing on the precipice of a cliff, staring into the unknown below. "I don't want to lose you, Em. You're one of the best things in my life."

"I don't want to lose you either," she replied, her gaze steady and searching. "But I can't be the one left behind while you two figure this out. I deserve more than that."

The determination in her voice sent a pang of guilt through me. "I know," I said, my voice barely above a whisper. "You deserve everything, and I—"

Before I could finish, the café door swung open with a gust of wind, and in walked a figure that felt like a blast from the past. It was Jess, her vibrant red hair practically glowing in the soft light, and behind her trailed Ryan, his trademark grin lighting up his face. My stomach knotted at the sight of them, knowing Jess would bring her own brand of chaos into our fragile moment.

"Look who it is!" Jess exclaimed, her enthusiasm infectious as she bounded over to our table. "What's this? A secret coffee date without us?"

"Totally clandestine," I said, my voice tinged with humor to mask the tension that had just resurfaced. "We were just planning our next caper."

"Oh, spill it!" Ryan chimed in, leaning over the table with an eager expression. "Are we robbing the nearest convenience store, or just revisiting our childhood escapades? Because I'm in for either!"

Emily's expression flickered between annoyance and amusement, her carefully constructed walls momentarily faltering. "You guys always have the worst timing," she said, though a smile tugged at her lips.

"Timing is everything, darling!" Jess declared, plopping down into a chair next to me, her exuberance filling the space like a firework explosion. "You should know that by now."

"Right," I said, trying to rein in the growing frustration. "Because the best time to discuss feelings is when our friends storm in like the cavalry."

Ryan shrugged, undeterred. "We're just here to rescue you from the impending doom of unresolved tension. I mean, c'mon. That look on your faces? I was half-expecting to see 'The End' flash over your heads."

"Thanks for the concern, but I think we've got this," I replied, casting a sideways glance at Emily, who seemed to be wrestling with a mixture of relief and exasperation.

Jess leaned closer, her expression suddenly serious. "Okay, let's set the scene. Are we talking romantic tension? Because I live for this. Or is it the type of tension that ends in tears? Because I have tissues."

Emily's eyes widened in disbelief, and I could barely contain my laughter. "Trust me, we'll keep the tears to a minimum."

"Fine, but I'll still be taking notes," Jess said with a mock-seriousness that made my heart feel lighter. "Can you imagine the future bestselling novel?"

"More like a tragicomedy," I quipped, grateful for the momentary distraction.

But even as we bantered, I felt the unease bubble back to the surface. Emily was quieter now, her eyes flitting between Jess and Ryan, a veil of uncertainty wrapping around her like a shroud. I could see the wheels turning in her mind, the thoughts colliding with the remnants of our earlier conversation.

And then it happened—a silence enveloped our table, thick and suffocating. Jess, sensing the change, leaned back, her expression shifting from playful to perceptive. "What's going on? You guys look like you've just survived a tornado."

"Just... working through some things," I managed, the weight of our unspoken truths pressing down on me.

"Yeah, right," Jess said, her brow furrowed in concern. "You can't fool me. I can smell tension from a mile away."

"Maybe we should leave it for later," Ryan suggested, glancing between us, his tone cautious. "Sounds like you've got more important stuff to deal with."

"Yeah," Emily agreed, her voice barely above a whisper. "Maybe we should."

And in that moment, the air crackled with unspoken words and unshed tears. I wanted to scream that it wasn't over, that we could still salvage our fragile truce. But as Jess leaned in, ready to dive back into the fray of conversation, I caught a glimpse of Emily's face, a mixture of determination and resignation, and I knew—this was only the beginning of a much deeper conflict.

The door swung open again, and a cold draft swept through the café. A figure stepped in, cloaked in shadows, the energy shifting around them like a gathering storm. My heart raced as I recognized the face. It was Tyler, the new kid—the one who had disrupted our fragile equilibrium and thrown a wrench into the already complicated machinery of our lives.

As he scanned the room, a sly smile crept across his lips, and for a split second, I felt like the ground had opened beneath me, ready to swallow us whole. In that instant, everything changed, and I couldn't shake the feeling that this was just the start of a whirlwind we had never prepared for.

Chapter 6: The Heart's Dilemma

The sun hung low in the sky, casting golden rays that spilled through the office windows, illuminating the scattered papers on my desk. It was a vibrant afternoon, the kind that normally inspired hope and ambition. Instead, I felt as if I were drowning in a pool of conflicting emotions, my heart torn between duty and desire. Each day brought with it a new set of challenges as a social worker, yet none of them compared to the turmoil brewing within me. I could almost hear the echoes of my heart pleading for clarity, but every attempt to listen only amplified the confusion.

The phone buzzed on my desk, its vibration jarring me from my thoughts. I glanced down and saw his name—Michael. My heart raced, a quickening pulse that felt both exhilarating and terrifying. How was it possible that his mere presence in my life could provoke such a storm? I had been wrestling with my feelings for him for weeks, and every time I thought I had a grip on the situation, he would enter my thoughts, unruly and uninvited. He was a spark, igniting something within me that I had buried deep under layers of loyalty to Emily.

Emily, my best friend, had been my anchor for as long as I could remember. We had weathered storms together—failed relationships, family dramas, and career crises. She had always been the steady force in my life, the one who would listen without judgment as I poured out my heart. The guilt of considering Michael, of wanting him, felt like a betrayal that weighed heavily on my shoulders. He was charming, with an easy smile that could light up a room and a laugh that danced like sunlight on water. But it was more than that. With Michael, there was a connection I hadn't felt with anyone before. It was magnetic and terrifying all at once, a force that pulled me closer even as it pushed me away.

I shook my head, willing the thoughts away and trying to refocus on my work. The cases piled up on my desk were filled with stories of heartbreak and struggle, reminding me of the importance of my role. I thumbed through the files, reading about families caught in cycles of abuse, children in need of homes, and individuals searching for a way out. My passion for helping others grounded me, giving me purpose. Yet as I skimmed the pages, I couldn't help but feel a nagging sense of inadequacy. Here I was, trying to help others find their way while I stumbled through my own emotional minefield.

Just then, the office door creaked open, and my supervisor, Lisa, peeked in. She was a whirlwind of energy, her bright red hair matching her vibrant personality. "Hey, you!" she chirped, stepping inside. "You look like you could use a break. Want to grab some coffee?"

"Sure," I replied, grateful for the distraction. As we made our way to the break room, I found myself chatting about mundane things—office gossip, the latest community event, and the annoying habit of my neighbor's dog barking at all hours. It felt good to share a laugh, to connect over the trivialities of life. Yet, as I poured my coffee, my mind drifted back to Michael, the way he could make me feel so alive, so free.

"Okay, spill," Lisa said suddenly, her perceptive gaze piercing through my facade. "You've got that look on your face—the one that says you're thinking about someone who isn't supposed to be on your mind."

I chuckled nervously, the heat creeping into my cheeks. "No, it's nothing like that," I lied, but the way her eyebrow arched told me she wasn't buying it. "Just work stuff."

"Work stuff, huh?" She smirked knowingly. "Is this about that handsome guy who popped into the office last week? The one with the killer smile?"

My heart skipped at the mention of Michael, a rush of warmth flooding my cheeks. "He's just a friend," I managed, even though the word felt foreign on my tongue.

"A friend who makes your heart race," Lisa teased, nudging me playfully. "You know, it's okay to want something for yourself. You've been so focused on helping others that I wonder if you've forgotten to help yourself."

Her words struck a chord, and I felt the weight of her insight. "It's complicated, Lisa. I care about Emily, and I don't want to hurt her. But Michael... he's different."

"Different can be good," she said, her voice softening. "Just remember that taking care of your heart is as important as taking care of others. You deserve happiness, too."

We sipped our coffee in companionable silence, the warmth of the drink matching the rising warmth in my chest. I pondered her words, aware that they were truth cloaked in simplicity. Yet, every time I considered stepping toward Michael, the thought of Emily's face stopped me in my tracks. It was a classic heart-versus-head situation, where my heart screamed for release, and my head insisted on loyalty.

After a few moments, I felt my phone vibrate again, a reminder of the world outside this safe haven. Reluctantly, I reached for it, half-expecting to see Michael's name once more. Instead, it was Emily, her message lighting up my screen: Can we talk later? I need your advice.

My stomach dropped. Was this the moment I'd been dreading? I replied quickly, heart racing. Of course. What's up?

As Lisa chatted animatedly about an upcoming office party, I felt my mind drift. The precarious balance of my heart and my commitments felt even more fragile, like a carefully spun web waiting for the wrong touch to unravel it completely. All I could think was that I needed to figure out what I wanted before the web collapsed under the weight of my indecision.

The sun dipped below the horizon, painting the sky in hues of orange and pink, as I sat at my desk, fingers hovering over the keyboard. Each keystroke felt like a confession, a silent acknowledgment of my turmoil. I could hear the soft hum of voices in the break room, laughter mixing with the clinking of mugs. Yet I remained cocooned in my thoughts, battling the tempest within.

Emily's message weighed heavily on my mind, a silent ticking clock counting down to our conversation. What did she want to talk about? The looming dread was accompanied by a flicker of hope that maybe she had sensed my inner conflict and was ready to help untangle this mess. I stared at the screen, my heart flipping at the idea of seeing her. She had a way of cutting through my confusion with her straightforwardness.

As the office slowly emptied, I grabbed my bag and made my way to the door. I paused, glancing out the window at the dimming light. Would it always be this hard to navigate the paths of love and friendship? I shook my head, trying to dispel the weight of indecision, and stepped outside. The cool evening air was refreshing, and I inhaled deeply, letting the sharp scent of pine and the distant sounds of laughter ground me.

I arrived at Emily's apartment, a cozy haven decorated with mismatched furniture and eclectic art that reflected her vibrant spirit. As I knocked, my mind raced through potential topics—our mutual friends, her latest obsession with a new TV show, anything but my emotional chaos. When she opened the door, her smile immediately put me at ease.

"Hey, you," she said, stepping aside to let me in. "I've been waiting for you. You hungry? I made a giant batch of chili."

"Chili sounds amazing," I replied, grateful for the familiar comfort of her presence. As we settled into the living room, she served up steaming bowls, and the rich aroma enveloped us.

We chatted about work, the latest office antics, and her plans for the weekend. Each laugh and shared story felt like a thread stitching up the frayed edges of my anxiety. Yet, as we finished eating, I could feel the conversation shifting, the unspoken words hanging between us like a tightrope stretched taut.

"Okay," she began, her tone serious yet warm. "I know something's bothering you. You can talk to me. You know that, right?"

I swallowed hard, the reality of the situation pressing down on me. "It's just... complicated," I finally admitted, my voice barely above a whisper.

"Complicated is my middle name. Just spill," she urged, leaning forward, her eyes sparkling with curiosity.

A part of me wanted to confess everything—the guilt, the desire, the chaotic longing for Michael—but I hesitated. I didn't want to burden her with my internal struggle. Instead, I chose to share the weight of my emotional maze. "I've been feeling... torn. Between wanting to support you and my feelings for someone else."

Her expression softened, and she reached out to squeeze my hand. "Who is this someone? I promise I won't freak out."

Taking a deep breath, I decided to lay it all bare. "It's Michael."

At the mention of his name, her brow furrowed, but she remained quiet, waiting for me to continue. "He's charming and funny, and when I'm with him, everything feels... lighter. But I can't shake the guilt of even thinking about him. I care about you so much, Em. I don't want to hurt you."

Emily leaned back, her fingers drumming thoughtfully on her thigh. "You know I want you to be happy, right? But I can't help but wonder if this is just some sort of distraction."

"It's not like that," I countered, my heart racing. "He makes me feel alive. I haven't felt that in so long."

"I get that," she said, her voice gentle. "But you need to be sure. Emotions can be tricky. You don't want to rush into something that might jeopardize what we have."

Her words hit home, and I felt the weight of her wisdom. "I know you're right. It's just so hard to see clearly when everything feels so overwhelming."

"Life is messy, and sometimes, we just have to embrace the chaos." She smiled, but there was an underlying seriousness to her expression. "What does Michael think about all this?"

I sighed, a mix of frustration and confusion bubbling up inside me. "I don't know! He's been so supportive and understanding, but I haven't even told him how I feel. I'm terrified of ruining what we have."

"Then maybe it's time you had that conversation," she suggested, leaning closer. "You deserve to know if this is real or just a fleeting spark. And who knows? He might feel the same way."

The thought was both thrilling and daunting. What if I took the leap, only to discover that my hopes were unfounded? Yet the more I pondered it, the more I realized that remaining silent would only deepen my inner turmoil.

As the night wore on, we shifted from serious conversations to playful banter, allowing laughter to weave through the air like a comforting blanket. I cherished these moments, the way we could dance between deep topics and lighthearted fun. But a part of me couldn't shake the unease, the sense that something was brewing just beneath the surface, waiting for the right moment to burst forth.

When the clock struck midnight, I reluctantly gathered my things, knowing I had to face the reality of my choices. "Thank you for tonight, Em. I really needed this."

"Anytime. Just promise me you'll think about what we talked about," she said, her expression earnest.

"I promise," I replied, even as I felt the weight of my own words. Leaving her apartment, I stepped out into the crisp night air, the chill wrapping around me like an old friend. The stars twinkled above, scattered like diamonds across a deep velvet canvas, and for a moment, I felt a sense of clarity wash over me.

But as I walked towards my car, I realized that clarity often comes at a cost. My phone buzzed again, and without thinking, I glanced at it, half-hoping for a message from Michael. Instead, it was a reminder of my ever-growing conflict. The night felt heavy, the weight of my heart pressing down on my chest as I grappled with the realization that every choice I made would lead me further down one path or another. The heart's dilemma was only just beginning.

The morning sun filtered through the blinds, casting striped shadows across my bedroom floor. It felt like the world outside had conspired to create the perfect backdrop for my emotional turmoil. I could hear the faint chirping of birds, their morning song a stark contrast to the storm brewing in my heart. The warmth of the sunlight was inviting, yet I felt a chill creeping in, a reminder of the unresolved tension between my feelings for Michael and my loyalty to Emily.

I rolled out of bed, determined to shake off the remnants of last night's discussion. The moment I stepped into the shower, the warm water cascaded over me like a soothing balm. I attempted to clear my mind, letting the steam envelop me, but Michael's smile kept resurfacing, its brightness blinding me to the weight of my reality.

After drying off and pulling on a comfortable sweater and jeans, I sat down with a steaming cup of coffee, hoping the familiar aroma would ground me. As I took my first sip, my phone buzzed on the table, shattering the brief moment of tranquility. I hesitated, half-hoping it was Michael, but braced myself to find it was just another work-related message.

It wasn't.

"Hey, can we meet today? I need to talk."

My stomach flipped. It was from Emily. Just yesterday, we'd delved into the complexities of my heart, and now she wanted to talk again? I typed a quick response, agreeing to meet her at our favorite café, and felt an uneasy flutter in my chest. Was she going to confront me about Michael? Or had she picked up on something more profound lurking beneath the surface?

As I drove to the café, the streets were filled with the familiar hustle and bustle of the city. I watched as people darted past, each lost in their own worlds, unaware of the emotional tempest I was navigating. The aroma of fresh pastries and coffee wafted through the air as I stepped inside, the warmth of the place wrapping around me like a comforting embrace.

Emily was already seated at a small table in the corner, her eyes scanning the menu but not really reading it. I took a deep breath, steeling myself for whatever she had to say. As I approached, she looked up and offered a tentative smile, but I could see the concern etched on her features.

"Hey," I greeted, sliding into the seat across from her. "What's up?"

She hesitated, taking a sip of her coffee as if searching for the right words. "I've been thinking about what we talked about last night," she began slowly, her gaze piercing through the atmosphere, searching for something beneath the surface. "And I wanted to make sure you're okay."

"I'm fine," I lied, but the quiver in my voice betrayed me.

"No, you're not," she shot back, her tone sharper than I expected. "You're dealing with a lot, and I just want to help. It's clear you're torn, and I can't help but worry that you're going to make a choice you might regret."

"I know," I said, exhaling sharply. "It's just... complicated. You know I care about you, right? But I can't help how I feel about Michael."

Emily studied me for a moment, her expression softening. "I want you to be happy, truly. But have you talked to him about how you feel?"

"Not yet," I admitted, feeling the weight of her gaze. "I'm scared to ruin what we have."

"Or what you have with me," she countered gently, her voice a soothing balm even as it cut deep. "If you don't take this chance, you'll always wonder what could have been."

The truth of her words hung in the air, heavy with unspoken consequences. I wanted to deny it, to cling to the comfort of familiarity, but I felt the truth resonating within me. "What if I take the chance and it blows up in my face?" I said, my voice barely above a whisper.

"Then at least you'll know," she replied, unwavering. "You can't keep holding onto this guilt forever. It's not fair to either of us."

We fell into a contemplative silence, the café bustling around us, the sound of laughter and conversation almost drowning out the weight of our discussion. My coffee grew cold as I wrestled with my thoughts, feeling as though I were perched on the edge of a cliff, staring down into the abyss of uncertainty.

"Maybe I should just... talk to him," I finally said, my voice tinged with resignation.

"Maybe you should," Emily said softly, a small smile creeping onto her face. "And if it goes well, I'll be your biggest cheerleader. If it doesn't, then we'll figure it out together. You've always been there for me, so it's only fair that I'm here for you."

As we finished our coffees, I felt a sense of resolve blossoming within me, a fragile but growing determination to confront my feelings head-on. I could do this. I had to.

Just as we stood to leave, my phone buzzed again, and I glanced down. It was a message from Michael: Can we talk today?

"Looks like the universe is pushing you," Emily said, her eyes twinkling with mischief.

"Yeah, or it's trying to send me off a cliff," I replied, trying to mask my anxiety with humor.

"Just be honest with him," she encouraged, her tone earnest. "You've got this."

I nodded, feeling both terrified and exhilarated. As we parted ways, I felt the weight of my choices bearing down on me. The sun shone brightly as I made my way to my car, illuminating the path ahead but casting long shadows behind me.

Arriving at the park where we often met, I parked and took a moment to gather my thoughts, my heart racing with anticipation and dread. Michael arrived shortly after, his handsome features softened by the sunlight, a mixture of hope and uncertainty flickering in his eyes.

"Hey," he said, his voice warm, wrapping around me like a favorite sweater.

"Hey," I replied, feeling the weight of the moment.

We walked a few paces in silence, the gentle rustle of leaves creating a symphony of sound around us. I could feel the tension rising between us, thick and palpable.

Finally, we found a bench, and as we sat, my heart pounded louder than ever. "I got your message," I said, trying to keep my voice steady.

"Yeah, I just... wanted to see how you've been. I've missed you."

The sincerity in his voice sent a shiver down my spine, and the longing in my heart flared to life again. "I've missed you too," I admitted, my eyes locking onto his.

He paused, taking a breath as if gathering his courage. "I've been thinking about what we talked about the other day. I really enjoy spending time with you, and I want to be more than just friends."

The words hung in the air, resonating within me like a heartbeat. Everything in my being urged me to leap forward, to embrace the possibilities before me. But then the lingering thought of Emily, the loyalty I felt towards her, sent a cold wave crashing over my enthusiasm.

"Michael..." I started, the conflict bubbling to the surface as doubt crept in.

But before I could finish, a loud crash echoed from across the park, followed by shouts. My heart raced as I turned, eyes widening in horror at the sight of a car skidding off the road, careening toward a group of children playing nearby.

"Run!" I screamed, instinct kicking in as I lunged forward, adrenaline surging through my veins. The world fell away, leaving only the desperate need to protect those around me. I sprinted, my heart pounding, unaware of the choices looming ahead.

Chapter 7: A Dangerous Liaisons

The café hummed with the comforting aroma of roasted coffee beans, mingling with the sweet scent of pastries cooling in the display case. Sunlight streamed through the large windows, casting a warm glow on the mismatched furniture, giving the place an eclectic charm that made it feel like a sanctuary amid the bustling town. I loved this spot, a cozy retreat where I could lose myself in thoughts or the latest novel tucked away in my bag. Yet today, my thoughts were far from peaceful, trapped in a whirlwind of emotions that threatened to spill over.

As I sat at my usual corner table, I could feel Emily's gaze piercing through the air, heavy with expectation. The sunlight danced on her auburn hair, framing her face and highlighting the mix of confusion and anger etched across her features. Her green eyes, usually vibrant and full of life, were stormy, swirling with unspoken words. I knew she was waiting for me to break the silence that stretched uncomfortably between us, a taut wire ready to snap.

"Why do you keep avoiding me?" she asked, her voice steady yet tinged with an edge that hinted at the storm brewing beneath the surface. "You know we can't keep pretending everything is fine."

The truth of her words hit me like a tidal wave. I had been dodging our conversations like a skilled athlete, avoiding the inevitable confrontation that loomed over us. It wasn't that I wanted to create distance; it was that I was terrified of the truths that would come spilling out if I dared to speak them. "I'm not avoiding you," I lied, the words tasting bitter on my tongue. "I just... needed some time to think."

"Think about what? About how you can keep this secret?" Her voice rose slightly, drawing the attention of a couple seated nearby. I winced but pressed on, the weight of my confession hanging heavy in the air.

"Emily," I began, my voice dropping to a whisper as I leaned across the table, desperate to keep this moment between us, "I can't keep this from you anymore. I'm... I'm attracted to your father."

The silence that followed felt like a living thing, wrapping around us in a suffocating embrace. I watched her expression shift, disbelief flaring in her eyes before being swiftly eclipsed by anger. It was a look I had never seen on her before, raw and jagged like shards of glass. "You can't be serious," she hissed, each word coated in a venom that stung.

"I know it sounds insane," I hurried to explain, my palms sweating against the cool ceramic of my mug. "But there's something about him—his charisma, the way he carries himself. I didn't ask for this to happen, but it did. And I can't just ignore it."

Her chair scraped against the floor as she leaned back, arms crossed tightly over her chest. "So you think it's okay to crush on my dad? To pretend our friendship means something when you're clearly after something else?" The accusation felt like a slap, and my heart sank, understanding her pain.

"I never meant to hurt you, Em," I pleaded, my voice shaking slightly. "You have to believe me. Our friendship has always meant everything to me, but I couldn't control how I feel. I tried. Trust me, I tried."

She inhaled sharply, and the look on her face twisted into something almost sorrowful, like a painting that had suddenly lost its color. "I don't know if I can believe you anymore," she admitted, her voice trembling with suppressed emotion. "You've crossed a line, and I can't just forget that. Not now, not ever."

Each word she spoke pierced through me, unraveling the bond we had built over countless shared moments. I felt the world around us blur, the clattering of cups and the laughter of nearby patrons fading into a distant hum. In that moment, it was just Emily and me, two people standing at the precipice of a rift that seemed impossible to bridge.

"Please, just give me a chance to explain," I urged, my throat tightening as desperation clawed at me. "This isn't just a fleeting attraction. There's something deeper, something that makes me want to explore it. I thought... I thought you would understand."

"Understand?" She laughed, a sharp sound that echoed in the space between us, filling the air with tension. "How could I understand that you're willing to throw away everything for a fantasy? He's my father, for God's sake!"

"Not a fantasy, Emily. He's not just your father. He's a man—complex and fascinating," I replied, my voice a mix of frustration and longing. "You can't deny that he has a presence. It's magnetic."

"Magnetic? Is that what you call it?" she snapped, her anger shifting into something else, something vulnerable. "You don't know him like I do. You don't see the mess behind that charm."

The truth hung between us like a thick fog, and I could see it settling in her eyes. "I don't want to hurt you, Em. I really don't. But I can't ignore how I feel. Not when it's this intense."

The words hung in the air, heavy with unspoken fears and uncharted desires. I felt a flicker of hope as her expression softened, just a fraction, a glimpse of the warmth that had always defined our friendship. "You think this will end well? That it's worth the risk?"

"I don't know," I admitted, my voice dropping to a whisper. "But I know that I can't walk away without exploring this, without knowing what could be."

The silence stretched again, thick and suffocating, as her gaze bore into mine, searching for something, anything, to hold onto. The café's background noise faded further as we stood on the edge of a precipice, where a single step could lead to unimaginable consequences.

The café's ambiance shifted like the tide, the tension around our table palpable enough to slice through the chatter and clinking of mugs. Emily's gaze shifted from my face to the window, where raindrops began to race each other down the glass, mirroring the storm brewing inside her. The sunlight had dulled, giving way to a slate-gray sky that hung heavy with unspoken words and unresolved feelings. I could practically hear the cogs turning in her mind, the gears of our friendship grinding against the revelation I'd just thrown at her like a grenade.

"I can't believe you would even consider this," she said finally, her voice a mixture of disbelief and frustration. "You've turned this into some kind of twisted romance novel."

"Twisted? Emily, it's not like I'm stalking him. It's not some dramatic teenage crush; this is—"

"Stop right there," she interrupted, shaking her head vehemently. "You think I'm just going to stand by and watch you ruin everything? My relationship with my dad, our friendship—it all hangs in the balance because of a moment of weakness on your part."

"Moments are fleeting," I countered, my pulse quickening. "But what if this is something real? Something we could explore together?" I was playing with fire, but a part of me was drawn to the heat, a moth fluttering toward the flame, hoping for a brighter outcome.

Emily leaned back in her chair, arms crossed tightly, as if physically barricading herself against my words. "You think he's going to feel the same way? He's my dad. He doesn't see you like that. You're just some—"

"Some what?" I demanded, my frustration boiling over. "Some girl he's known for a while? Some friend of his daughter's? You think that's all I am to him?"

"Right now, that's all you are," she shot back, her eyes flashing like emeralds under the gathering storm clouds. "And the fact that you're even entertaining these thoughts is more than just concerning; it's reckless."

Reckless. The word hung between us like an accusation. I looked down at my hands, tracing the patterns on the table's surface, willing the anxiety to melt away. "What do you want me to say?" I asked, my voice softer now. "That I can magically turn off my feelings? Pretend they don't exist? Because I can't. I wish I could."

Emily sighed, the tension in her body relaxing just a fraction. "This isn't just about you anymore, though. This affects everyone."

"Like I said, I didn't choose this. It just happened."

"Maybe you should think before you let your emotions get the better of you." She looked away, her fingers tapping nervously on the table, a nervous rhythm that mirrored my own anxious heartbeat. I could see the conflict on her face—part of her wanted to lash out, but another part was still trying to reconcile our friendship with this unforeseen twist.

The door to the café swung open, and a gust of wind swept in, carrying with it the scent of impending rain. My heart leapt momentarily at the sight of Michael striding in, his tall frame silhouetted against the light. His presence was magnetic, and for a moment, I forgot all about the churning emotions swirling between Emily and me.

"Hey!" he called, his voice rich and inviting, pulling my gaze away from Emily. "Just finished up a meeting. How's it going in here?"

I felt Emily's tension spike as she squared her shoulders, narrowing her eyes at me as if daring me to betray our conversation. "Perfect timing, right?" she muttered, sarcasm dripping from her words. "Just what I need."

"Do you want something?" I shot back, not wanting Michael to sense the thick fog of conflict hanging over us. "We were just having a chat."

"Yeah? About what?" Michael asked, his curiosity piqued as he approached our table. His attention darted between the two of us, a flicker of concern crossing his face.

"Nothing important," Emily replied too quickly, her tone all sharp edges. "Just... catching up."

"Catching up, huh?" Michael chuckled, his warm smile disarming. "I could get used to this friendly dynamic."

I shot Emily a desperate look, silently pleading with her to keep her cool. "Maybe we should head out for a bit, let things cool down?" I suggested, desperately trying to steer the conversation away from the tension that had erupted between us.

"Sure," Michael agreed, oblivious to the storm brewing beneath the surface. "How about we grab lunch? I could use a break from all that endless talking."

Emily glanced at me, her expression a mix of annoyance and resignation, and I knew I was walking a tightrope. The last thing I wanted was for Michael to be caught in the crossfire of our conflict.

"Sounds great," I forced a smile, masking the turmoil roiling inside. We stood up, and as I took a step toward the door, I felt Emily linger behind for just a moment, her breath catching as she wrestled with her own thoughts.

The rain had started to fall softly, creating a soothing rhythm against the pavement outside. As we walked side by side, I could feel the weight of Emily's silence pressing in, wrapping around us like an unwelcome cloak. I could sense her struggle, the way she wanted to confront me again but held back out of respect for Michael's presence.

"So, what's the plan?" Michael asked, breaking the silence as we stepped onto the sidewalk, his casual tone brightening the gray day.

"Maybe we could try that new burger place a few blocks over?" I suggested, hoping to steer the conversation toward neutral territory.

"Burgers sound perfect," he said, a grin lighting up his face. "I hear they have some crazy combinations."

We walked in silence for a moment, and I could feel Emily's anxiety radiating beside me. It was a strange mix, her tension battling against Michael's relaxed demeanor, creating an almost electric atmosphere that crackled with unsaid words.

"I love burgers," I finally said, attempting to inject some levity into the situation. "What's your take on the classic cheeseburger versus the gourmet versions?"

"I'm all about the classic," Michael replied, his eyes sparkling with mischief. "You can't beat a good cheeseburger. But if you're feeling adventurous, why not add some jalapeños?"

Emily rolled her eyes, unable to contain a smile despite the heaviness still looming in the air. "Really? You're going to bring spice into this? That's your solution?"

"Absolutely," Michael laughed, glancing at her sideways. "Life's too short for bland food. You have to live a little!"

As we continued to walk, I could feel Emily's defenses beginning to lower, the slightest cracks appearing in her steely exterior. Maybe Michael was right. Maybe we needed to break away from the seriousness and just enjoy each other's company.

But beneath it all, the knowledge of my feelings lingered, a shadowy figure that refused to be ignored. I couldn't help but glance sideways at Emily, searching for a sign that she would eventually forgive me, that our friendship could withstand this unexpected turn. The rain fell softly around us, washing away the remnants of our earlier confrontation, but I knew deep down that the real storm was far from over.

The burger place turned out to be a bustling little gem, with its neon lights flickering against the rain-soaked pavement. The aroma of sizzling patties and fried onions wafted through the open door, mingling with the sound of laughter and clinking dishes, creating a welcoming atmosphere that was impossible to resist. I felt the tension ease slightly as we stepped inside, the warmth wrapping around us like a cozy blanket.

Emily slid into a booth, her posture still rigid, arms folded tightly across her chest as if bracing herself against the world. Michael settled across from her, effortlessly charming and unaware of the emotional earthquake just beneath the surface. "What do you recommend?" he asked, scanning the menu as if it were a treasure map. "I hear the triple-decker burger is legendary."

Emily raised an eyebrow, her lips twitching in a reluctant smile. "Legendary, huh? Are you sure you can handle that much burger?"

"Oh, please," he scoffed, feigning offense. "I was born ready for a culinary challenge."

"Culinary challenge? Or a heart attack?" she teased, her eyes lighting up for a moment, reminding me of the vibrant girl I adored, the one who had been overshadowed by the storm we were navigating.

"Why not both?" I interjected, trying to latch onto the light-hearted banter. "If you're going to indulge, you might as well go all in."

Michael laughed, his deep voice reverberating off the walls, lifting the mood just a notch. I watched the easy way he interacted with Emily, the comfort they shared, and felt a pang of longing coupled with an overwhelming sense of guilt. This was the man I was drawn to, yet he was also the root of the problem threatening to unravel everything between us.

Once we placed our orders, the waiter departed, and an awkward silence descended upon us again, thickening the air with unspoken truths. I toyed with the edge of my napkin, desperately searching for something to break the tension, when Michael suddenly turned to me, his eyes serious.

"Is everything okay between you two? I noticed something was off earlier."

"Just a little misunderstanding," I quickly replied, forcing a smile. "Nothing we can't work through, right, Emily?" I glanced at her, hoping for her to chime in, to reassure me that our friendship still had a fighting chance.

"Sure," she said, her tone flat. "Just a misunderstanding."

"Good." Michael nodded, seemingly satisfied but still looking a touch concerned. "Because I hate to see friends at odds. Life's too short, you know?"

"Yes, it is," Emily said quietly, her gaze falling to the table as if the wood grain held all the answers.

Before I could think of a way to steer the conversation toward safer waters, our burgers arrived, stacked high with all the fixings. The sight was almost overwhelming—a mountain of flavor that begged to be devoured. Michael's eyes sparkled with excitement as he dove into his food, discussing the best ways to layer toppings with such enthusiasm that I couldn't help but smile. But even as he chatted about how crispy bacon paired perfectly with a spicy aioli, I could feel Emily's unease lurking beneath the surface.

"I read an article about burger pairings," he said, wiping a stray piece of lettuce from his chin. "Apparently, the right drink can elevate the whole experience. Who knew?"

"Yeah, I mean, you can't go wrong with a classic soda, but who's to say a craft beer wouldn't just blow your mind?" Emily offered, her sarcasm rearing its head, an almost protective shield against the vulnerability threatening to breach her walls.

"Craft beer? Now we're talking!" Michael laughed, his eyes dancing between us, trying to bridge the growing rift with humor. "I'll admit, I have a soft spot for the local brews. They're like a party in your mouth."

"Great, now you've made me want to try a beer with my burger," I said, chuckling. "But what if I'm not ready for a party? What if I just want a quiet evening in?"

Emily shot me a look that mixed amusement with disbelief. "You, quiet? That's rich."

Just as I was about to reply, a loud crash erupted from the back of the restaurant, shattering the light-hearted atmosphere. My heart raced as I turned to see a group of patrons scrambling from a table, one of them clutching a bleeding arm. Chaos erupted as people rose from their seats, eyes wide with shock, and the waiter rushed to help.

"Stay here," Michael ordered, standing up instinctively. "I'll check it out."

"Wait!" I reached for his arm, but he was already moving toward the scene, leaving Emily and me behind in a whirlwind of confusion and fear.

"Is it always like this?" Emily asked, her voice trembling as she watched Michael disappear into the crowd. "You know, a restaurant filled with potential disasters?"

"Not typically," I replied, my own heart pounding as I tried to assess the situation. "But this is definitely a new level of excitement."

As we leaned over the table, craning our necks to see what was happening, the atmosphere shifted. Whispers fluttered through the crowd, mingling with the sound of someone yelling for a doctor. The tension from earlier faded, replaced by a collective concern that washed over everyone present.

"Should we go help?" I asked, uncertainty gnawing at my insides.

"No," Emily said sharply, her eyes wide. "Let them handle it. It could be dangerous."

But before I could respond, Michael reappeared, his face pale and eyes wide with shock. "It's bad," he said, his voice shaky. "Someone might have been hurt intentionally. We need to—"

"Intentionally?" I echoed, my mind racing with possibilities. "What do you mean?"

Michael hesitated, glancing back toward the scene, then lowered his voice, his expression grave. "I think it was a robbery gone wrong. The guy who got hurt was trying to stop them."

My stomach dropped, and I could see the fear flicker in Emily's eyes. "What does that mean for us?"

"I don't know," Michael admitted, running a hand through his hair in frustration. "But we need to get out of here. Now."

Before we could react, the sound of sirens wailed in the distance, a cacophony of chaos that mingled with the shouts of restaurant staff. Panic surged through me as I grasped Emily's hand, the warmth of her skin a stark contrast to the chill creeping up my spine.

"Let's go!" I urged, pulling her along as we navigated through the panicked crowd, our hearts racing in sync. But just as we reached the door, a shadow loomed ahead, a figure stepping out from the chaos.

"Not so fast," the voice sneered, low and threatening, sending a jolt of fear through my veins.

I looked up to see a man standing in the doorway, his face obscured by the dim lighting and the rain-soaked gloom outside. A flicker of recognition danced at the edge of my mind, but before I could place him, Emily squeezed my hand tighter, and I knew we were far from safe.

"Run!" I shouted, adrenaline flooding my system as I turned to push her toward the exit, but the man took a step forward, his intentions dark and unreadable, a storm brewing in his eyes.

Chapter 8: The Depths of Desire

The air in the dimly lit café was thick with the rich scent of roasted coffee beans, mingling with the sweet notes of pastries warming in the oven. The soft hum of chatter wrapped around me like a familiar blanket, providing a sense of comfort I desperately needed. I settled into my usual corner, a small round table tucked beneath the overhanging branches of a whimsical indoor tree, the leaves a vibrant shade of green that seemed almost too vivid for the season. It was my refuge, a place where I could hide my thoughts among the steam rising from my mug of coffee.

As I stared into the depths of the dark liquid, the warm ceramic against my palms, memories of Michael flooded my mind. There was something intoxicating about him—his easy smile, the way his laughter seemed to dance through the air like a gentle breeze. We had fallen into a rhythm that felt both reckless and exhilarating, our secret meetings adding an electric charge to the otherwise mundane days. Every moment together was a whirlwind, a mix of whispered confessions and stolen glances, the world outside fading into a distant hum.

The bell above the café door chimed, breaking my reverie. I glanced up, heart racing, half-hoping to see him striding through the door, that easy confidence radiating off him. Instead, a gust of wind swept in, rustling the pages of the newspaper laid out on the adjacent table. I let out a sigh, the absence of his presence weighing heavy on my chest. I couldn't help but feel like a ship lost at sea, adrift without a compass, desperately trying to navigate through this tangled web of desire and uncertainty.

In the weeks since Emily had distanced herself, Michael and I had found an unspoken bond that thrived in the shadows. Each encounter was laced with urgency, as if we were the last two survivors of a shipwreck, clinging to each other in a world that had become hostile and unwelcoming. The thrill of our connection simmered just beneath the surface, like a secret too potent to share, and yet, as our intimacy deepened, so too did the anxiety gnawing at the edges of my heart. Were we merely two lost souls escaping the weight of our respective realities, or was there something more profound blossoming between us?

"Lost in thought, are we?" A voice broke through my musings, smooth as silk yet tinged with playful mischief. I looked up to find Clara, my best friend, her bright eyes sparkling with curiosity. Her presence was a welcome distraction, a tether to reality that I often needed in moments like this.

"Just contemplating life's little dilemmas," I replied, attempting a nonchalant smile while my stomach twisted in knots. Clara slid into the chair opposite me, her expression shifting to one of mock seriousness.

"Life's little dilemmas, huh? Are we talking existential crises or the dilemma of whether to add an extra shot of espresso to your latte?" She leaned forward, feigning gravity in her tone, and I couldn't help but chuckle. Clara had a way of lightening even the heaviest of moods, her humor a soothing balm to my swirling thoughts.

"More like the complicated love life of a girl caught between friendship and passion," I admitted, my gaze drifting back to the window. Outside, the sun was beginning to set, casting a warm golden glow over the streets, a beautiful contrast to the inner turmoil brewing within me.

"Michael?" Clara's tone shifted, a knowing glint in her eye. It was as if she could see right through my carefully constructed facade, peeling back the layers of uncertainty that clung to me like an old sweater I couldn't quite shake off.

"Yeah, Michael." I sighed, surrendering to the wave of vulnerability that washed over me. "Things are... intense. It's like every moment we spend together feels so right, yet so wrong at the same time."

"Welcome to the world of adult relationships," Clara replied, her grin widening. "You think it's all roses and butterflies, and then suddenly you're knee-deep in complications and heartache. Sounds like you're living the dream!"

"Dream or nightmare, it's hard to tell sometimes," I mused, the tension in my chest tightening. "I don't want to hurt anyone, but every time we're together, it feels like we're forging something beautiful, despite the shadows lurking around us."

"Have you talked to him about it?" Clara asked, her expression softening. "I mean, what does he want? What do you want?"

I hesitated, my thoughts tumbling over each other like leaves in a windstorm. "I want to believe that this connection is real, that it's not just a temporary escape from everything that's been happening. But I'm terrified, Clara. What if it's just a distraction? What if I'm chasing a fantasy?"

Clara leaned back, crossing her arms as she regarded me thoughtfully. "It's okay to be scared. Relationships are messy, and they don't come with guarantees. But you need to communicate. You can't keep pretending like everything's fine when it's not. Talk to him. Lay it all out on the table."

Her words lingered in the air, a challenge and a comfort all at once. I knew she was right; the weight of unspoken fears was becoming unbearable. Yet, the thought of voicing my insecurities to Michael felt daunting. Would he understand? Would he laugh it off, thinking I was overthinking things again? Or worse, would he agree that we were just two souls caught in a fleeting moment?

The door swung open again, and my heart leaped, a thrill of hope igniting within me. But it was only a group of college students, laughing and chattering as they crowded in. I forced myself to focus on Clara instead, to ground myself in our conversation. "Okay, I'll think about it," I said, though even as I spoke, the tightness in my chest didn't loosen its grip.

"Good. Just remember, sometimes the most beautiful things come from facing our fears head-on," Clara encouraged, her voice warm with sincerity.

As she spoke, I couldn't help but wonder if facing those fears would bring me closer to Michael or push us further apart. The uncertainty hung in the air like an uninvited guest, and as I took a sip of my now lukewarm coffee, I realized that the time had come to decide if I was brave enough to dive into the depths of desire, or if I would let it slip away like grains of sand through my fingers.

The soft glow of the streetlights filtered through the trees, casting playful shadows on the pavement as I walked home, the cool evening air wrapping around me like a comforting shawl. The echoes of Clara's advice resonated in my mind, stirring the pot of anxiety simmering in my chest. What was it about love that was so deliciously complex? I had never expected my heart to feel like a game of tug-of-war, each pull either drawing me closer to Michael or sending me spiraling into uncertainty.

Every step felt heavier as I replayed our last encounter. The warmth of his breath on my skin, the way he looked at me as if I were the only person in the universe—it was intoxicating. Yet, beneath that intoxicating surface lay an undercurrent of guilt, a nagging voice that whispered I was treading on dangerous ground. My heart yearned for him, but the shadows of my choices loomed large, threatening to eclipse the light we had ignited.

As I reached my apartment, I found myself hesitating at the door, my hand lingering on the cool metal doorknob. I could almost hear Michael's laughter echoing in my mind, feel the heat of his body next to mine as we shared moments that seemed to stretch time itself. Yet those fleeting instances were shadowed by the looming question of what came next. Would we be able to build something real, or were we simply trying to escape our respective realities, each holding on to the other like a lifeline?

With a sigh, I stepped inside, the familiar scent of lavender from my candles filling the air, a soothing balm against the chaos in my thoughts. I tossed my bag onto the couch, the soft thud echoing in the stillness of my space. As I wandered into the kitchen, I began the comforting ritual of brewing a cup of chamomile tea, hoping it would help quiet the tumult raging within me.

Just as the kettle began to whistle, my phone buzzed, jolting me from my reverie. The screen lit up with a message from Michael. My heart raced as I swiped it open.

Can we talk?

Those three words sent a jolt of electricity through my veins. I stared at the screen, a mix of excitement and dread bubbling up inside me. What did he want to talk about? Did he feel the same confusion I did? The kettle continued its shrill protest, drawing me back to reality as I hastily poured the steaming water over my tea bag, the fragrant steam curling up towards my face.

I took a moment to steady my nerves, inhaling deeply before typing my response.

Of course. When and where?

I hit send, my heart pounding as I awaited his reply. It was a strange sensation, this mingling of anticipation and anxiety, like standing on the edge of a diving board, peering down at the water below, unsure if I should leap or back away.

The reply came swiftly.

How about that little park by the café? In an hour?

A smile crept across my face, a flicker of warmth cutting through the chill of uncertainty. That park was our secret haven, a place where the world seemed to fade away and our laughter filled the air like music. It was where we first began to blur the lines between friendship and something more, and the thought of returning there sent butterflies flitting through my stomach.

With a newfound determination, I set about getting ready. I changed into a cozy sweater that felt like a warm hug, letting my hair fall in loose waves around my shoulders. As I glanced in the mirror, I practiced a smile, a mix of hope and uncertainty. What if tonight was the night we laid everything bare, untangling the knots that had formed between us? I wanted to believe it could be.

The walk to the park felt shorter than usual, each step driven by a cocktail of excitement and dread. The moon hung low in the sky, its silvery light spilling over the path, illuminating the way ahead. When I arrived, the park was serene, bathed in soft shadows, the gentle rustle of leaves whispering secrets to the night.

And there he was, leaning casually against a tree, the faint light catching the edges of his features, making him appear almost ethereal. His eyes sparkled with that familiar mix of mischief and warmth as I approached, and my heart skipped a beat.

"Hey," I greeted, trying to keep my voice steady as I reached him.

"Hey," he replied, that infectious smile spreading across his face. "I was starting to think you'd changed your mind."

"Never. Just needed to prepare myself for this monumental conversation we're about to have," I quipped, trying to inject some humor into the moment to ease the tension coiling in my stomach.

Michael chuckled, and the sound wrapped around me like a familiar melody. "I don't know if I'd call it monumental, but it's definitely important. At least, it is for me."

We fell into step beside each other, walking further into the heart of the park, where the trees stood tall and the air felt electric. I could feel the weight of his words hanging between us, an unsaid acknowledgment of the feelings we had both been tiptoeing around.

"Can I be honest with you?" he asked, his voice dropping to a more serious tone. I nodded, my heart pounding in anticipation. "I've been thinking a lot about us, about what we're doing."

Here it was, the moment I'd both dreaded and longed for. "Me too," I admitted, the confession tumbling out before I could stop it. "I mean, I really like you, Michael, but it's complicated."

"Complicated is an understatement," he replied, running a hand through his hair in that endearing way I had grown to love. "But I can't help but feel like what we have is something worth exploring. I just... I don't want to lose what we have, you know?"

His words hung in the air, fragile yet potent, and I felt the sharp pang of vulnerability creeping in. "I don't want to lose it either, but I can't help but wonder if we're just trying to fill a void left by others."

Michael stopped walking, turning to face me fully, the intensity in his gaze pinning me in place. "What if we're not? What if this is something real? Something we can build on?"

His words washed over me, soothing yet igniting a flicker of fear. What if we were venturing into something deeper, something that could shatter both our worlds? But there was also that undeniable spark, the chemistry that sparked between us like fireworks on a summer night. I could almost see it in the air, swirling around us, pulling us closer.

"Then let's take it slow," I suggested, my voice steadier than I felt. "No pressure. Just... let's see where this goes."

He nodded, a grin breaking across his face, and I felt a rush of relief mingling with excitement. In that moment, the world outside faded away, and all that remained was the two of us, standing on the precipice of something extraordinary. The uncertainty remained, swirling like autumn leaves around us, but perhaps that was part of the journey—learning to navigate the unpredictable winds of desire together.

The night air hummed with a delicate tension as we stood beneath the sprawling branches of the park's ancient oak trees. Moonlight filtered through the leaves, casting dappled shadows on the ground and creating a mosaic of light and darkness around us. It was the perfect backdrop for the conversation we were navigating, a kind of natural stage where vulnerability and hope mingled like the scents of the blooming jasmine nearby.

"Slow sounds good," Michael said, his voice rich and deep, a comforting warmth against the cool evening breeze. I could see the relief washing over him, and it mirrored the flutter of hope blooming in my chest. "I don't want to rush anything and ruin what we have."

"Right," I agreed, the sincerity of his words wrapping around me like a favorite blanket. "It's just... things are complicated, and I don't want to make things messier than they already are."

A moment of silence stretched between us, thick with unspoken worries. I glanced up at him, his features softened in the pale light. The way he looked at me—intensely yet tenderly—made my heart race. It was a look that said he understood, that he too was standing on a tightrope, balancing between desire and fear.

"Complicated might be my middle name," he replied, a teasing lilt in his tone, but there was a hint of seriousness in his eyes. "But let's take it one day at a time. We can start by grabbing coffee together tomorrow, just like old times."

I chuckled, the tension easing a fraction. "Just coffee? No secret rendezvous in the middle of the night?"

"Unless you want to add some excitement to the routine," he quipped, a smirk dancing on his lips. "I can always suggest the local donut shop. They have an amazing chocolate-glazed that's practically a work of art."

"Only you could turn a simple coffee date into an adventure with pastries involved," I shot back, feeling the warmth of a genuine smile spread across my face.

Michael's laughter echoed through the quiet park, and for a moment, the world outside faded away. But as the sound lingered, it also brought with it a reminder of the reality we were both trying to navigate. Emily's absence felt heavy in the air, the unspoken complexities of our situation pulling at the edges of our playful banter.

"Speaking of adventures," I began, hesitating as I broached the topic that had been nagging at me since the moment we stepped into the park. "What about Emily? I mean, where does she fit into all of this? It feels... unfair to her."

Michael's expression shifted, the playful spark in his eyes dimming as he pondered my words. "I wish it were easy. Emily's been a big part of my life, but it's different now. I care about her, but what we had was—"

"Complicated?" I finished for him, raising an eyebrow.

"Exactly," he said, a hint of exasperation creeping into his tone. "I've been caught in a tug-of-war between two people I care about, and it's exhausting. I don't want to hurt anyone, but I can't ignore what's happening between us. I just... don't know how to fix it."

His honesty struck a chord within me, resonating with the fear I had tried to bury. "Maybe there's no fixing it. Maybe we just have to find a way to coexist, to make this work without destroying the pieces we both care about."

He looked at me then, his gaze piercing through the uncertainty like a lighthouse in a storm. "You make it sound so simple."

"Maybe it's not," I admitted, crossing my arms as I leaned against the tree. "But I can't shake the feeling that there's a way through this mess, even if it's not clear yet. I just... I want to figure it out without losing you in the process."

The weight of my words hung between us, and I felt as if we were on the precipice of something monumental, something that could change everything. But then, like the sudden crack of a twig underfoot, a sharp sound shattered the intimate moment we had created.

We both turned our heads toward the sound, the playful energy evaporating like mist in the morning sun. A shadow flickered at the edge of the park, just beyond the reach of the streetlight's glow. My heart raced as I squinted into the darkness, trying to discern the shape lurking there.

"Did you see that?" I asked, my voice barely above a whisper, adrenaline surging through me.

"Yeah, I did," Michael replied, his tone shifting from relaxed to alert. He stepped closer, instinctively placing himself between me and the darkness. "Let's just—"

But before he could finish, the figure stepped into the light, revealing a tall silhouette with sharp features and an air of undeniable menace. My breath caught in my throat as recognition washed over me.

"Emily?" I breathed, shock rippling through me. The girl I thought I'd left behind was standing before us, her expression a mix of anger and hurt.

"What the hell are you doing here?" Michael snapped, his protective instinct flaring as he stepped forward, his posture tense.

"I came to find you," she said, her voice steady but laced with an undercurrent of emotion. "To find both of you. I know what's been going on, and I need to talk."

The air felt thick with unspoken words, a tension that could snap at any moment. I exchanged a glance with Michael, uncertainty flickering in his eyes as the weight of the situation settled heavily around us.

"Emily, it's not what you think," I began, my heart racing as I sensed the delicate balance we had struck teetering on the edge of chaos.

"Then tell me what it is," she challenged, her gaze fierce and unwavering.

And in that moment, everything I had feared about our secret was laid bare before us. The shadows of desire and guilt twisted together, threatening to pull us all into a whirlwind of emotions we weren't prepared to face. As I opened my mouth to speak, I felt the ground shift beneath us, a storm brewing that could either bring us closer or tear us apart for good.

Chapter 9: Shattered Illusions

The sun hung low in the sky, casting long shadows across the asphalt, where whispers seemed to cling like a stubborn fog. I stood at the edge of the school courtyard, my heart racing as I watched Emily storm across the lawn. The vibrant greens of the grass felt like a distant memory, faded by the storm brewing in her stormy blue eyes. She had a fire in her step that morning, each stride radiating a mix of determination and fury that made my stomach churn. Just days before, we had shared laughter and promises in secret, but now that warmth felt as distant as the horizon.

The moment I had dared to hope that our love might become something more than stolen glances and hushed conversations, the world had conspired against us. Emily was a force of nature, and now it was as if she had transformed from the shy girl I had fallen for into a hurricane, intent on tearing down everything in her path. I was trapped in a tempest of emotion—pride, fear, and an aching need to protect what we had built.

"Michael!" Her voice cut through the chatter of students, and all eyes turned toward us. I winced, knowing the full weight of what she intended to do. I had watched her shrink back from confrontation before, but this time she was a lioness, ready to claw her way to the truth. I felt a flush of embarrassment ripple through me, mixing with the adrenaline that surged in my veins. "We need to talk!"

Panic danced in my chest as I met her gaze, hoping to convey that this wasn't the way. The school was our sanctuary, or at least it had been. Now it felt like a battleground. The air around us was thick with the scent of overripe fruit from the nearby apple trees, mingling with the sound of laughter and whispers that echoed across the courtyard. I felt their stares like arrows, each one aimed to wound.

"Emily, wait!" I called out, but she had already forged ahead, her resolve unshaken. There was an undeniable strength in her, one that I admired even as I feared it. I caught snippets of conversation as we crossed the threshold into the heart of the school, a cacophony of shock and disbelief swirling around us.

"Did you hear? They're together!"

"No way. It can't be true."

"He was with Sarah just last week!"

Each remark landed like a punch, each word a reminder of the precariousness of our situation. I could feel the cracks in our world widening, threatening to swallow us whole. We had danced around the truth for too long, and now it was out there, raw and bleeding.

"Why are you doing this?" I managed to ask as we reached a more secluded hallway, away from prying eyes. I could hear the soft hum of the overhead lights, a stark contrast to the chaos brewing in my mind. "Can't we just keep this between us for a little longer?"

"Keep it secret? You think I want to hide? I'm tired of living in the shadows, Michael!" Her voice was low but fierce, echoing off the walls as if the very building could feel the weight of her words. "I thought we were in this together, but you keep acting like you're ashamed of me."

Shame? I wanted to argue, to tell her that nothing could be further from the truth. But the truth was complicated—our world was a minefield of expectations, and every step we took felt like a gamble. I had thought I could protect her, that I could shield us both from the inevitable fallout. But watching her now, I realized that she was fighting for something I was afraid to fully embrace.

"Emily, it's not about being ashamed. It's about—" I struggled to find the right words, feeling the weight of their gazes pressing down on us like a heavy cloak. "It's about protecting what we have. I don't want to lose you."

Her expression softened for a fleeting moment, and I saw the girl who had captured my heart—the one who had shared secrets beneath the stars, who had whispered dreams of our future as we lay in the grass. But that flicker was quickly extinguished. "You're already losing me," she said, her voice breaking like fragile glass.

It was true; I could feel the distance growing between us, like an invisible chasm we had both created. I reached out, desperate to bridge that gap, but she flinched away, as if my touch was a brand. It was a blow I hadn't anticipated, one that sent ripples of regret through me.

"Please," I said, desperation creeping into my voice. "Let's just take a step back. We can figure this out without involving everyone else."

But her resolve only hardened, and I watched as the flames of her anger reignited, burning brighter than before. "No! I won't stand by while you hide from the world. I deserve more than being your secret. I deserve to be loved openly, and I deserve to love you openly, too."

Her words struck me like lightning, illuminating the dark corners of my heart where doubt had festered. There was a choice to be made, one that would either bring us together or tear us apart. I felt the weight of the world crashing down, and in that moment, I realized how precarious our love truly was.

As the tension crackled in the air, the unmistakable sound of footsteps drew nearer. A small crowd had gathered, intrigued by the spectacle unfolding. I could feel their judgment like a noose tightening around my neck. I wanted to scream, to tell them to back off, but all I could do was stand there, paralyzed by fear and uncertainty.

Emily's eyes darted toward the group, and in that instant, something shifted. The fierce determination on her face faltered for just a heartbeat before she straightened her back, a warrior ready for battle. "I'm done hiding, Michael. This is who I am. Take it or leave it."

And just like that, she turned and walked away, her silhouette framed against the buzz of the school, a symbol of everything I had failed to protect. The whispers followed her, swirling like leaves in the wind, and I stood frozen, gripped by the chilling realization that the love I had cherished was now a double-edged sword, threatening to cut deeper than I could have ever imagined.

I stood in the remnants of our fractured moment, the air heavy with tension and unspoken words. Emily's silhouette faded into the crowd, leaving behind a silence so profound that I could hear my heart thudding against my ribcage. The faces surrounding me mirrored a mix of curiosity and malice, and I felt as though I had been thrust into a cruel stage play where the audience was both spectator and critic. Each whisper twisted the knife a little deeper, unraveling the fragile thread of connection that had tethered me to Emily.

I turned away from the gathering storm of students, searching for a refuge in the nearest empty classroom. The walls, adorned with faded posters of past achievements, felt oddly comforting, like a relic from a time when life had been simpler, unclouded by secrets and shame. The familiar scent of chalk dust hung in the air, and as I sank into one of the old wooden desks, I attempted to gather my thoughts, but they swirled around me like autumn leaves caught in a gale.

Why hadn't I fought harder to keep her close? The truth settled heavily on my chest, an unwelcome weight. I had been trying to shield us both from the inevitable fallout, but Emily was right—hiding was a betrayal of our love. It struck me then, as I replayed her words in my mind, that I had underestimated her strength. This wasn't just about me anymore; it was about her, about her right to love and be loved openly.

Lost in thought, I barely heard the classroom door creak open. It wasn't until Sarah, my so-called friend, slid into the room that I snapped back to reality. She leaned against the doorframe, arms crossed, a mix of concern and intrigue etched across her face. "You look like you've seen a ghost, Michael. Or maybe just the aftermath of a really bad decision."

I offered a weak smile, but it didn't reach my eyes. "You could say that. I think I just signed up for the drama club without auditioning."

"You can't avoid this, you know." Her voice was surprisingly soft, cutting through my haze. "Emily is not going to back down. She's fierce, and she deserves to be heard."

I ran a hand through my hair, feeling the weight of every unspoken sentiment pressing down. "I know. I just didn't expect her to come out swinging like that. She's always been so reserved, and now—"

"Now she's done playing it safe," Sarah interrupted, her gaze steady. "You need to figure out what you want. Do you really love her, or are you just scared of what everyone else thinks?"

That question hung in the air like a specter, and I flinched at the raw honesty of it. "Of course I love her. But..." I trailed off, grappling with the tangled mess of emotions within me. "But it's complicated. This isn't just a romance; it's a war zone. We're up against gossip, judgment, everything."

"Right, and the best thing to do is hide in this classroom until it all blows over?" She raised an eyebrow, her expression skeptical. "Michael, if you care about her, fight for it. Love isn't just about the easy parts; it's about being there when things get tough."

The door swung open again, this time with an enthusiasm that was entirely unwelcome. It was Matt, one of my so-called friends, whose grin faded as he took in the atmosphere. "What's going on in here? I heard Emily went nuclear on you."

"Just a little misunderstanding," I muttered, wishing I could slide further into my seat and disappear.

"Misunderstanding? More like a declaration of war," Matt said, smirking. "You might want to prepare for battle, soldier. Rumor has it, she's not going down without a fight, and everyone's choosing sides."

"Great, just what I need," I replied, sarcasm leaking into my voice. "A battlefield full of my friends armed with gossip. How am I supposed to navigate that?"

Matt leaned against the desk, an exaggerated air of nonchalance about him. "Easy. You pick your side. Either you're with her or you're against her. Just don't be surprised when people show their true colors."

A knot formed in my stomach at the thought of losing friends over this, but I couldn't deny the truth in his words. I had to make a choice. "So, you think I should just jump into the fray?"

"Why not? If you're going to do this, do it right," he said with a shrug. "Besides, if Emily's ready to go all out, you should match her energy. Show her you're in it together."

The more I thought about it, the more the idea resonated within me. Sarah's words echoed in my mind, urging me to step out of the shadows. Emily deserved more than half-hearted affection. She needed to know I was all in.

As if on cue, the classroom door swung open again. This time, it was Emily herself, her expression a tempest of emotions. She looked like a warrior stepping onto the battlefield, with fire dancing in her eyes. The moment she entered, the air shifted, charged with the palpable tension between us. I stood, instinctively drawn to her presence, but she held up a hand to stop me.

"Michael, I—" she began, her voice trembling slightly, but her determination was unwavering.

"Wait," I interrupted, cutting through the silence. "I've been thinking, and you're right. We can't keep hiding. If this is going to work, we need to be honest about what we want. I want you, Emily. I want to be with you, no matter what it takes."

She blinked, momentarily taken aback, and I could see the flicker of hope in her eyes. "You mean that?"

"Absolutely," I said, my heart pounding in my chest. "I know it won't be easy, but I refuse to let anyone dictate how we feel about each other. I'm ready to face this together."

Her expression softened, and the tension in the room seemed to ease just a fraction. "Together?" she echoed, her voice almost a whisper.

"Yeah. No more hiding, no more shame. Just us, facing whatever comes our way."

A smile broke through the storm, a brilliant beacon cutting through the darkness. "I've been waiting to hear you say that," she admitted, her voice steadying.

But just as relief washed over me, I heard the unmistakable sound of laughter echoing from the hallway, cruel and mocking. I turned instinctively, and my heart sank as I saw a group of students gathered outside, their eyes glued to us like vultures waiting for the inevitable. The whispers rose to a crescendo, and just like that, the moment felt shattered, splintered into a million pieces that danced mockingly around us.

Emily's face fell, and I realized that our declaration of love had just become a spectacle. "They're watching us," she said, her confidence wavering.

"Let them," I replied, but doubt crept in like an uninvited guest. Would this ever be just ours again?

And with that question looming, I reached for her hand, holding on tightly. "No matter what they say, we know the truth."

Emily nodded, a fire igniting in her gaze once more. We were standing at the edge of something monumental, and while the path ahead was strewn with uncertainty, I could feel a shift within me. This was no longer just about us; it was about the choices we would make together, the battles we would fight side by side, ready to face whatever storms awaited us.

The hallways buzzed like a disturbed beehive, every student a potential threat as I navigated the sea of judgmental stares and hushed conversations. Emily walked beside me, her grip on my hand fierce, but her confidence seemed to ebb and flow with each whispered comment that drifted through the air. I could feel her heart racing in tandem with mine, a shared pulse of determination and anxiety. The moment of solidarity we had forged in the classroom felt fragile now, teetering on the brink of collapse as the reality of our situation hit hard.

"Why are they acting like we just declared war?" she muttered, her eyes flaring with indignation. "It's just a relationship, not a hostage negotiation."

"Welcome to high school," I replied, trying to lighten the mood despite the turmoil swirling in my chest. "Where love is treated like a scandal worthy of a soap opera."

She huffed, her frustration palpable. "Next thing you know, they'll be sending out press releases. 'Local couple shatters expectations and hearts!'"

I couldn't help but chuckle, but the laughter was short-lived. Our peers were notorious for their cruelty, and the murmurs swelled to a cacophony as we walked past groups of students. I caught snippets of conversations—words like "traitor" and "fool" punctuated the air, sharp enough to slice through the already thin veil of confidence we clung to.

As we approached our lockers, a familiar face appeared in the crowd—Sarah, with her usual air of confidence now tainted with a hint of pity. "Hey, are you two okay?" she asked, stepping in closer.

Emily flashed her a tight-lipped smile. "Just peachy. Nothing like a little public shaming to start the day."

"I didn't mean to—"

"Look, Sarah," I interrupted, my patience fraying, "we're handling this. Can you just... I don't know, not act like it's the end of the world?"

Sarah studied me for a moment, her expression shifting from concern to determination. "Okay, but you need to think this through. Everyone is talking. Some people might even think they're doing you a favor by 'helping' you break it off."

"That's ridiculous!" Emily exclaimed, her voice rising. "Why can't they just let us be?"

"Because they don't understand," Sarah replied, her tone softening. "And honestly, some of them are just waiting for a reason to pounce. You need to prepare for the fallout."

"What are you suggesting?" I asked, feeling a wave of anger mixed with the realization that she might be right.

"Maybe you should consider laying low for a bit," Sarah said cautiously. "Give it time for the heat to die down. Maybe, just maybe, people will forget about it. You could pretend you're just friends for a while."

"Pretend?" Emily's voice dripped with sarcasm. "I don't want to hide who I am. I'm not ashamed of us!"

"No one's saying you should be," Sarah responded, her eyes darting around, aware of the prying ears nearby. "But love is about compromise too, isn't it?"

"Compromise?" I echoed incredulously. "So what? We should just pretend we're strangers to make it easier for everyone else?"

A chill settled in the pit of my stomach as the reality of our situation sunk in deeper. The thought of playing a part in someone else's theater of gossip felt like betrayal, yet Sarah's warning echoed painfully true.

Before I could respond, the school bell rang, signaling the start of our next class. The crowd shifted, and as students filed into the building, I felt the weight of the decision pressing down like a boulder.

"Let's just get through today," I said, forcing my voice to remain steady. "We'll figure it out later."

Emily nodded, but I could see the doubt creeping into her eyes. We headed into the classroom, our shoulders brushing against each other, a silent reminder of the connection we shared amid the chaos.

The class was a blur of scribbled notes and half-hearted participation, the teacher's voice blending into a monotonous drone as my mind raced with everything that had transpired. I caught glimpses of Emily stealing looks at me, her frustration flickering like a candle's flame in the wind. I wanted to reach for her, to assure her that we were in this together, but every time I moved, I felt the eyes of our classmates glued to us, waiting for the next spectacle.

By the time lunch rolled around, the atmosphere felt even more charged. We stepped into the cafeteria, the noise palpable, filled with laughter and the clatter of trays. Yet, all I could focus on was the disapproving gazes flitting our way. I led Emily to a corner table, the only spot that felt somewhat safe, but the feeling of being on display didn't wane.

"So, what's the plan?" Emily asked, her tone a mixture of defiance and frustration as she picked at her salad.

"Honestly? I don't know," I admitted, feeling like I was fumbling in the dark. "I thought we could take it one step at a time. Maybe we—"

But my words were drowned out by the sudden arrival of Matt, who plopped down across from us, a grin plastered on his face. "You two are the talk of the school. I had to come see for myself. How's the relationship drama unfolding?"

"Real nice of you to drop by," Emily said, her sarcasm cutting through the tension. "Got any sage advice, or just here to gawk?"

"Hey, I'm just here for the show," he replied with a wink. "But seriously, it's kind of wild. You've got a fan club and a hater club now. You're practically famous."

"Great," I muttered, feeling the heat rise in my cheeks. "Fame is exactly what I need right now."

"Look," Matt said, leaning forward, "you two need to take control of this narrative. Don't let them dictate your story. You can either let the gossip consume you or you can turn it into something."

"What does that even mean?" Emily asked, her brow furrowing.

"It means you can own it. Make it your own," he said, excitement flickering in his eyes. "You could start a blog, or maybe a vlog! Something where you share your story—like a couple's journey against the odds. You'd have a following in no time!"

"A vlog?" Emily echoed, incredulous. "You think I want to broadcast my life to everyone?"

"It's better than hiding, isn't it?" he replied, undeterred. "People love a good underdog story. You'd be surprised how many folks might actually support you."

"And how many would just want to watch us fail?" I shot back, frustration boiling to the surface. "What's the point of putting ourselves out there if we're just going to be the next gossip?"

As our conversation spiraled into a heated debate, I noticed a figure lingering near the entrance of the cafeteria. It was Sarah, her face a mask of concern as she scanned the room. I felt a knot tighten in my stomach as her gaze landed on us. She leaned in to whisper something to a girl next to her, and then suddenly, a loud voice rang out.

"Hey, everyone!" Sarah shouted, and the chatter fell to a hush. "Guess what? Emily and Michael are together, and it's causing quite the stir! Let's give them a round of applause for being brave enough to love in public!"

The applause that followed was mockingly sparse, accompanied by a few snickers and whispers that sliced through the air like ice. My heart raced as the attention shifted, the spotlight now glaring on us in a way that felt both exhilarating and terrifying.

"Sarah, what are you doing?" I hissed, but she just smiled, a glint of mischief in her eyes.

"Trying to give you a moment," she replied, stepping back as the murmurs rose again. "You need to own this. Make it your story, not theirs."

But as I glanced at Emily, I saw the uncertainty reflected in her eyes, and the weight of the moment loomed large. The world felt unsteady, as if teetering on the edge of a knife. We had faced so much together, but this was a new battlefield, and I could sense the tides were shifting.

Just then, the cafeteria doors swung open, and in walked Tyler, the school's reigning heartthrob, with an entourage that radiated confidence. He scanned the room, and when his eyes landed on us, a smirk twisted his lips.

"Looks like the lovebirds are feeling bold," he called out, his voice dripping with sarcasm. "What a brave choice, huh? Kissing and telling. Must be a new trend."

Laughter erupted from his group, and I could feel the heat rising in my cheeks. I glanced at Emily, whose expression had hardened.

"Shut up, Tyler," I snapped, feeling a surge of protectiveness.

But before he could respond, Emily stood up, her expression fierce. "You know what, Tyler? I'm done being ashamed of who I am.

If you can't handle it, that's your problem. Maybe it's time for you to grow up."

Gasps rippled through the crowd as she turned on her heel and strode toward the exit, leaving a stunned silence in her wake. I stood frozen, caught between admiration and fear.

"Emily!" I called after her, but the

Chapter 10: Fractured Trust

The air was thick with tension, a palpable weight pressing against my chest as I paced the dimly lit hallway of my once vibrant home. Each step echoed like the distant rumble of thunder, signaling the storm brewing both outside and within me. I could still hear the remnants of the confrontation replaying in my mind, each word carving deeper wounds than the last. "How could you?" was the refrain that echoed through my thoughts, reverberating like a cruel taunt. It felt surreal, like a scene from a bad movie where the protagonist's life unravels before their eyes, and all I could do was watch.

The wallpaper, once a cheery shade of yellow, now appeared drab and lifeless, a reflection of my mood. I ran my fingers along the fraying edges, tracing the patterns that had been a source of comfort for years. But comfort was a fleeting memory now, overshadowed by the looming specter of betrayal. I had trusted Emily completely, and that trust had shattered like glass underfoot. As I glanced out the window, rain began to fall in rhythmic bursts, tapping against the glass as if trying to penetrate the fog that had enveloped my heart.

I moved to the kitchen, seeking solace in the familiarity of the space. The aroma of freshly brewed coffee filled the air, a bittersweet reminder of mornings spent laughing and sharing secrets over steaming mugs. I had always thought of this room as a sanctuary, a place where worries melted away in the warmth of companionship. But today, it felt foreign, the silence suffocating. I poured a cup, watching the dark liquid swirl, contemplating whether caffeine could mend what felt irreparably broken.

With each sip, I felt the heat of the coffee course through me, stirring dormant emotions. I recalled the last time I had seen Emily—her eyes ablaze with hurt, her voice trembling with accusations. She had stormed out, leaving me standing there, rooted to the spot, grappling with the realization that our friendship had been irrevocably altered. It was as if a tempest had ripped through our lives, leaving behind a landscape dotted with remnants of what had once been whole.

As the clock ticked away the seconds, I found myself lost in thought, grappling with Michael's silence. He had always been my rock, the one I turned to when the world became too chaotic. But since that fateful night, he had retreated, his easy laughter replaced with a solemnity that felt like a dark cloud hanging over us. I craved the intimacy we once shared, the late-night conversations that flowed like water, but now they felt forced, strained under the weight of unspoken words.

In a moment of defiance, I reached for my phone, scrolling through the messages that had flooded in since the confrontation. Friends had chosen sides, and the group chat buzzed with a cacophony of opinions, each one more scathing than the last. My heart sank with every notification, the betrayal running deeper than I had anticipated. It was as if I had been cast into the role of the villain in a story I never wanted to write.

Just as I was about to throw my phone across the room in frustration, a notification flashed. It was from Emily. My heart raced, a flutter of hope mingling with dread. Perhaps this was it—perhaps she had come to her senses, willing to mend the rift between us. But as I opened the message, my stomach dropped.

"Stay away from me. You don't know what you're doing."

Those words hung in the air, heavy and suffocating, a dagger twisting in my gut. I could almost hear her voice, laced with venom, the betrayal like acid on my tongue. How had we spiraled so far so fast? My fingers trembled as I typed out a response, desperation clawing at me. "Emily, please. Let's talk. I need to explain." I hit send, but deep down, I knew it wouldn't change anything. The damage was done, and the chasm between us felt insurmountable.

In that moment of despair, I glanced out the window again, and my gaze caught on Michael as he stepped out of his car, rain drenching him almost instantly. His dark hair clung to his forehead, and for a fleeting moment, I felt the urge to rush outside, to embrace him and forget the turmoil that had taken root in our lives. But as he looked up, our eyes met, and I saw the weight of uncertainty etched across his face. It was as if he was caught in a web of indecision, unsure of which path to take.

I opened the door, the cool air whipping around me, mingling with the scent of rain-soaked earth. "Michael!" I called out, the urgency in my voice slicing through the stillness. He paused, his expression shifting from surprise to something that resembled apprehension. He took a tentative step toward me, the distance between us still painfully wide. "Can we talk?" The words felt inadequate, an invitation that held the weight of a thousand unspoken questions.

He hesitated, his brow furrowing as he glanced back toward his car. I could sense the internal struggle waging war within him, the tug-of-war between loyalty and uncertainty. "I... I don't know if that's a good idea," he finally said, his voice barely above a whisper, and my heart sank at the distance those words created.

"Please," I implored, taking a step forward, desperate to bridge the gap. "I can't lose you too." There was a crack in his armor then, a flash of vulnerability that made my chest ache. It was a reminder that beneath the layers of hurt, we still cared for one another.

As the rain continued to fall, the two of us stood at a precipice, teetering on the edge of everything we had built together, caught between a past we cherished and a future clouded by uncertainty. In that moment, I realized that the journey ahead would not be easy. Trust, once fractured, could be mended, but the road would be long and fraught with challenges. And as the first drops of rain began to mix with the tears I refused to shed, I knew that the storm was far from over.

I stood on the porch, rain still cascading in rhythmic sheets, the world around me softened to a watercolor blur. Michael's expression lingered like an unfinished sentence, and I felt a mixture of relief and anxiety wash over me. There he was, standing at the edge of my universe, his presence both a comfort and a reminder of everything that had slipped through my fingers. I gestured toward the swing that hung from the porch's overhang, its chains creaking softly in the wind. "Let's at least sit. The rain's not going to let up anytime soon."

He nodded, a hesitant smile breaking through the tension as he joined me. The swing swayed under our weight, a delicate motion that mirrored the uncertainty we both felt. "I didn't think you'd actually come outside," he said, a playful lilt to his voice that suggested he was trying to lighten the mood, even if it fell flat. "I was half expecting a dramatic reenactment of a scene from a soap opera."

"Believe me, if I could pull off dramatic, I'd be on Broadway by now." I chuckled lightly, but my heart was heavy with the unspoken words that danced just beyond the surface.

The rain began to lighten, transforming into a gentle drizzle that created a soothing melody against the wooden slats of the porch. "So," I began, choosing my words carefully as if they were fragile glass. "How are you handling... all of this?"

He sighed, running a hand through his wet hair, pushing it back from his forehead. "It's been rough. Everyone's whispering about you, and honestly, it makes me feel like I'm in the middle of some ridiculous high school drama."

"Tell me about it," I replied, my tone laced with sarcasm. "I didn't sign up for this reality show either. If I had known betrayal was part of the package, I would have opted for the stay-at-home life with a Netflix subscription."

Michael's laughter was genuine, breaking through the cloud of unease that had settled between us. "You know, you'd be great on reality TV. Just imagine the dramatic confessional moments."

"'I'm here for the friendships, but all I got was this crummy betrayal,'" I mimicked, placing a hand dramatically on my heart as if I were delivering a monologue.

"Perfect! You can even cry a little for effect," he teased, his eyes sparkling with mischief. But that lightness faded quickly, replaced by the familiar heaviness that had characterized our interactions lately. "But seriously, I don't know how to navigate this. It's like walking on eggshells around everyone. People think I'm choosing sides, but I just... I care about both of you."

"I understand. It's not fair to you, either." I bit my lip, feeling the weight of the world bearing down on me. "I didn't want it to be like this. I never wanted to hurt her."

"Neither did I," he replied, his voice low and earnest. "But now it feels like our entire friend group is splintering."

"I used to think we were all so tight-knit, like a tapestry. Now it feels more like a quilt full of mismatched patches, and every time I look at it, I'm reminded of how ugly it's become."

Michael nodded, his gaze distant as if he were caught in the threads of our shared history, each moment a stitch that had woven us together. "Maybe we can do something about that. Like, I don't know, a group outing? Something that reminds everyone of how much fun we used to have?"

I snorted softly, the sound a little more bitter than I intended. "Yeah, because nothing screams 'fun' like an awkward group outing where everyone's silently judging each other. It'll be like an episode of 'Survivor: Friend Edition.'"

"Okay, maybe that's a bad idea," he conceded, a sheepish grin breaking through. "But we need to come up with something, because I can't just stand by and watch this happen."

I turned to him, our eyes locking for a heartbeat, and in that moment, a flicker of hope sparked between us. "You're right. I want to fix this. But I'm not sure how."

Michael leaned back, crossing his arms over his chest, a thoughtful look creeping onto his face. "What if we reach out to Emily? Maybe if we can talk things through, we can salvage something from this mess."

"Talk to Emily?" I hesitated, the idea sending a ripple of anxiety through me. "Do you really think she'd be open to it?"

He shrugged, his expression softening. "If she cares about you—and she does—then it's worth a shot. I know you two are at odds right now, but it doesn't have to stay that way."

I sighed, the thought swirling in my mind like a whirlwind. "I want to believe that. But I don't know if I'm ready to face her again. What if she just throws more accusations at me?"

"Then we deal with that. Together," he said, his tone firm. "I won't let you face this alone. We'll figure it out, one step at a time."

The sincerity in his voice brought a warmth that radiated through my chest. It was easy to forget how supportive he had been, even in the midst of the chaos. "Okay," I said finally, finding a flicker of resolve. "Let's try reaching out to her. I just hope she's willing to listen."

The rain had slowed to a gentle patter, the world outside transforming into a serene backdrop that mirrored the quiet resolve blossoming between us. Michael leaned closer, the swing swaying softly as he held my gaze. "If there's one thing I know, it's that real friendships can weather the storm. We just have to navigate through the rough patches."

"Rough patches, huh?" I replied, a smirk tugging at my lips. "Sounds like we're in for a bumpy ride."

"Bumpy is my specialty," he said, the mischief returning to his eyes. "Just think of me as your emotional seatbelt."

I laughed, the sound bubbling up from a place deep within me. "I guess that makes me the driver of this emotional road trip. Buckle up, then. It might get wild."

"Wild is an understatement."

As we sat there, the rain finally relenting and the first hints of sun breaking through the clouds, I felt a sense of clarity wash over me. Whatever lay ahead, I knew we would face it together. The path to rebuilding trust would be fraught with challenges, but the strength of our connection would guide us. In that moment, the prospect of healing seemed just within reach, shimmering like a distant star on the horizon.

The next morning dawned bright and deceptively serene, the kind of day that seemed at odds with the tumult brewing inside me. I stood at the kitchen window, staring out at the sun-drenched yard, where the flowers bloomed vibrantly, oblivious to the storm that had rattled my world. I could almost convince myself that everything was fine, that yesterday's chaos was just a figment of my imagination. But the shadows of doubt and betrayal lingered like an unwelcome fog, creeping into my thoughts.

I poured myself a cup of coffee, the rich aroma filling the air, and took a moment to savor the warmth of the mug in my hands. Each sip was a fleeting comfort against the backdrop of anxiety that loomed over me. The kitchen clock ticked rhythmically, a constant reminder of the minutes slipping away as I braced myself for what lay ahead. Today was the day I would reach out to Emily.

The phone sat on the counter, its screen glowing with notifications. I had put off texting her, afraid of what her response might be. As I stared at it, the weight of indecision pressed down on my shoulders. "It's just a message," I murmured to myself, trying to summon the courage that felt so elusive. "You can do this."

I picked up the phone, hesitated for a moment, and finally typed a simple message: Hey, can we talk? I think we need to clear the air. My finger hovered over the send button, anxiety bubbling up in my throat. Would she even respond? Would she slam the door on any hope of reconciliation? With a quick exhale, I pressed send, the notification ping echoing like a gunshot in the quiet kitchen.

Minutes passed, each one stretching into an eternity. Just as doubt began to creep in, my phone buzzed with a new message. My heart raced as I opened it, but the words that met my eyes were not what I had hoped for. I'm busy. Maybe later.

The brevity of her response stung, each word like a tiny dagger. I stared at the screen, disappointment flooding my senses. Maybe later? The uncertainty gnawed at me, filling the air with a suffocating tension. The chance of mending our friendship felt as fragile as a spider's web, quivering with each gust of wind.

"Good job, genius," I muttered to myself, tossing my phone onto the counter with an exasperated sigh. "Maybe later" was a classic brush-off, and I had no idea how to interpret it. Part of me wanted to throw in the towel, retreat back into the shadows where the chaos couldn't reach me, but a flicker of determination sparked within.

I needed to take action, to show Emily that I valued our friendship enough to fight for it. I poured another cup of coffee, downing it in one go before gathering my things. If she wouldn't come to me, maybe I could go to her. I hopped into my car, the engine humming to life as I made my way to her apartment, my heart racing with each passing block.

As I drove, memories of happier times played like a montage in my mind—the spontaneous ice cream runs, late-night movie marathons, and deep conversations that made us feel invincible. Those moments felt so distant now, like a beautiful dream I was struggling to grasp. I parked outside her building, a quaint little place nestled between a bakery and a bookstore, both places that had always brought us joy. But today, everything felt off, as if the world was holding its breath in anticipation.

I walked up the steps, my heart thudding loudly in my chest. With every knock on her door, I felt the weight of our friendship resting on my shoulders. Would she even want to see me?

After what felt like an eternity, the door creaked open, and there stood Emily, her hair tousled and eyes puffy as if she hadn't slept well. She looked surprised to see me, her expression a mix of annoyance and curiosity. "What are you doing here?" she asked, crossing her arms defensively.

"I came to talk," I replied, trying to keep my voice steady despite the tremor in my hands. "I think we really need to figure this out."

"I'm not sure there's anything left to figure out," she said, her tone icy, and I felt the chill seep into my bones.

"Can we at least try?" I pleaded, my voice softer now, almost a whisper. "I miss you, Em. I miss us."

Her defenses wavered for just a moment, and I caught a flicker of something in her eyes—hurt, longing, perhaps a trace of hope. But it vanished as quickly as it came. "I don't know if I can trust you right now," she said, her voice firm but tinged with sadness.

"Trust takes time, I get that. But I don't want to lose you without at least trying to talk it out."

The silence hung heavily between us, thick enough to cut with a knife. I could almost see the gears turning in her mind, her conflict playing out behind her guarded expression. "Fine," she finally said, her voice low. "Let's talk. But only for a little while."

We settled on her small couch, the air thick with unspoken words as I perched at the edge, trying to gauge her mood. I reached for the coffee table, and in a moment of impulse, I grabbed the remote and switched on the TV, hoping a distraction might ease the tension. The news blared loudly, a stream of alarming headlines that felt painfully fitting given our current predicament.

As the anchors discussed the latest town gossip—a missing dog, a local hero saving a cat from a tree—I caught a glimpse of a familiar face in the background, and my stomach dropped. It was Michael, standing just outside the bakery across the street, talking animatedly with some friends.

"Isn't that—" I began, but Emily's gaze had already turned toward the window, her expression shifting from apprehension to shock.

"Why is he here?" she asked, her tone edged with suspicion.

"I don't know," I admitted, watching as Michael laughed, oblivious to the storm brewing just beyond the glass. "I thought he might be at home."

"I can't believe he would just show up here," Emily snapped, her fingers curling into fists on her lap. "What does he want?"

"Maybe he's trying to talk to you too," I suggested, but Emily shook her head, her frustration palpable. "I didn't ask for this, and I'm done with playing games," she shot back, rising to her feet.

Just as she turned toward the door, ready to confront him, there was a sudden crash outside, followed by a frantic shouting. The news anchor's voice echoed in the background as I caught glimpses of people running, their faces twisted in panic.

"What the hell?" Emily gasped, rushing to the window. I followed her, and our eyes widened in horror as we saw smoke billowing from the bakery.

"Something's wrong," I whispered, the gravity of the moment pulling us both into a frenzied reality.

The commotion outside escalated, shouts merging into a cacophony of confusion. I grabbed Emily's arm, adrenaline surging through me. "We have to see what's happening."

As we bolted out the door, the world outside transformed into chaos, with sirens wailing in the distance and people scrambling for safety. And there, amid the chaos, I spotted Michael again, his expression grim as he helped someone to their feet. My heart raced, torn between the need to find him and the urgency of the crisis unfolding before us.

"Stay close!" I shouted to Emily, but as we pushed through the throngs of panicked townspeople, I couldn't shake the feeling that this was just the beginning. Trust had been shattered, but now, something far more dangerous threatened to unravel everything we had fought to preserve.

The ground beneath us trembled as we turned a corner, and the sight that met our eyes was more than I had ever bargained for. In the midst of the chaos, I saw a figure emerging from the shadows, cloaked in an ominous aura, and a shiver ran down my spine. The day had taken a turn I never saw coming, and the secrets hidden in our past were about to come crashing into our present in ways we couldn't begin to imagine.

Chapter 11: Hiding in Plain Sight

The night air was thick with salt and secrets as I led him down a narrow, winding path that twisted through the dense underbrush, each step drawing us deeper into our private world. The faint sound of waves crashing against the shore teased our ears, promising refuge. Underneath the canopy of stars, I could almost convince myself that this was how things were meant to be—an enchanted escape from the weight of our everyday lives, far from the prying eyes of our friends and family.

The cove appeared like a hidden treasure, framed by rugged cliffs that rose sharply from the sand. The moon hung low, its silvery light dancing across the water, illuminating our faces and revealing the breathless anticipation in his gaze. I could feel the heat of his body beside me, an electric current that buzzed through the air, amplifying the thrill of our clandestine rendezvous.

"Are you sure this is the right spot?" he asked, his voice low, teasing me as he stepped closer. I could see the glint of mischief in his eyes, a spark that matched the fire within me.

"Trust me," I replied, a smile curling at the corners of my lips. "It's not every day you get to have your very own private beach."

His laughter, warm and infectious, echoed in the stillness. "Private, huh? I can't wait to see how you've set the stage for this little getaway."

I shrugged, feigning nonchalance, but my heart raced as I led him closer to the water's edge. "It's all about the ambiance, right? Soft waves, a cool breeze, and maybe a little moonlight magic."

The sand felt soft and cool beneath our feet as we stepped closer to the shoreline. I kicked off my sandals, relishing the sensation of the grains slipping between my toes. There was something utterly liberating about shedding the confines of our lives, even if just for a few stolen hours. The ocean beckoned, its rhythmic pulse like a heartbeat, thrumming in time with the rush of excitement coursing through me.

As we settled into the sand, the world melted away—our worries, our responsibilities, and the expectations that seemed to weigh us down at every turn. I turned to him, my breath hitching slightly as I took in the way the moonlight danced in his hair, highlighting the sharp angles of his jaw and the curve of his lips. "You know," I said, feigning a casual tone, "there's something about the ocean that makes everything feel possible."

He chuckled softly, his eyes locking onto mine, dark and mesmerizing. "Or maybe it's just you. You've got this whole aura about you tonight."

"Is that so?" I raised an eyebrow, teasingly flipping my hair back. "I like to think of myself as the Ocean Queen, ruler of this hidden kingdom."

His laughter rang out, mingling with the sound of the waves, and for a moment, I felt invincible. But as we sat there, the laughter fading into a comfortable silence, the reality of our situation seeped back in, like the chill of the evening air creeping in around us.

"We can't keep hiding like this," I murmured, the weight of my thoughts finally spilling out. "Eventually, people will notice we're gone, and..."

"And they'll talk," he finished, a shadow crossing his face. The lightheartedness from earlier faded, replaced by a tension that clung to us like the humidity of the night.

I sighed, wrapping my arms around my knees, feeling the familiar pang of fear twist in my gut. "Do you think it's worth it? This... whatever this is?"

His gaze softened, and he leaned closer, resting a hand on my knee, a gentle touch that ignited a wildfire within me. "You feel it too, don't you? The connection? It's not just a fling, not for me."

The words sent a rush of warmth through my veins, but the doubt still lingered. "I just worry that this is all a fantasy. One day, we'll have to face our reality again, and I don't know if I'm ready for that."

He hesitated, then let out a slow breath. "What if we make our own reality? What if we decide what this means, instead of letting everyone else define it for us?"

My heart raced at the suggestion, the idea of carving our own path both thrilling and terrifying. "You really think we could do that?"

"Why not?" he said, a hint of determination in his voice. "I'm not afraid of the consequences. I just want to be with you, wherever that takes us."

For a moment, the world felt like it could shift on its axis with just those words. The warmth of his hand on my knee felt like an anchor, grounding me amidst the chaos of my thoughts. Yet, as much as I wanted to believe in this new reality, the fear gnawed at me. What would our friends think? Would we lose everything we had built?

Before I could respond, a sudden sound shattered our moment—a rustle in the nearby bushes followed by a figure emerging from the shadows. My heart raced, panic setting in as I instinctively shifted away from him, our bubble of intimacy ruptured. "What was that?"

His expression turned serious, eyes scanning the treeline. "I don't know, but we should probably—"

Before he could finish, a figure stepped into the moonlight, revealing a familiar face, one that sent a shiver down my spine. It was someone from our social circle, someone who would definitely not be pleased to find us here, together in our secret hideaway. My heart sank as I recognized the unmistakable glint of betrayal in their eyes, and just like that, the sanctuary we had created crumbled before us.

The air thickened with tension, a palpable force that made the hair on the back of my neck stand on end. I felt exposed, like a deer caught in the headlights, as the figure stepped closer, their silhouette becoming clearer under the moon's relentless gaze. It was Clara—my friend, my confidante—her expression a curious blend of surprise and amusement.

"Well, well, well, what do we have here?" she said, her voice dripping with mock innocence. I could almost see the wheels turning in her mind, the realization dawning that this wasn't just a friendly meet-up.

"Clara," I said, trying to sound composed, though my heart raced like it was auditioning for the Olympics. "This isn't what it looks like."

"Really? Because from where I'm standing, it looks like you two are getting awfully cozy. Planning a secret romantic escape? Or just a hot tub time machine?" She waggled her eyebrows, a grin plastered across her face, and for a split second, I hated her playful spirit and the levity she brought to the moment.

He moved slightly in front of me, a silent protector, his presence warm and grounding, yet fraught with uncertainty. "Clara, it's not like that. We just—"

"Oh, spare me the semantics!" she interrupted, holding up a hand. "This is too good to pass up. You two have been acting like lovesick teenagers for weeks, and now I stumble upon you in a romantic hideaway?"

"Okay, maybe we have been a little...sneaky," I admitted, the blush creeping up my cheeks betraying my attempts at nonchalance. "But it's complicated. We're just trying to figure things out away from the judgment of everyone else."

"Complicated, huh?" Clara's expression softened, and I could see the gears in her head shifting from playful to concerned. "Look, I get wanting to escape. This social scene is exhausting, and everyone has their opinions. But running off like this? You know it'll blow up in your faces eventually."

"Yeah, thanks for the pep talk, Clara," I said, attempting a smile that fell flat. "But maybe a little chaos is exactly what we need right now."

"Or it's a recipe for disaster," she shot back, crossing her arms. "You know how people talk. If they catch wind of this, it'll be all over Instagram faster than you can say 'awkward.'"

He stepped closer to me, our shoulders brushing, and I could feel the unspoken bond between us—torn between the thrill of our secret and the stark reality of what Clara was saying. "Clara, we're not trying to hurt anyone. We just... needed a moment to breathe."

"Breathing's great, but you might want to consider the consequences," she said, her tone shifting to one of genuine concern. "You know how quick the rumor mill can be. I'm not here to ruin your fun, but you've got to be careful."

I opened my mouth to respond, but a sudden wave crashed dramatically against the shore, drowning out my words. The sound of the ocean was both a comfort and a reminder of the storm brewing just outside our hidden paradise.

"Look, Clara, we appreciate your concern," I said, finding my footing amidst the chaos of emotions. "But we're in this together, and I think we deserve a chance to figure it out—on our terms."

She sighed, her defenses crumbling slightly. "Fine, but just know I'll be watching. The last thing I want is for you two to get hurt because you decided to play with fire."

"Noted," he said, his voice smooth, but I could see the tension still lingered in his posture. As Clara turned to leave, I felt an inexplicable weight settle in my chest.

"Wait, Clara!" I called out, desperation lacing my voice. "Can you keep this to yourself? Just for a little while?"

She paused, glancing back over her shoulder, her expression softening. "Of course, I'm not a monster. Just... be careful, okay?"

The moment she disappeared into the shadows, the cove felt more isolated than ever. The air buzzed with unspoken words, and as I turned to him, my heart raced with uncertainty.

"Guess that went well," he said, attempting a lighthearted tone that didn't quite mask the tension in the air.

"Yeah, well, Clara has a knack for making everything feel like a ticking time bomb." I ran my fingers through my hair, frustration bubbling beneath the surface. "I'm not sure how much longer we can keep this up. I want to be with you, but the weight of hiding it feels suffocating."

"Maybe it's time to stop hiding," he said, the conviction in his voice igniting a flicker of hope within me. "What if we faced it together? We can't keep running forever."

His words hung in the air, and for a moment, the prospect of breaking free from the chains of secrecy felt intoxicating. But then, a familiar fear washed over me like a cold tide, drowning out the warmth of possibility. "And what if it doesn't go well? What if the fallout is worse than what we have now?"

"Then we deal with it together," he replied firmly, reaching out to take my hand, his fingers intertwining with mine as if anchoring me to the moment.

The warmth of his touch sent ripples of comfort through my veins, and for a heartbeat, I felt invincible, ready to take on the world. "Okay, maybe you're right. Maybe it's time to stop hiding in plain sight."

"Besides," he said, his trademark smirk breaking through the tension, "if we're going to be a hot topic, we might as well be the best kind of scandal."

I laughed, the sound breaking the heavy atmosphere. "A scandal worth gossiping about, huh? What a way to make an entrance."

"Exactly. We'll be the drama everyone secretly craves."

As we shared a smile, a thrill of excitement coursed through me. The idea of stepping into the light felt simultaneously terrifying and exhilarating. But beneath that excitement, a quiet dread lingered, whispering reminders of the consequences that lay ahead. In that moment, I realized that the risk of living openly with him was a gamble I was finally willing to take, even if it meant facing the storm head-on.

Just as I began to breathe a little easier, the shadows of doubt crept back in. It was one thing to speak boldly of love and acceptance, but the real world was not so forgiving. And as the waves lapped at the shore, I couldn't shake the feeling that the tide was about to turn.

The thrill of defiance hung in the air like the salty tang of the ocean breeze, lifting the weight from my shoulders for the first time in what felt like forever. We were ready to plunge into the unpredictable chaos that awaited us. I squeezed his hand tighter, a gesture that conveyed more than words ever could—a promise, an agreement, a leap into the unknown.

"Let's make a pact," I suggested, my voice barely above a whisper as the sound of the waves crashed rhythmically against the shore. "No matter what happens, we face it together. No backing down."

He grinned, that spark igniting in his eyes. "I like the sound of that. Together, as the ultimate power couple of our social scene."

"More like the unintentional chaos squad," I shot back, chuckling at the absurdity of it all.

As we basked in the moment, I felt a flicker of hope surging through me, drowning out the cacophony of fears threatening to take root. We both knew the risks—we had seen friendships crumble under the weight of jealousy and judgment—but the idea of standing side by side, united against the world, was intoxicating.

But just as I began to envision a new reality, one where we could love openly without fear, a distant voice shattered my reverie. "There you are!"

I turned sharply, my heart plummeting into my stomach. It was Max, my brother's best friend and a notorious gossip-monger. His presence was like a sudden storm cloud blotting out the sun. "Thought you could hide away without me, did you?"

His tone was playful, but the glint in his eyes suggested he wasn't merely here for small talk. I felt a rush of panic wash over me. "Max, this isn't what it looks like."

"Oh, but it looks exactly like what I think it is," he retorted, stepping closer with a cocky smirk. "A rendezvous in a secret cove? Scandalous! If I didn't know any better, I'd say you two were having a romantic escape."

I exchanged a quick glance with him, anxiety pooling in the pit of my stomach. My heart raced as I watched the amusement on Max's face shift to a more calculating expression. "You've been busy, haven't you? What happens when everyone finds out?"

"Max, please," I implored, my voice trembling. "We're not ready for this. Can you keep it to yourself?"

He leaned back against a rock, crossing his arms as he regarded us like a chess piece caught in the middle of a game. "That depends. What's in it for me?"

His question hung in the air, heavy with implication. I could feel the panic rising, threatening to spill over. "Are you blackmailing us?"

"Blackmail is such a strong word," he replied, feigning innocence. "Let's call it leveraging a good story. The social scene could use some spice, don't you think?"

"You're unbelievable," I shot back, my voice low and fierce. "You wouldn't do this to us. We thought you were our friend."

"Friend? Oh, sweetheart, I'm an opportunist," he said with a wink. "And this? This is gold. You two are practically a tabloid waiting to happen."

The atmosphere shifted, growing colder and more charged. I could feel the tension radiating from him, but it was as if the weight of our predicament pressed down on my chest, squeezing the air from my lungs.

"Max, you can't," he said, stepping forward. "We're not a story. We're—"

"A relationship built on secrets?" Max interjected, enjoying the discomfort that swirled around us. "What kind of foundation is that? It's like building a house of cards, darling. One breath, and it all comes tumbling down."

"Shut up, Max!" I shouted, the words escaping before I could rein them in. The sharpness of my voice startled him, and for a moment, surprise flickered across his face.

"Wow, look who found her voice," he remarked, chuckling lightly. "You're feistier than I thought. I like that."

"Just leave us alone," I hissed, irritation boiling over. "If you breathe a word of this, you'll regret it."

"Oh, I'm quaking in my boots," he replied, sarcasm dripping from his words. "But how about this? I'll keep quiet—for now. In return, you let me be the first to know all the juicy details. The behind-the-scenes drama of the year."

"Why would we agree to that?" he asked, his voice steady, though I sensed the tension radiating from him.

"Because the alternative is me spilling the beans, and we both know that would be disastrous," Max said, his grin widening. "No one likes to be the subject of rumors, especially when they're so messy."

"Fine," I muttered, reluctantly conceding. "Just... don't make this harder than it has to be."

"Sweetheart, I'm all about making things interesting," he replied with a wink. "But don't worry, your secret is safe—for now."

As Max turned to leave, I felt an overwhelming sense of dread settle in my stomach, the thrill of defiance quickly replaced by a sinking sensation. Our beautiful escape was slipping through my fingers, tainted by the reality of our situation.

"Wait," I called after him, desperation creeping into my voice. "What do you want from us, really?"

He paused, glancing over his shoulder. "Just a good story, my dear. Just a good story."

With that, he disappeared into the shadows, leaving us in a precarious silence. The waves crashed louder now, a stark reminder of the chaos that surrounded us.

"What just happened?" he asked, his voice laced with disbelief.

"I don't know," I replied, a chill crawling up my spine. "But we've got to figure this out before Max decides our fate for us."

"We will," he said, determination etching itself across his features. "But we have to be careful. If we want this to work, we can't let anyone dictate our story."

As I looked into his eyes, the gravity of the moment washed over me. My heart raced at the thought of losing what we had, all while the world loomed ominously around us.

But just as I began to regain my composure, a shrill scream pierced the air, echoing through the cove. It was a sound filled with panic, slicing through the stillness of the night like a jagged knife. I felt my heart drop, instinctively looking in the direction it came from.

"Did you hear that?" I whispered, dread pooling in my stomach.

He nodded, his face paling. "Yeah, and I don't like it."

Before I could respond, the sound of hurried footsteps thundered across the sand, drawing closer. My pulse quickened, adrenaline surging as the unknown threat loomed ever closer.

"What if that's Max?" I asked, anxiety flooding my voice.

"Then we need to move," he said, urgency propelling us into action.

But as we turned to run, a shadow emerged from the darkness, and I froze, the world around me narrowing down to the looming figure blocking our escape.

Chapter 12: The Ultimatum

The air was thick with tension as I stood in front of Emily, my best friend and confidante. Her arms were crossed tightly over her chest, her expression a fierce mask of determination. The sunlight streamed through the café window, casting a warm glow on the rustic wooden tables and the eclectic decor that surrounded us. It was a stark contrast to the storm brewing inside me, where loyalty battled fiercely with a budding connection I could no longer ignore.

"Choose, Zoe," Emily said, her voice steady but her eyes betraying a hint of vulnerability. "It's either him or me." Her words hung in the air, heavy and suffocating. A barista nearby frothed milk, the sound a sharp reminder of how mundane life continued around us, oblivious to the chaos unfolding in our small corner of the world.

Michael had become more than just a friend; he was a flame that drew me closer, igniting feelings I had buried deep beneath layers of self-doubt and fear. We had spent countless late nights exploring each other's thoughts and dreams, our laughter mingling with the fading echoes of the bustling city outside. It was intoxicating, the way he saw me—truly saw me—beyond the façade I often wore. Yet, here I was, facing a choice that felt like standing at the edge of a precipice, the ground crumbling beneath my feet.

I took a deep breath, trying to steady the rapid thudding of my heart. "Emily, can't we just talk this out?" My voice came out softer than I intended, a desperate plea rather than the firm argument I wanted it to be. She shook her head, her long hair catching the light and framing her face in a halo of frustration.

"No more talking. You know what he did. You can't just ignore it because he's charming." Her tone was sharp, laced with the heat of betrayal. I could feel my stomach twisting in knots at the mention of Michael's name, a name that had started to feel like home.

"Charming? You make him sound like a rogue from a romance novel. He's not some villain, Emily. He's—"

"He's the reason I lost my scholarship!" Her voice escalated, drawing the attention of nearby patrons. I winced, glancing around at the curious eyes peering our way, but Emily seemed too engrossed in her anger to notice. "You're willing to throw everything away for him? What about me? What about us?"

It wasn't just her scholarship that hung in the balance; it was our friendship, a bond forged through years of shared secrets, laughter, and unspoken promises. I felt a pang of guilt settle in my chest. Had I been so wrapped up in my whirlwind with Michael that I had overlooked her pain? I glanced down at the table, the wood worn and scratched, much like my heart felt at that moment.

"I didn't mean to hurt you, Emily. You know that," I said quietly, my words barely escaping my lips. The realization hit me hard: I had never intended for my happiness to come at her expense. But the thought of losing Michael, of losing that connection, made my skin crawl.

"I don't care about your intentions," she snapped, her eyes narrowing as she leaned closer, her voice low and intense. "I care about what he did, Zoe. If you keep hanging around him, I will tell everyone. You think I'm bluffing? I'm not. This isn't just about you anymore. You have to pick a side."

The coffee shop felt like a prison, the walls closing in as the weight of her ultimatum pressed down on me. I had never been good at making decisions, often preferring to drift along with the current rather than take a stand. But this time, the current felt like it was dragging me under.

I could almost hear Michael's laughter in my mind, the way his eyes sparkled when he spoke about his dreams. It made me question everything. Had I been naive? Did I really know him? Or was I simply infatuated with the idea of him, the escape he represented from the mundane reality of my life?

"Emily, please," I pleaded, my voice trembling. "What do you want me to say? That I'll cut him out of my life just because you're angry? That I'll turn my back on something real?" I felt a tear threaten to escape, but I blinked it away. I wouldn't let her see me cry. Not now, not when everything felt like it was crumbling around me.

She looked at me, her expression softening for a fleeting moment, but the steel resolve quickly returned. "I want you to choose. You've been with him for weeks, but you don't see the truth. I can't watch you get hurt by someone who doesn't care about you."

"Maybe he does care!" I shot back, the fire igniting within me. "Maybe he cares more than you think. You don't know him like I do!"

"Exactly! And you don't know him like I do!" Her voice cracked, the anger bubbling beneath her surface. "You think love is enough to fix everything? It's not. I thought he was one of us, but he's a snake in the grass, Zoe. And I refuse to let him ruin you, too."

The words struck a chord deep within me, resonating with a truth I hadn't wanted to confront. The thrill of our stolen moments together clashed with the reality of the chaos that seemed to follow Michael wherever he went. I felt lost, suspended between two worlds—the life I had built with Emily and the spark of something unpredictable and exhilarating with Michael.

"I can't just cut ties, Emily," I whispered, the fight slowly draining from my voice. "I wish it were that simple." The realization of the enormity of my choice weighed heavily on my chest. Each beat of my heart echoed the decision I dreaded to make, as uncertainty swirled around us like a gathering storm.

The café around us buzzed with the clinking of cups and the soft murmur of conversations, but all I could hear was the thunderous roar of my heart, pounding a frantic rhythm of confusion and fear.

Emily's piercing gaze seemed to dissect my every thought, laying bare the turmoil swirling within me. I watched as she pulled a lock of hair behind her ear, the small gesture almost endearing amidst the tempest we found ourselves in. The contradiction of our friendship—a history built on trust and laughter now overshadowed by distrust—made my stomach churn.

"I just don't understand how you can be so blind, Zoe." Her words were laced with frustration, and I could sense the hurt beneath them, a raw nerve exposed. "I thought you were smarter than this."

"Smarter? Maybe I'm just too busy trying to figure out what's right for me," I shot back, the edge in my voice surprising even myself. The truth was, I felt lost, teetering on the brink of two very different realities. I could hear Michael's laughter echoing in my mind, each note resonating with warmth and comfort, yet Emily's warnings rang out like an alarm, sharp and unyielding.

"Right for you or right for him?" Emily challenged, her brows knitting together as she leaned in closer. "Because I don't see how being involved with someone like him can possibly be good for anyone but him. It's like watching a train wreck, and I can't just stand by and let it happen."

I took a breath, feeling the weight of her words. "And what if you're wrong? What if he's not who you think he is?" My voice trembled, the desperation creeping in as I fought to hold onto a thread of hope that maybe, just maybe, Michael was more than the mistakes of his past.

Emily scoffed, rolling her eyes. "Oh, right! Because we all know that charm can mask a whole host of issues. Look, I'm not trying to ruin your fun, but sometimes fun comes with consequences. You're playing with fire, Zoe, and you might end up getting burned." Her expression softened, a flicker of genuine concern breaking through her frustration. "I just don't want to see you get hurt. I can't stand by while you ignore the obvious."

The reality of her ultimatum settled over me like a heavy fog. "So, this is it, then? I either choose you or him?" I asked, incredulous. The thought felt utterly absurd, as if I were in a bad rom-com, forced to pick between a charming lead and my loyal best friend.

"Yes! That's exactly it!" she replied, her voice unwavering. "You need to figure out what really matters to you. Is it loyalty to a friend or a whirlwind with someone who doesn't have your best interests at heart?"

The café door chimed, drawing my attention for a brief moment as a gust of wind ushered in a chilly breeze, almost as if nature itself was trying to interrupt our tense standoff. I could see people pass by, lost in their own lives, blissfully unaware of the emotional turmoil brewing between us. The world outside continued spinning while I felt frozen, caught in the crosshairs of a decision I wasn't ready to make.

"Why can't you just trust me?" I asked, my voice softer now, almost pleading. "You've always said you support my choices, no matter how crazy they are. Why can't this just be another crazy choice?"

"Because this isn't just a crazy choice! This is a decision that could ruin you! I can't stand by and watch you throw everything away. It's not just my opinion; it's the reality of the situation." Her frustration was palpable, each word slicing through the air like a knife.

"Fine! Then tell me what to do, Emily! Please, just tell me what to do!" I shouted, feeling the burn of unshed tears prickling at the corners of my eyes. The sensation was foreign; I prided myself on my emotional fortitude, yet here I was, an unraveling mess in a coffee shop, arguing with my best friend over the intricacies of love and betrayal.

"I can't tell you what to do!" she replied, exasperated. "You have to figure it out for yourself. You have to understand what he's done and how it affects you. I can't make that choice for you, but I will be here to support you, no matter what you decide. Just... don't expect me to sit quietly while you march into the fire."

A silence enveloped us, and in that space, I could almost hear the clock ticking down the seconds to my impending decision. I had never been good at confrontations, at navigating the murky waters of relationships that threatened to drown me.

"I just..." I started, words tangling in my throat. "I wish things were simple. I wish I could see a clear path forward." I wrapped my hands around my coffee cup, the warmth seeping through the ceramic and into my palms, grounding me, even if only slightly.

"I wish it were simple, too," she said, her voice softening as she leaned back, crossing her arms tightly over her chest as if protecting herself. "But life isn't a fairy tale, and sometimes you have to make the tough choices that lead to the most growth. Trust me, I know."

"I don't want to hurt you," I whispered, vulnerability spilling over the edges of my carefully crafted defenses. "You're my best friend. I can't imagine losing you over this."

Emily sighed deeply, her shoulders slumping slightly. "You won't lose me. But I need you to think about what's at stake here. I can't pretend everything is fine while you walk around in a haze, infatuated with someone who's already caused damage."

The barista called out an order, the normalcy of it all pulling me momentarily from the depths of my despair. Outside, a group of kids on bicycles raced by, laughter bubbling up like a sweet melody that felt a world away from the heaviness inside the café. I wished for a moment that I could join them, to leave all of this behind, to escape into the innocence of youth where choices were simple and consequences felt distant.

"I just need time," I finally said, my voice steadier. "I need time to figure this out. If I can't do that, then maybe I don't deserve either of you."

Emily's expression softened again, the hard edges of her resolve melting away to reveal the caring friend beneath. "You deserve happiness, Zoe, but it's up to you to choose what that looks like. Just don't shut me out, okay? We're in this together."

The thought of losing her as I navigated this tangled mess was unbearable. I reached across the table, taking her hand in mine, squeezing it tightly, a silent vow that I wouldn't turn my back on her, no matter where this chaotic journey led. It felt like a fragile lifeline, a thread tying us together even as I stood on the precipice of a choice that could change everything.

The café hummed with a comforting rhythm, but the warmth of its atmosphere felt alien as I faced Emily, our hands clasped tightly across the table. The scent of freshly brewed coffee filled the air, mingling with the sweet aroma of pastries that lined the glass case nearby. I should have found solace in this familiar setting, but instead, it served as a stark reminder of how quickly things could spiral out of control. I had always loved the soft chatter of the patrons, the clinking of cups, and the way the world outside blurred into a vibrant tapestry of life. But today, those sounds faded into a dull backdrop, drowning beneath the weight of our conversation.

"I just don't want to see you get hurt," Emily repeated, her voice edged with concern that tugged at my heart. "You're better than this, Zoe. You deserve someone who won't drag you into chaos."

"Is that really how you see Michael? As chaos?" The words slipped out before I could catch them, a defensive reflex I couldn't quite suppress. "I thought you knew me well enough to know I thrive in chaos. It's where I feel alive."

"Alive?" she shot back, her eyebrows arching high in disbelief. "You think drama equals excitement? You're not in some ridiculous TV show, Zoe! This is real life, and it comes with real consequences. You're standing on a ledge, and I can't just watch you jump."

Her metaphor hung in the air, casting an ominous shadow over my thoughts. Did I really have the strength to choose between my friend and the man who made my heart race with a mere glance? I had spent so long pretending to be the fearless adventurer in my own story, but the truth was, I was terrified.

"Look," I said, forcing the air from my lungs in a shaky exhale, "you know what he means to me. He's not just some passing fling. We have this connection, something I can't quite explain. It's..."

"Intense?" Emily interjected, her tone dripping with skepticism. "Intense is one way to describe someone who's probably got a dozen secrets lurking behind that charming smile. Do you even know his past?"

"Maybe I'm willing to overlook it!" The words burst out of me, loud enough to catch the attention of the barista, who glanced our way with a raised eyebrow. I took a moment, allowing the embarrassment to wash over me, before continuing in a quieter tone. "We're all flawed, Em. We all have our baggage. I'm just tired of pretending to be perfect."

"I'm not asking you to be perfect," she said, her voice calming as she softened her stance. "I'm just asking you to be smart. Please."

The plea in her eyes struck a chord, the familiar ache of loyalty battling against the intoxicating pull of something new and exhilarating. I could almost picture Michael's face, his smile, the way his laughter felt like a balm on my worst days. Could I really risk everything for that?

"What if he's changed?" I asked, leaning in as if the answer lay just within reach. "What if he's not the person he used to be? People grow, right?"

Emily paused, her expression contemplative. "You're willing to gamble on a what-if? You could lose everything. You could lose me."

The thought settled heavily between us, and I felt my defenses begin to crack. "Losing you would destroy me, Em," I admitted, my voice breaking. "You're my anchor, and I don't want to hurt you. But I also don't want to throw away something that feels... special."

"Then how do we figure this out?" Emily asked, her voice softer now, almost tender. "You're going to have to make a choice soon. Maybe you should just let him go. If he cares about you, he'll understand."

"Or maybe he won't," I said, shaking my head. "Maybe he'll think I'm just like everyone else, abandoning him when things get tough." The thought felt like a dagger to my chest. I didn't want to be that person, not to him or to myself.

As I wrestled with my emotions, the door swung open again, and the icy wind swept through the café, sending a shiver down my spine. My gaze flicked toward the entrance just as Michael walked in, his presence commanding attention like a sudden flash of lightning. The moment our eyes met, a jolt of electricity coursed through me, igniting the space between us.

"Zoe!" he called, a broad smile breaking across his face as he stepped inside, shaking off the cold. The warmth of his energy was a stark contrast to the chill of my predicament. "I was hoping to find you here. I have something to tell you."

The world around me faded as he approached, leaving Emily's warning hanging in the air like a dark cloud. I felt a surge of affection for him, one that battled fiercely against the gravity of my reality.

"Michael!" I responded, forcing a smile, but my heart raced with a mix of excitement and dread. "What's going on?"

He stepped closer, his expression shifting to something more serious. "I've been thinking about us, about everything," he said, lowering his voice as he glanced between me and Emily. The intimacy in his gaze made my heart flutter, but a sinking feeling settled in my gut.

"Is that so?" I asked, trying to keep my tone light, even as the gravity of the situation pulled me down.

"I think we should take a step back," he said, and my breath caught in my throat. "I've been doing some soul-searching, and I realize I've been dragging you into my mess. I don't want that for you."

A wave of confusion washed over me. "Michael, what do you mean? You're not making any sense. I thought we were—"

"We are," he interrupted, running a hand through his hair, a gesture that always made my heart skip a beat. "But it's complicated. I've been approached about some things... some people from my past who want to get involved again. I can't drag you into that chaos. You deserve better."

Emily's eyes widened in disbelief, and I could feel her holding her breath, awaiting my reaction. "You're talking about leaving?" I asked, incredulous. "You can't just decide what's best for me! That's not fair!"

"Maybe it's not fair, but it's what's best. I care about you too much to let you get hurt because of me." His voice held a weight that resonated with the depths of my heart, yet it felt like a trap, a way to push me away before I could make my own choice.

"Michael," I started, but the words stuck in my throat, battling against the tempest of emotions swirling inside me. "I can't believe you'd do this. You're just going to walk away because it gets hard?"

"It's not about walking away," he insisted, desperation creeping into his voice. "It's about protecting you. This isn't just a game for me, Zoe. I have real demons to face. You should be free to chase your own dreams without my baggage weighing you down."

As his words hung between us, I felt a tightness in my chest, the walls I had built around my heart trembling under the weight of his confession. Did he really think leaving would protect me? Did I even want to be protected?

"I can't just stand here and watch you make decisions for me, Michael!" I exclaimed, anger flaring as I stepped back, the table now a chasm between us. "I'm not some fragile thing that needs to be shielded from reality!"

His face contorted with frustration, and I saw the flicker of pain in his eyes. "Then what do you want from me? Because I can't keep dragging you down. Not anymore."

"I want the truth!" I shouted, my heart pounding with emotion. "I want to know if what we have is worth fighting for! But if you think running away is the answer, maybe you're right. Maybe you don't really want this!"

The room fell silent, the words hanging heavily in the air. Emily shifted uncomfortably beside me, her expression a mix of concern and disbelief. Michael's gaze bore into mine, and in that moment, everything felt like it was teetering on the edge of a precipice, ready to plunge into the unknown.

Just then, a familiar figure stepped into the café—one I had hoped never to see again. My heart raced, and for a brief moment, I felt the ground beneath me shift, everything spiraling out of control.

Chapter 13: A Father's Shadow

The air in the house had shifted, thickening with an unspoken tension that seemed to cling to the walls like an unwelcome guest. I watched as Michael moved about the kitchen, his movements methodical yet restless, like a clock ticking toward an inevitable strike. The sunlight poured through the window, illuminating the dust motes that danced in the golden light, but even that warmth felt insufficient to bridge the growing distance between us.

"Are you going to stare at me all day, or are you going to say something?" he asked, a hint of impatience threading through his voice. His tone was sharp, yet I could sense the vulnerability lurking beneath. It was as if he was daring me to break the silence, to shatter the glassy facade he had carefully constructed.

I leaned against the doorframe, letting the moment stretch, feeling the cool wood against my back grounding me in reality. "I thought you might want some coffee. You know, to fortify yourself against the onslaught of my company." My attempt at humor landed with a soft thud, but I pressed on. "Or we could have a proper conversation. You know, the kind that doesn't involve you pretending to be busy while I drown in my own thoughts."

He chuckled softly, the sound tinged with bitterness. "Pretending is easier, don't you think? It's less messy than reality."

"Messy is where all the good stuff lives," I replied, pushing off the doorframe and crossing the room to stand beside him. "You can't expect everything to be neat and tidy, especially not when emotions are involved. I mean, look at us." I gestured between us, letting my hand linger in the space that felt more like a chasm than a bridge.

Michael let out a heavy sigh, resting his hands on the counter as if it were the only thing anchoring him to this moment. "I miss Emily," he finally admitted, his voice cracking under the weight of his confession. "I miss who we were before everything changed. She was my light, you know? I thought I could manage everything—parenthood, work, life—but it feels like I'm losing her every day."

The words hung in the air like a fog, enveloping us both. I had heard snippets of this before, the longing and regret etched into the lines of his face. But hearing it now, raw and unfiltered, stirred something deep within me. "And you think distancing yourself from me is the answer?"

He turned to me, surprise flickering in his eyes. "It's not like that. I don't want to push you away. It's just—"

"Just what? You're terrified of getting hurt again? Of falling for someone who might not stick around?" I interrupted, frustration bubbling to the surface. "Look at the way you're acting! You're like a man teetering on the edge of a cliff, and I'm the one trying to pull you back. But you keep inching closer to the abyss."

"You don't understand," he said, his voice strained. "Being a father means putting someone else's needs before your own. Emily is my priority, and I can't afford to get distracted. I can't let you get hurt because of my mess."

"Michael," I said, my voice softening as I placed a hand on his arm, feeling the tense muscle beneath my touch. "You're not a mess. You're human. And I get that you're afraid. But it's okay to let someone in. I'm not here to take Emily's place; I'm here to support you both. We can figure this out together."

He turned to me, his eyes searching mine for something—understanding, perhaps, or hope. "You make it sound so simple."

"Maybe it could be, if you let it." I took a deep breath, trying to quell the anxiety knotting my stomach. "Just imagine for a moment what it could be like, having someone to lean on when it gets tough. It doesn't have to be perfect. We can navigate the chaos together."

For a heartbeat, I saw a flicker of something in his gaze, a glimmer of the man I had fallen for amid the shadows of doubt. Then it dimmed, and he stepped back, creating more distance between us than I had expected. "I can't. I don't want to drag you into my problems. You deserve better than this."

Before I could respond, the sound of footsteps echoed from the hallway, light and hurried. Emily bounded into the kitchen, her golden hair shining like a halo, her laughter spilling over the room like sunlight. She froze mid-laugh when she saw the two of us, the air thick with unspoken tension. "What's going on?" she asked, her tone innocent yet probing, as if she could sense the undercurrents swirling between us.

Michael glanced at me, a silent plea for composure passing between us. "Just discussing plans for dinner," he replied, his voice steady but lacking the warmth that usually accompanied it.

Emily's brows furrowed slightly, but she shrugged it off, her carefree nature too bright to be dimmed for long. "Great! I'm starving! What's for dinner?"

As I watched her enthusiasm, my heart twisted in my chest. She deserved a father who was wholly present, one who didn't feel the need to hide behind walls of guilt and sadness. And yet, here I was, tangled in the very web I had hoped to help untangle.

"Let's make something together," I suggested, the words tumbling out before I could rethink them. "How about a taco bar? Everyone loves tacos!"

"Perfect! I'll chop the veggies!" Emily exclaimed, darting to the fridge with an energy that was infectious. I couldn't help but smile as she rummaged through the drawers, her face a mix of concentration and joy.

Michael and I exchanged glances, the tension still lingering, but somehow, this small shift felt like a victory. As Emily hummed a cheerful tune, I felt the cracks in our fragile dynamic start to fill, if only just a little.

In the warmth of the kitchen, surrounded by laughter and the promise of a meal shared, I clung to the hope that we could weave something beautiful from the frayed edges of our lives, a tapestry of connection and understanding, even if it took time and patience to fully stitch together.

As the evening unfolded, the kitchen buzzed with an unexpected energy. Emily had seized the reins of our taco-making venture, her enthusiasm igniting a warmth that wrapped around us like a cozy blanket. I stood by, chopping tomatoes and onions, while she narrated an elaborate tale about a talking taco truck she dreamed up, complete with quirky characters and outrageous adventures. It was the kind of whimsical narrative that only a child could concoct, and I found myself laughing, the sound echoing in the cozy confines of our kitchen.

"Wait, wait! So, the taco truck could talk, but what did it say?" I asked, half-expecting her to roll her eyes at my eager involvement.

"It said, 'Let's taco 'bout how delicious I am!'" she replied, giggling at her own pun. The laughter spilled over us, a balm for the strain that had thickened the air earlier.

Michael, who had been meticulously browning the ground beef, cracked a small smile at Emily's infectious delight. For a moment, the shadows receded, and it was just us—a family navigating the chaos of life through the power of laughter and food. I glanced at him, hoping to catch a glimpse of the man I'd fallen for, but I could still see the faintest trace of worry etched in the corners of his mouth.

"Alright, let's spice things up," I said, my eyes gleaming mischievously. "Who wants to be the first to get creative with toppings? Remember, the more bizarre the combination, the better the taste!"

Emily's eyes sparkled with mischief, and before I could blink, she was rummaging through the fridge. "I'll take that challenge!" she declared, her voice dripping with determination. "How about marshmallows and pickles?"

"Disgusting!" Michael exclaimed, shaking his head with a mock grimace. "Now I have to wash my mouth out with soap just hearing that."

"Don't knock it until you try it!" she countered, her hands on her hips, a miniature version of someone prepared to defend their culinary choices in a courtroom.

"Please don't try it," I chimed in, barely containing my laughter. "We need our dinner to stay in one piece and not turn into a science experiment. How about some cheese and maybe—just maybe—guacamole instead?"

As the tacos took shape, laughter bubbled around us, each burst a reminder that joy still had a place in our lives. But just as I began to feel the weight of the day lifting, the kitchen door swung open, and in walked Emily's best friend, Jenna, her usual whirlwind of energy palpable even before she entered the room.

"Did someone say tacos?" Jenna exclaimed, her eyes widening with delight. She was a whirlwind of colorful leggings and oversized sweaters, a riot of personality that could brighten the gloomiest of days. "I can smell them from a mile away!"

"Only the best tacos for our resident food critic," I teased, tossing a tortilla toward her, which she deftly caught.

Jenna plopped onto a stool, her enthusiasm filling the space. "You guys are so lucky! I was just telling my mom how unfair it is that I get sandwiches while you feast on gourmet tacos."

Michael, still stirring the pot, glanced over with a playful grin. "Just remember, you can't be a taco snob when you've had a peanut butter sandwich for lunch."

Jenna laughed, flipping her hair over her shoulder. "Touché! But if I had a taco truck, I'd take it on the road! Just picture it: Jenna's Totally Tasty Tacos, with a side of my secret sauce!"

"Is it the sauce that makes everyone question your taste?" Michael shot back, laughter dancing in his voice.

"Oh, hush! You're just jealous because I'm the culinary genius here," she retorted, her tone playful yet confident. "I'll bring my secret sauce over next time, and we'll see who's the real taco master!"

Just as the playful banter continued, Emily turned to Michael, her expression suddenly serious. "Dad, can I ask you something?"

The lighthearted atmosphere shifted, a softening tension washing over us as Michael wiped his hands on a towel and focused his full attention on Emily. "Of course, sweetheart. What's on your mind?"

She hesitated, her little fingers twisting together, betraying the weight of her thoughts. "Why do you look sad sometimes? You don't have to hide it from me. I'm not a little kid anymore."

Michael's smile faltered, and I could see the emotional toll her words took on him. He opened his mouth, but the words seemed to get tangled up somewhere between his heart and mind. "I just... I worry about things, Em. Grown-up things that don't make sense."

"I'm not afraid of grown-up things," Emily insisted, her voice firm. "I can help if you let me. I'm brave, just like the characters in my stories!"

Her innocent bravery cut through the air, a reminder that sometimes the strongest voices came from the smallest figures. Michael's expression softened, and for a brief moment, I saw the barriers start to crumble. "You're right, you are very brave. It's just... sometimes it's hard to share everything."

"Can I help with the sharing part?" Emily asked, her eagerness palpable. "I want to help you not be sad. I love you, Dad."

His eyes glistened with unshed tears, and he nodded, a silent acknowledgment of her unwavering support. "I love you too, kiddo. I'll try to talk more, I promise."

The moment hung suspended in time, a fragile yet profound connection threading between them. It was one of those rare instances where everything felt right, where the world outside faded, and all that remained was the deep bond between father and daughter, a reminder that love could conquer even the darkest of shadows.

I busied myself with arranging the tacos, letting the warmth of the scene wash over me. I was the outsider in this moment, yet I felt privileged to witness their exchange. It was beautiful, a dance of healing that offered a glimpse of hope amid uncertainty.

Just as I was reveling in this familial moment, the front door swung open again, this time revealing Emily's mother, Kate, her presence casting a different kind of shadow over the gathering. She stepped in with an air of authority, her sharp gaze sweeping across the room, assessing the situation with an intensity that could slice through steel.

"What's going on here?" she demanded, her tone laced with a mixture of curiosity and suspicion. "I could hear laughter from outside, and I thought I'd walked into the wrong house."

"Just taco night!" Jenna piped up cheerfully, her usual charm rolling off her tongue with ease. "We're having a blast!"

Kate raised an eyebrow, clearly unimpressed. "Is that so? And how many tacos are you planning to devour, Jenna?"

"Oh, only enough to ensure that I steal some of Michael's culinary glory!" she joked, a glimmer of mischief dancing in her eyes.

Yet the playful tone didn't fully pierce through the tension. I could feel the air shift once again, the dynamics of the room evolving as Kate's gaze landed on Michael. A flicker of apprehension crossed her features, a reminder of the unspoken history that loomed over us.

Michael straightened, his expression turning cautious. "We were just... talking. About dinner."

"Dinner is lovely, but we need to talk about something important," she replied, her voice cutting through the banter like a sharp knife.

And just like that, the buoyancy of our taco night faded, leaving in its wake the inevitable storm that was brewing on the horizon.

The atmosphere in the kitchen thickened as Kate's presence solidified the tension that hung like a heavy curtain. She stood with her arms crossed, her gaze piercing through the dim light. Michael's posture stiffened as he faced her, the warmth of our previous laughter slipping away like a forgotten dream. I could feel the air grow cold, like the sudden hush of a crowded room when the music stops and everyone waits for the next note.

"Mom, we were just—" Emily began, her youthful enthusiasm dimming under her mother's scrutiny.

Kate waved her hand dismissively, cutting off whatever defense Michael had been about to conjure. "Save it. We need to talk about what's going on with you two. I'm not blind; I see the way you look at each other. It's... inappropriate."

I watched as Michael's face paled, the color draining from his cheeks. "It's not like that, Kate," he protested, his voice strained but steady. "We're just friends trying to navigate a complicated situation."

"Friends? Is that what you're calling it now?" Her tone dripped with skepticism, and I felt the tension coil tighter in the room. Emily shifted uncomfortably, her small hands fidgeting with the edges of her shirt, caught between her parents like a pawn in an unwinnable game.

"I mean it," Michael insisted, stepping forward as if to shield Emily from the storm brewing in Kate's eyes. "We've had to support each other through some tough times, and it doesn't mean—"

"Doesn't mean what? That you're both falling for each other? Because let's be honest, that's exactly what's happening," she shot back, her words sharp enough to slice through any lingering camaraderie.

Emily's eyes darted between her parents, confusion etching her features. "But Mom, it's not like that! We're just having fun together. Why does it have to be more?"

The vulnerability in her voice was palpable, and I felt a surge of protectiveness for the little girl who had somehow become an unwilling participant in this adult drama. "Emily's right," I interjected, hoping to diffuse the rising tensions. "What Michael and I have is purely supportive. We're all just trying to help each other heal."

Kate's eyes narrowed, locking onto me with a fierce intensity. "And you're okay with this? You don't think it's strange to be so involved with him, considering—"

"I think it's complicated, just like life," I said, a bit more forcefully than I intended. "But that doesn't mean it can't be healthy. We're navigating this as best we can."

Her brows furrowed, but for a moment, I saw a flicker of doubt in her gaze. "This isn't just about you. You might think it's harmless, but it affects Emily. She's a kid caught in the middle of a situation that's already strained."

"Mom, I can handle this!" Emily piped up again, her voice steadying as she squared her shoulders. "I want to help Dad and be a part of this. I'm not scared. I love him, and I love that we can talk to each other like friends!"

The declaration hung in the air, both innocent and brave. I could feel Michael's eyes soften as he took in his daughter's unwavering support. But Kate remained unyielding, her posture tense as if preparing for a fight. "You think you're being brave, but it's not just about love, Emily. Relationships are messy, and this could backfire on you. You need to be careful."

"Isn't that what you always say? That life is about taking risks?" Emily countered, her voice rising in defiance, tinged with youthful wisdom. "I'm not going to hide from the people I care about just because it's uncomfortable for you!"

The standoff between Kate and Emily was electric, crackling with emotions that could ignite the room. I glanced at Michael, whose expression mirrored the conflict within me—caught between the need to protect his daughter and the desire to defend our connection.

"Emily, it's not about hiding; it's about being sensible," Kate pressed, her voice softer now, yet still resolute. "There are boundaries that should never be crossed."

"Maybe we should start respecting each other's boundaries," Michael replied quietly, a hint of irritation creeping into his tone. "You're talking about Emily as if she's not part of this conversation. She has her own feelings, her own thoughts about what's happening."

Kate's expression hardened, and I could sense the shifting sands beneath our feet. The kitchen had transformed into a battleground, where loyalties were tested and the stakes grew higher. I took a step back, feeling like an outsider in a family feud that was escalating beyond my comprehension.

The silence that followed felt heavy, suffocating, until Emily broke it, her small voice laced with determination. "I just want everyone to get along. Why does it have to be so hard? Can't we just eat tacos and be happy?"

The weight of her innocence cracked something in me, and I couldn't help but smile despite the tension. "You're right, Em. We should be focusing on the important stuff, like who gets the last taco."

"Fine," Michael relented, his expression softening. "Let's eat first, and then we can talk about the rest of this."

But before we could indulge in the small victory of camaraderie, Kate's phone buzzed sharply against the counter, cutting through the fragile peace we had attempted to establish. She glanced at it, her expression shifting to something more serious.

"Excuse me," she said, her tone turning grave as she stepped away to take the call. The distance she created felt palpable, the energy in the room shifting again as we exchanged bewildered glances.

"Do you think everything's okay?" Emily whispered, worry knitting her brows.

"I'm sure it is," Michael replied, though his voice lacked conviction. "Just give her a moment."

Minutes felt like hours as we waited, the silence stretching, filled only by the muffled sounds of Kate's conversation. Then, suddenly, she returned, her face pale and drawn.

"We need to go. Now," she said, urgency tinging her words as she rounded on Michael. "It's about your father."

"Dad?" Michael's face blanched, worry crinkling his brow. "What do you mean?"

"I don't have time to explain. Just grab what you need, and let's go!"

Confusion twisted in the pit of my stomach. "What's happening?"

"There's been an incident. It's serious," Kate snapped, a crack in her usual composure revealing her own fear.

The gravity of her words settled heavily over us, and just like that, the warmth of our earlier gathering evaporated into the ether. Emily glanced at me, her eyes wide with confusion and fear, the evening's laughter replaced by a sense of impending doom.

Michael grabbed Emily's hand tightly, his gaze flickering between his daughter and Kate. "I need to know what's going on," he demanded, the strength of his voice faltering under the weight of uncertainty.

"Not here. We'll explain everything on the way," Kate insisted, urgency driving her words.

But as they turned to leave, a loud crash erupted from outside, rattling the very foundation of the house. The windows rattled in their frames, and I felt my heart leap into my throat.

"What was that?" I whispered, my voice barely audible over the growing chaos.

And then, without warning, the front door burst open, revealing a shadowy figure silhouetted against the dim light outside. I couldn't tell if it was friend or foe, but as I took a step back, my heart raced, knowing that whatever was about to unfold would change everything.

Chapter 14: Shifting Sands

I arrived at the café, the smell of freshly brewed coffee mingling with the sweet aroma of pastries, each scent vying for attention in the bustling morning air. The soft clinks of cups and the low hum of chatter provided a comforting backdrop, yet today, the familiarity of it all felt suffocating. I'd barely had time to settle into my seat when Michael's message pinged my phone, a simple request that tugged at my heartstrings and sparked an uneasy anticipation. "We need to talk. Meet me at our usual spot." The words hovered in my mind like a specter, leaving a bitter taste lingering in my throat.

The warmth of the café faded as I stepped outside, the sharp autumn breeze wrapping around me like a reminder of the chill lurking in my reality. With each step toward our rendezvous, I felt the weight of my dual life pressing down harder. Balancing my responsibilities as a social worker and the burgeoning relationship with Michael had become a tightrope act; one misstep could send everything tumbling. The world outside continued its busy rhythm, people moving with purpose while I felt suspended, caught between obligations and the electrifying pull of my heart.

I reached the park where we often met, its vibrant foliage a stark contrast to the turmoil within me. Leaves danced playfully in the wind, a vibrant array of oranges, yellows, and reds. The serene pond glimmered under the afternoon sun, the surface shimmering like a thousand tiny diamonds, but all I could see was the reflection of the chaos brewing in my heart. As I approached our usual bench, my eyes landed on him, but the moment was shattered when I noticed Emily sitting beside him.

A sudden knot twisted in my stomach, sending icy tendrils of anxiety racing through me. She sat there, radiating confidence and effortless charm, her laughter cascading through the air like a melodious chime. She and Michael shared a private moment, their heads bent together, conspiratorial whispers drifting toward me like the autumn leaves tumbling to the ground. A rush of jealousy ignited within me, hot and consuming, as I wrestled with the urge to turn around and retreat. But retreating wasn't an option. Not now.

"Hey," I managed, forcing my voice to remain steady as I approached. Michael's face brightened at the sight of me, but the warmth in his expression faltered as Emily turned to look at me, her smile slipping just slightly, a glint of surprise dancing in her eyes.

"Look who decided to join us!" Michael exclaimed, gesturing to the empty space on the bench. "I was just telling Emily about your latest project at the shelter. She's really interested in what you're doing."

"Oh really?" I replied, my tone laced with feigned enthusiasm, masking the tension that twisted my insides. "That's sweet of you, Michael."

Emily's eyes sparkled with a mix of intrigue and challenge as she scrutinized me, her smile returning with renewed vigor. "I've heard so much about the amazing work you do. It must be fulfilling, helping people find their footing."

"It has its moments," I said, my heart racing as I tried to gauge her intentions. "It's definitely not without its challenges."

The conversation danced between us, light and airy at first, but beneath the surface, I felt the weight of unspoken words. My stomach churned as we navigated this unfamiliar territory, three of us intertwined in a web of friendship, rivalry, and something far more complicated. As I engaged with Emily, I couldn't help but notice the way Michael leaned closer to her, the effortless camaraderie that seemed to flow between them, making the air around me crackle with tension.

"So, what's next for you?" Emily asked, tilting her head slightly, her curiosity genuine yet edged with something sharper. "I can't imagine how you juggle everything."

"Honestly, I'm still trying to figure that out," I admitted, my voice catching slightly as I forced a smile. "The last few weeks have been a bit overwhelming."

The truth hung between us, unacknowledged yet palpable. I felt trapped in a tug-of-war, my heart divided between the intoxicating connection with Michael and the unsettling reality that I might lose everything I'd fought to build.

As the conversation shifted, Michael's hand brushed against mine, an innocent gesture, yet it sent shockwaves through my body. My heart leaped, both in excitement and dread. I glanced at Emily, and in that split second, I saw it—a flicker of something unreadable in her expression. Was it jealousy? Concern?

"I know the shelter means a lot to you, but you have to prioritize your own happiness too," Emily said suddenly, her voice steady but her eyes revealing a depth of understanding that unsettled me. "It's important to find balance."

"Balance," I echoed, the word rolling off my tongue like a bitter pill. "It's easier said than done."

The tension coiled tighter, and I felt the urge to escape, to flee this uncomfortable tableau. Yet, I was rooted in place, caught in the magnetic pull of Michael's presence, the uncharted territory of Emily's interest, and the flickering fear of losing it all.

"I have an idea," Michael interjected, his voice cutting through the heavy atmosphere like a knife. "Why don't we all go grab some ice cream? It's been ages since I indulged in a little sweetness."

"Sounds perfect!" Emily chimed in, her eyes sparkling with excitement. "I could definitely use a scoop of something to sweeten the day."

I nodded, forcing a smile that felt like a mask. The thought of ice cream—my favorite indulgence—was appealing, but the shadows of uncertainty loomed larger than any dessert could chase away. As we stood and walked toward the ice cream shop, I stole glances at

Michael, his easy charm captivating Emily as I struggled to hold onto the fragile thread of our relationship.

With each step, I felt the delicate balance of my world shift, the shifting sands beneath my feet threatening to swallow me whole. In this moment, surrounded by laughter and bright colors, I realized that the storm brewing inside was far from over.

As we strolled toward the ice cream shop, the late afternoon sun cast a golden hue over everything, making the world feel like a perfectly staged Instagram filter. The sidewalk was dotted with fallen leaves, each one crinkling underfoot as if protesting the chill that hinted at the inevitable arrival of winter. Emily walked beside Michael, her laughter ringing out, and I felt a tug of resentment at how easily she seemed to fill the spaces I'd once claimed. I tried to drown it out with thoughts of the sweet coldness of ice cream, but the competition felt so much sharper in her presence.

We arrived at the small shop that had become a staple of our meetings. The colorful menu board hung overhead like a carnival prize, each flavor beckoning with the promise of delight. My eyes darted over the choices—classic vanilla, tangy lemon sorbet, and the ever-mysterious "mystery flavor," which I was convinced was just vanilla with a flair for the dramatic.

"Any chance you're going to surprise me with a scoop of that mystery flavor?" Michael asked, nudging my shoulder playfully.

"Only if you're feeling adventurous," I shot back, allowing a hint of a smile to curve my lips.

He grinned, that familiar spark in his eyes. "I'm always up for a challenge."

Emily interjected, her voice light and teasing. "How about I stick with a classic? Can't go wrong with chocolate fudge brownie."

"Classic? Is that your go-to move, Emily? Playing it safe?" I said, raising an eyebrow.

"Oh, please," she replied, rolling her eyes dramatically. "There's nothing wrong with being practical. Besides, someone has to keep things grounded here."

"Grounded?" I echoed, trying to inject some sarcasm into my tone, but the quirk of her smile softened the barb. "Sure, until you blow up the whole thing with spontaneous decisions."

The banter flew back and forth, and while I tried to play it cool, the unease continued to coil in my gut. It was as if I were watching a performance unfold, one I had somehow stumbled into without a script. With each exchange, I felt the invisible barrier between us—one that I desperately wanted to dismantle but couldn't quite figure out how.

As we ordered, Michael kept glancing between Emily and me, his eyes darting as if he were trying to navigate a maze he hadn't anticipated. "What do you think, Anna?" he asked, turning his focus to me. "Should I dare to try that mystery flavor?"

"Absolutely, if you're feeling brave," I said, though my stomach knotted at the thought of how our lives were becoming an intricate web of choices and risks. The ice cream server handed over our cones with a flourish, and I couldn't help but notice how effortlessly Emily leaned into the playful exchange, her easy confidence starkly contrasting my simmering tension.

As we settled at a small table outside, the sun dipping lower in the sky, I took a tentative lick of my cone. The rich, creamy blend of caramel and sea salt exploded on my tongue, a delicious distraction from the whirlwind of thoughts whirling in my mind. Emily was engrossed in conversation with Michael, and I found myself observing them, trying to decipher the connection between them.

"Did I ever tell you about the time I tried to make homemade ice cream?" Michael asked, his voice warm and inviting, yet a hint of mischief sparkled in his eyes.

"I don't believe you have," Emily replied, leaning forward with genuine interest. "But I'm dying to hear about it."

"Oh, it was a disaster," he laughed, a genuine sound that made my heart sink a little deeper. "I thought I could make it without a machine—just shake a bag in a bag method. But let's just say that after ten minutes of shaking, my arm felt like it was about to fall off, and the end result tasted like salty milk."

"Salty milk? Sounds delightful," Emily chimed in, her laughter brightening the chilly air. "Next time, stick to the store-bought stuff."

"Good advice," he replied, and the chemistry between them crackled like static electricity.

As they exchanged stories, I felt a pang of nostalgia for our own lighthearted moments—the late-night ice cream runs, the goofy road trips, and the comfortable silences that spoke volumes. But that connection felt like it was slowly dissolving in the rising tide of my insecurities. Each laugh shared between them was a reminder of the secret we had yet to acknowledge, one that felt heavier with each passing second.

"Anna, do you have any embarrassing cooking stories?" Michael asked, pulling me back into the moment.

"Oh, where do I even start?" I replied, adopting a playful tone to mask my growing discomfort. "Let's see. There was that time I thought I could impress my friends with a homemade pasta dish. Spoiler alert: I ended up with a flour explosion and a kitchen that looked like a scene from a disaster movie."

Emily snickered, her laughter infectious. "I'm sure you did it with flair, though!"

"Only if you count flour all over my face as flair," I shot back, reveling in the familiar warmth of humor while I felt the pressure of the unspoken looming above us like dark clouds.

Just then, the playful atmosphere shifted as a group of rowdy teenagers passed by, their voices loud and boisterous, clashing with the serenity of the moment. One of them, a guy with a mop of curly hair, glanced at our table and let out a low whistle. "Hey, check out the lovebirds!" he called, laughter trailing behind him like a careless wind.

I felt the heat rise to my cheeks, and I shot a glance at Emily, who appeared unfazed, her brow furrowing slightly as she raised an eyebrow at the group. "Charming," she muttered under her breath, but the teasing spark in her eyes belied any real annoyance.

Michael, ever the smooth talker, shot a casual wave at the teenagers, his expression unfazed. "They think we're adorable. Can't blame them."

"Adorable?" I echoed, my tone a mix of disbelief and amusement. "I'm not sure we're ready for that label yet."

Emily leaned back, her laughter bubbling up again, "Well, I don't know. If you two keep sharing those ridiculous stories, you might just convince them!"

In that moment, I felt a fleeting sense of connection wash over us, an acknowledgment of the tangled emotions that lurked beneath the surface. I caught Michael's gaze, and something unspoken passed between us, a shared understanding of the precariousness of our situation. Yet even in that fragile space, the tension remained, an undercurrent that was impossible to ignore.

We finished our cones, the sweet remnants lingering on our tongues, but I couldn't shake the feeling that the moment was just a pause in an ongoing storm. The world around us continued to spin, but my heart raced with the anticipation of what lay ahead, unsure if the path forward would bring clarity or chaos.

The ice cream shop had a small garden out back, a hidden pocket of tranquility surrounded by thick hedges and colorful flowers that swayed gently in the breeze. Michael suggested we retreat there, seeking a bit of privacy away from the raucous laughter of the teenagers and the bustling street beyond. I nodded, grateful for the change of scenery, but as we settled onto a weathered wooden bench, the tension that had been simmering since I'd seen Emily began to bubble to the surface once more.

"So, tell me, what's the deal with you two?" Emily's voice cut through the air, sharp and direct, a hint of amusement dancing in her eyes. I shifted uncomfortably, an involuntary reaction to the sudden spotlight on us.

"Us? There's no deal," I replied, forcing a casual tone. "Just friends enjoying ice cream, right, Michael?" My heart raced as I shot him a sidelong glance, willing him to play along.

"Right," he agreed quickly, but the flicker of uncertainty in his gaze told a different story. "Just friends. Nothing more." His smile faltered slightly, and the weight of our hidden relationship pressed down like a heavy blanket, stifling any attempts at levity.

Emily leaned in, her interest piqued. "You're telling me there's nothing between you? Because the way you look at each other says otherwise."

I opened my mouth to deny it, to weave a clever retort that would diffuse the situation, but nothing came out. Instead, I felt my heart thump in my chest, a mix of excitement and fear. This wasn't just a casual outing anymore; it felt like we were navigating treacherous waters, and I was clinging to the hope that I wouldn't capsize.

"Honestly, it's complicated," I finally admitted, allowing my vulnerability to seep through. "But we're figuring it out."

"Complicated is my middle name," Emily quipped, a teasing grin lighting up her features. "But I think I know a bit about complex relationships. You're not the only one in a bit of a twist here."

"What do you mean?" Michael interjected, his expression shifting to one of genuine curiosity.

Emily hesitated, her expression growing serious. "Just that sometimes, the lines between friendship and something more get blurry, especially when feelings are involved."

The air thickened, and I felt the walls of the garden closing in around us. This was more than just idle chatter; it felt like a revelation waiting to spill over. I could sense Michael's discomfort at the direction the conversation had taken, and yet, there was something undeniably engaging about Emily's honesty.

"Okay, let's say hypothetically that someone were caught in a complicated triangle," I ventured, my tone playful yet cautious. "What would you do?"

Emily shrugged, her smile fading slightly. "Honestly? I'd just be real. Life's too short to play games. But I'd also try to figure out who truly makes me happy, you know?"

"Very wise for someone who eats chocolate fudge brownie," I replied, trying to lighten the mood. But the flicker of seriousness in her eyes made it clear she was more than just a sweet tooth.

"Thanks, but it's hard to stay wise when you're trying to decipher the emotional baggage of everyone around you," she said, a hint of exasperation creeping into her voice. "Especially when people don't say what they really mean."

The truth hung in the air, taut and charged. I wanted to scream that I wasn't trying to keep secrets, that I wanted nothing more than to be honest, but the fear of losing everything held me back. The swirling emotions within me mirrored the vibrant colors of the flowers around us—wild, chaotic, and beautiful all at once.

We continued to nibble on our cones, the sweet coldness a welcome distraction, but the air was thick with unspoken words. Michael suddenly stood, the abruptness of his movement startling me. "You know what? Let's get to the point. Anna, you need to know something. I've been thinking—"

Just then, a loud crash shattered the moment, a nearby table tipping over, sending cups and cones flying. Emily jumped, her eyes wide with surprise. The commotion drew our attention, and we turned just in time to see a couple of guys from the earlier group of teenagers laughing hysterically, clearly responsible for the chaos.

"Nice one, guys! Real smooth!" one of them shouted, his voice dripping with sarcasm as they stumbled away, leaving a mess behind.

Michael let out an exasperated sigh. "What is it with kids these days?"

"Not a clue," Emily replied, rolling her eyes but laughing at the absurdity. "But at least they're entertaining."

I took a breath, trying to shake off the tension that had just surged back to life. "Maybe it's a sign. You know, sometimes things have a way of revealing themselves when you least expect it."

Michael gave me a sideways glance, one that held a deeper meaning I wasn't sure how to unpack. "Or sometimes they blow up in your face. Like that ice cream cone," he said, gesturing to the remains of a fallen sundae, remnants of whipped cream and sprinkles strewn across the pavement.

We all shared a laugh, a collective relief settling in, but it was short-lived. I could feel the weight of Michael's unfinished thought hanging between us, like a precarious thread that could snap at any moment.

"So," I prompted, trying to guide the conversation back to the edge we'd nearly crossed. "What were you saying before the ice cream disaster?"

"Right," he said, his brow furrowing as if searching for the right words. "I was just saying that—"

Before he could finish, Emily's phone buzzed violently against the table, slicing through the tension like a knife. She glanced at the screen, her expression shifting from amusement to concern. "Oh, it's my mom," she said, biting her lip. "I should take this."

"Sure, go ahead," Michael replied, though I could see the disappointment shadowing his features.

Emily stood, walking a few steps away to take the call. I watched her as she paced, her voice a low murmur, the concern on her face growing more pronounced. I turned to Michael, whose expression mirrored my own uncertainty.

"What do you think she's so worried about?" I asked, the unease returning in waves.

"I have no idea," he replied, his brow knitting together. "But something feels off."

Emily returned, her expression strained. "Sorry about that. Just some family stuff," she said, brushing it off.

"Everything okay?" I asked, instinctively stepping closer, ready to offer support.

"Yeah, it's just..." she trailed off, her gaze shifting to the ground. "My sister's having some issues at school. I think it's more serious than she's letting on."

Before I could respond, Michael stepped in, his voice firm but gentle. "You should check in on her. Family's important, and you can't help others if you're carrying that weight alone."

"Yeah, you're right," she said, her voice barely above a whisper. "I should go."

"Do you want us to come with you?" I offered, though I feared I knew the answer.

"No, it's okay. I'll handle it."

And with that, she turned and walked away, leaving me and Michael in a silence that felt heavy and loaded.

"Let's go after her," he said, glancing at me with a determination that flickered like a flame in the dark.

"Right, because that will definitely help," I replied, sarcasm spilling out before I could rein it in.

But Michael was already moving, and I followed, my heart pounding as we approached Emily. Just as we rounded the corner, the ringing of my phone sliced through the air, an unfamiliar number flashing on the screen. I hesitated, caught between the urgency of the call and the growing concern for Emily.

"Are you going to answer that?" Michael asked, his voice tight with anticipation.

I looked at the phone, then back at him. "I should—"

But before I could finish, the ground beneath us seemed to tremble, a rumble vibrating through the air, followed by a loud crash echoing from the direction of the café. In a split second, everything changed, and the world around us plunged into chaos once more, leaving me frozen in place, heart racing, as the reality of our shifting sands threatened to pull us under.

Chapter 15: Confrontation

The air was thick with anticipation, each heartbeat echoing in my ears as Emily stormed into the room, her presence a tempest that sent ripples through the very fabric of our reality. The dim light filtered through the window, casting shadows that danced ominously on the walls, mirroring the turmoil that churned within us. Emily stood before us, her fiery gaze ablaze with indignation, every inch of her radiating a fierce determination that both captivated and frightened me.

"Do you even hear yourselves?" she spat, her voice sharp enough to cut through the tension like a hot knife through butter. Each syllable dripped with contempt, and I felt the weight of her words settling over me like a heavy cloak. "You're tearing apart your lives for what? A fleeting fantasy that was never meant to be?"

The words hung in the air, a heavy pall that suffocated any semblance of a response. I stole a glance at Michael, who stood stoically beside me, his jaw clenched tight enough to turn his knuckles white. He had always been the silent strength, the unwavering support in the tempest of my emotional turmoil. But now, he was as much a prisoner of this confrontation as I was.

"Emily," I finally managed, my voice a fragile whisper against the tumult. I wanted to reach out, to bridge the chasm that had suddenly widened between us, but the flicker of her fury was like a wildfire threatening to consume everything in its path. "It's not what you think. We—"

"We what?" she interrupted, hands on her hips, a fierce defiance etched across her features. "You think this is some grand love story? This isn't a romance novel, and you aren't characters in one of those happy-ending tales. This is real life, and you're both playing with fire."

I flinched at her words, feeling the heat of shame rise in my cheeks. Was that how we looked to her? Like a couple of lovesick fools with our heads buried in the clouds, oblivious to the chaos we were causing around us?

"I'm not trying to play games, Emily," I replied, my voice gaining strength. "What Michael and I have isn't a whim. It's not just some passing fancy. There's more to it—"

"More to it?" she scoffed, laughter laced with bitterness bubbling up from somewhere deep within. "More than the destruction you're causing? More than the friends you're losing? You think this is love? It looks more like a train wreck to me."

Her words stung like icy rain, each accusation piercing through my defenses. I had known this moment would come, the reckoning where the facade we had built around our relationship would shatter under scrutiny. But knowing didn't ease the ache that bloomed in my chest.

Michael shifted, his silence now a palpable force between us, almost as if he were a statue carved from stone, unmoving but full of unspoken words. I longed for him to speak, to offer some defense or maybe even a counterpoint to Emily's blistering critique, but he remained locked in place, his eyes darting between Emily and me, uncertainty written all over his face.

"Emily," he finally said, his voice low and steady. "I never meant to hurt you. Or anyone. But we can't just ignore what we feel. I can't ignore it."

I turned to him, surprised to see the vulnerability in his eyes, a softness that had been masked by his usual bravado. There was an intensity in his gaze that spoke of a yearning for understanding, a desperate plea for Emily to see past the chaos and recognize the truth of our connection.

"Feelings?" Emily laughed, a bitter sound that reverberated in the quiet room. "Feelings don't matter when they come at the cost of everything else. You two are like moths to a flame, and all you're doing is burning everything down around you."

Her words sank deep, wrapping around my heart like a constrictor. I wanted to scream, to defend our love, to shout that we were not just reckless souls blindly dancing towards destruction. But deep down, I could feel the truth of her accusations, the weight of our choices settling heavily upon my shoulders.

"Maybe you're right," I admitted, my voice trembling. "Maybe we are just... lost. But don't you see? We're trying to find our way, together. Isn't that worth something?"

Emily's expression softened for just a moment, a flicker of something—regret, perhaps—flashed across her features. But it was quickly snuffed out, replaced by the steadfast resolve of someone who had been hurt one too many times.

"Together?" she echoed, her tone laced with incredulity. "What about the rest of us? What about your friendships? What about the lives you're disrupting?"

The question hung in the air, a chilling reminder of the collateral damage that our relationship had wrought. Friends had drifted away, their faces clouded with confusion and hurt, and now Emily stood before us, a representative of all that was unraveling.

Michael finally broke his silence, his voice low and earnest. "I didn't mean to hurt anyone, but I can't change how I feel. Neither can you, Emily. You know how it is."

"Is that so?" she shot back, crossing her arms defensively. "You can't just choose to ignore the fallout. This isn't just about you. It's about all of us. You need to take responsibility."

Her words struck a chord, resonating deep within me. The weight of my actions, the choices that had led us here, felt like a noose tightening around my throat. What had begun as a spark, an exhilarating leap into the unknown, had morphed into a complex web of heartache and conflict.

And as I looked between them, the fiery tempest that was Emily and the quiet storm that was Michael, I realized that I was standing at a crossroads. What had once felt like a path paved with possibility now lay fraught with peril, and the direction I chose would echo far beyond this moment, touching every life entwined in our story.

The weight of Emily's words hung in the air like a thick fog, suffocating the space around us. Her passion ignited something deep within me, a cocktail of guilt and defiance swirling together like a tempest. I could feel Michael's presence beside me, a solid anchor in this storm of emotions, but even his steady demeanor seemed to flicker under the intensity of the moment.

"You don't get it," I managed, my voice steadier now, fueled by the adrenaline coursing through me. "This isn't just some reckless fling. It's real, and I'm not ashamed of that." My heart pounded against my ribcage, each beat a reminder of the risks we had taken.

"Oh, it's real, all right," Emily shot back, her eyes flashing with a blend of fury and sadness. "But you're too wrapped up in this fantasy to see the wreckage you're leaving in your wake."

There was a piercing honesty in her words that cut deeper than I would have liked to admit. The fallout of our choices was palpable, a living, breathing entity that wrapped itself around our lives, squeezing out the joy and replacing it with a heavy sadness. Friends had become distant shadows, drifting away as we dove headfirst into our romance, but the allure of what Michael and I had felt too intoxicating to abandon.

Michael finally spoke, his voice calm yet unyielding, as if he were a lighthouse guiding a lost ship. "We're trying to figure things out, Emily. It's not like we planned for this to happen." He gestured between us, the movement both protective and assertive. "But it has happened, and you're not going to convince us it was a mistake."

"You're playing with fire, and you're both too blind to see you're going to get burned," she retorted, her voice rising, a battle cry infused with desperation.

In that moment, the room felt charged, the atmosphere thick with unspoken truths. I could see the shadows lurking behind Emily's anger, the hurt that had driven her to this confrontation. The friendship we once shared now felt like a fragile web, stretched to its limits and threatening to snap at any moment.

"Emily, this isn't just about us," I interjected, my heart racing. "It's about you too. Don't pretend you don't care. You're hurt, and I get it, but we can't go back to what we had before. Not now."

Her expression softened for a heartbeat, vulnerability flickering across her features like a candle fighting against the wind. "I care because I don't want to see you both ruin your lives. I thought we were friends. We were supposed to look out for each other, not burn the whole place down."

The silence that followed was deafening. I could feel the tension curling around us, wrapping us in an uncomfortable embrace, each of us caught in our thoughts, trapped in the aftermath of our choices. My heart ached for the friendship we had lost, a bond that had once felt unbreakable now teetering on the brink of collapse.

"Maybe it's already too late for that," I murmured, my voice barely above a whisper. The admission hung between us, a bitter truth that refused to be ignored.

Emily stepped closer, her frustration bubbling beneath the surface, desperate for clarity. "Do you even realize what you're throwing away? Do you think love is all it takes? You're both so wrapped up in this whirlwind that you can't see the reality right in front of you."

"Maybe the reality is that we're trying to figure out what we want," Michael chimed in, his patience thinning. "And we're doing it together, whether you like it or not."

"Do you really think this is a wise decision?" Emily pressed, her eyes narrowing, searching for a crack in our resolve. "What happens when the dust settles? When you both wake up and realize the mess you've made?"

I felt the heat of her words burning into me, but there was an unexpected spark of defiance that ignited in the pit of my stomach. "Maybe we'll figure that out when we get there," I shot back, the words spilling from my lips like water from a broken dam. "But we won't know until we try."

"Trying is one thing," she retorted, her voice filled with scorn. "But what if it all goes wrong? What if you end up hurting each other worse than anyone else ever could?"

The question hung heavily in the air, a chilling reminder of the risks we faced. I could see the flicker of fear in her eyes, the shadow of concern that lurked just beneath the surface of her fury. It was a painful reflection of my own worries, the constant hum of anxiety that thrummed through my veins, but I couldn't let that stop me.

"We have to take that risk," I said, trying to infuse my words with a conviction I didn't fully feel. "Isn't that what life is about? Taking chances?"

"Taking chances is one thing," Emily said, her voice softening, becoming almost pleading. "But this... this is reckless. You're both betting everything on a feeling that might just be a fleeting moment. And if it blows up in your faces, don't come crying to me."

Her tone shifted, a subtle vulnerability seeping through the cracks of her anger, and I could see the storm brewing just beneath her facade. There was something more, a depth of emotion that suggested this was more than just about us.

"Emily, we're not just chasing a feeling," I replied, my heart racing. "This is real. And yes, it's scary, but isn't that what makes it worth pursuing?"

For a moment, we were locked in an unspoken battle, each of us fighting our own inner demons while trying to grapple with the complexities of our intertwined lives. Emily's lips parted, as if she wanted to respond, but the words faltered, caught somewhere in the tangled web of her emotions.

Finally, she took a step back, her shoulders sagging as if the weight of the world had settled onto them. "I just don't want to see you both end up like me," she whispered, her voice breaking slightly. "I've been there, and it's a dark place. I wouldn't wish that on anyone."

The room fell silent, and the truth of her statement struck like lightning, illuminating the shadows that loomed over us. It wasn't just anger that had brought her here; it was a deep-seated fear rooted in her own experiences.

"I'm sorry," I said, my voice sincere, my heart aching for the friend I once knew. "I didn't realize how much this was hurting you. We're still friends, Emily. We want you in our lives, but you can't keep pushing us away like this."

Her gaze softened, and for a moment, the tension eased, replaced by a fragile connection that flickered between us like a candle in the dark. "I just want what's best for you both," she replied, her voice barely above a whisper.

"And we want what's best for you too," Michael added, his voice gentle yet firm. "But you have to trust us to find our own way."

The three of us stood there, the silence enveloping us like a warm blanket, each of us grappling with the complexities of love, friendship, and the intricate dance of emotions that pulled us together and tore us apart.

The silence that enveloped us was almost unbearable, punctuated only by the distant hum of life outside—cars rolling down the street, laughter echoing from the nearby park, and the occasional bark of a dog, oblivious to the emotional maelstrom brewing between us. It felt like we were standing on the edge of a precipice, a rift that threatened to pull us all apart.

"I can't keep doing this," Emily finally broke the stillness, her voice low yet fierce, as if she were voicing a resolution rather than an admission. "I won't sit by and watch you both ruin your lives because of some misguided notion of love. I care too much for you to just stand back and let it happen."

The sincerity in her eyes, bright and filled with a mixture of frustration and affection, chipped away at my defenses. She wasn't just angry; she was heartbroken, her concern for us wrapped tightly around her emotions like a security blanket she couldn't quite let go of. I could feel the heat of her words brushing against me, a reminder of everything I had fought to build alongside Michael.

"What if it's not misguided?" I asked, unable to contain the tremor in my voice. "What if this is exactly what we need?"

Emily's expression flickered, confusion mingling with resolve. "You really believe that? That you can just ignore everything else and chase after a feeling?"

"Sometimes, feelings are all we have," Michael interjected, his voice calm but firm. He stepped slightly closer to me, as if drawing strength from our proximity. "We're not asking for your blessing, Emily. We just want you to understand that this is more than just a moment for us."

The defiance in his tone was infectious, fueling my own resolve. I had grown weary of defending our relationship, yet here we were, engaged in a battle for our right to feel, to love, and to embrace the tumult of emotions that had entwined our lives.

Emily's eyes narrowed, her frustration boiling just beneath the surface. "What about your lives? What about everything else that matters? Your friendships, your families, your futures?" Her voice broke slightly, revealing the vulnerability hidden behind her fierce facade. "This isn't just some adventure. This is your life!"

And there it was, the truth. Our lives felt like a tightrope, and the further we ventured into this uncharted territory, the more perilous the journey became. But as scary as it was, I refused to believe we were mere fools chasing an illusion.

"You're right," I admitted, a wave of honesty washing over me. "This is serious. It's not just some passing phase for us. We're trying to build something real. And that scares me just as much as it scares you."

The words hung in the air, thick with unspoken tension. Emily's posture softened for a fleeting moment, a glimmer of understanding breaking through her defenses. "I just don't want to see you hurt," she whispered, her voice trembling slightly.

"Then don't push us away," I replied, desperation creeping into my tone. "Help us instead. Help us navigate this chaos, not tear it apart."

Her eyes darted between Michael and me, the turmoil of conflicting emotions playing out on her face. "You don't understand. I feel like I'm losing you both. This isn't how it was supposed to be."

There was an almost palpable sense of desperation in her plea, and I wanted to reach out, to soothe the ache I could see pooling in her gaze. "You're not losing us, Emily. We're all still here, standing right in front of you. Just... let us be who we are, together."

But as I spoke, I felt a shift in the atmosphere, a chill creeping into the warm, sticky air that surrounded us. The moment was fragile, teetering on the brink of something either transformative or utterly destructive.

Suddenly, a loud bang echoed from outside, a sound sharp enough to make us jump. My heart raced, adrenaline pumping through my veins as I glanced toward the window, where shadows flickered, dancing in the dying light. Emily's expression morphed from confrontation to confusion, and she moved toward the window, her curiosity piqued despite the rising tension.

"What was that?" she asked, her voice trembling slightly, the earlier anger momentarily forgotten.

"I don't know," I replied, anxiety creeping into my chest. "It sounded like it came from the park."

Michael moved to the window next to Emily, his brow furrowing as he peered outside. "Looks like something's happening," he murmured, tension knotting his shoulders.

The three of us crowded by the window, straining to catch a glimpse of what was unfolding just beyond our walls. The park was alive with commotion. A group of people had gathered, their voices rising in alarm, and the flicker of flashing lights illuminated the gathering shadows, creating an eerie glow that contrasted with the encroaching night.

"What's going on?" I breathed, a sense of foreboding settling over me like a thick blanket.

"I can't tell," Emily replied, squinting into the distance. "It looks like... police?"

My heart sank. In our small town, police involvement usually meant trouble—real trouble. Something had shifted outside, an unseen wave of chaos that threatened to spill into our carefully curated world.

"What if it's serious?" Michael asked, his voice edged with concern. "What if something's happened to someone we know?"

We shared a look, the tension between us instantly shifting from personal conflict to a collective sense of worry. The moment of connection we had just forged felt tenuous, fragile against the backdrop of an unknown threat.

Just then, a sharp scream pierced the night air, slicing through the clamor and freezing us in place. My stomach dropped, dread pooling in my gut like poison.

"Let's go see," I said, urgency flooding my veins.

Emily nodded, her eyes wide, the fear etched in her features mirroring my own.

Before we could take a single step, the front door burst open, and a figure rushed inside, breathless and wild-eyed. It was Ryan, our mutual friend, and his frantic presence sent our hearts racing.

"They need help!" he gasped, urgency dripping from his voice. "You have to come now!"

In that moment, everything shifted once again, and the confrontation that had seemed so pivotal moments before now felt trivial in the face of something far greater, something that could unravel our lives even more.

As we stood there, a collective breath held in anticipation, I could feel the ground shifting beneath us, the chaotic storm of our emotions fading into the background. Something dangerous was afoot, and the night had only just begun.

Chapter 16: Secrets Unearthed

The late afternoon sun filtered through the trees, casting dappled shadows across the forest floor as I wandered deeper into the woods. The scent of damp earth mixed with the crispness of autumn leaves, filling the air with a nostalgic perfume that reminded me of childhood adventures. I brushed aside low-hanging branches, each crackle underfoot sending a familiar thrill up my spine. There was a sense of liberation in the stillness, a promise that within this sanctuary, I could unearth truths hidden beneath layers of time and memory.

Michael's confrontation with Emily had left an indelible mark on my heart, a jagged line of unease that made it hard to breathe. It wasn't just about their past; it was the way he flinched at the mere mention of her name, as if it were a brand seared into his soul. I needed to understand this man who had swept into my life like a tempest, stirring emotions I had buried beneath my pragmatic exterior. His secrets, like the shadows that danced around me, beckoned me closer, whispering tales of a past I was desperate to uncover.

I remembered the first time we met, his laughter ringing out like a melody that clung to the air, wrapping around me like a warm embrace. The way he leaned in, his voice low and conspiratorial, made me feel as though we shared an unbreakable bond. But with Emily's name hanging heavily between us, I was left grappling with a chasm that threatened to swallow us whole. Determined to bridge that gap, I decided to delve into the depths of his history, armed with nothing but a notebook and an insatiable curiosity.

As I walked, I thought back to the late-night conversations we had shared, the intimate glimpses into his life that felt like pieces of a puzzle. There were stories of childhood escapades and fleeting moments of joy, but they were always tinged with an undercurrent of sorrow. It was as if he wore a mask, expertly concealing the scars that had shaped him. I needed to peel back those layers, to see the man behind the facade, to understand the shadows that lurked in his past.

My first stop was the small café on Main Street, a quaint little spot adorned with fairy lights and mismatched furniture that exuded an air of charm. I slipped inside, the warm air enveloping me like a cozy blanket, and approached the barista, a bubbly woman named Sarah with a penchant for gossip. She had a knack for knowing everyone's business, and I hoped she might shed some light on Michael's life before he arrived in town.

"Hey there, what can I get for you?" she chirped, her eyes sparkling with curiosity as she wiped down the counter.

"A cappuccino, please. And, um, do you know Michael Bennett?" I asked, trying to sound casual despite the flutter of nerves in my stomach.

Her eyebrows shot up, a smirk playing at the corners of her lips. "Ah, Michael. The brooding artist, right? He keeps to himself mostly, but there are whispers about him. The man has a history, you know."

"Whispers? What kind?" I leaned in closer, desperate for any shred of information.

She glanced around, as if ensuring no one was eavesdropping. "Well, there was a lot of talk when he first moved here. Something about a family fallout. He used to live in the city, had a gallery there. But one day, poof! He just left, and nobody really knew why."

"Did he have a falling out with his family?" I asked, a knot forming in my stomach.

Sarah shrugged. "That's the rumor. He doesn't like to talk about it. Just shows up here, paints in solitude. It's like he's running from something."

Her words hung in the air, heavy with implications. I thanked her and took my cappuccino, the foam art swirling like a storm brewing in my mind. I needed more than just rumors; I craved the truth. A name flickered in my memory—one of Michael's old friends from the city, a woman named Claire. I'd seen her mentioned in passing, an artist who had once shared the stage with him in a prestigious gallery. If anyone had the answers I sought, it would be her.

As I made my way to my car, I pulled out my phone and searched for her contact information. After a few moments of scrolling, I found her number and hesitated. Would she be willing to divulge Michael's secrets? I took a deep breath, steeling myself. Sometimes, the truth hurt, but it was the only way forward.

"Claire?" I greeted when she picked up, my voice laced with nervous energy. "This is... um, I'm a friend of Michael's."

"Oh! Michael! What a talented soul. How is he doing?" Her tone was warm, but a hint of sadness echoed beneath her words.

"He's... well, he's struggling with some things. I was wondering if you could share a bit about his past?"

There was a brief silence on the other end before she sighed. "That boy has a complicated history. I'd be happy to help. But you should know, some things are better left buried."

Her caution sent a shiver down my spine, but I pressed on. "Anything you can share would mean a lot."

As Claire unraveled the tapestry of Michael's past, my heart ached for him. I learned of a family torn apart by tragedy, of dreams shattered under the weight of expectations, and of the heartache that had driven him away. The pieces began to fit together, forming a picture of a man not only shaped by his choices but by the ghosts of his history.

With each revelation, my determination to help him grew stronger. I couldn't change his past, but I could be there for him, help him face those shadows instead of running from them. A fierce warmth spread through me as I imagined standing by his side, ready to tackle whatever demons loomed in his mind.

With renewed resolve, I made my way back home, the path before me illuminated by the fading sun. I was no longer just a curious observer; I was a participant in a story that was unfolding—a story that needed courage and compassion to rewrite its ending. Michael had suffered long enough in silence, and it was time for me to step into the light and show him that healing could begin with a single, brave step forward.

The shadows in the café shifted as evening approached, casting a cozy glow on the intimate conversations taking place at the mismatched tables. I cradled my cappuccino, letting the warmth seep into my palms while I mulled over Claire's revelations about Michael. Her words echoed in my mind, a haunting melody that tugged at my heartstrings. I imagined him as a child, a small boy with a big smile, weaving dreams through his artwork, only to have those dreams splattered by the harsh realities of family life. It made me want to protect him, to shield him from the jagged edges of his past that still threatened to cut deep.

Leaving the café, I wandered through the bustling streets, where autumn leaves danced in the brisk wind, swirling like confetti at a parade. Each step felt charged with purpose as I envisioned my next move. I wanted to confront Michael not with accusations or pity but with understanding. I was determined to be the steady hand he could lean on, the voice that whispered, "You're not alone." But I had to approach this delicately. His scars weren't for show; they were part of who he was.

As I reached the gallery where he worked, the familiar scent of paint and varnish wrapped around me like a second skin. Michael was often ensconced here, pouring his heart into canvases that reflected his inner turmoil. I hesitated at the entrance, recalling our last conversation. There had been a darkness in his eyes, a flicker of something that hinted at vulnerability. With a deep breath, I stepped inside, the door chiming softly behind me.

The space was quiet, the kind of quiet that felt like the calm before a storm. I scanned the room and spotted Michael in the corner, bent over a canvas splashed with colors that fought for dominance. He wore an old, paint-splattered apron, his brow furrowed in concentration. I admired him for a moment, the way he lost himself in his work as if it were a lifeline. But my admiration was soon shadowed by the memories of the day's revelations, memories that pressed on my heart like a weight too heavy to bear.

"Hey, Picasso," I said, injecting a lightness into my voice as I approached. "What's the masterpiece of the day?"

He looked up, surprise flaring in his eyes, quickly replaced by a guarded smile that didn't quite reach his eyes. "Just trying to make sense of the chaos," he replied, a hint of self-deprecation threading through his words. "You know how it is. Sometimes the colors just refuse to cooperate."

"Maybe they're having an identity crisis of their own," I teased, leaning against the wall, my heart racing at the thought of broaching the subject that lingered between us like an uninvited guest.

"Or maybe they just don't trust me," he said, his voice dropping to a whisper. There was a vulnerability there, one I hadn't seen before, and I knew it was my moment to step in.

"Michael," I began, my tone softening as I approached him, "I had a talk with Claire today."

His expression shifted, tension coiling in the air. "Claire?" he repeated, a hint of wariness creeping into his voice. "What did she say?"

"Just that you had a tough upbringing," I replied carefully. "That you left the city to escape... something."

He stiffened, his gaze dropping to the floor. "It's not something I like to discuss," he muttered, as if the words themselves were poison on his tongue.

"I get that," I said, hoping to ease the weight of the moment. "But you don't have to bear it alone. I'm here, you know? Whatever it is, you can tell me."

His eyes darted to mine, the storm of emotions swirling behind them. "It's complicated," he finally said, a mixture of defiance and desperation in his tone.

"Complicated is my middle name," I replied, forcing a smile. "Come on, if you can throw paint around like that, you can at least share a few colors from your life."

For a heartbeat, silence enveloped us, thick enough to slice with a knife. Then he sighed, running a hand through his hair, which was starting to curl in the humidity of the studio. "Fine. But promise me you won't judge."

"Cross my heart," I said, making an exaggerated motion as I mimed the act of crossing my heart and waving my pinky. "Pinky swear, even."

He let out a half-hearted chuckle, the tension in his shoulders easing just a fraction. "Okay, here goes. My family... well, it's a mess. I grew up with a mother who had big dreams for me. Art was never in the picture; it was all about business and legacy. When I decided to pursue art instead of following her plans, let's just say it didn't go over well."

"Was that when you left?" I asked, intrigued.

"Not right away. It took time for the storm to brew," he explained, his voice growing steadier. "But the day I got the call about my sister, that was the day everything shattered. I didn't just leave the city. I left my family behind."

The weight of his words settled in the room, thick and heavy like a storm cloud about to burst. "Your sister?" I prompted gently, knowing this was the moment where I had to tread carefully.

"Emily," he said, his voice barely above a whisper. "We used to be close, but when I chose art, it drove a wedge between us. I thought I was doing what was best for me, but it cost me her. When she needed me the most, I wasn't there."

I swallowed hard, the revelation hitting me with the force of a freight train. "You blame yourself, don't you?"

He nodded slowly, anguish etching lines across his face. "I do. I thought leaving would save me, but in reality, it just left me more lost. I didn't think I'd ever be ready to face her again."

"Michael, you can't carry that burden forever," I said, my heart aching for him. "You deserve a chance to heal. And if Emily is still in your life, maybe there's still a chance to reconnect."

His gaze met mine, and for the first time, I saw a flicker of hope mingling with the shadows. "You really think so?"

"I do," I replied, my voice firm yet tender. "But you have to take that first step. It won't be easy, but you won't be alone this time. I'll be right here, cheering you on."

As the vulnerability between us shifted, a sense of possibility bloomed in the air, wrapping around us like a warm embrace. He stepped closer, the unspoken connection between us deepening, filling the space with a gentle warmth that felt as though we were on the precipice of something beautiful. In that moment, I realized that love wasn't just about the grand gestures or stolen kisses; it was about standing together in the quiet chaos, ready to face whatever came next.

The evening settled around us like a soft blanket, the dim light in the gallery accentuating the vibrant colors of Michael's paintings. The air was thick with unspoken words, and I could feel the weight of our conversation hanging between us, a fragile bridge we were slowly constructing together. With a newfound sense of connection, I dared to hope that maybe we could navigate the tumultuous waters of his past side by side.

"Can I see it?" I asked, gesturing toward the canvas he'd been working on. The colors danced together, a chaotic swirl that seemed to reflect the storm brewing within him.

He glanced at it, hesitating for a moment before nodding. "It's not finished, but you can take a look."

As I stepped closer, the vivid strokes pulled me in. The piece was a tempest—deep blues and purples clashed with fiery reds and yellows, each brushstroke pulsating with emotion. It felt raw and vulnerable, as if he had poured his heart onto the canvas without reservation.

"It's incredible," I said, turning to him with wide eyes. "What's it about?"

Michael stepped beside me, his shoulder brushing against mine, sending a delightful spark of electricity through the air. "It's... complicated," he replied, echoing the theme of our earlier conversation. "It's a reflection of everything I feel. Anger, love, loss... it's all jumbled together. I guess it's how I process what happened with Emily."

I studied his profile, the way his brow furrowed as he spoke, revealing a depth of pain I wanted to soothe. "Have you thought about showing it to her?" The words slipped out before I could rein them in, my heart pounding as I waited for his reaction.

His gaze hardened, shadows crossing his features. "I can't. Not yet. I'm not ready for her to see that side of me. I don't even know if she wants to see me again."

"Then it's time to change that," I urged, feeling a surge of determination. "You owe it to yourself—and to her—to let her see who you are now. Not just the brother she lost, but the man you've become."

He turned to me, surprise flickering in his eyes. "And what if she doesn't want to? What if I'm just a reminder of everything that went wrong?"

"Then you fight for it," I said, my voice firm. "You don't just walk away because it's easier. Love isn't about perfection; it's about honesty and facing your fears."

His expression softened, and a flicker of something like hope ignited in the depths of his gaze. "You really think I can do this?"

"I know you can," I replied, smiling. "And I'll be right there with you. Every step of the way."

The warmth of our moment hung in the air, fragile yet filled with promise. But as quickly as that warmth enveloped us, it was interrupted by the shrill ring of Michael's phone. He glanced at the screen, the light illuminating his face, but his expression shifted from warmth to something colder and more guarded.

"It's my dad," he muttered, tension creeping back into his voice. He answered with a curt, "Hello?" The change was immediate; his body stiffened, the openness we had just shared slipping away like sand through fingers.

I watched as his face hardened, his eyes narrowing with each word exchanged. Whatever his father was saying clearly troubled him, a shadow creeping back across his features. I could see the way his fingers clenched around the phone, the tightness in his jaw.

"Listen, I'll deal with it later," Michael said, his voice clipped. "No, I'm not coming back. Not now. I've got things to sort out."

The silence that followed felt thick and suffocating. He hung up abruptly, a look of frustration etching lines across his brow. "Sorry about that," he said, attempting to shake off the tension. "Family stuff. You know how it goes."

"Do I?" I shot back, raising an eyebrow. "Your dad doesn't seem like the type to just check in for a friendly chat."

His expression shifted to one of frustration mixed with something deeper—resentment, perhaps? "He's not exactly my biggest fan," Michael replied, running a hand through his hair in frustration. "I thought leaving would distance me from all that, but I guess it's not that easy."

"Maybe it's time to face it head-on, then," I suggested, stepping closer again, feeling the palpable tension swirling around us. "You can't keep running from your family, Michael. Not forever."

"Maybe that's all I know how to do," he countered, his voice a low murmur.

The intensity of our conversation felt like a boiling pot ready to overflow, and just as I opened my mouth to respond, he turned abruptly, a shadow crossing his face as he glanced toward the entrance. I followed his gaze, and my heart sank as I spotted a figure stepping into the gallery—a woman whose striking resemblance to Michael left no doubt in my mind.

Emily.

The moment hung in the air, charged with unspoken tension and uncharted emotions. She stood in the doorway, hesitating, uncertainty flickering in her eyes. The air thickened between us as Michael's body froze, caught between the past and the present.

"Michael?" she finally called, her voice a blend of hope and apprehension. "Is it really you?"

I glanced at Michael, whose expression was a tapestry of emotions, each thread pulling him in a different direction. He looked as if he were caught in a storm—wary, longing, and terrified all at once.

"Emily," he breathed, barely above a whisper. The world around us faded, the colors dimming as the reality of the moment sank in.

This was it. The moment I had hoped for—the confrontation that could either mend broken bonds or shatter them further. I could almost feel the weight of their shared history pressing down upon us, and I knew that whatever happened next would change everything.

Just then, the gallery door swung shut behind Emily, the sound echoing like a gavel striking the final verdict in a long-running trial.

She stepped further inside, uncertainty mingling with a fierce determination.

"Can we talk?" she asked, her voice steady but vulnerable, the words laden with the weight of years lost.

Michael remained rooted to the spot, torn between stepping forward and retreating into the safety of his pain. I felt the tension snap like a taut string, the air thick with anticipation, every heartbeat echoing the stakes of this moment. I wanted to reach out, to guide him, but I knew this was a journey he had to take on his own.

"Michael?" she pressed, her eyes shimmering with unshed tears, and suddenly I realized that I wasn't just a bystander in this reunion; I was an unwilling participant, standing on the precipice of a fragile bridge between them, knowing that one misstep could lead to a devastating fall.

And as Michael's gaze shifted from Emily to me, uncertainty flared in his eyes. Would he step into the past, or would he forge a new path forward? The question hung heavy in the air, crackling with tension, as the ground beneath us trembled, ready to shift in unpredictable ways.

Chapter 17: In the Eye of the Storm

The door creaked open, revealing Michael in a tailored shirt that clung to his shoulders like it was made for him alone. His hair, tousled but somehow intentional, caught the dim light, casting a halo effect that momentarily dimmed the noise of our gathering. I'd invited a motley crew—friends I thought might lighten the mood, even as my heart sank at the sight of him. In a room full of people, his presence created an isolation bubble, a sharp contrast to the warmth that had filled my apartment moments earlier.

"Hey, everyone," he said, his voice smooth as honey yet laced with a tension that made my skin prickle. The jovial chatter faltered, replaced by a heavy silence that felt as if it had been woven into the very fabric of my living room. It was one of those moments when time stilled, and everyone held their breath, waiting to see how the drama would unfold.

I felt the weight of their eyes on us, each gaze a silent question. What were we? Were we broken or simply bent? I took a sip of my wine, the chilled liquid burning down my throat, and forced a smile that didn't quite reach my eyes. As if on cue, Jess broke the silence with her usual exuberance, her laughter slicing through the tension like a hot knife through butter.

"Michael! You finally decided to grace us with your presence! We were beginning to think you'd joined a cult or something." She nudged me playfully, but her eyes flickered with concern, silently asking if I was okay. I appreciated her effort, though it was almost futile against the storm brewing between Michael and me.

"Yeah, sorry about that. I got stuck in traffic." He shrugged, his easy demeanor in stark contrast to the storm brewing within me. I wanted to laugh, to join in the mirth, but my emotions felt like a blender on high speed, mixing confusion, anger, and a sprinkle of longing.

"Traffic? In this town? That's a new one," Ryan chimed in, his grin wide as he handed Michael a beer. "You must be cursed."

The laughter rippled through the room, lightening the mood, but it felt insubstantial against the weight of my apprehension. I watched Michael's face, searching for signs of that familiar warmth, the one that had once felt like home, but now only seemed to cast shadows. He accepted the beer, raising it slightly in a mock toast before taking a long swig, eyes darting around the room as if searching for something—or someone—to anchor him.

The gathering resumed its jovial cadence, a lively blend of music, laughter, and chatter, but I couldn't shake the feeling that we were all performing. Each laugh was a note in a symphony that masked the underlying dissonance. I drifted through conversations, my mind a million miles away, replaying the moment we had stood toe-to-toe in the café, words flying like knives, cutting deeper than I had intended.

"Hey, you good?" Lucas, always attuned to my moods, sidled up beside me, his brow furrowed with concern. "You've been awfully quiet."

"Just trying to figure out the room's vibe," I said with a tight smile, my fingers toying with the stem of my glass. "You know, blend in with the background."

He frowned, the playful edge of his demeanor vanishing. "Don't let him get to you. You've got more support here than you think."

I nodded, appreciating his words but knowing that support couldn't erase the tension crackling like electricity between Michael and me. As if on cue, I glanced across the room to find him locked in conversation with Jess, her animated gestures punctuating the air between them. The sight twisted something deep in my gut. The small, nagging thought that maybe she understood him better than I did wrapped around my heart like a vice.

"What's happening?" Lucas whispered, following my gaze. "Do you want me to intervene?"

"No, it's fine," I replied, though my heart raced at the thought of losing Michael's attention to someone else, even if it was someone I trusted. "I just... I thought things would be different."

As the evening wore on, I became acutely aware of how the laughter grew louder, more raucous, an attempt to drown out the silence that had grown between us. I was caught in a whirlwind of conflicting emotions—love, resentment, fear, and a strange longing for what had been. The others were blissfully unaware, lost in their own lives, while I felt like a lighthouse in a storm, flickering uncertainly amid the chaos.

In a moment of recklessness, I decided to take a bold step. "Alright, everyone! Time for a game!" My voice rang out, and a hush fell over the group, heads turning toward me. "Let's play 'Truth or Dare.' It'll be fun!"

"Or revealing," Michael interjected, a smirk playing on his lips as he leaned against the doorframe, arms crossed. The challenge in his eyes sent a thrill of adrenaline coursing through me, igniting the competitive fire I had buried beneath layers of uncertainty.

"Let's keep it light, shall we?" I shot back, my smile sharper than intended. "And maybe we'll unearth some secrets along the way."

As we settled in, the game kicked off with hesitant dares and light-hearted truths, laughter bubbling up like a brook after a rain. With each revelation, I felt the weight of the room shift, the tension easing, if only a little. But when the game reached its peak, I could see the storm clouds gathering again. Michael was challenged to reveal a secret, and the silence that followed was palpable.

"Alright, then," he said, leaning forward, a gleam of mischief in his eye. "I dare you to tell us about your biggest regret."

The room held its breath, a collective gasp weaving through the air. I held my breath too, each second stretching into an eternity as Michael's gaze found mine, dark and stormy. It was a dare that felt loaded with unspoken words, a truth that had been simmering beneath the surface.

As Michael leaned against the doorframe, his posture casual yet charged with an electric energy, I could practically hear the gears in everyone's heads turning. Was I brave or foolish for daring him to speak his truth? The silence draped over us like an expensive velvet curtain, heavy and full of unvoiced thoughts. I could sense the weight of the moment settling in, a palpable thing that made me acutely aware of every heartbeat in the room.

"Regret?" Michael finally broke the silence, his tone feigning nonchalance. "That's rich. You all must be starving for drama. You sure you want to hear my deepest, darkest regret?" He cast a teasing glance around the group, but I knew better than to be lulled by his playful demeanor. His eyes flickered with something deeper, an emotion barely restrained behind the facade of humor.

"Please, enlighten us," Jess goaded, her curiosity sparkling in the dim light. "You've always been full of secrets. It's about time you spilled one."

I watched as Michael's expression shifted, the playful glint replaced by a seriousness that made the air grow thick with tension. It was as if he were standing on the edge of a precipice, contemplating whether to leap or retreat. "Fine," he said finally, his voice steady yet tinged with vulnerability. "I regret not fighting harder for what I wanted."

Gasps punctuated the room, laughter fading into a reflective silence. I held my breath, every nerve ending in my body alight with anticipation. "And what was that?" I challenged, my tone light yet probing, wishing to peel back the layers he had wrapped around himself.

He hesitated, an emotion flashing in his eyes that was all too familiar—fear. "A person," he said, his gaze fixed on me, unyielding. The room held its breath again. "I guess I should've tried harder to make things right before..." He trailed off, and I could almost hear the unspoken words echoing around us. Before everything fell apart, before we got caught in this messy, emotional cyclone.

"Before what? Before you decided I wasn't worth it?" I shot back, unable to restrain the sting of resentment from creeping into my voice. It wasn't fair. Why did he get to define this narrative? Why did I feel so helpless to change it?

"Let's not turn this into a blame game," Lucas interjected, sensing the shift in the room, his protective instincts kicking in. "This was supposed to be a fun evening, right? Light and carefree?" He offered a forced smile, trying to shepherd us back into safer waters.

"Fun? Oh, please. I didn't sign up for a therapy session," Julian piped in from the back, his trademark smirk in place. "Where's the fun in that?" The group erupted into a series of half-hearted chuckles, but the tension remained, an invisible thread connecting Michael and me, taut and vibrating with unacknowledged feelings.

"Let's switch it up," I suggested, desperation creeping into my voice. "How about we do something a little less... existential?" I grinned at the group, hoping to dissolve the building pressure. "Truth or dare? Let's up the ante."

"Fine," Michael said, crossing his arms, his lips curving slightly in a reluctant smile. "But I'll have my revenge later."

"Oh, I'm counting on it," I replied, trying to match his playful tone, though my heart raced with uncertainty. The game resumed, shifting between light-hearted truths and ridiculous dares, laughter bubbling through the air like champagne. With each passing round, the weight of Michael's earlier revelation hung heavy, teasing me, pulling me back toward a truth I had buried deep beneath my bravado.

As the game progressed, I watched as Lucas and Jess traded dares that had them leaping around the room like children. The infectious energy began to seep into my bones, easing the tension knotting my stomach. Until, of course, the dare landed squarely in my lap.

"Dare," Ryan said, his eyes sparkling with mischief. "I dare you to take a shot of that horrid green drink Michael brought last time. You know, the one that tasted like regret mixed with the tears of your enemies."

"No way! That stuff is vile!" I protested, laughter spilling from my lips. "What do I look like? A masochist?"

"Only if you make it entertaining," Michael teased, leaning forward as if the idea intrigued him. "But I'll join you if you're feeling brave."

"Count me out! I still remember the last time," I shot back, memories flooding back of a drunken escapade that had involved far too much singing and not enough self-control.

"Ah, c'mon! For the sake of the game," Jess piped in, her eyes sparkling with mischief. "You'll thank me later. Or not."

"Fine, but only because I'm not one to back down from a challenge," I relented, pouring the vivid green concoction into two shot glasses. The liquid glimmered ominously, swirling like a toxic fairy potion. I raised my glass, and we downed the shots in unison, the foul taste sending shockwaves through my system.

"Ugh, why does this taste like something I'd scrape off the bottom of my shoe?" I sputtered, laughter erupting as I tried to regain my composure.

"Because it's probably made from whatever was left in my fridge after three months," Michael quipped, his smile teasing yet softening the sharp edges of the evening. "At least it's not a complete waste, right?"

"Right!" I laughed, wiping my mouth dramatically. The tension seemed to dissolve momentarily, replaced by the lightness of the absurdity we had just embraced.

But just as I felt the air lift, the doorbell rang, slicing through our laughter like a knife through butter. The unexpected chime made my heart drop; I exchanged glances with Michael, both of us sensing that whatever—or whoever—stood on the other side of that door could change everything.

"I'll get it," Lucas volunteered, moving toward the door, but the unease hung in the air like a dark cloud, pregnant with the promise of something unwelcome.

"Hope it's not another random salesman," Ryan joked, but the laughter that followed felt shaky, the room tense again as we waited for Lucas to return. Each passing second stretched into eternity, and the lively atmosphere shifted into an uncomfortable anticipation.

Lucas swung the door open, a grin plastered on his face, but the expression faded as quickly as it appeared. Standing on the threshold was a figure cloaked in shadow, their features obscured by the dim light spilling from my apartment. It was the kind of moment that felt ripped from a suspenseful film—a stranger appearing just as we were on the brink of something monumental.

"Uh, can I help you?" Lucas asked, his voice wavering slightly. I could see the uncertainty flicker across his face, his usual bravado evaporating like mist under a hot sun.

The figure stepped into the light, revealing a tall girl with sharp features and a determined glint in her eye. "I'm looking for Michael," she said, her tone a mix of urgency and irritation, as if she were accustomed to being taken seriously.

All eyes turned to Michael, whose expression morphed from playful to alarmed in the blink of an eye. "What's going on?" he demanded, his voice dropping to a low rumble, a protective instinct awakening within him.

"I need to talk to you. It's important," she insisted, her gaze darting around the room, taking in the group like she was assessing a battlefield.

"Who are you?" I couldn't help but interject, my voice sharper than I intended. The newcomer seemed out of place, her air of urgency stark against the backdrop of our casual gathering.

"I'm Beth. A friend," she replied, but the hesitance in her voice hinted at something more complicated. "I heard there was a gathering, and I needed to warn Michael about what's happening."

"Warn me?" Michael echoed, stepping forward. The protective shield he'd put up was slowly being chipped away, his curiosity piqued. "About what?"

"About Emily," Beth said, glancing at me as if I were the very embodiment of trouble. "She's not who you think she is. You need to be careful."

The room buzzed with murmurs, an undercurrent of tension rising like a tide. I felt as if I had been splashed with cold water, the laughter from moments before draining away, leaving me cold and exposed. "What do you mean?" I pressed, my heart racing, each beat echoing in my ears.

Beth held her ground, a fierce intensity in her gaze. "You think she's just trying to ruin things for you? It's more than that. She's got plans, and they don't involve just you and your friends. It's bigger than this—bigger than what you all realize."

"Plans?" I scoffed, irritation bubbling to the surface. "You think I'm the villain here? I'm just trying to live my life. If anything, it's Emily who's been a total thorn in my side."

"Emily isn't the problem, Michael," Beth said, her voice firm and unwavering. "She's trying to help. But she's caught in something that's dangerous. You don't know the whole story."

"Then tell me!" I challenged, my voice rising. The room felt stifling, each breath a struggle against the growing tension. "What the hell is going on?"

"Calm down," Lucas interjected, his hand on my arm, grounding me. "We're all friends here, right? Let's just hear her out."

"Fine," I relented, but I couldn't shake the anger bubbling beneath the surface. "Go on, Beth. What's the big mystery?"

"Emily is part of something that involves all of us. And it's not just about her feelings for you or the rumors you think she's spreading." Her gaze shifted to me, intense and probing. "She's been investigating some things that go beyond high school drama. Trust me when I say that things could spiral out of control quickly."

"What things?" Michael asked, his concern evident as he stepped closer to Beth, his body language betraying a protective instinct.

"Things that you don't want to be involved in," she replied, her voice lowering conspiratorially. "There are factions at play—people who would do anything to protect their secrets. Emily's caught in the crossfire, and you're all in danger because of her."

"Danger? What are you talking about?" My voice trembled slightly as the weight of her words sunk in. I felt the walls closing in, the shadows lengthening as a sense of dread settled over me.

"Look," she said, raising her hands in a placating gesture, "I don't have all the answers. But I know enough to say that you should keep your distance. Emily might not be the innocent bystander you think she is. She has connections you aren't aware of."

The silence that followed her words was deafening. Everyone exchanged glances, confusion and concern etched on their faces. I felt Michael's eyes boring into me, searching for a sign, some glimmer of the girl he thought he knew. But the weight of Beth's revelation sat like a stone in my stomach, heavy and unyielding.

"You're saying she's dangerous?" Michael asked incredulously, the protective warmth of his earlier bravado replaced by an edge of uncertainty.

"I'm saying you should be cautious," Beth replied, her tone becoming more urgent. "This isn't just about your relationships. It's about something much larger."

I could feel Michael wavering, the air thick with unspoken doubts. The laughter from earlier felt like a distant memory, replaced by a sense of foreboding that loomed over us. "You don't know Emily like I do," he said, a hint of defensiveness creeping into his voice.

"Maybe not," Beth admitted, her eyes narrowing slightly. "But I know danger when I see it, and right now, I can feel it surrounding you all."

Just then, the door swung open, and the cold wind howled into the room, cutting through the atmosphere like a blade. A sudden gust sent papers scattering from the coffee table, creating a chaotic flurry that mirrored the turmoil swirling inside me. Everyone turned toward the door, the sudden shift in air intensifying the uncertainty hanging over us.

"Is this a bad time?" a voice called from the doorway, laced with sarcasm. It was Emily, her silhouette framed against the darkened hallway, a playful smirk plastered across her face. But the tension in the room shifted instantly, and I could see it flicker in her eyes as she took in the scene—our startled expressions, the heavy silence, and the unspoken accusations woven into the fabric of the air.

The moment stretched, a taut line between what was and what could be, as her gaze locked onto mine. "What did I miss?" she asked, the smile fading into something more serious, a question hanging between us like an unresolved chord, ripe with tension and anticipation.

As I opened my mouth to respond, a sharp crack echoed outside, the sound cutting through the room like thunder. The lights flickered, and the atmosphere shifted dramatically, as if a storm had moved in without warning. The windows rattled, and I caught a glimpse of a shadow darting past—something dark and ominous lurking just beyond our view.

"Emily!" I shouted, the name slipping from my lips as the storm intensified, both outside and within. Something was coming, something that would shake the very foundations of everything we thought we knew. And as I looked around at the anxious faces of my friends, I realized we were standing on the precipice of a revelation that could change everything.

Chapter 18: A Heart Divided

The moonlight spilled through the slats in my window, casting a quilt of silver and shadows across my room. I lay in bed, staring at the ceiling as the weight of expectations pressed down like a heavy blanket. The clock ticked relentlessly, each second echoing the turmoil in my mind. On one side, loyalty tugged at me, a steadfast companion that whispered reminders of Emily's unwavering friendship. On the other, the intoxicating allure of my feelings for Michael wrapped around me, warm and sweet like a promise of summer rain.

My heart danced uneasily between them, caught in an unrelenting game of tug-of-war. I could picture Emily, her laughter ringing like a melodic chime, and how it brightened even the darkest days. But then there was Michael, with his mischievous grin and the way he made my heart race like I was sprinting through the wildflower fields behind our school. I closed my eyes, trying to summon clarity, but all I found was the soft cadence of my breathing mingled with the muted sounds of the night.

Our world had become a tangled mess of emotions, each thread pulling tighter as the days slipped away. The summer had ignited something within me—something fiery and desperate. Each stolen glance at Michael sent tremors through my heart, the thrill of our moments together sending sparks dancing through the air. But the memories of laughter shared with Emily, our late-night talks about everything and nothing, weighed heavily on my conscience. I could already hear the conversation replaying in my head, how Emily's eyes would shimmer with hurt if she knew the extent of my feelings for Michael.

The unexpected twist of fate had brought us together one sunny afternoon, the kind where the sky seemed to vibrate with possibility. We were all gathered at the old oak tree in the park, the branches swaying gently above us, when Michael casually tossed a crumpled paper airplane my way. It soared past Emily, who laughed, a beautiful sound that filled the space between us. That laughter was the spark that ignited my interest in him. It was all innocent fun at first—a few shared jokes, some playful jabs. But then there was that moment when our hands brushed while reaching for the last slice of pizza, and the air crackled with something electric.

Those initial moments grew into an undeniable connection, one that felt as though it had been scripted by fate itself. I couldn't help but think of the universe, a mischievous architect pulling strings behind the scenes, placing Michael in my path just when my heart had begun to thirst for something more. Yet here I lay, teetering on the precipice of a decision that felt monumental, as though the fate of our small circle of friends hinged entirely on my shoulders.

The next morning, the sun broke through the clouds, spilling light into my room like a herald announcing the day's arrival. As I prepared for school, I felt a simmering anxiety twist in my stomach. My phone buzzed with a message from Emily, "Can we talk?" The words sent a jolt of panic through me, but I responded with a casual, "Sure, what's up?"

Arriving at school felt like stepping into a carnival of emotions. Laughter floated in the air, mingling with the scent of fresh grass and blooming flowers. I navigated through the bustling hallways, nodding at familiar faces while my heart drummed an erratic beat. I spotted Michael by the lockers, a group of friends gathered around him, their laughter echoing against the cinderblock walls. He looked effortlessly charming, the kind of boy who made you believe the sun shone just for him.

"Hey, stranger," I called out, forcing a smile that felt more like a mask than an expression of joy.

"Hey!" He turned, his grin brightening the mundane surroundings. "You ready for the weekend? I've got a surprise planned." His eyes sparkled with mischief, and I felt a flutter of excitement in my chest.

"Surprise? Now you've got me curious," I replied, trying to ignore the knot in my stomach.

Before he could respond, I caught sight of Emily approaching. Her expression was neutral, but there was an undercurrent of tension in the air, as if we were both aware of the unspoken words lingering between us.

"Can we talk now?" she asked, her voice steady but her eyes betraying a hint of worry.

"Sure, just a second," I said, forcing myself to look back at Michael. "I'll catch you later?"

"Definitely," he replied, his smile fading slightly as he sensed the change in atmosphere.

As I followed Emily to a quieter corner of the school, I felt the weight of my decision pressing down like a lead anchor. "What's on your mind?" I asked, attempting to inject some lightness into the moment.

"I've been noticing some things," she started, her tone carefully measured. "You've been... different lately. More distracted. Is everything okay between us?"

The question hung in the air, heavy with implications. I opened my mouth to respond, but the truth felt lodged in my throat, a bitter pill that wouldn't go down. The silence stretched, fraught with tension, as I tried to navigate the labyrinth of my thoughts.

"I mean, I just..." I stammered, searching for the right words. The truth was, I couldn't bear to watch her face fall, the realization that I was caught in a web of emotions that was tearing us apart.

Emily's expression softened, a mixture of concern and understanding illuminating her features. "You can talk to me, you know that, right?"

And as I looked into her earnest eyes, I knew I had a choice to make—one that would echo through our lives long after this conversation had ended. In that moment, the fabric of our friendship felt fragile, straining under the weight of secrets and unspoken words. My heart ached, knowing that whatever I chose would forever alter the landscape of our intertwined lives.

The silence between us stretched like a taut wire, vibrating with the unspoken words that hovered in the air. Emily crossed her arms, a small defensive gesture that twisted my stomach into knots. "You know I'm here for you, right? I just don't want you to pull away," she said, her voice laced with concern, echoing the very thoughts that had kept me awake the previous night.

"Of course I know that," I replied, the warmth of our friendship a bittersweet comfort. "It's just—"

"Just what?" she pressed, tilting her head as if she could physically untangle the mess of emotions swirling in my mind. "You've been acting weird. I'm not a mind reader, you know."

"Weird? Me? Never." I forced a laugh, hoping to lighten the mood, but it felt more like a deflection. Emily's brows knit together, clearly unconvinced by my feeble attempt at humor.

"Look, I'm just saying, if something's bothering you, it's better to talk about it now than wait until it explodes later," she said, her tone softening, making her sound like the caring friend I had always relied on.

I hesitated, wrestling with the tidal wave of my feelings for Michael, the pull of our laughter, the thrill of his presence, and the ache of knowing Emily would be hurt if she knew. "It's complicated," I finally admitted, feeling the weight of those two words hang heavily in the air.

"Complicated how?" She leaned in slightly, her curiosity piqued.

I bit my lip, weighing the consequences of my next words. "You know how things change. Sometimes, feelings get... messy."

"Messy how?" She pressed, her eyes searching mine for clarity.

"Let's just say I've been spending a lot of time with Michael."

"And?" Emily's expression morphed into one of concern tinged with jealousy, a mix that was almost palpable.

"Okay, maybe I like him. Like, really like him." The admission slipped from my lips before I could stop it. It hung in the air between us like a fine mist, both refreshing and suffocating.

Emily's eyes widened, a flash of hurt crossing her features before she masked it with a bright smile. "Oh! So you like him, huh? That's... great. Really. I mean, it's about time someone swept you off your feet!" Her tone was a tad too chipper, betraying the bitterness lurking beneath.

"Emily, I—" I began, but she held up a hand to stop me.

"Let's not make this a thing. You do you," she said, her voice a little too light as she took a step back, creating a chasm that felt insurmountable.

I could see the disappointment settling in her eyes, the tiny fissures in our friendship widening. "It's not like that. I didn't mean for this to happen. I just... I didn't know how to tell you."

"Well, now you know," she replied, her words sharper than I expected. "Just... go for it then. If he makes you happy, I can't stop you, right?"

"Emily, I don't want this to ruin what we have," I pleaded, feeling the weight of our history press down on me like an anchor.

"What we have?" she echoed, crossing her arms again, a fortress of defensiveness rising between us. "Is that what you call this? Because it feels like you're about to leap off a cliff, and I'm not sure if you even care if I'm holding the rope or not."

"I care! You know I do!" I exclaimed, frustration bubbling to the surface.

"Then why does it feel like I'm losing you?" Her voice quivered slightly, and I wanted nothing more than to reach out, to pull her back from the edge of her hurt.

"Because I'm still figuring things out! I didn't mean to—"

"Maybe you should have thought about that before you started having feelings for someone else," she shot back, her words a sharp arrow aimed straight at my heart.

"Emily..." I sighed, searching for the right words, but they escaped me like wisps of smoke. How could I explain the intoxicating pull I felt toward Michael without invalidating the beautiful friendship I cherished with Emily?

"Look, I'm not mad," she said, her voice softer now, but still trembling with emotion. "Just... be honest with me. If you decide to go after him, just know that it'll change everything between us."

The truth of her words hit me like a freight train. I wanted to shout that nothing could change the bond we shared, the years of laughter, tears, and memories. But deep down, I understood that I was standing at a crossroads, and whichever path I chose would lead to a reckoning.

"I'll be honest," I said finally, my voice steadying. "But I need some time to figure out what that means."

"Time," she repeated, her gaze flickering away. "Yeah, I get that. Take all the time you need, but just don't forget who you're leaving behind."

As she walked away, the distance between us felt infinite. I watched her retreat, her shoulders squared with determination, but her aura tinged with vulnerability. The hall buzzed around me, laughter and chatter filling the air, but I felt an overwhelming sense of isolation.

I turned to find Michael again, the energy around him magnetic. He was deep in conversation with some friends, animated and alive, a stark contrast to the heaviness weighing down my heart. The choice

I faced loomed large, but so did the excitement of what could be. I approached him, adrenaline coursing through me like a river.

"Hey, can I steal you for a minute?" I asked, injecting a level of lightness I didn't quite feel.

"Sure, what's up?" Michael flashed that dazzling smile that made my knees feel like jelly.

"Just wanted to see if you're still up for that surprise this weekend."

"Absolutely! It's going to be epic. Just you wait." His enthusiasm was contagious, and I found myself smiling despite the storm brewing inside.

"Can you keep a secret?" I asked, my heart racing as I realized I was about to share something that could change everything.

"Is it a good secret or a bad secret?" he asked, his eyes dancing with mischief.

"A bit of both," I replied, biting my lip.

He leaned closer, his expression turning serious. "Well, I'm all ears."

And as I stood there, caught between two worlds, I realized that whatever I decided in that moment, the ripples would spread far beyond this instant. Would I plunge headfirst into the unknown with Michael, risking everything? Or would I take a step back, preserving the bond I had with Emily? The answer hung just out of reach, teasing me like a melody I couldn't quite remember. The choice felt monumental, and in that moment, I knew I had to decide who I wanted to be—not just for myself, but for the two people I cared about most.

As Michael leaned closer, his curiosity almost palpable, I felt an electric thrill course through me. The moment felt charged, as if the universe was holding its breath, waiting to see what I would say next. "You know how we've been hanging out a lot lately?" I started, my voice slightly trembling.

"Yeah, and it's been awesome! I mean, who knew you could throw a frisbee like a champ?" he grinned, his playful tone easing some of the tension I felt in my chest.

"Well, there's something else. Something that's been on my mind." I took a deep breath, aware that this could change everything. "I really like you, Michael. Like, a lot. And I know that probably doesn't come as a surprise, but I need you to know that it's not just a fling for me."

Michael's expression shifted, surprise flickering in his eyes before a warm smile spread across his face. "Wow, really? I'm glad to hear that because I was starting to think you were going to play hard to get forever." He laughed, and the sound washed over me like a balm.

"Well, I wasn't trying to be difficult. I just didn't want to mess things up. You know how things can get... complicated." I couldn't help but glance back at Emily, who was now deep in conversation with someone else, the distance between us feeling more pronounced than ever.

"Complicated is my middle name," Michael replied, his tone light and teasing, but I could see the flicker of seriousness in his eyes. "So, are you saying we're officially a thing now?"

"I think so," I said, the words tasting both sweet and terrifying on my tongue. It felt like a leap of faith, and I could almost hear the thrill of the crowd cheering as I jumped.

"Awesome," he said, reaching out to take my hand. His touch sent a jolt of warmth up my arm, and for a moment, the world around us faded into the background. The laughter of our friends, the chatter of classmates—all of it blurred as we stood there, connected in our bubble of newfound intimacy.

But as the moment stretched on, my mind wandered back to Emily. Her laughter used to come so easily, but now it felt tinged with uncertainty. I wanted to tell her everything, to make her understand that my feelings for Michael didn't diminish our friendship. But I knew that saying those words would come with its own set of consequences.

"We should probably tell Emily," I said, suddenly feeling the weight of my decision pressing down on me again. "I don't want her to find out later and feel like I was hiding something."

Michael hesitated, the smile fading a fraction. "Do you think she'll be okay with it?"

"I hope so," I said, my voice barely above a whisper. "But she deserves to know. She's my best friend."

With a resigned nod, Michael squeezed my hand. "Okay, let's do it together. I'd hate for you to face her wrath alone." His attempt at humor didn't quite land, but it did bring a flicker of reassurance.

We made our way toward Emily, the air thick with unspoken tension. I could feel my heart pounding in my chest, each beat echoing the weight of what I was about to do. "Hey, Em," I called, forcing a casualness into my tone. "Can we talk?"

She turned, her expression instantly shifting to one of guarded curiosity. "What's up?"

"Michael and I—" I started, but the words seemed to twist in my throat. I glanced at Michael, who nodded encouragingly, and then back to Emily, whose eyes narrowed slightly.

"Michael and I have decided to give this thing between us a shot," I finally blurted out, the confession tumbling from my lips like a waterfall.

The silence that followed felt deafening. Emily blinked, her expression morphing from surprise to a complex cocktail of emotions—hurt, confusion, and something else I couldn't quite place. "So, you're dating now?" she asked, her voice eerily calm.

"Um, yeah," I said, trying to sound confident but failing miserably. "I didn't want to keep it from you. I mean, we've been spending so much time together, and I just felt like it was the right thing to do."

Emily's eyes flashed, and I could see the turmoil brewing beneath the surface. "Right thing for who? Because it sure as hell doesn't feel right for me."

"Em, I—" I began, but she held up her hand, cutting me off.

"No, let me finish. I thought we were in this together. I thought we were best friends." Her voice shook, revealing the cracks in her composure. "And now you're just going to throw that away for some guy? For Michael?"

"It's not like that," I protested, desperation creeping into my voice. "You mean the world to me. I didn't want this to hurt you."

Emily scoffed, crossing her arms tightly across her chest. "Well, congratulations. You've succeeded. It hurts like hell."

The sting of her words cut deeper than I expected, twisting my insides with regret. "I didn't want to betray you. You're my best friend. I love you!" I exclaimed, my voice rising in pitch as panic set in.

"Do you? Because it sure doesn't feel that way," she shot back, her eyes glistening with unshed tears. "You're choosing him over me, and it feels like I'm losing everything. We've been through so much, and now you're just... moving on."

The heartbreak in her voice twisted something inside me, making me feel small and lost. I opened my mouth to respond, but nothing came out. I didn't know how to mend the rift that was rapidly widening between us.

"Emily, please," I begged, feeling the tremors of my own emotions surfacing. "I don't want to lose you. I can't lose you."

Just then, a loud crash echoed from down the hall, pulling all our attention away from the confrontation. A group of students had knocked over a stack of chairs, laughter and chaos erupting around us like fireworks. Emily flinched at the noise, her expression momentarily distracted.

"What was that?" she said, her brow furrowing.

"I don't know," I replied, relieved for the distraction, but the feeling was fleeting.

Before I could say anything more, Michael stepped forward, concern etched on his face. "You okay, Em?" he asked, his voice gentle.

Emily's gaze shifted to him, and for a split second, I could see the walls she had built around her emotions begin to crack. "I just... I need a minute," she said, her voice softer now but still laced with pain.

"Take all the time you need," he replied, glancing at me.

As Emily walked away, I felt a knot of anxiety form in my stomach. "I didn't mean to hurt her," I murmured, turning to Michael. "What if she doesn't come back?"

"We'll figure it out," he said, though his tone lacked the usual confidence. "Let's give her some space."

But as the laughter of our classmates faded into a dull roar, I couldn't shake the feeling that this wasn't just about my friendship with Emily. I was caught in a tempest of emotions, and it felt like everything I cared about was spiraling out of control.

Just then, Emily reappeared at the edge of the hallway, her expression grave. "I need to talk to both of you," she said, her voice low and urgent. The air crackled with tension as we both stepped closer, sensing the shift in her demeanor.

"Is everything okay?" I asked, anxiety gnawing at my insides.

"Something's happened. Something big," she said, her eyes darting around as if searching for something—or someone.

"What do you mean?" Michael asked, his brow furrowing.

Before she could answer, a commotion erupted from the entrance of the school, and the three of us turned to see a group of students gathered, faces pale and eyes wide. Someone pushed through the crowd, and I recognized Jason, his face flushed and panicked.

"There's trouble," he shouted, his voice cutting through the air like a knife. "Something's gone wrong! We need to leave!"

My heart raced, the urgency in his tone igniting a primal instinct to protect those I loved. "What do you mean?" I yelled back, fear creeping into my voice.

But before he could respond, the electricity in the air shifted, and I felt a chilling realization wash over me. Whatever was about to unfold would change everything.

As the crowd began to scatter, I turned to Emily and Michael, our expressions mirroring the same mixture of dread and determination. "We need to stick together," I said, the gravity of the moment weighing heavily on us.

And just as we began to move toward the door, a loud explosion shook the building, sending a shower of dust and debris raining down. The world erupted in chaos, and I knew, in that split second, that everything had just changed.

Chapter 19: The Calm Before the Storm

The sun hung low in the sky, casting a warm, golden glow that wrapped around the quaint little town of Briarwood like a soft, familiar blanket. Autumn leaves crunched beneath my feet as I walked the familiar path to the café, where the scent of freshly brewed coffee mingled with the sweet aroma of pastries. The air was crisp, invigorating, almost electric, yet beneath this idyllic façade, a tempest brewed, threatening to unravel everything I had fought so hard to maintain.

Inside the café, the gentle hum of conversation and the sound of clinking mugs created a cozy atmosphere, but my heart felt like a rock sinking in a deep ocean of uncertainty. I scanned the room, my eyes searching for Michael, who had become an integral part of my life—a comfort, a confidant. Yet lately, he felt like a ghost haunting my days. Each fleeting glance and faint smile exchanged between us felt more like a distant memory than the connection I once cherished.

The barista, a bubbly woman named Claire, greeted me with her usual cheerfulness, her bright smile cutting through my melancholy. "The usual?" she asked, already reaching for my favorite blend.

"Sure, Claire. Thanks." I forced a smile, hoping it would mask the anxiety gnawing at my insides.

As I settled into my favorite corner table, sunlight streaming through the large windows, I couldn't help but replay the last few days in my mind. Michael had withdrawn, his laughter replaced by silence, his warm touches now just fleeting memories. I had tried to draw him out, to coax him back into our world with gentle words and shared laughter, but each time I approached, he stepped back as if my presence was a puzzle he couldn't solve. It was infuriating and heartbreaking all at once.

I sipped my coffee, the warmth spreading through me, momentarily distracting me from my worries. Outside, children played, their laughter ringing like music. Couples strolled hand-in-hand, and elderly neighbors exchanged pleasantries, the town buzzing with life. Yet here I sat, alone amidst the bustle, feeling the weight of a thousand unsaid words pressing down on me.

Suddenly, the door swung open, and Michael walked in, his presence commanding the room despite the casualness of his jeans and worn leather jacket. My heart leaped, then faltered as I took in his expression—a mix of frustration and sorrow. He scanned the café, his eyes landing on me, and for a moment, time stood still. I could see the flicker of something in his gaze, a spark of the warmth that had once ignited our connection.

"Hey," he said, his voice low, almost hesitant as he approached. The tension was palpable, a taut string threatening to snap.

"Hey." I tried to keep my voice steady, but it wavered slightly, betraying my nervousness.

He slid into the seat across from me, the space between us feeling more like a chasm. "How's work?" His question was perfunctory, lacking the usual warmth.

"It's fine. Busy, but fine," I replied, pushing a strand of hair behind my ear, my pulse quickening under his scrutiny. "What about you? You've been... quiet."

A sigh escaped him, heavy and laden with unsaid thoughts. "Just thinking." He leaned back in his chair, arms crossed defensively. "About everything."

"Everything?" I echoed, my heart racing. "You mean us?"

He hesitated, eyes flickering to the side, avoiding mine as if they held too much weight. "Yeah, something like that."

The air between us thickened, the tension knotting tighter. My heart pounded against my ribcage, and I could feel the urge to reach out, to bridge the gap that had grown like a canyon between us. "Michael, if something's wrong—"

"It's not just that," he cut me off, his voice rising slightly, frustration coloring his words. "It's everything, Amelia. The pressure, the expectations... It's like I'm being pulled in a million different directions."

I nodded slowly, attempting to understand. "I get that, but you don't have to do this alone. We're a team, remember? We can figure it out together."

His gaze finally met mine, and for a moment, the world around us faded away. "But what if I'm not the person you think I am?" The vulnerability in his voice pierced through the heaviness.

"Then show me who you are," I challenged softly, the words escaping before I could reconsider. "I'm here, waiting. You don't have to hide from me."

He leaned forward, the tension crackling in the air between us. "What if I told you that I'm scared? Scared of letting you down, scared of losing you."

"Then let me in," I urged, desperate for connection, my voice barely above a whisper. "You're not going to lose me."

A flicker of hope ignited in his eyes, but it was overshadowed by a deeper shadow, an unspoken fear that loomed over us like a thundercloud. "It's not that simple."

And just like that, the storm I had sensed on the horizon seemed to break, unleashing a torrent of emotions neither of us was prepared to face. I felt the ground shift beneath me, a sense of foreboding creeping into my thoughts. This was not just a moment of misunderstanding; it was the beginning of a reckoning, a confrontation with truths we had both avoided for too long.

Outside, the world continued to bustle around us, blissfully unaware of the tempest brewing within our small corner of existence. As I searched his eyes for answers, I knew that whatever was coming would change everything—and the realization settled over me like the chill of an impending winter storm.

The unease hung like a thick fog, clouding the vibrant moments that should have filled our days with joy. As I settled into my routine, the world outside continued to sparkle with the energy of late summer. The park across the street thrummed with laughter and the sounds of children playing, while the golden leaves of the maple trees began their slow descent, painting the ground in warm hues. Yet here I was, ensnared in a web of tension that felt tighter with each passing hour, my heart a pendulum swinging between hope and despair.

Michael's silence was a shadow looming over our shared space. Even the familiar buzz of our shared coffee breaks had dimmed to a muted whisper. I would watch him as he stared out the window, his expression inscrutable, as if he were searching for answers hidden in the patterns of the clouds. I felt as if I were watching a fascinating movie that had lost its plot, leaving only fragmented scenes of emotions I could hardly decipher.

One evening, after yet another day of unspoken words and lingering glances, I found myself standing in front of my mirror, scrutinizing my reflection as if it held the answers to our rift. My hair, usually a wild cascade of curls, was now pulled back into a tight ponytail, the effort to look polished feeling increasingly futile. I couldn't shake the sensation that I was an actress in a play where the script had gone awry, the words escaping me just when I needed them most.

With a determined sigh, I decided to shake things up. If Michael was going to keep retreating, then perhaps it was time to challenge him to come out of his shell. I donned my favorite dress—bright and floral, a stark contrast to the grayness clouding our lives. The outfit felt like a burst of sunshine against the encroaching darkness. With a deep breath, I slipped into my sandals and headed to the café, ready to reclaim my footing.

When I arrived, the familiar scent of coffee mingled with the sweet, buttery aroma of pastries, instantly warming my heart. I found a table by the window, the light spilling over me like a warm embrace, and pulled out my notebook, flipping it open to a blank page. It was my sanctuary, a place where thoughts flowed freely without judgment.

As I scribbled notes on possible activities we could do—hiking, an impromptu road trip, or a simple movie night—I sensed a familiar presence behind me. It was Michael, standing just outside the café, his expression hesitant, as though the threshold between us had morphed into a chasm too wide to cross.

"Hey," I called, waving him over, my heart racing at the possibility of breaking the spell that had bound us.

"Hey," he replied, his voice a hesitant echo of my own. He walked over slowly, each step a deliberate choice. "I didn't know you'd be here."

"Surprise!" I said, trying to inject some cheer into the air that felt too heavy. "Thought I'd come to plot our great escape."

He raised an eyebrow, a flicker of curiosity breaking through his solemn demeanor. "Escape?"

"Exactly. We need to get out of our heads and away from this... this tension," I said, gesturing wildly with my pen. "I was thinking a little adventure could do us good. What do you say? A drive along the coast? Some fresh air?"

His lips twitched, caught somewhere between a smile and a frown. "Sounds tempting, but do you really think running away will solve anything?"

"Maybe not solve," I said, leaning forward. "But it might help us see things differently. Sometimes you need to change your view to get a clearer picture."

He sighed, the battle of emotions etched on his face. "I don't want to run from my problems, Amelia. I just—" He paused, searching for the right words. "I don't know how to deal with everything that's happening."

"Then let's figure it out together," I urged, my heart thundering at the vulnerability that hung in the air between us. "We're stronger as a team, remember? You've been there for me; I want to be there for you."

He leaned back in his chair, considering. The silence stretched between us, a fragile thread teetering on the brink of breaking. Finally, he nodded, albeit reluctantly. "Okay. Let's do it."

I felt a rush of triumph, a spark igniting in the dull haze of our previous conversations. "Great! We'll make a day of it. No plans, no pressure—just us and the open road." I grinned, buoyed by the potential for adventure, the thrill of spontaneity lighting a fire beneath my apprehensions.

As we shared a pastry, the atmosphere shifted, the tension easing just slightly. We talked about everything and nothing, the banter returning in small, tentative bursts. For every step forward, however, there was still that heavy undertow pulling us back, the knowledge that the storm still loomed.

That evening, as we drove along the coastal road, the sun dipped low, painting the horizon with vibrant oranges and pinks. The ocean sparkled under the fading light, a vast expanse of possibility stretching before us. I felt the weight of unspoken fears recede just a little as we laughed and reminisced about our favorite memories. Each shared moment felt like stitching together the fabric of our connection, patching the holes that had formed in the recent storm.

"Remember that time we got lost on our way to that music festival?" I asked, chuckling at the memory of us wandering aimlessly, laughter bubbling up between us like a refreshing spring.

"Yeah," he replied, a genuine smile breaking through. "We ended up at that random diner instead. I think we might have eaten our weight in pancakes."

"Best decision ever," I grinned, the warmth of his laughter a balm to my spirit.

But as we continued driving, the horizon darkened, the sun slipping away too quickly, shadows creeping in. I glanced at Michael, who had fallen silent again, his brow furrowed as he stared at the road ahead, lost in thought.

A heavy silence settled around us, threatening to pull us back into the depths we had just started to escape. The tension swelled, and I felt the urge to break it, to reach out and grasp the thread connecting us. But the moment hung suspended, as if the universe was holding its breath, waiting for us to make a choice.

As the road unwound before us, I could feel the cool night air seeping through the open windows, bringing with it the salty tang of the ocean. The rhythmic sound of waves crashing against the shore provided a backdrop to our shared silence, one that felt both heavy and fraught with possibility. Michael's fingers drummed idly against the steering wheel, and for a moment, I could almost hear the unsung song of his thoughts.

"Do you think the ocean knows all our secrets?" I mused, attempting to pierce the quiet that had settled like a thick blanket between us. "I mean, it's vast enough to hold everything we've never said."

He glanced at me, a flicker of amusement dancing in his eyes. "If the ocean is eavesdropping, I hope it has a good memory. Otherwise, we're doomed to repeat our mistakes."

I laughed, grateful for the glimmer of light in his expression. "Well, let's hope it's more forgiving than us."

He nodded, the corners of his mouth tugging up slightly, but it didn't quite reach his eyes. The distance still felt palpable, the secrets buried beneath layers of uncertainty pressing down on us like the weight of the world. I glanced at him, wishing I could pull the truths from his mind like a magician revealing hidden cards, but I was left only with the quiet hum of the engine and the flickering streetlights lining the road.

After a few moments of silence, I dared to reach for the conversation that had been simmering just beneath the surface. "So, what are we doing, Michael? What's really going on with us?" My heart raced as I waited for his response, the air thick with anticipation.

He inhaled sharply, as if my question had punctured the bubble of calm we'd managed to create. "I don't know," he admitted, his voice barely above a whisper. "I feel like I'm walking on a tightrope, and I can't figure out what's on the other side."

"Then let's talk about it." I leaned forward, trying to inject a sense of urgency into the moment. "I'm here, and I want to help. But I need you to meet me halfway."

His grip tightened on the wheel, knuckles whitening as he battled with his emotions. "It's complicated, Amelia. Sometimes, I don't even know where to start."

"Start with what you're feeling. Start with the truth." The words spilled out of me, laced with both frustration and concern. "I can't do this without you."

He glanced sideways at me, vulnerability flickering in his gaze like a candle in the wind. "What if the truth changes everything? What if it shatters what we have left?"

The weight of his words hung heavily in the air, a palpable fear that echoed my own insecurities. "Maybe it needs to be shattered," I challenged gently. "Maybe we need to start over with something real."

Michael exhaled, a resigned breath that seemed to carry the weight of the world. "I've been holding back because I didn't want to hurt you. But I think we're past that now, aren't we?"

A surge of hope coursed through me, propelling me forward. "Yes! We are. You're not going to hurt me by being honest. It's what I want."

He took a moment, his gaze fixed on the winding road ahead. "Fine," he said finally, his voice steadying as if he had made a decision. "I've been feeling lost. Like I'm not the person I thought I was. There's so much I'm dealing with, and it's overwhelming."

I nodded, my heart racing with a mix of sympathy and anticipation. "You can talk to me. Whatever it is, I promise I won't judge."

"I just..." He hesitated, searching for the right words, and I could see the internal battle playing out behind his eyes. "I don't want to drag you into my mess."

"Too late for that," I shot back, trying to lighten the mood, but my smile faded as I saw the seriousness in his expression. "I'm already here, Michael. We're in this together."

He took a deep breath, as if summoning the courage to reveal the deepest part of himself. "My past isn't exactly... tidy. There are things I've done—mistakes I've made—that I'm not proud of. And I'm afraid that if I tell you, you won't look at me the same way again."

"Try me," I replied, heart pounding in my chest. "I promise you I'll still be here."

He nodded, and I could almost see the gears turning in his mind. "Last year, I was in a really dark place. I made choices that hurt people, choices I thought I could live with. But every time I think about them, it feels like I'm suffocating under the weight of it all."

The vulnerability in his voice cut through the tension like a knife. I reached for his hand, intertwining my fingers with his, grounding us both in that moment. "You're not alone, Michael. Whatever it is, we can work through it together."

He looked down at our clasped hands, his expression softening. "I want to believe that. I really do."

But before he could say more, a blaring horn erupted from behind us, pulling us from our moment of intimacy. The driver of a truck swerved into the other lane, glaring at us as they sped past. Michael's focus shifted back to the road, tension surging once more as we approached a narrow curve.

"Just a little distracted," he murmured, and the moment hung heavily in the air.

Suddenly, headlights appeared around the bend ahead, illuminating a figure standing in the middle of the road. A surge of adrenaline shot through me, and I instinctively grasped the dashboard. "Michael! Look out!"

He slammed the brakes, and the tires screeched against the asphalt. Time slowed, the figure morphing from a shadow into a recognizable form—a woman in a long, flowing white dress, her hair swirling like a dark cloud around her as she stood in stark contrast against the fading light.

"Get back!" I shouted, but the words felt lost in the chaos.

The impact was jarring as we skidded to a halt, the world around us blurring in a cacophony of screeching tires and rising panic. The figure didn't move, standing resolute, her eyes fixed on us with an unsettling intensity.

"What the hell?" Michael breathed, staring wide-eyed at the apparition before us.

I held my breath, unsure if I was dreaming or if we had driven straight into the heart of a horror movie. As the figure began to move closer, my heart raced, the storm I had felt brewing now crashing over us like an unstoppable wave.

With a sense of dread creeping into my bones, I turned to Michael, my voice trembling. "What do we do?"

But before he could respond, a chilling whisper floated through the air, words I couldn't decipher, yet felt deeply familiar. I felt the world tilt, and I knew in that moment that whatever was coming next would shatter everything we thought we knew.

Chapter 20: The Tempest Within

The moment the storm broke, the skies opened up, mirroring the tempest within me. I stood by the window, mesmerized by the relentless downpour that drummed against the glass, a rhythmic echo of my racing thoughts. Each raindrop felt like a fragment of the chaos swirling inside, as if the universe was conspiring to externalize my internal struggle. I could hardly breathe, each inhale heavy with the weight of unsaid words and unresolved feelings. I closed my eyes, trying to block out the noise of the storm, but it only amplified the tumult within.

Just then, my phone buzzed against the countertop, slicing through the silence like a knife through butter. I glanced at the screen, and my heart jumped. It was Michael. I hesitated, my thumb hovering over the screen as a wave of nostalgia washed over me. Memories of laughter, shared secrets, and moments that felt suspended in time flooded my mind. Yet, the specter of our last conversation loomed larger, a shadow that twisted the joy of remembrance into something heavy and bittersweet. I inhaled deeply, steeling myself before answering.

"Hey," I said, trying to keep my voice steady, but it cracked like the thunder outside.

"Can we meet?" His voice crackled through the line, an urgent plea wrapped in vulnerability. "At the beach? Please."

The beach. Our sacred place. A sanctuary where the world melted away, leaving only us and the whispering waves. The memory of sun-drenched afternoons and laughter floated into my mind, but now, the thought of the beach in the midst of a storm sent a shiver down my spine. It felt reckless, dangerous. And yet, something deep within me—a longing I couldn't quite articulate—urged me to say yes.

"Isn't that a bit... crazy? It's pouring out there," I replied, glancing out the window as lightning cracked across the sky, illuminating the landscape in stark relief.

"I know, but I need to talk to you. It's important." There was a vulnerability in his tone that tugged at my heart. I remembered the warmth of his laughter, the way his eyes sparkled with mischief, and the way he could make the world seem infinitely brighter. I could hear the desperation beneath his words, and it pulled at something deep inside me.

"Fine," I relented, the decision bubbling up from some hidden well of strength I hadn't realized was there. "I'll be there in ten."

As I grabbed my coat and shoes, I caught a glimpse of myself in the mirror—wild hair, flushed cheeks, and eyes that sparkled with determination. I looked like someone ready to face a storm, both outside and in. The wind howled as I stepped out into the elements, rain soaking through my clothes within moments, but I welcomed the chill against my skin. It was a reminder that I was alive, that I could feel something—anything—beyond the swirling void of my uncertainty.

The path to the beach was slick and treacherous, each step a gamble as I navigated the puddles that formed like miniature lakes along the way. The familiar scent of salt and rain intertwined in the air, an intoxicating mix that filled me with anticipation and dread. My heart raced as I approached the shoreline, the roar of the waves drowning out my thoughts. I spotted Michael standing near the edge, silhouetted against the gray sky, water cascading down his face.

"Michael!" I shouted, my voice barely piercing through the storm. He turned, and for a moment, time seemed to suspend, his gaze locking onto mine with a fierce intensity. The world faded, leaving just the two of us and the raging ocean.

"I'm glad you came," he said, his voice steady despite the tempest raging around us. He took a step closer, the wind whipping his hair back, framing his face in a halo of chaos.

"What's going on? You sounded... different," I managed, my heart pounding in my chest.

"I've been thinking about everything—about us," he replied, his eyes searching mine as if trying to read the very essence of my soul. "And I realized I can't just walk away from what we had. It means too much to me."

The waves crashed violently against the shore, each surge a reminder of the tumult in my heart. "But what about everything that happened? The distance? The hurt?"

He took another step forward, his expression resolute. "I know. I messed up. I thought pushing you away was the right thing to do. But now, standing here, I see how wrong I was. I've spent too much time trying to convince myself that I could live without you."

The sincerity in his voice sent a jolt of electricity through me. My heart raced, battling against the storm of uncertainty. "You can't just drop a bombshell like that and expect everything to be okay," I said, frustration spilling out as the rain continued to drench us.

"I know it's not that simple. But we need to figure this out. Together," he insisted, his tone firm, yet the vulnerability beneath it tugged at my heartstrings.

As the rain drummed louder, I felt my defenses crumbling. The emotions I had buried rushed to the surface, threatening to spill over. "Together?" I echoed, disbelief lacing my voice. "What does that even mean anymore?"

"It means being honest, facing the storm, and whatever comes after," he said, his gaze unwavering. "I want to fight for us, for what we had. I miss you, and I think... I think we can find our way back."

The sincerity in his eyes struck a chord deep within me, a longing that I had tried to suppress. But the fear still lingered, whispering doubts that echoed louder than the crashing waves. "What if we can't?" I asked, my voice barely above a whisper, the vulnerability pouring out like the rain around us.

He stepped closer, our faces inches apart, the world around us fading into a distant roar. "Then we try anyway," he said, his breath warm against my chilled skin. "I don't want to let fear decide our fate. I want to be brave, for both of us."

In that moment, standing in the heart of the storm with the man who had once meant everything to me, I felt the walls I had built beginning to crack. The thunder rumbled in the distance, but it paled in comparison to the storm brewing between us. My heart raced with the thrill of possibility and the weight of my own fears, an exhilarating blend that ignited a flicker of hope in the depths of my heart.

The rain continued to pour in relentless sheets, each drop a reminder of the uncertainties swirling in my mind. Michael's words hung in the air like a promise yet to be fulfilled, and I could feel the tension of the moment wrapping around us like a blanket. The storm raged on, but as I stood before him, drenched to the bone, it was as if the chaos outside became secondary to the tempest brewing between us.

"Do you hear that?" he asked, his voice barely above the roar of the ocean. "It's like the world is trying to drown out everything we've left unsaid."

I couldn't help but smile, despite the seriousness of the moment. "Or maybe it just wants to keep us from getting too comfortable." I ran a hand through my wet hair, attempting to regain some semblance of control. "Because, really, who doesn't love a little dramatic weather for a heart-to-heart?"

Michael chuckled, the sound warming me even in the storm. "A bit on the nose, don't you think? But I'd take this over silence any day." He stepped closer, the space between us diminishing as the waves crashed like applause around us.

"Silence has its charm, though," I replied, crossing my arms to ward off the chill that crept in, though it wasn't just the cold air that sent shivers down my spine. "It's the things left unsaid that tend to fester."

"I guess that makes us a pair of festering wounds," he said, an edge of humor lacing his tone, but there was an earnestness beneath it that struck a chord. The flicker of a smile on his lips held a mix of hope and fear, and I realized that the storm wasn't just a backdrop; it was the embodiment of our fractured connection—raw, unfiltered, and desperately alive.

"What are we doing, Michael?" I asked, the weight of my words pressing against my chest. "You called me here in the middle of a storm. It feels... significant."

"Because it is significant," he replied, his gaze unwavering. "We've been avoiding this conversation for too long. I want to be honest about everything—about us, about how I feel." He hesitated, glancing down for a moment before meeting my eyes again. "I don't want to just be a memory for you, something you look back on with a sigh. I want to be part of your now."

My heart raced at his admission, a rush of conflicting emotions surging through me. "But what does that even mean? How do we go from being two people lost in the fog to something more?"

"By wading through the fog together," he said, the earnestness in his tone unwavering. "I know it sounds cliché, but life is too short for half-measures. I'd rather face the storm with you than walk away from it alone."

The sincerity in his words wrapped around me like a lifeline. My instincts screamed to push him away, to guard my heart against potential heartache, yet something deeper within urged me to lean in closer. I wanted to believe him, to embrace the possibility that we could rewrite our story.

"Okay, but you know it's not going to be easy, right?" I shot back, trying to temper my growing excitement with a dash of realism. "You don't just get to say 'I miss you' and expect fireworks. We've got some serious ground to cover."

He smirked, that familiar playful glint returning to his eyes. "Fireworks? Maybe we can save those for the Fourth of July. For now, let's settle for a good old-fashioned stormy reunion."

As the rain lashed at us, we shared a quiet moment, allowing the tension of the past to settle between us like the mist on the water. I could feel the air thrum with unspoken promises and the weight of our shared history, a tapestry of joy, confusion, and love woven through every thread.

But just as I felt the tension easing, the wind whipped up again, howling like a banshee as if warning us that we were not alone in this moment. A jagged bolt of lightning lit up the horizon, illuminating the dark ocean and casting a fleeting glow on Michael's face.

"Did you see that?" he shouted over the wind, pointing toward the waves that began to churn violently. The once-gentle surf now resembled a furious beast, rising and falling with an alarming intensity.

"Yeah, I did!" I yelled back, a mix of awe and fear clawing at my throat. "That's not just a summer storm. It's like the ocean has something to say."

As if in answer, a loud crash echoed, sending a spray of water up the shore. We both stepped back instinctively, hearts racing. The world around us felt alive, electric with energy that matched the chaos within me. "Maybe we should go back," I suggested, glancing back at the shore where our footprints had been washed away.

"Not yet," Michael replied, determination etched in his features. "We can't let the storm decide for us. We're here now, and I don't want to lose this moment."

Just then, as if the universe decided to play its own game, a figure appeared in the distance, silhouetted against the tumultuous backdrop. My heart sank at the sight, confusion morphing into apprehension as I squinted through the sheets of rain. "Michael, do you see that?"

He followed my gaze, and I could see the realization dawn on his face. "What the hell?" he muttered, an edge of concern creeping into his voice. "Who could be out here in this weather?"

As the figure drew closer, I felt a wave of dread wash over me. The storm intensified, the wind howling like a siren, warning us of the impending confrontation. I braced myself, my mind racing with possibilities, as the figure emerged from the curtain of rain, revealing a familiar face that sent a chill down my spine.

"Clara?" Michael exclaimed, his voice tinged with disbelief. "What are you doing here?"

My heart dropped as Clara stepped closer, soaked to the skin but with an air of defiance that radiated from her. She was the last person I expected to see at our sacred place, especially during a storm. "I came to find you, Michael!" she shouted, her voice rising above the crashing waves. "We need to talk!"

As the storm raged on, the air thickened with tension. The wind whipped around us, carrying Clara's words like a thunderclap, forcing us to confront everything we had tried to avoid. My heart pounded in my chest, the unexpected turn of events tightening the grip of uncertainty.

"Clara?" Michael's voice cracked with surprise, and I felt my heart drop like a stone, the weight of this unexpected intrusion crushing any flicker of hope I had nurtured moments before. The storm roared around us, amplifying the tension that hung thick in the air.

"What are you doing here?" I managed to ask, my voice steady despite the quaking of my insides. Clara was the last person I wanted to see in this moment—a hurricane of complications in an already tumultuous situation.

"I came to find you," she repeated, her eyes locking onto Michael's with a fierce intensity that sent an involuntary shiver down my spine. "We need to talk about what happened."

Michael shifted uneasily beside me, the warmth of our previous moment now feeling like a fragile bubble on the verge of popping. "Clara, not now. This isn't the time," he said, the urgency in his tone betraying his discomfort.

"It is the time!" she shot back, her voice rising above the wind. "If we don't sort this out, it could ruin everything."

Everything. The word hung in the air, heavy with implications. I glanced at Michael, his expression a mix of confusion and resolve, and felt the knot in my stomach tighten. The storm wasn't just a physical presence; it felt like a metaphor for the turmoil brewing within our little triangle.

"Maybe you should just go," I said, trying to keep my tone measured, though irritation crept in. "We were in the middle of something important."

"Oh, I can see that," Clara replied, her voice dripping with sarcasm. "What's more important than figuring out why you suddenly vanished?" She turned to Michael, her expression softening for a moment. "You can't keep running away from this. You need to face it."

Michael ran a hand through his hair, frustration etched into his features. "And what do you think showing up here in the middle of a storm is going to accomplish?"

"I think it's going to force us to confront the mess we've created," Clara retorted, her eyes narrowing. The rain continued to drench us, but it seemed to fade into the background as the tension between us escalated. "We can't just ignore the past because it's inconvenient."

"Convenience? This isn't about convenience, Clara!" Michael's voice was louder now, rising over the howl of the wind. "This is about moving forward and not getting stuck in old wounds."

"Is that what you think? That running away is moving forward?" she shot back, her gaze unwavering. "You're both so focused on the past that you're blind to the present."

I took a step back, the cold spray of ocean water hitting my face like a slap. "This is not how I envisioned our talk going," I said, my voice sharp with frustration. "I thought we were having a moment, and now it feels like we're in a telenovela."

"A telenovela?" Clara raised an eyebrow, a smirk twitching at the corners of her lips. "How quaint. If only it were that glamorous. Right now, it feels like we're in an episode of 'Survivor.'"

"Great, just what I needed. A reality check amidst the storm," I muttered under my breath, casting a glance at the churning sea.

"Listen," Michael interjected, his tone suddenly serious, drawing both of our attention. "We're all here, caught in this storm together, and we need to get things straightened out—no more dodging or running. Clara, you need to tell me what you came here to say."

Clara hesitated, glancing between us, the intensity of the moment shifting as the wind howled like a wailing banshee. "I know I haven't been the best at dealing with things," she finally admitted, her voice softening, vulnerability creeping in. "But I'm here because I care about both of you, and I can't stand the thought of losing what we had."

"Losing what?" I asked, unable to keep the sharpness out of my voice. "What exactly are we supposed to be holding on to?"

"Friendship," she said, her gaze earnest. "Love, the connections we've built over the years. It doesn't have to be black and white. There's a middle ground."

Michael stepped closer, the tension crackling between us like static. "And what does that middle ground look like, Clara? Because right now, all I see is confusion and hurt."

"I just—" she began, but the storm seemed to intensify, the wind shrieking as if trying to drown her words. Suddenly, a blinding flash of lightning illuminated the beach, illuminating the moment in stark contrast.

"What was that?" I shouted over the roar of the ocean, the intensity of the storm escalating as if sensing our turmoil.

"It's just a storm," Clara replied, but her voice held a tremor that betrayed her confidence.

"No, it feels like something else," I said, my instincts firing like alarm bells. "We shouldn't be here. Not now."

As if to punctuate my words, the ground beneath us rumbled ominously, and I felt a sudden rush of air whip past me. I turned just in time to see a massive wave surge towards us, taller than any I had ever seen.

"Run!" Michael shouted, grabbing my arm, and I didn't hesitate, my heart racing as we sprinted away from the encroaching water. Clara stumbled after us, the three of us racing against nature's fury, the roar of the storm drowning out our voices.

We dashed toward the nearby cliffs, but the terrain was treacherous, slick with rain and chaos. My breath hitched as I glanced back, fear clenching at my heart. The wave crashed down with a deafening roar, sending a spray of water high into the air.

"Keep going!" Michael yelled, pulling me closer as we dodged rocks and debris, but Clara's presence beside us felt both grounding and chaotic, an unpredictable element in our fragile alliance.

Just as we reached the cliffs, another bolt of lightning struck, illuminating a dark figure perched on the rocks above us. My heart raced, a different kind of dread filling the pit of my stomach. "What the hell is that?" I gasped, pointing as the figure came into sharper focus.

It was a person—a woman, cloaked in a dark shroud, her face obscured by shadow. She seemed to shimmer against the backdrop of the storm, as if she were both part of it and separate from it.

"Who is she?" Clara asked, her voice shaking as the stranger lifted her head, revealing eyes that glowed like embers in the night.

"Stay back!" Michael shouted, instinctively stepping in front of me, but the woman only smiled, an unsettling expression that sent chills down my spine.

"I've been waiting for you," she said, her voice a haunting melody that cut through the storm.

And just like that, everything we thought we knew unraveled, leaving us standing on the edge of the unknown, with the storm raging around us and the mysterious figure beckoning us forward into the heart of chaos.

Chapter 21: Torn Apart

The salty tang of the sea air whipped around me as I stumbled onto the beach, my clothes clinging to my skin like a second layer. Each step I took sent splashes of icy water cascading from my sneakers, and my heart raced—not from the chill, but from the storm brewing within me. The sky roared, dark clouds swirling ominously above, mirroring the tumult of emotions I couldn't quite untangle. In that moment, I was alive, raw, and exposed, the very essence of chaos reflected in the tumultuous waves crashing against the shore.

There he stood, Michael, a dark silhouette against the flashing brilliance of lightning that illuminated the night. His posture was tense, rigid with an energy that crackled in the air. He looked almost ethereal, as if he were conjured from the storm itself—a tempestuous figure battling the weight of his own stormy thoughts. I took a deep breath, bracing myself for whatever words would tumble from his lips. There was something inherently magnetic about him, something that pulled at the threads of my heart even as I felt them fraying.

"Why are you here?" His voice was strained, a whisper swallowed by the howling wind. It seemed to carry the weight of every unspoken worry, every miscommunication that had haunted us for weeks. He shifted his weight from one foot to the other, glancing toward the horizon, where darkness met the frothy, turbulent sea.

"I had to see you," I replied, my voice barely rising above the roar of the ocean. I stepped closer, the wet sand squishing beneath my feet, but the closer I got, the more I sensed a distance—a gulf that felt insurmountable. "I thought... I thought maybe we could talk."

"Talk?" His eyes flashed in the darkness, stormy blues reflecting the tempest around us. "Is that what you call it? Because every time we try to talk, it ends up in an argument." His words stung, but I couldn't dismiss the truth wrapped in his frustration. We had danced around the same issues for too long, each confrontation layered with unvoiced fears.

"I'm not trying to argue. I just want to understand where we stand," I pleaded, feeling the swell of emotion rising within me like the tide. "We can't keep pretending everything is fine when it's not. We both feel it."

He looked at me, really looked at me, and the silence stretched between us, thick as the storm clouds above. I could see the struggle etched across his features, the desire to break free battling against the deep connection that had always tethered us together. "It's suffocating," he finally admitted, his voice a low rumble that seemed to echo the distant thunder. "I don't know if I can handle this anymore, Zoe. I love you, but it feels like we're drowning."

Those words hit me like a cold wave crashing against my heart. I had spent so many nights dreaming of a life filled with laughter and shared moments, yet here we stood, at the brink of something beautiful, only to have it twisted by our fears. "You're not drowning, Michael. We're in this together. I thought we were fighting for something real," I said, the desperation creeping into my voice.

"Maybe that's the problem." His gaze fell to the sand, and the flickering light from the storm caught the glimmer of unshed tears in his eyes. "What if it's too real? What if we're just two ships passing in the night, bound to collide but never truly meet?"

His metaphor struck me, sharp and unexpected, and for a moment, the world around us faded. It was just him and me, standing on the precipice of what could have been, both terrified of the leap required to reach the other side. The wind howled like a lost soul, but within that chaos, I felt a flicker of hope, igniting a fire in my chest that begged to burn brighter.

"I don't want to be a passing ship," I breathed, stepping closer still. "I want to anchor us. I want to fight for this." My fingers grazed his arm, a tentative bridge reaching out for the warmth of connection, but as if the universe conspired against us, the sound of an approaching car engine shattered the fragile moment.

The headlights pierced through the storm, illuminating our little world just before it was swallowed by darkness once more. Panic washed over me, the heavy weight of reality crashing in as I recognized the unmistakable vehicle. Emily's car. My heart sank as I saw the silhouette of her figure through the rain-spattered windshield, a storm of her own brewing within.

As she stepped out, her expression shifted from confusion to betrayal in the blink of an eye. "What the hell is going on here?" she shouted over the wind, her voice carrying a sharp edge that cut through the tension like a knife.

"Emily, wait—" I began, but she was already striding towards us, eyes blazing with hurt and anger. I could see the disbelief in her expression, the way her lips quivered as if she were holding back a storm of her own. This was a tempest I had never anticipated, one that threatened to tear apart everything we had tried to build.

Michael's shoulders tensed, and in that split second, I understood the implications of our tangled emotions, the precariousness of our situation. This was not just about us anymore; this was a three-way intersection where choices could lead to heartbreak, loss, or, if we were lucky, understanding. The thunder rolled ominously overhead, a fitting soundtrack to the tumultuous reality that was unfolding before us.

"I can explain!" I called out, desperate to salvage what remained of our fragile conversation, but the look on Emily's face told me everything I feared. With one swift motion, the world I had hoped to create with Michael began to unravel, leaving behind only jagged edges and echoes of a love that could have been.

The rain drummed against the ground like a frantic heartbeat as Emily approached, each step heavy with accusation and uncertainty. I felt my stomach drop, the moment that had been so charged with potential now tainted by her presence. The air crackled with tension, and I could sense the shift in the atmosphere, as if the world itself held its breath, waiting for the storm to break.

"Zoe, is this what it looks like?" Emily's voice sliced through the night, sharp enough to cut glass. The shock in her eyes shifted to something darker, a cocktail of hurt and rage. She stood there, drenched and defiant, framing a stark contrast to Michael and me, who seemed lost in a realm of unspoken words and raw emotions.

"Em, it's not—" I started, but the words clung to my throat, suffocated by the weight of the moment. Michael's hand slipped away from mine, retreating as if the very act of touching me had ignited a powder keg of chaos.

"Not what? Not what it looks like? Because it looks like you're about to share some deep, heartfelt revelation, and I just waltzed into a soap opera." Her eyes blazed with indignation, but I could see a flicker of vulnerability beneath her bravado, a glimpse of the friend I had always cherished.

"We were just talking," Michael interjected, stepping forward in a futile attempt to defuse the tension. "I swear, it's not—"

"It's not what, Michael? Is this just a conversation, or are you finally telling her how you feel?" Emily's laughter was brittle, a laugh devoid of humor. "Because it certainly looks like you two were about to dive into the deep end without a life jacket."

"Emily, please," I pleaded, stepping toward her. "It's complicated. We were just trying to sort things out. I didn't mean for you to find us like this." My words spilled out, frantic and desperate, but she shook her head, the resolve in her eyes like steel.

"I thought we were better than this, Zoe. I thought you were different." The hurt in her voice lanced through me, each word a dagger that twisted in the open wound of our friendship.

"Different how?" I shot back, irritation flaring amidst the guilt. "Because I'm human, too? I have feelings, and I'm trying to figure this out just like you."

"Maybe you should have thought about that before you got all cozy with my ex," she snapped, the accusation hanging heavily in the damp air.

Michael glanced at me, and in that fleeting moment, I saw our collective confusion mirrored in his eyes. I wanted to scream, to tell Emily that it wasn't just about him and me, that the connection we shared was tangled in layers far more complicated than a simple romance.

"Emily, I didn't choose this," I said, trying to keep my voice steady as the storm raged around us. "I didn't choose any of this. You think I wanted to hurt you?"

"Then what was this?" she gestured wildly, the rain streaking down her face, mixing with the tears she clearly struggled to hold back. "What were you two doing here, under the storm, whispering sweet nothings like it was some secret rendezvous?"

Before I could respond, the thunder cracked overhead, a furious growl from the heavens that felt like an echo of the turmoil between us. Michael, sensing the rising tension, stepped closer to me again, attempting to shield me from the storm, both outside and within.

"Zoe and I were just trying to talk about us, about our feelings," he said, his voice steadying despite the tempest around us. "I didn't mean to involve you in this mess. I promise, I wanted to be honest, but everything feels so heavy, and I didn't know how to approach it."

"By hiding behind a storm?" Emily retorted, her voice rising. "You're so afraid of being real that you choose to play games instead of owning up to what you really want. And now you're trying to pull Zoe into your confusion."

The rain poured down harder, and I could feel it drenching my clothes, but it didn't come close to the soaking I felt from the confrontation. "It's not a game, Emily," I insisted, my heart pounding in my chest. "We were trying to figure things out, and maybe we shouldn't have been doing it here, but it's real for us. It's not just a whim or a secret crush."

Michael caught my gaze, and in that moment, the world fell away, leaving just us. I felt a deep connection to him, but I couldn't shake the weight of Emily's heartbreak. I glanced back at her, the pain etched across her features sending a fresh wave of guilt crashing over me.

"Maybe you should have thought about that before you got cozy with my ex," she repeated, her voice quieter now, the fight momentarily fading. "I didn't just lose a boyfriend; I lost a friend in you, Zoe. You're my best friend, and now..." Her voice cracked, revealing a crack in her armor, and it hit me like a brick wall.

"I'm so sorry, Em." I took a step toward her, reaching out, desperate to bridge the chasm that had suddenly opened between us. "I never wanted to hurt you. This isn't how I envisioned it. I wanted to talk to you first. I wanted to be honest."

"Honesty? What do you know about honesty?" she shot back, her expression wavering between fury and pain. "I thought we were supposed to be in this together, and now you're picking sides."

"No one's picking sides!" Michael interjected, frustration lacing his voice. "This isn't about sides; it's about feelings. You both mean something to me, but I can't pretend this isn't happening."

The storm raged on, a symphony of chaos surrounding us as we stood there, a trio caught in an emotional whirlwind. I was torn between my loyalty to Emily and the undeniable bond I felt with Michael, and the weight of that realization pressed down on me like a storm cloud ready to burst.

"Zoe, do you really care about him?" Emily asked, her voice trembling as she searched my eyes for answers. "Do you really want to go down this road, knowing what it means for our friendship?"

I took a deep breath, the salty sea air mixed with the scent of rain filling my lungs, anchoring me. "I don't know, Em. I didn't plan for any of this to happen. I care about both of you, but it feels like I'm caught in a tempest where no one is winning."

A moment of silence hung between us, charged with emotion, uncertainty, and an unyielding sense of impending change. Just then, the thunder cracked loudly overhead, as if the universe was signaling a shift, and I realized we were standing at a crossroads, each choice heavy with consequences.

In that instant, I understood that whatever direction we took, nothing would ever be the same again. The storm would pass, but its echoes would linger, shaping our paths, intertwining our stories in ways we couldn't yet comprehend.

The air pulsed with unspoken words, each moment stretching like the tension before a storm. As Emily glared at us, I felt my heart hammering in my chest, a frantic rhythm battling the roar of the ocean. She looked like a tempest herself, soaking wet and fierce, a mix of betrayal and hurt radiating from her like the electric energy crackling in the air around us.

"Zoe, why would you do this?" Her voice trembled, teetering on the edge of anger and heartbreak. "You know how I felt about Michael."

"Em, it's not like that!" I rushed to say, desperately trying to hold onto the thread of our friendship. "I didn't plan for any of this to happen. We were just trying to figure things out."

"Figure things out?" she repeated incredulously, arms crossed defiantly over her chest. "You two were about to take a leap off the emotional cliff while I was supposed to be left hanging in midair? Do you really think I'm that naive?"

I opened my mouth to defend myself, but the words stuck in my throat. Deep down, I knew I had let her down. "It was never my intention to hurt you. I swear," I managed, feeling the weight of the world pressing down on me.

Michael, caught in the crossfire, looked between us with a mix of helplessness and concern. "We both care about you, Emily," he said, his voice low but steady. "But we also need to be honest about what's happening. It's not fair to any of us to pretend everything is fine when it's not."

"Honest?" Emily's laugh was sharp, a bitter edge cutting through the rain. "You call this honesty? You want to be honest when it suits you, but you hide behind each other when it gets tough. I thought I could count on both of you."

"Stop putting this all on Zoe," Michael snapped, frustration spilling over. "This isn't just about her. It's about all of us trying to navigate something that's become incredibly complicated. We need to talk, really talk, and figure out what this means for our friendship."

The tension hung thick in the air, and for a moment, the only sound was the relentless pounding of the waves. I could feel the currents of our emotions swirling around us like the storm itself, pulling at my heartstrings. But Emily wasn't finished.

"Talk?" she echoed, her voice rising. "Is that what you think we need? A group therapy session? Because all I see is betrayal, and that's not something you just chat away over coffee."

"I know this looks bad," I pleaded, frustration creeping into my voice. "But it's not black and white! Relationships aren't easy. Sometimes they twist in unexpected ways, and we have to navigate those twists."

"Maybe you should have thought about that before cozying up to my ex." The words cut deep, a reminder of the fracture forming in our once-solid friendship.

A flash of lightning illuminated the sky, revealing the anguish etched on Emily's face. I could see her heart breaking, piece by piece, and it twisted painfully in my chest. "I'm sorry," I whispered, hoping to bridge the chasm between us.

Emily stepped back, her arms wrapping tightly around herself, a physical barrier that echoed the emotional distance now between us. "You're sorry? That doesn't change the fact that you chose him over me."

"It's not about choosing!" I retorted, the hurt spilling out despite my attempts to contain it. "I'm trying to figure out my own feelings here, too! I didn't want to hurt you, Em. I just... I just don't know what I want right now."

"Clearly," she muttered under her breath, her gaze shifting to the crashing waves. "This is a mess, and we're all standing in it."

Michael stepped forward again, trying to close the distance, but I could see the concern in his eyes—a mix of frustration and worry for both of us. "We all deserve to be happy," he said softly, his voice filled with an unexpected gentleness. "But we can't do that if we don't communicate. It's not about you versus me, Em. It's about figuring out how we move forward."

Emily's shoulders relaxed ever so slightly at his words, as if the storm inside her was calming, but her eyes still glistened with unshed tears. "And what if moving forward means losing one of you? What if it means losing everything?"

I took a breath, knowing the truth would hurt but believing it was time to confront the reality of our situation. "Maybe... maybe we have to consider that risk," I said cautiously. "Nothing worth having is ever easy."

A moment passed, heavy with the gravity of our choices, the air electric with tension. "You think I want to lose you?" Emily asked, her voice now softer, tinged with uncertainty. "You both mean a lot to me."

"Then let's talk about it," I suggested, my heart racing as I looked from Michael to Emily. "Let's be honest about what we want. Let's not let fear dictate our choices."

"Easier said than done," Emily replied, shaking her head, but there was a hint of hope glimmering in her eyes.

"We're all scared," Michael admitted, his gaze steady. "But if we don't try, we'll lose each other anyway."

"Right now, we're losing each other anyway," Emily shot back, the anger flaring anew. "You both can't see how this is tearing us apart! I feel like I'm stuck in the middle of a tornado, and I have no idea which way to turn."

I glanced at Michael, seeking his support, and he nodded, determination set in his jaw. "What do you want, Emily?" he asked, his tone challenging yet inviting. "What would make this better for you?"

Emily took a deep breath, and for a moment, the storm seemed to pause, waiting for her answer. "I want honesty," she said finally, her voice steadying. "I want to know if we can be friends again. I want to know if you both really care about me or if this is just about you two figuring out your feelings."

The vulnerability in her voice cut through the chaos like a beacon of light, illuminating the path ahead. "We do care about you," I reassured her, heart racing. "But we can't move forward without talking it out. It may hurt, but honesty is what we need."

As the words left my mouth, a sudden silence enveloped us, the rain easing, allowing the sounds of the ocean to rise in a gentle crescendo. I felt the tension shift, an unsteady truce forming amidst the storm.

But just as I thought we were making progress, a distant noise caught my attention—an engine roaring to life, breaking through the soft lull of the waves. I turned, my heart sinking, as headlights cut through the darkness, illuminating the beach like a spotlight.

"Who's that?" Emily asked, her voice suddenly tense again, eyes widening in alarm.

"I don't know," I breathed, my heart racing anew, every instinct screaming that this was a pivotal moment. The car barreled toward us, its intentions unclear, and just as it drew near, it slammed to a stop. The door swung open, and a figure emerged, silhouetted against the night.

"Zoe!" The voice echoed across the beach, sharp and urgent. It was Jack, my brother, looking wild-eyed and panicked. "You need to get away from here! Now!"

Panic surged through me, and I instinctively moved closer to Emily and Michael, a knot of fear tightening in my stomach. "What's happening?" I called out, dread creeping in.

"It's not safe!" Jack shouted, glancing around as if expecting someone—or something—to jump out of the shadows.

"Why? What do you mean?" I pressed, my heart pounding in my chest as the storm around us resumed, rain pounding down in sheets.

"They're coming," he said, urgency flooding his voice. "We have to go. Now!"

And just like that, the night erupted into chaos, the echoes of our emotional confrontation eclipsed by a far greater danger lurking just beyond the reach of our understanding.

Chapter 22: Echoes of Betrayal

The wind howled outside, a chaotic symphony of nature that matched the turmoil inside me. Shadows danced across the room, cast by the flickering candlelight that seemed to mock our situation, their brief illumination revealing the strain etched on Emily's face. Her eyes, once warm and inviting, now burned with a fierce intensity, a tempest of emotions that swirled like the storm raging beyond the glass panes.

"How could you?" she spat, her voice sharp enough to cut through the thick tension. Each accusation was like a knife, piercing my heart and leaving behind a dull ache that refused to fade. I opened my mouth to defend myself, to explain the reasons behind our decisions, but the words clanged in my throat like a heavy metal door, refusing to budge.

Michael shifted uneasily beside me, the embodiment of calm amidst the storm. He had always been my rock, but now, his protective stance felt like a cage closing in around me. The moment he stepped between us, I sensed the fault lines shifting beneath our feet, the delicate balance of our lives fracturing under the weight of her anger. "Emily, let's just talk this through," he said, his voice smooth as honey, attempting to soothe the tempest brewing in her eyes.

But Emily wasn't interested in soothing words. She had her fists clenched at her sides, her posture taut like a coiled spring. "Talk? You think we can just talk this through?" The incredulity in her voice was palpable. "You're hiding everything! You're part of this mess, and you want to brush it under the rug with a few pretty words?" The rawness of her emotion struck me, igniting a flicker of regret deep within my gut.

Her fingers twitched, as if she might reach for something—a weapon, a truth, or perhaps the remnants of our friendship. I searched for the right words, a way to reach her, to dismantle the growing chasm between us. "Emily, I never meant for you to get hurt," I finally managed, my voice cracking under the weight of unspoken apologies. "We thought we were protecting you."

"Protecting me?" she echoed, the word laced with bitterness. "You think keeping me in the dark is protecting me?"

The accusation stung, and I felt Michael's presence slip away, replaced by the sharp awareness of my own failings. The room spun, and with it, the memories of laughter and secrets shared flooded back. I remembered our late-night conversations filled with dreams, and the way her smile could illuminate the darkest corners of my mind. How had we come to this?

As if sensing my spiraling thoughts, Emily stepped closer, her voice dropping to a whisper, yet carrying the weight of thunder. "You think I'm just going to sit back and let you manipulate me? You've crossed a line, and I'm not going to let you walk away unscathed."

The determination in her stance made my heart race—she was no longer the girl I had known, but a force of nature ready to unleash a storm of her own. I glanced at Michael, whose gaze darted between us, a silent plea for peace lingering in his eyes. But this was no ordinary argument; it was a battle of wills, and I could feel the ground shifting beneath my feet, threatening to swallow us whole.

"Emily, please," I said, desperation creeping into my voice. "We're on the same side. You have to trust us."

Her laughter rang out, a harsh and bitter sound that echoed off the walls. "Trust? You expect me to trust the people who've been lying to me?" The words dripped with disbelief, and I felt the world tilt precariously. The air grew heavy, each breath thick with unspoken fears and accusations, as if the storm outside had crept into our hearts and settled there.

"Then what do you want?" I demanded, the heat of my frustration spilling over. "What's the point of this confrontation if not to find some resolution? You want to expose us—fine! But that won't solve anything."

Her eyes narrowed, a storm brewing beneath the surface. "You think I want to expose you? No, I want you to understand that I won't be a pawn in your game. You can't keep me in the dark anymore."

Michael interjected, trying to diffuse the tension. "We're not playing games, Emily. We're trying to keep you safe." His voice was steady, but I could see the tension coiling within him, ready to snap at the slightest provocation.

"Safe? By lying to me? By keeping me from the truth?" She turned to him, her expression fierce. "You're both fools if you think I'll back down now."

The temperature in the room dropped, and I could almost hear the ice forming around us. The storm outside raged on, lightning flashing in the distance, illuminating the turmoil within. My mind raced, the implications of our secrets colliding with the reality of our fractured relationships. I could feel the pressure building, a storm of our own brewing, and I knew we had to confront it head-on or risk being consumed by it.

"Emily, listen," I said, stepping forward despite the fear gnawing at my insides. "We're in this together. Whatever it is you think you're trying to do, it won't work unless we're united."

Her gaze softened for just a moment, a flicker of the Emily I knew beneath the stormy facade. "And if I don't trust you?"

"Then we'll be lost," I replied, my voice a whisper, the truth of it hanging heavy in the air. "All of us."

Silence settled in, punctuated only by the distant rumble of thunder and the relentless howling of the wind. The weight of our choices pressed down on us, each breath laced with the tension of what was left unsaid. In that charged moment, I knew the battle lines were drawn—not just between us, but within ourselves. We were teetering on the edge, and the next step could lead us to salvation or destruction.

But as the storm raged on outside, we stood at the precipice, unsure of what lay ahead. All I could hope for was that love, in whatever form it took, could weather the storm.

The silence that followed felt like a held breath, a moment suspended in time as Emily's accusations hung in the air, thick with betrayal and hurt. I could see her chest rising and falling rapidly, her emotions a kaleidoscope of fury and disappointment. Michael shifted slightly, a silent signal that I should take the lead, but the pressure of the moment rendered me momentarily mute.

"Emily," I finally said, my voice steadier than I felt, "this isn't what you think. We're not the enemy here." The words came out, but they felt inadequate, floating helplessly in the space between us.

"Oh, really?" she shot back, crossing her arms tightly over her chest, as if trying to physically shield herself from the truth. "Because from where I stand, it looks like you two have been playing games at my expense. If you think I'm going to let that slide, you're dead wrong." Her voice dripped with a mix of sarcasm and pain that cut deeper than any dagger could.

Michael stepped forward, but I could see the conflict in his eyes; he was caught between wanting to soothe the storm brewing inside Emily and the protectiveness he felt towards me. "We thought we were doing what was best for you," he said, his voice low, attempting to strike a chord of understanding.

"Best for me?" she scoffed, the laugh bitter and sharp. "You mean best for yourselves. Keeping me in the dark, playing the heroes while I'm left to figure this mess out alone."

The truth in her words was a hard pill to swallow, and I felt my defenses crumble slightly. "We were trying to keep you safe," I said, desperation creeping into my tone. "There are things at play here that are bigger than all of us."

"Safe? By lying?" she echoed, the disbelief palpable. The tension snapped like a taut wire, and I took a step closer, my heart pounding with the desire to bridge the chasm growing between us.

"You don't understand," I pressed. "We thought if we kept you away from this, you wouldn't get hurt. We wanted to protect you from the fallout."

"Fallout?" she shot back, shaking her head. "How can you even say that? You've been lying to me! If I get hurt, it's because of you two, not some mysterious 'fallout.'"

At that moment, a gust of wind rattled the windows, howling like a wounded beast, and I felt the weight of the storm pressing against us, as if the very elements were mirroring our tumultuous emotions.

"Emily," Michael tried again, stepping forward, his expression earnest. "What we didn't tell you was—"

"Save it!" she interrupted, raising a hand, her eyes narrowing. "I don't want to hear another excuse. You've made your choice, and now I have to make mine."

My breath caught in my throat as I realized what that could mean. A flicker of fear darted through me. "What are you planning?" I asked, my heart racing. "You can't just go and—"

But she cut me off again, her voice a mix of defiance and desperation. "Watch me."

With that, she turned sharply, her silhouette framed against the tempest outside. The door slammed behind her with a finality that echoed through the room, leaving an oppressive silence in its wake.

"Great. Just great," I muttered, rubbing my temples as the adrenaline began to wane, leaving behind a dull ache. Michael sighed beside me, a heavy sound that filled the empty space between us.

"We have to go after her," he said, determination flooding his tone.

I shook my head, panic swirling within me. "What if she's serious? What if she really exposes us? The last thing we need is for our lives to be turned inside out."

Michael shot me a sharp look, frustration flaring. "What do you propose we do? Just let her run off and do something reckless?"

"It's her decision," I replied, feeling the weight of the words settle heavily on my shoulders. "She's right about one thing—she deserves to know the truth. But maybe she needs to process this on her own first."

"While she's out there in a storm?" Michael's voice was laced with disbelief. "We can't just sit here and do nothing."

I took a deep breath, trying to quell the rising tide of anxiety. "Let's give her some space. She'll come back, and when she does, we can talk this through. We need to approach her when she's ready, not when emotions are running high."

A moment of tense silence passed between us, the reality of the situation settling like a thick fog. Outside, the storm raged, lightning illuminating the darkened sky in brief, brilliant flashes, casting eerie shadows that danced along the walls.

"Okay," Michael finally conceded, though the tension in his shoulders remained. "But I'm not leaving her side for long. The last thing we need is for her to make a decision that could jeopardize everything."

I nodded, grateful for his unwavering loyalty even as the worry gnawed at me. We were standing on the precipice of a decision that could unravel everything we had fought for, and I could feel the weight of the moment settling around us.

The hours passed slowly, the storm outside mirroring the turmoil within. Each rumble of thunder felt like a reminder of our fractured relationship, the echoes of our earlier confrontation lingering in the air. My heart ached with the knowledge that Emily was out there, alone and hurt, while we remained here, caught in a web of our own making.

As the storm began to wane, I found myself pacing the room, the adrenaline from earlier fading into a heavy sense of dread. "What if she doesn't come back?" I murmured, more to myself than to Michael.

"She will," he reassured, though I could hear the uncertainty in his voice. "She needs time to cool off. We all do."

But as the hours dragged on, that reassurance began to feel increasingly fragile, like a thin veneer over the anxiety bubbling beneath the surface. I could almost feel the tension radiating from the empty spaces she once occupied, each tick of the clock echoing the fear that we might lose her—along with everything we held dear.

Finally, the door creaked open, and my heart leaped. Emily stood in the doorway, rain-soaked and wild-eyed, her hair a halo of chaos. The moment felt electric, charged with unspoken words and unacknowledged emotions, as if the storm outside had unleashed something far more tumultuous within her.

"I need to talk," she said, her voice barely rising above the remnants of the storm.

The weight of the world seemed to settle back onto our shoulders, and I knew this moment would change everything. As she stepped inside, the air around us crackled with the possibility of redemption or ruin, and I took a tentative step forward, ready to face whatever came next.

The air crackled with tension, each second stretching into infinity as Emily stood drenched in rain, her defiance radiating from every soaked fiber of her being. I felt my heart stutter, a rush of conflicting emotions swirling within me—relief that she was back, mixed with the fear of what this confrontation would unleash. The storm had not just raged outside; it had seeped into our lives, and now we were standing on the precipice, teetering dangerously close to an abyss.

"Emily," I breathed, taking a cautious step toward her. The room felt smaller, walls inching in, pressing down on us as if the very house was holding its breath. "I'm glad you're here. We need to talk."

She raised an eyebrow, a sharp edge of skepticism cutting through her soaked hair. "Talk? Is that what you call it? Because last time I checked, your idea of 'talking' involved a whole lot of deceit and avoidance."

"Okay, fair point," I conceded, the heat creeping up my neck. "But this isn't about avoidance; it's about trying to keep you safe."

"Safe?" She laughed, a bitter sound that echoed around the room. "You think keeping me in the dark is going to keep me safe? If anything, it puts me in more danger."

I opened my mouth to argue, but the words caught like thorns in my throat. This was a battle I had to tread carefully, the stakes higher than I had ever anticipated. Michael stood beside me, arms crossed, his expression a mix of concern and wariness.

"Can we just take a step back?" he interjected, breaking the tension, his voice steady yet cautious. "Let's remember why we're doing this. There are things happening out there that are far more dangerous than the secrets we've kept."

"Why does everyone always want to ignore the elephant in the room?" Emily shot back, her eyes narrowing. "What's the point of pretending that everything is fine when it's not? Secrets never protect anyone; they just fester until they explode."

"Fester?" I echoed, frustration bubbling to the surface. "Is that really how you see it? We didn't mean for this to blow up in your face. We were trying to shield you, to give you a normal life, and we thought we were doing a good job."

Her expression softened momentarily, the storm clouds in her eyes parting just enough for me to glimpse the girl I had known before all this chaos. "A normal life? You think being kept in the dark is normal? Do you have any idea how isolating that feels?"

The admission struck me, leaving a raw ache in its wake. "I'm sorry, Emily," I whispered, wishing I could rewind time and undo the tangled web we had woven. "I just—"

"Don't." She held up a hand, cutting me off. "No more apologies. Just tell me what's really going on. Why was I kept in the dark, and what are you two really protecting me from?"

The air thickened, a heavy blanket settling over us as I exchanged a glance with Michael. He looked back at me, his brow furrowed, weighing his words carefully. "There are people involved—powerful people—who don't play by the same rules we do. They have agendas that could threaten not just us but everyone we care about."

"Like who?" Emily challenged, stepping forward, determination etched into her features.

"Think of it this way: If you knew a storm was brewing, would you tell someone standing in the eye of it?" Michael countered, his voice low but firm. "Our goal was to protect you from being caught in the middle."

Emily shook her head, disbelief shadowing her expression. "By pretending everything is fine? By hiding the truth?"

"Look," I interjected, frustration pouring out. "We're not asking you to agree with us. We just need you to understand that everything we've done was to keep you from getting hurt. You think you're ready for the truth, but can you really handle what's out there?"

She hesitated, her bravado faltering as if she were weighing the gravity of my words. "You don't get to decide that for me," she said quietly, and in that moment, I saw the flicker of uncertainty in her eyes.

Before I could respond, a loud crash echoed from outside, followed by a surge of wind that rattled the windows. We all turned, hearts racing, as the door swung wide, revealing a figure standing in the threshold, silhouetted against the stormy night.

"Just in time for the party," a voice drawled, dripping with sarcasm.

"Julian?" Emily gasped, the surprise evident in her voice.

"Sorry to crash the heartfelt reunion," he said, stepping inside, water streaming from his clothes, creating a small puddle on the floor. "But I couldn't help but overhear your little conversation. It seems like you've all been keeping secrets."

The tension shifted again, coiling tightly as Julian leaned against the doorframe, a smirk playing on his lips. He had a knack for entering at the most inopportune moments, and tonight was no exception.

"Julian, this isn't a game," I warned, my irritation flaring. "This is serious."

"Oh, I can see that," he said, raising his hands in mock surrender. "But trust me, the truth you're so desperately clinging to isn't nearly as safe as you think it is. You all have no idea what's really going on."

Emily narrowed her eyes, the remnants of her anger bubbling back to the surface. "And you do? Enlighten us, please."

"Ah, the brave little hero," Julian teased, a glint of mischief in his eyes. "You think you're ready for the truth? Let's just say the storm isn't just out there; it's also brewing right here."

"What do you mean?" Michael stepped forward, his voice low and cautious, ready to confront whatever Julian was about to unleash.

Julian leaned closer, his expression turning serious. "What you don't know can hurt you. Those powerful people you've been trying to protect Emily from? They're already in this room. They've been watching, waiting for the right moment to strike. And trust me, they're far more dangerous than you've ever imagined."

A chill ran through me, and I could feel the very air shift, heavy with unspoken truths and impending danger. I glanced at Emily, who stood frozen, processing the weight of Julian's words, her expression a mixture of disbelief and concern.

Just then, a loud rumble of thunder shook the house, and the lights flickered ominously, plunging us into darkness for a brief moment. The flickering candles cast shadows that danced wildly around the room, mirroring the chaos in our minds.

As the lights steadied, Julian's face was suddenly grave. "It's time to choose a side, and it's time to decide how far you're willing to go to protect those you care about. Because the storm is coming, and it won't wait for you to make up your mind."

The implication hung in the air, heavy and foreboding, and I felt a knot form in my stomach as reality crashed down around us. This was no longer just about secrets and lies; it was about survival.

In that moment, a piercing scream erupted from outside, slicing through the tension like a knife. Emily's eyes widened, fear etched across her face. "What was that?"

I turned towards the door, heart pounding in my chest, the sense of impending doom settling over us like a dark cloud. "We need to find out," I said, adrenaline surging as I took a step toward the door.

But before I could reach the handle, the ground beneath us trembled, a low rumble resonating like the growl of a wild beast. The room shook, sending a cascade of books tumbling from the shelves, and I caught a glimpse of the horror unfolding outside.

"Whatever's coming," Julian warned, "it's already here."

And with that, the door burst open, revealing a sight that sent a wave of terror crashing over us, freezing us in place. The storm was just the beginning; something far more sinister had arrived, and we were standing at the edge of an abyss, with no way to predict what would happen next.

Chapter 23: In the Shadows

The chill of early autumn wrapped around me like a well-worn blanket, comforting yet suffocating. I found myself tucked away in the corner of my favorite café, a quaint little spot adorned with flickering candles and mismatched furniture, each piece holding stories of the countless souls who had sought solace within its walls. The aroma of freshly brewed coffee mingled with the sweet scent of pastries, wrapping me in a cocoon of warmth while I stared blankly at my laptop screen, the cursor blinking impatiently, as if mocking my inability to produce even a single word.

My clients' stories, once vibrant and full of life, felt distant, mere echoes of the energy that had once ignited my passion. Instead of the excitement of crafting narratives for others, I was lost in the shadows of my own mind, my thoughts spiraling back to the confrontation that had unraveled everything. The memory of Michael's eyes—those piercing, deep-set eyes that had once filled me with warmth—now felt like daggers piercing my heart. I could still hear his voice, the way he had said my name, half a question and half a plea, as if he were trying to reach me from the depths of a chasm I had unwittingly created.

In the wake of our fight, I became a ghost drifting through my own life, my laughter silenced, my smile an echo of its former self. Friends began to drift away, their whispers curling around me like smoke, leaving me isolated in the very world I once loved. Invitations piled up, unopened, on my kitchen table, remnants of social gatherings I couldn't bear to attend. What was the point? To feign joy amidst the strained glances and the hushed conversations? I was a castaway in a sea of normalcy, marooned by my own choices, each day blurring into the next.

My resolve to immerse myself in my work faltered as the days turned into weeks. Late nights at the café became my refuge, where

I could hide behind my laptop and let the hum of conversation and the clatter of cups drown out my turbulent thoughts. I crafted stories for my clients with meticulous care, my fingers dancing across the keyboard as I poured my heart into their experiences, while my own lay in tatters. Each project I completed felt like a small victory, a reminder that I still had the ability to create beauty, even if my life felt anything but beautiful.

The café, with its faded photographs and the warm glow of hanging lights, became my world, and the barista, an old man with twinkling eyes and a penchant for dad jokes, my only confidant. He would lean over the counter, a knowing smile creeping across his face as he poured my coffee. "You know, it's okay to let the light in sometimes," he would say, wiping the foam from his hands. "Even the brightest days have their shadows." His words lingered in the air, a gentle nudge toward a truth I wasn't ready to face.

Yet there was something about the way he looked at me, as if he could see past the carefully constructed facade I wore, that both frightened and fascinated me. I took solace in the routine—the clinking of cups, the soft chatter of patrons, and the warmth of the coffee against my fingertips—but as the days stretched on, the heaviness in my chest grew harder to ignore.

One particularly gray afternoon, as rain tapped softly against the window, a familiar figure entered the café, shaking droplets from his hair. My heart raced, caught between disbelief and dread. It was Michael. He looked out of place yet achingly familiar, his features sharper against the backdrop of the café's warmth. I froze, my hands clenching around the warm cup as I willed myself to disappear.

"Is it too late to apologize?" His voice cut through the ambient noise, low and sincere. I couldn't bear to look up, couldn't face the storm brewing in his eyes. The weight of our last conversation hung thick in the air, suffocating the space between us. I could almost hear the unspoken words, the things left unsaid, clawing at the edges of my resolve.

"Why now, Michael?" I managed to whisper, my voice barely rising above the hum of the café. "You made your choice." I could feel the heat rising to my cheeks, a mix of anger and vulnerability spilling over as the walls I had so carefully erected began to crack.

He stepped closer, his gaze unwavering, that familiar spark of determination igniting the air around us. "Because I was wrong, and I didn't realize what I had until it slipped through my fingers. I thought I could handle it all on my own, but I can't. Not without you."

The world around me faded as I processed his words, the barista's laughter and the rustle of newspaper pages becoming a distant murmur. My heart thundered in my chest, the familiar ache creeping back, mingling with the hope I had buried deep within. Could it be possible that he genuinely wanted to repair what had been broken? Or was it just the shadow of regret whispering sweet nothings, hoping to ensnare me once more?

I took a deep breath, steadying myself against the whirlwind of emotions. "I need time," I said finally, each word a weight I had to bear. "Time to figure out what I want and what we can even be after everything." The truth of it felt like a knife twisting in my gut, but it was a necessary honesty, a step toward the light I had been too afraid to seek.

Michael nodded, his expression softening, and in that moment, I saw a flicker of the person I once knew—the boy who had made me laugh until I cried, who understood the depths of my passions and fears. Perhaps he was still there, buried beneath the rubble of our past. But could I trust that he wouldn't disappear again when the shadows returned?

As I stood there, the scent of rich espresso and freshly baked pastries swirling around us, Michael's eyes held a mix of desperation and sincerity that tugged at my heart. He was, in many ways, still the boy I had known—the boy whose laughter could light up the darkest corners of my mind. But that was before the storm, before the words that had shattered the fragile bond we had built. My chest tightened as I considered the possibility of opening that door again, only to have it slammed shut in my face.

"I don't even know what that means for us anymore," I managed, keeping my voice steady, though inside, my emotions were a swirling tempest. "We were so... messy." The word hung between us, heavy and full of the history we shared. My heart raced as I braced myself for his response.

Michael took a step back, running a hand through his hair in that way he always did when he was trying to figure out the right thing to say. "Yeah, messy is one way to put it. I'd say it was more like a tornado hit a house of cards. But maybe—maybe we can rebuild? You know, with sturdier cards?" His smile was tentative, but there was an earnestness in his gaze that made my heart flutter despite myself.

I couldn't help but chuckle softly. "Are we really going to build a house of cards? I can already see it collapsing." I shook my head, trying to ease the tension, but the truth lingered. "You know what happened last time we tried to build something, Michael. I can't just jump back in without knowing if the foundation is even solid."

He nodded, the weight of my words settling over us. "I get it. But I think... I think the time apart has taught me something. I realized how much I took you for granted. You were always there, and I was too wrapped up in my own stuff to appreciate it. Now I'm here, trying to figure out how to make it right."

"Make it right," I echoed, tasting the words on my tongue. "That sounds easy, doesn't it? Like we could just wave a magic wand and poof—everything is perfect again." The irony didn't escape me. I wanted to believe that magic existed, that somehow we could erase the pain, but deep down, I knew it wasn't that simple.

His gaze intensified, and for a moment, I felt the electric pull between us again, that gravity that had drawn us together in the first place. "I'm not asking for perfection. Just a chance. I miss you, and I'm willing to do the work if you are." The vulnerability in his tone struck a chord within me, and I felt the barriers I had so carefully erected begin to tremble.

"I don't know, Michael," I whispered, looking down at my cup, tracing the rim with my finger. "I'm afraid of getting hurt again. What if we fail again? What if this time it's worse?" My voice wavered as I spoke the truth that had haunted me for weeks.

"Life is messy. It's like a three-year-old with finger paints. There's always going to be some splatter," he said, his eyes sparkling with mischief. "But isn't that what makes it interesting? If we waited for everything to be perfect, we'd never get anywhere."

"Are you seriously comparing our relationship to finger painting?" I shot back, raising an eyebrow, half-amused and half-annoyed.

"Hey, it's a solid analogy! Just think about it. You start with a blank canvas, and then you dive in, get your hands dirty, and create something beautiful. Sure, there might be a few smudges, but isn't that part of the charm?" He grinned, a genuine smile that made my stomach flutter.

"Okay, Picasso," I retorted, unable to suppress a smile despite my lingering doubts. "But if we're going to paint this picture together, we need to agree on the colors. No more red flags or green monsters lurking in the background."

His expression shifted, and I saw the seriousness return to his eyes. "Agreed. I'll do whatever it takes to make sure there are no surprises this time. I'll be transparent, I promise. No more running away when things get tough. I can't promise it'll be easy, but I can promise it'll be real."

Real. The word echoed in my mind, reverberating through my heart like the toll of a distant bell. I wanted real. I craved the authenticity we once shared, the laughter and the late-night talks that made the world fade away. But could I trust him to keep his promise? Could I trust myself to step back into that whirlwind of emotions?

Before I could answer, the bell above the café door jingled, and in walked Jenna, my best friend since childhood, her vibrant red curls bouncing with each step. She had an uncanny ability to brighten any room, and her presence shifted the atmosphere instantly. "Well, well, if it isn't the star-crossed lovers having a heart-to-heart!" she exclaimed, her voice teasing yet warm. "Should I get a banner made or something?"

"Very funny, Jenna," I shot back, trying to hide the warmth creeping up my cheeks. "We were in the middle of something profound."

"Ah, profound!" she mused, stepping up to the counter to order her usual caramel macchiato. "That's code for 'the two of you are dancing around the real issues.'" She turned to Michael with a mischievous smile. "If you're here to win her back, you'd better come prepared. She's tough."

"I wouldn't expect anything less," he replied, meeting Jenna's gaze with a confident smile. "I'm ready for the challenge."

"Challenge accepted!" Jenna declared, sipping her drink and leaning against the counter. "Just remember, if you break her heart again, I'll unleash the wrath of a thousand teenage rom-coms on you."

Michael laughed, the tension momentarily dissipating in the warmth of friendship. "Noted. I'll be on my best behavior, I promise."

As I watched the banter unfold, I couldn't help but feel a flicker of hope rising within me, battling against the shadows that had clouded my heart. Maybe this was a turning point, a moment where the past could become a foundation for something new. Maybe I could allow myself to step into the light again, to embrace the uncertainty and the beauty of what could be. But as the words lingered in the air, I knew the journey wouldn't be easy, and the path ahead was still shrouded in the fog of the unknown.

The café buzzed with life as Jenna's laughter filled the air, but my heart raced with uncertainty. Michael leaned against the counter, his smile warm yet tentative, while Jenna launched into her tales of recent misadventures—an awkward date involving a wrong turn into a retirement home, a mishap that had us all in stitches. For a moment, the weight of my worries lifted, and I found solace in the familiarity of laughter, the joy of friendship pushing back against the shadows that loomed large in my mind.

"Honestly, who knew old men could throw such impressive parties?" Jenna declared, her eyes sparkling. "They had a dance-off, and let me tell you, those walkers can really glide!"

"Maybe they were secretly training for the senior Olympics," Michael joked, a glint of mischief in his eyes. "You know, when they get tired of bingo, they switch to the cha-cha."

Their playful banter danced around me, but beneath the surface, I felt the unshakeable tension between Michael and me, a current running just below our laughter. I couldn't deny the spark that still flickered between us, an undeniable pull that tethered me to the past while I desperately sought a way to move forward. But how could I reconcile the remnants of our shared history with the reality of my guarded heart?

Just as I opened my mouth to speak, to perhaps lay down some of my fears and doubts, a commotion erupted near the café entrance. The bell jingled frantically as the door swung open, and a gust of wind burst into the warm space, carrying with it a figure wrapped in a long coat, their face obscured by a hood. The energy shifted; conversations halted, and all eyes turned toward the newcomer, a palpable tension filling the air.

"Who is that?" I whispered to Jenna, my curiosity piqued. "They look like they just stepped out of a mystery novel."

"I'd say they're here for some dramatic reveal," she replied, her gaze fixated on the stranger. "Or maybe a villain audition for a low-budget horror film."

The figure stepped closer, revealing an angular face framed by dark hair. The hood slipped back to expose piercing blue eyes that scanned the room, locking onto mine with a weight that felt almost tangible. My heart stuttered in my chest as recognition washed over me. It was Evan, Michael's older brother, who had long been a shadow in the background of our lives. Rumors swirled around him like a storm cloud—whispers of trouble and secrets that sent shivers down my spine.

"Evan?" Michael said, his voice a mix of surprise and apprehension. "What are you doing here?"

Evan's gaze flickered between us, a half-smirk forming on his lips that didn't reach his eyes. "I heard there was a family reunion in progress. Figured I'd crash the party."

Jenna raised an eyebrow, clearly sensing the undercurrent of tension. "Well, welcome, I guess. Just in time for the thrilling conclusion of our café sitcom. Care for a seat, or are you planning to steal some pastries and vanish into the night?"

"I'm here for more than pastries," Evan replied, his tone suddenly serious. He leaned closer, lowering his voice, as if the walls themselves had ears. "I need to talk to you, Michael. It's important."

The shift in the atmosphere was electric, the air thickening with unspoken words and anxious glances. Michael straightened, the playful banter evaporating as concern etched itself onto his face. "What's going on? You look—"

"Like I've seen better days? Yeah, I get that a lot." Evan interrupted, casting a wary glance around the café. "But we need to discuss something—something that can't wait. I'm not here to stir up drama, but this is serious."

My heart raced as I exchanged glances with Jenna, her eyes wide with curiosity and concern. Whatever was happening, it felt monumental, like a dam ready to break. Michael shifted uncomfortably, and I could see the internal battle waging behind his determined facade. I could almost hear the thoughts racing through his mind: Should he push Evan away, or should he listen to what his brother had to say?

"Can't we talk about this later?" Michael replied, his voice strained. "We're in the middle of something here."

"Trust me, this can't wait," Evan insisted, his expression now hardening. "I've got information—about the company, about our father. Things you need to know. You'll want to hear this."

The café hummed with the buzz of anticipation as I shifted uncomfortably in my seat, caught in a whirlwind of emotions. Part of me was desperate to escape the scene, to flee from the heaviness that threatened to suffocate me. But another part—a deep, instinctual part—felt drawn to the unfolding drama. This was a world I had once known so intimately, filled with the kind of secrets that could shatter lives.

"Fine. Let's step outside," Michael said, his voice laced with resignation. He looked back at me, uncertainty flickering in his eyes. "Stay here. I'll be back."

"Yeah, because that's worked out so well in the past," I muttered under my breath, but my sarcasm fell flat as I watched them walk toward the door, Evan's presence casting a long shadow over the café.

As they disappeared outside, Jenna turned to me, her expression shifting from playful to serious. "What do you think is going on?"

"I wish I knew," I admitted, running a hand through my hair in frustration. "I can't shake this feeling that whatever it is, it's going to change everything."

"Then we should eavesdrop." Jenna's eyes sparkled with mischief, and I couldn't help but chuckle at her enthusiasm.

"Jenna, no," I protested half-heartedly, but she was already slipping out of her seat, a determined look on her face.

"Come on, we'll just lean against the wall and pretend we're looking at the menu. It's not like they're discussing the weather!" she replied, dragging me along with her.

We inched toward the door, pressing ourselves against the wall just outside the café, straining to catch snippets of the conversation. The wind whipped around us, and the air felt charged with anticipation, each word spoken between Michael and Evan sending shivers down my spine.

"I need you to listen," Evan was saying, his voice low but urgent. "It's about the business, about everything that's happening. You're not going to believe me, but we're in serious trouble."

"Why should I trust you?" Michael snapped back, his voice sharp. "You disappeared when we needed you most. You can't just waltz back in here and expect me to fall in line."

"I didn't choose to disappear! I was trying to protect you," Evan retorted, the tension in his voice thickening the air. "Things are more dangerous than you realize. If you don't take this seriously, it could cost you everything."

I glanced at Jenna, her eyes wide, mirroring my own shock. The stakes were higher than I had anticipated, and the weight of their words pressed down on me like a suffocating blanket. My mind raced with possibilities. What trouble could Evan be referring to? And what did it mean for Michael—and for me?

"Maybe I don't need your protection anymore," Michael replied, his voice firm. "Maybe I can handle my own life."

Evan sighed, the sound heavy with frustration. "This isn't just about you. It's about the family. It's about what they're planning, and it's worse than you think."

My heart pounded in my chest, and just as I opened my mouth to say something, anything, to break the tension, a loud crash echoed through the air, reverberating off the walls of the café. Jenna and I shared a panicked glance, the world around us blurring into chaos.

"What was that?" I gasped, adrenaline surging through me.

"Let's find out," she said, her expression resolute.

Before I could protest, she pulled me toward the door just as a crowd began to gather outside, murmurs of confusion and alarm rising. I could see Michael and Evan, their expressions etched with shock, staring at something beyond my view. My heart raced as I braced myself for whatever revelation awaited, but a shiver of dread crept through me.

Then, a voice sliced through the din, sharp and commanding. "Everyone, step back!" It was a stranger's voice, but something about it felt menacing, a dark omen that promised upheaval.

As I pushed my way through the crowd, the scene unfolded before me, and the reality of what lay ahead hit me like a freight train. A figure stood in the street, cloaked in shadow, and in that moment, I realized that the chaos was just beginning. The shadows that had clung to my life were about to engulf me once more, and I was left standing at the precipice, unsure of which way to turn.

Chapter 24: A Glimmer of Hope

The air was thick with the scent of pine and damp earth, a fragrant reminder that autumn had draped its colorful cloak over Cedar Ridge. I navigated the winding trails of our town's expansive park, my heart a percussion instrument against my ribs, each beat echoing my uncertainty. Leaves crunched underfoot, crisp and brittle, creating a symphony that felt almost mocking in its lightness. Here I was, wrestling with the weight of my own doubts, while nature flaunted its beauty as if to say, "Look at me! Everything has its season."

It was hard to ignore the tension coiling in my chest. I had thought the narrative of Emily's life would unfold like one of those heartwarming stories in movies—complete with grand gestures and tearful reconciliations. Instead, it felt like a soap opera caught in an endless loop of misunderstandings and heartbreak. I was determined to rewrite this tale, to drag Emily from the depths of despair, yet with each passing day, the task felt more Herculean. The weight of her pain had become an uninvited guest in our lives, hovering like a shadow.

I paused at the edge of a small pond, the surface shimmering with reflections of the fiery foliage above. A family of ducks paddled lazily by, oblivious to the storm brewing in my heart. Their carefree existence taunted me. "What are you doing, Lily?" I muttered under my breath, scolding myself for wallowing in self-pity. I had spent enough time feeling helpless; now it was time to act.

The news of Michael's attempts at reconciliation hit me like a bolt from the blue. Our mutual friend, Jess, had mentioned it in passing during a study session, her eyes twinkling with the kind of hope that felt foreign to me. "He's trying to talk to her, you know," she had said, almost conspiratorially, her voice low and inviting. "He really wants to make things right." Those words lingered in my mind, swirling like the leaves caught in a playful breeze.

I knew Emily. She was stubborn, fierce, and as beautiful as the sunset that now painted the sky in brilliant oranges and purples. But her heart was fragile, wrapped in layers of hurt and disappointment. Michael had wounded her deeply, and while I believed in second chances, I also understood that forgiveness was a labyrinthine journey, fraught with missteps and hesitations.

Deciding to confront the truth, I made my way to her favorite café, a quaint little spot called The Willow Nook. The bell above the door chimed softly as I stepped inside, the aroma of freshly brewed coffee wrapping around me like a warm hug. The walls were adorned with local art, each piece telling a story that felt intimately connected to our town. I scanned the cozy space, searching for Emily's familiar silhouette, and soon spotted her nestled in a corner, her fingers wrapped tightly around a steaming mug.

"Hey," I greeted, sliding into the seat across from her. Her eyes flickered up, shadows lingering in their depths, and I felt a twinge of sorrow for my friend.

"Lily," she replied, her voice a mixture of warmth and wariness. "What brings you here?"

I leaned forward, the gravity of my words pressing against my chest. "I heard something today. About Michael."

The change in her demeanor was palpable. She stiffened, her expression closing like a flower at dusk. "I don't want to talk about him," she replied curtly, her tone icy.

"Just hear me out," I urged, my voice a gentle plea. "I think he's trying to make amends. Jess mentioned he wants to talk to you, to find a way back." I watched her face for any sign of hope, any flicker of interest.

She scoffed, a sound that resonated with disbelief. "And why would I want to do that? He hurt me, Lily. Deeply." Her eyes shone with unshed tears, and I felt the walls around her heart grow thicker.

I took a deep breath, weighing my words carefully. "I know he did. But maybe... maybe there's a path to forgiveness. You deserve to feel whole again, Em. Holding onto this pain is only going to hurt you more."

Emily's gaze softened for a moment, a vulnerability surfacing that tugged at my heartstrings. "It's not that simple. What if I can't forgive him? What if it only brings more hurt?"

"Then you'll have clarity," I countered, feeling the words surge within me like a dam breaking. "You'll know that you tried. Sometimes the act of forgiving isn't about the other person; it's about freeing yourself from the weight of resentment. And I promise you, you won't be alone in this."

Her brow furrowed as she considered my words, the battle between her heart and her mind raging visibly across her features. The sunlight streamed through the window, casting golden hues around us, illuminating the unspoken hope that flickered in the air like the glow of a candle.

"Do you really think it's possible?" she asked, her voice barely above a whisper.

"I do," I replied firmly, letting my conviction wrap around us like a protective blanket. "But it starts with you. You have to decide what you truly want, Emily."

The silence stretched between us, filled with the sound of clinking cups and soft chatter. I could see her wheels turning, her heart wrestling with the chains that bound it. In that moment, I realized that perhaps the glimmer of hope I had felt was not just for Emily and Michael, but also for myself. I, too, had been holding onto my fears—fear of losing her, fear of stepping into uncharted territory. But maybe this was our chance to break free, together.

Emily's expression shifted, her eyes glistening with unshed tears, but this time they weren't tears of despair; they were tears of contemplation, a testament to the complexity of human emotions.

The afternoon sun began its descent, casting long shadows that danced among the trees lining the café's patio. The golden light filtered through the leaves, painting the ground in a mosaic of light and shadow, as if nature itself conspired to create the perfect backdrop for a pivotal moment. Emily stirred her coffee, watching the liquid swirl, and I could see the gears of her mind turning, a tumult of thoughts battling for attention.

"Forgiveness, huh?" she said finally, a hint of sarcasm coloring her tone. "That's rich coming from you. The queen of holding grudges." A playful smirk tugged at her lips, but I could tell it was a fragile mask over her deeper feelings.

I chuckled, raising an eyebrow. "True, I can be a little dramatic. But maybe I've learned a thing or two from all that angst. Besides, it's easy to clutch onto anger like a favorite sweater. It feels comfortable, but it's scratchy, and eventually, it makes you miserable. So why not try a softer fabric for a change?"

Emily rolled her eyes, but the corners of her mouth twitched upward, betraying her amusement. "A fashion metaphor for forgiveness? Really, Lily?"

"Why not? Life is a tapestry, and we all need a bit of color," I replied, leaning back in my chair, enjoying this small reprieve from the heavy conversation. But I could feel the tension still lurking, an unseen weight that pressed against our shared laughter.

"You think I should just throw on the bright colors and forget about everything?" Her voice lowered, revealing a glimpse of her vulnerability. "What if I can't get past the dark threads?"

"There's beauty in every thread, even the dark ones," I said, my heart racing. "They make the light ones pop. Maybe it's not about forgetting but about weaving those experiences into something stronger, something uniquely yours."

She stared at me, her expression softening as if she were reconsidering everything. "You make it sound so simple."

"It's not," I said, my own voice turning serious. "It's like climbing a mountain. Each step is a struggle, and sometimes you slip and fall, but if you keep going, the view from the top is worth every scraped knee."

A silence settled between us, punctuated only by the distant chatter of other patrons and the clinking of cups. I knew she was weighing my words, and a part of me was terrified she might not see the value in them. Just as I was about to break the quiet, her phone buzzed on the table, pulling her attention away. The moment passed, and I felt a pang of frustration at the interruption.

She picked it up, her face draining of color as she read whatever was on the screen. "It's him," she said, her voice barely a whisper. "Michael wants to meet."

I leaned in, my heart thumping in my chest. "What do you want to do?"

Emily's fingers curled around the edge of the table, her knuckles white. "I don't know. Part of me wants to scream at him. Part of me wants to run away."

I nodded, feeling the weight of her dilemma. "You could always tell him you're too busy with, I don't know, a documentary on the mating habits of sloths."

A ghost of a smile appeared, but the tension remained. "You know I'm not going to do that."

"Okay, so what's the plan, brave soul? You could go, let him apologize, and see if there's a chance to clear the air," I suggested, my voice firm but encouraging.

"What if I crumble? What if he says something that just... I don't know, unravels me?"

"You won't crumble. You're stronger than you give yourself credit for," I reassured her. "And if he does unravel you, I'll be right here, ready to stitch you back together."

She took a deep breath, and for a fleeting moment, I saw the glimmer of her old self return—the Emily who faced challenges head-on and laughed in the face of fear. "Maybe I should," she finally said, determination creeping into her voice. "But I need backup."

"Always," I replied, my heart swelling with pride. "Just text me when you need me. I'll be your personal cheerleader from the sidelines. I can even bring pom-poms!"

Emily chuckled, the sound brightening the dim corners of our conversation. "I can't believe you just suggested pom-poms."

"Hey, every good confrontation needs flair!" I grinned, and for a moment, the heaviness lifted, allowing the light to seep in.

As we left the café, the golden hour wrapped around us like a comforting shawl. The world felt ripe with possibility, each step we took echoing with renewed hope. Emily's phone buzzed again, and this time, it was a message from Michael. The sunlight caught her profile, illuminating her features, and I couldn't help but admire her strength, the way she carried her burdens even while battling her fears.

"Are you ready for this?" I asked, falling into step beside her as we wandered down the tree-lined street.

"Not even a little," she admitted, her voice steady despite the flicker of anxiety in her eyes. "But if I don't try, I'll never know."

"You're right. And remember, this is your story. You get to decide how it unfolds."

As we approached the park where they'd agreed to meet, the atmosphere shifted. The air felt electric, charged with the weight of unspoken words and unresolved emotions. I could sense her heart racing as we neared the bench where Michael would be waiting. The trees stood sentinel around us, their leaves whispering secrets as if they knew the turmoil ahead.

Emily stopped just short of the clearing. "Lily, what if it doesn't go the way I hope?"

"Then we regroup, reevaluate, and maybe go get ice cream. Because who doesn't love ice cream?" I said, attempting to lighten the mood with a wry smile.

"That's a solid plan," she replied, the corners of her lips twitching. "So, just remember, ice cream's on the line here."

With a nod of determination, she took a deep breath, steeling herself for the impending conversation. I could feel the gravity of the moment—this was her turning point, the precipice from which she would leap into either the unknown or the arms of hope. As she stepped forward, I felt my own heart echo her rhythm, pounding with a blend of anxiety and excitement, ready to support her whatever the outcome.

Emily stepped into the clearing, and the world around us blurred as I focused solely on her. The park's familiar sights faded into the background—the rustle of leaves, the distant laughter of children, the echo of footsteps on the gravel path. Michael was already there, leaning casually against a tree, his expression a mix of anticipation and uncertainty.

"Do you see that?" I whispered, my eyes darting toward the tall oak that framed the scene. "He looks like he's trying to pull off the brooding artist look, but it's just... awkward."

Emily snorted, a sound that was both endearing and relieving. "I guess I should give him credit for trying."

As she walked forward, I felt a knot of anxiety settle in my stomach. This was the moment—her moment. I couldn't shake the feeling that whatever happened next would ripple through our lives, shaping the days ahead in ways we couldn't yet foresee. She slowed her pace, glancing back at me with wide eyes that flickered with a mix of determination and sheer terror.

"Go on. I'll be right here," I reassured her, trying to sound more confident than I felt.

With a nod, she squared her shoulders and approached Michael, each step heavy with the weight of unspoken words. I took a few steps back, positioning myself so that I could still see them without intruding. The distance felt necessary, like a protective barrier against the emotional fallout that was bound to follow.

"Hey," she said, her voice wavering slightly.

"Hey," Michael replied, his smile faltering as he took in her tense posture. "Thanks for meeting me."

A tense silence lingered between them, stretching like the elastic band of a slingshot. I could almost hear the internal dialogue—her heart screaming for the chance to forgive while her mind wrestled with the scars left behind.

"I didn't think you'd want to," Emily finally said, her words breaking the silence.

Michael raked a hand through his hair, a nervous gesture that tugged at my heartstrings. "I wasn't sure you would either. But I've been doing a lot of thinking, and I really want to talk about what happened... about us."

His eyes, usually so full of confidence, now glimmered with vulnerability, and I felt my breath catch. What could he possibly say that would make this right?

"You mean the mess you made of everything?" she shot back, her tone sharp. I could almost see the steel in her spine reinforcing itself.

He nodded, swallowing hard. "Yes, exactly. I've been a complete idiot, and I don't expect you to forgive me right away. But I want you to know that I'm trying. I've been talking to Jess, trying to figure out how to make things right."

"Jess?" she echoed, incredulity painting her features. "You think talking to Jess gives you a free pass? She's not your therapist, Michael."

He looked down, a flicker of shame crossing his face. "I know, but she told me I needed to face you and stop hiding. I didn't realize how much I'd hurt you until it was too late."

Emily crossed her arms, her posture mirroring the walls she had built around her heart. "You know, it's a little late for epiphanies."

"I know it is," he admitted, his voice breaking slightly. "But I'm here now. Please, let me explain. I've been an idiot, but I want to change."

"You're asking me to believe that you can change?" Emily's voice trembled, a blend of hurt and disbelief.

"Not just for you—my whole life needs to change. I've realized I've been running from everything that matters, and I don't want to run anymore."

His sincerity wrapped around me like a fragile thread, and I found myself rooting for him, hoping that he could be the person Emily needed. But the doubt etched on her face showed she was less convinced.

"I can't just forget everything, Michael. You've left me in the wreckage of your choices," she said, her voice trembling with emotion.

"But I want to help you rebuild. I can't promise it'll be easy, but I'm willing to fight for you." His eyes locked onto hers, a desperate plea for understanding that made my heart race.

Emily hesitated, the internal struggle playing out on her face. "And what if I don't want you to fight for me? What if I want to forget?"

"You don't really mean that," he urged gently, his voice steady despite the tremor of uncertainty. "Deep down, you know you want something more than this pain."

Her lips pressed into a thin line, a fortress built on years of hurt and disappointment. "What if I can't go back? What if the pieces don't fit anymore?"

"Then let's find new pieces. Together." The vulnerability in his voice caught my breath in my throat, and I felt the air thicken with the weight of their shared history.

Silence enveloped them again, and I strained to hear her reply. Just as Emily opened her mouth, the moment shattered. A sudden rustle from the bushes nearby caused both of them to jump, and I instinctively ducked behind a large rock, my heart racing.

"Did you hear that?" Michael asked, glancing around.

"Yeah," Emily replied, her brows knitting together in confusion and concern. "It sounded like someone—or something—was watching us."

My stomach dropped. What if someone was lurking in the shadows? I peered around the rock, desperate for a glimpse of whatever had interrupted this pivotal moment.

Suddenly, a figure burst from the underbrush, and I stifled a gasp. It was Ryan, his face pale and eyes wide with urgency. "Lily! Emily! You need to come quick!"

"What is it?" I called out, my voice shaking as I joined them, leaving the relative safety of my hiding place.

"There's trouble at the old mill. We need to go. Now."

The weight of Ryan's words hit us like a cold wave, crashing over the fragile moment between Emily and Michael. Their argument faded, replaced by a sense of impending chaos.

"What do you mean, trouble?" Emily asked, her previous conflict forgotten, replaced by concern for her friends.

Ryan swallowed hard, glancing around as if to ensure no one else was nearby. "I can't explain right now. Just trust me—there's something out there. Something dangerous."

Michael stepped forward, his expression shifting from remorseful to alarmed. "I'll go with you."

"No!" Ryan's voice cut through the tension. "It's too risky. You don't know what you're getting into."

Emily's eyes darted between the two, a mixture of fear and determination swirling within her. "What are we talking about? Just tell us!"

Ryan's face hardened, his next words tumbling out like stones, heavy with urgency. "People are disappearing from the town, and I think it's connected to the old mill. We need to investigate before it's too late."

A chill raced down my spine as I glanced at Emily, her expression mirroring my fear. The danger was real, and this wasn't just about reconciling past hurts anymore. It was about survival.

"Let's go," Emily said, her voice a newfound spark of determination. "We'll deal with this first."

And just like that, the fragile moment was gone, replaced by the daunting unknown. As we raced away from the clearing, I couldn't shake the feeling that whatever awaited us would alter everything once again, plunging us deeper into the darkness of our tangled lives.

Chapter 25: A Risky Proposition

The café was a cozy little nook with a faded blue awning and mismatched chairs that seemed to whisper stories of countless heart-to-heart conversations and laughter that once spilled out onto the cobblestone street. The scent of freshly brewed coffee mingled with the sweet aroma of pastries, creating a warm embrace that almost masked the tension brewing between us. I picked at the edges of my napkin, feeling the rough texture beneath my fingers, a futile attempt to distract myself from the gravity of our upcoming conversation.

Michael sat across from me, his brow furrowed as he absently stirred his coffee, the spoon clinking against the ceramic mug like a metronome counting down the seconds to an inevitable confrontation. I couldn't help but notice the shadows lurking beneath his eyes, a reflection of the doubts that danced between us like a pair of sparring partners. His dark hair, usually tousled in that effortlessly charming way, seemed to carry a weight today, as if each strand was a burden he wasn't ready to share.

"I think it's time we talk about Emily," I said, forcing the words out as if they were thickened honey, slow and sweet but heavy on my tongue.

His gaze snapped up, a flicker of surprise followed by a cautious acknowledgment. "You think we can just sit here and have a civilized discussion about her?" he asked, a hint of sarcasm threading through his voice. "As if she's not the elephant in the room with a glittering crown on her head?"

I smiled, grateful for the lightness he tried to inject into the moment, even if it felt more like a smoke signal than an actual flame of hope. "Well, it's better than letting her take up all the space between us without so much as a word." My heart raced; I had never been good at this—navigating emotions and hidden tensions was like trying to dance on a tightrope strung between two skyscrapers. One misstep, and I could plummet into chaos.

He chuckled softly, though it lacked genuine amusement. "True. It's just—she's... complicated. More complicated than a crossword puzzle on a Monday morning." He leaned back, crossing his arms as if bracing himself for the incoming storm.

"I know," I said, my voice softening. "But we can't keep avoiding her. Ignoring the problem isn't going to make it disappear. It's only going to grow, like that one weed in the garden you pretend isn't there until it's taken over everything."

Michael's eyes flickered with acknowledgment, the corners of his lips lifting slightly. "You have a way of turning everything into a gardening metaphor. If only we could just pull her out of our lives like a stubborn weed."

"Believe me, if it were that easy, I'd have done it by now." I sighed, taking a sip of my coffee, the heat curling around my fingers. "But Emily is more than a weed; she's a wildfire. We need a plan to handle her before everything goes up in flames."

"Okay, Miss Fire Chief," he said, raising an eyebrow in playful challenge. "What's your brilliant plan, then?"

I leaned in closer, my voice dropping to a conspiratorial whisper. "We invite her here. We lay everything out on the table—no secrets, no games. Just honesty. If we don't confront this now, it'll eat away at us until we're hollow."

Michael studied me, and for a moment, I could see the gears turning behind his eyes, weighing my words against the possibility of disaster. "You really think that'll work?"

"It's our best shot," I insisted, my heart pounding in sync with the ticking clock on the wall. "I'd rather take the risk than sit here wondering what could have happened. We owe it to ourselves—and to her."

After a long pause, he sighed, the tension easing slightly from his shoulders. "Alright. We'll do it. But if she starts throwing fireballs, you're taking the first hit."

I couldn't help but laugh, the sound bubbling up and lightening the atmosphere. "Deal. But you'd better be ready to catch the flames if it gets too hot."

With a plan in motion, I texted Emily, the message sitting in the air like an uninvited guest, waiting for her response. As I stared at my phone, the butterflies in my stomach began to flutter violently. I'd faced many challenges, but confronting Emily—her sharp tongue, her piercing gaze, and her ability to twist words like a magician with a deck of cards—was perhaps the scariest of all.

We chose to meet in the early evening, when the sun dipped low and the café glowed like a lantern against the deepening twilight. The anticipation of her arrival knotted my stomach, each minute stretching longer than the last. I watched as the door swung open, and my breath caught in my throat.

Emily stepped inside, a whirlwind of vibrant energy wrapped in a bright scarf that fluttered behind her like a flag declaring war. She scanned the room, and when her gaze landed on us, a flicker of recognition danced across her features, swiftly replaced by something more guarded.

"Surprise," I managed to say, forcing a smile that felt more like a grimace.

"Surprise, indeed," she replied, her tone dripping with a blend of sarcasm and curiosity. "What's the occasion? A reconciliation or an intervention?"

"Why not both?" Michael quipped, a teasing smile on his lips.

She crossed her arms, her posture radiating defiance. "I'd rather not be part of either, thank you very much."

The tension coiled tighter, like a spring about to snap. But beneath her bravado, I sensed a flicker of vulnerability. Whatever walls she had built around herself, I was determined to breach them, one brick at a time.

"We just want to talk," I said, keeping my voice steady. "We're tired of avoiding each other. It's time we face the truth, whatever that may be."

Emily's eyes narrowed, a hint of curiosity mingling with her suspicion. "And what truth is that? That you two are on the same side now, united against me?"

"No," Michael replied, his voice calm yet firm. "It's about figuring out how we can move forward. Together."

Her expression shifted, the sharp edges softening just a fraction. I hoped that beneath the bravado, beneath the wildfires and the thorns, there was a chance for healing—a chance for us all to find common ground in the tangled mess we had created.

As we sat there, the air heavy with unspoken words, I realized that this was the moment that could either bind us together or unravel everything. And somewhere in the depths of my heart, I believed we could find a way through the flames.

Emily perched on the edge of her seat, her fingers drumming a chaotic rhythm against the table, creating an almost musical backdrop to the heavy silence. It was as if she could summon a storm with just the right beat, and I couldn't tell if the electricity in the air was due to the unresolved tension or the impending downpour outside. The sky had darkened, casting a dim light over the café, and the soft patter of rain began to punctuate our awkward gathering.

"I didn't expect you two to turn this into some kind of support group," she said, arching an eyebrow. "You know, 'Feelings Anonymous: Come for the Coffee, Stay for the Drama.'"

Michael chuckled, and I shot him a warning glance, hoping he wouldn't venture too far into humor when we were barely treading water. "We're not here to roast marshmallows over our emotional campfire," he replied, his voice light but careful. "We really just want to talk."

Emily leaned back, crossing her arms defensively. "And you think this is going to solve everything? Just sit around with lattes and air out our dirty laundry?"

"Maybe not everything," I jumped in, trying to lighten the mood without veering into sarcasm. "But it's a start. We can't keep pretending that things are fine. That's a surefire way to make them worse."

Her lips curved into a bemused smile, the kind that said she was amused yet skeptical. "I'm all for honesty, but honesty has a funny way of turning into a bloodbath. Are you sure you two are ready for that?"

"Wouldn't be the first time," Michael quipped, and for a moment, I saw a flicker of something in Emily's eyes—perhaps it was the ghost of shared laughter, buried beneath layers of misunderstandings and hurt.

"Look," I said, my voice steadying. "I know we've all had our issues, but we're here because we care. I want to understand what's been happening between us."

"Caring is a slippery slope," Emily replied, leaning forward, her gaze piercing. "One minute you're sharing secrets, and the next you're dragging each other through the mud."

"Then let's get muddy," Michael said, feigning bravado. "Better to trudge through it together than pretend we're all squeaky clean."

Emily laughed, the sound rich and surprising. "You have a way of making everything sound so simple, don't you? Like life is just a picnic in the park."

"If only," I said, shaking my head with a smile. "But seriously, this isn't about perfect resolutions. It's about peeling back the layers, even if it's messy. So, let's just lay it all out."

She hesitated, the flicker of vulnerability crossing her face. "Alright, but remember, you asked for it."

With a deep breath, Emily dove in. "Let's start with the obvious: I know you two have been whispering behind my back. I could practically hear the murmurs." Her voice was steady, but the crack in it was unmistakable.

"Whispering? We were more like frantic note-passing in class," I shot back, trying to infuse some levity. "But seriously, it's not about you; it's about us trying to figure out how to be honest with each other."

"I get that," she replied, a mixture of frustration and understanding simmering in her voice. "But do you really think it's that easy? One conversation and we all hold hands and sing Kumbaya?"

"Better than letting the resentment fester," Michael added, leaning forward, his elbows resting on the table, intent. "We're all adults here, right? We can handle a little discomfort."

The corners of Emily's mouth twitched, torn between amusement and exasperation. "Ah, yes. The fine art of adulting—because it's so effortless."

"Hey, we're all just winging it," I said, my tone half-serious. "If we can make it through high school, we can tackle whatever this is."

Emily shook her head, a hint of a smile breaking through her serious façade. "You really believe that, don't you? That if you just throw a little confidence at a problem, it'll magically disappear?"

"Well, that and a sprinkle of determination," I replied, grinning. "And coffee. Always coffee."

"Right, because caffeine solves everything," she shot back, her playful sarcasm cutting through the tension.

With her walls beginning to soften, I pressed on. "So, let's address the elephant in the room—what happened after the party? The moment when everything shifted."

She sighed, the lightheartedness fading slightly as her eyes turned serious. "It was like watching a movie where you know the ending is going to break your heart. One moment, everything felt fine, and then—" She paused, her voice catching. "Then it all just spiraled."

I nodded, wanting her to keep going. "And how did that make you feel?"

"Like I was losing my mind," she admitted, her voice raw but steady. "I felt isolated, like I was watching you two from the outside, and you were both moving on without me."

"That wasn't our intention," I said gently, hoping to bridge the gap. "We were just trying to navigate things the best way we knew how."

"By excluding me?" she challenged, the fire returning to her gaze.

"It was never about excluding you," Michael interjected, his tone earnest. "It was about figuring things out in our own heads first. We didn't want to drag you into our confusion."

"Funny how that didn't work out, huh?" she retorted, her expression a mix of hurt and understanding.

"Right," I agreed. "But we're here now, and I think we can work through this. We've all made mistakes, but there's no point in keeping score."

Emily's expression softened, the wall of defensiveness crumbling just a bit. "You really think we can fix this?"

"I don't just think it; I know it," I replied, feeling a surge of determination. "But it's going to take all of us being honest—like, truly honest."

"Okay, then," she said, a newfound resolve in her tone. "Let's hear it. I'm all ears."

The rain outside began to drum more insistently against the windows, creating a rhythm that echoed the rising tension of our conversation. The atmosphere buzzed with the electricity of what was left unspoken, and as I looked into Emily's eyes, I could see the flickering embers of hope struggling to ignite.

"Fine," I said, taking a deep breath. "Let's start with why I've felt so lost since everything happened. It's not just about you or Michael; it's about me feeling like I'm losing both of you."

"Yeah, well, newsflash: you're not the only one," Emily countered, but her tone was less combative, almost vulnerable.

Michael stepped in, a calm presence amidst the storm. "Then let's make a pact. No more sidestepping. If we can't be honest with each other, what's the point?"

Emily nodded slowly, her expression earnest. "Alright. Honesty it is. Let's rip off the Band-Aid."

As we sat in the dim café, surrounded by the soft glow of flickering lights and the sweet scent of pastries, we were no longer just three friends on the precipice of destruction. We were three souls trying to find their way back to one another, ready to confront whatever truth awaited us, armed only with the promise of honesty and the hope of redemption.

As the tension in the café thickened, I felt a palpable shift in the air, like the moment before a storm breaks. The rain outside had intensified, transforming the gentle patter into a symphony of chaos, each droplet a reminder of the emotions swirling around us. Emily, her arms crossed, leaned back in her chair, studying us with an intensity that felt like a spotlight.

"Let's do this," she said finally, her voice steady but laced with an undercurrent of vulnerability. "Let's lay everything out. No more dancing around the truth."

Michael nodded, and I caught the glimmer of resolve in his eyes. It was as if we were stepping onto a tightrope, each of us holding the other accountable, balancing precariously between honesty and heartache.

"Alright," I said, my heart pounding against my ribs. "I'll go first. I've been feeling... lost. Like I'm caught between the two of you, and I don't know how to navigate it anymore. It's like I'm in a maze with no exit."

"Welcome to the club," Emily interjected, her voice a mix of sarcasm and sincerity. "I've felt like a juggler with too many flaming torches. Just when I think I've got one handled, another one comes crashing down."

Michael shifted in his seat, his brows furrowing as he searched for the right words. "I get that. And honestly, I didn't want to add more chaos to your lives. I thought distancing myself might help, but it only made things worse."

"Distancing? You mean running away," Emily shot back, her tone playful but edged with truth. "You can't hide from a fire by moving to another room. It just ignites somewhere else."

I couldn't help but chuckle, the absurdity of our situation cutting through the thick tension. "Well, look at us—three fire marshals sitting here, trying to extinguish our own emotional inferno. Who knew we'd need a plan to rescue each other?"

Emily grinned, her earlier tension softening into something more approachable. "If we're going to tackle this, we might as well have a fireman's pole for quick escapes when things get too hot."

"And possibly a water hose?" Michael added, a playful spark igniting in his eyes.

"A hose, a ladder, and maybe a trampoline," I quipped, feeling lighter as our shared laughter bridged the chasm of misunderstanding. "But in all seriousness, I'm glad we're talking. It feels like we're finally chipping away at the walls we've built."

"True," Emily conceded, her expression growing serious again. "But we can't just brush over the past. I need to know why you pulled away from me, Michael. I felt abandoned."

He winced, the words cutting deep, and I could see the internal struggle playing out in his eyes. "I thought I was doing the right thing. I didn't want to hurt you more than I already had. It felt safer to step back."

"Safer?" Emily echoed, incredulous. "Safer for whom? You think shutting me out protected me? All it did was leave me feeling like I was drowning."

"I see that now," he admitted, his voice barely above a whisper. "But I thought I was doing you a favor. It was easier to pretend everything was fine."

"Easier for you," I interjected gently, wanting to steer the conversation into healing territory rather than letting it spiral into blame. "It's clear we all have some unpacking to do."

Emily nodded, her resolve returning. "Then let's lay it all out. The good, the bad, and the ridiculously awkward. No holds barred."

"Okay, then," Michael said, his voice gathering strength. "Let's talk about the night everything fell apart. We were all there, but somehow we missed each other. I still don't understand how things went so wrong."

I felt the air shift, the weight of that night pressing down on us like a physical presence. "I remember feeling blindsided. We were all supposed to be in it together, but then it felt like I was fighting to hold on while you both were slipping away."

Emily sighed, her expression darkening. "That night felt like a bomb going off. One moment, we were laughing, and the next, it was chaos. And it wasn't just the party; it was everything building up to it."

"Exactly," I said, my heart racing as I recalled the atmosphere that night. "We were all on edge. The unresolved tension had been brewing for weeks, and when it erupted, it left us all shattered."

"And instead of picking up the pieces, we just retreated into our corners," Michael added, his voice tinged with regret.

The café buzzed around us, the sounds of clinking cups and quiet chatter fading into the background as we honed in on our shared turmoil. "So how do we fix it?" I asked, my voice steady, though my heart was racing with uncertainty. "How do we navigate this mess we've created?"

"We talk," Emily said, her voice fierce. "We be raw and honest, even if it hurts. We don't back down. This is our chance to clear the air before the smoke chokes us."

"Agreed," I said, emboldened by her determination. "No more skirting around feelings. If we can't be real with each other, we're doomed to repeat the same mistakes."

As the rain continued to pour outside, creating a soothing backdrop, we embarked on a candid exploration of our feelings—confessions spilled forth like the rain cascading down the windows. The weight of unspoken thoughts and emotions lightened as we shared the turmoil that had colored our interactions.

Michael opened up about his fears of losing both of us, the tightrope he had been walking while trying to keep us both close. "I thought I was protecting you, but instead, I pushed you away. I didn't realize how much it hurt until it was too late."

"Right," Emily agreed, her voice softening. "And I spent so much time feeling like an outsider that I didn't even notice the rift growing until it was too late. I was so focused on my own hurt that I didn't think about yours."

"And I felt so lost," I admitted, "that I didn't know how to reach out for help. Instead, I built walls thinking it would keep me safe."

We shared stories, experiences, and regrets, each confession a step toward rebuilding the fragile connections that had frayed. I could feel the tension easing, the darkness giving way to light as we forged a path toward understanding.

But just as it seemed we were on the brink of a breakthrough, the door swung open with a loud clatter, a gust of wind trailing in as a figure stepped into the café. The bell above the door chimed, breaking the intimacy of our moment.

My heart raced as I turned to see who had arrived, a sudden chill washing over me. A familiar face emerged from the shadows, someone I hadn't expected to see.

"What are you doing here?" I asked, my voice thick with disbelief as I recognized the unmistakable features of someone from my past—a ghost I thought had faded into the background of my life.

Emily and Michael exchanged confused glances, their expressions mirroring my shock as the figure moved closer. Whatever fragile peace we had just begun to forge felt like it was on the brink of crumbling, and I could only hope that the reappearance of this unexpected guest wouldn't send us all spiraling back into chaos.

Chapter 26: Unraveling Threads

The café was a cacophony of sound, laughter spilling from every corner as the smell of freshly brewed coffee mingled with the sweet, buttery scent of pastries cooling on the counter. I sat at a small table by the window, my fingers tapping anxiously on the wooden surface, a nervous rhythm that matched the fluttering in my stomach. Outside, the world bustled on, completely unaware of the emotional tempest brewing just a few feet away. I glanced at the door, half-expecting Emily to burst in, her fiery spirit trailing behind her like a comet's tail. When she finally arrived, however, it was like a storm rolling in—a sudden drop in temperature and the palpable crackle of electricity in the air.

Emily swept into the café, her presence commanding attention. Her auburn hair caught the light, shimmering like copper in the morning sun, framing a face that was often lit by mischief but today was shadowed by fury. As she approached, I felt a mix of dread and sympathy. I had never seen her so agitated, her normally bright eyes dark with hurt and betrayal.

"Can we just get this over with?" she snapped, sliding into the chair across from me. The tension between us was a taut string, vibrating with unsaid words. I opened my mouth to speak, to explain, to reach out, but the words lodged in my throat, stifled by the weight of her gaze.

"Emily, I—"

"Don't. Just don't." Her voice was steady but edged with an urgency that sent a shiver down my spine. "You think I don't know what's been going on behind my back? The whispers? The lies? It's like I'm living in a bad soap opera, and you two are the stars."

The accusation hung between us, heavy and suffocating. I could feel the heat rising to my cheeks, a mix of embarrassment and shame. This wasn't how I envisioned our reunion. I had hoped for understanding, for reconciliation, not this raw confrontation that felt like an earthquake beneath my feet.

"Emily, please," I tried again, desperation creeping into my voice. "You're misunderstanding everything. It's not what you think."

"Oh really?" Her laugh was harsh, a brittle sound that shattered my resolve. "Then enlighten me. Because all I see are two people who have decided that I'm not worth being honest with."

The memories flooded back—the late-night conversations with Michael that had spiraled into uncharted territory. How could I explain that the connection I had with him felt like a lifeline, even as it threatened to drown me in guilt? It was complex, messy, and utterly human, yet Emily's hurt was a palpable force that made it impossible to defend myself.

I clenched my fists beneath the table, feeling the heat radiate from my skin as I took a deep breath, forcing myself to maintain some semblance of calm. "I never meant to hurt you, Em. You have to know that. We were just trying to navigate this crazy thing together. It wasn't meant to come between us."

"Navigate? Is that what you call it?" She leaned forward, her voice low and fierce. "You think this is just a matter of navigating feelings like it's some kind of relationship GPS? Because it feels more like betrayal. Like you both thought I wouldn't notice or care."

The café felt like it was shrinking, the other patrons blurring into a background of noise. I wanted to reach across the table, to take her hands in mine and make her see that I hadn't intended to deceive her. But the way she pulled back, arms crossed, spoke volumes about the gulf that had grown between us.

"It was never supposed to be like this," I murmured, almost to myself. "I just wanted us to be okay."

Her expression softened for the briefest moment, the anger giving way to a flicker of sadness. "What do you think I want?" she replied, her voice now tinged with vulnerability. "I wanted us all to be okay. I wanted to trust you both. But now?"

The weight of her words settled around us like a fog, choking out the air. There was a tenderness in her tone, a reminder of the friendship we once had, a connection that felt like home. "Emily," I said, my voice cracking, "I never wanted to put you in this position. You're my best friend. You mean the world to me."

"But it feels like you've chosen him over me."

"I haven't!" My voice rose, surprising even me. "This isn't a choice. It's... it's complicated!" I could see the storm in her eyes, the way it threatened to break loose again.

"Complicated," she echoed, her tone dripping with sarcasm. "That's one way to put it. Or maybe you're just both too cowardly to face what you've done. Do you know how much that hurts?"

The revelation stung. It pierced through the anger and left me raw. The truth was, I didn't fully understand what was happening between Michael and me either. He was a balm to my restless heart, yet every moment spent with him felt like a betrayal to Emily, like I was tearing at the seams of a fabric we had woven together.

"I didn't want to hurt you," I insisted, the words tumbling out in a desperate rush. "I thought I was protecting you. I thought we could find a way through this together."

"Together?" She laughed bitterly, shaking her head. "Together looks a lot different when one person is kept in the dark. You're both keeping secrets from me, and I'm just supposed to sit back and accept it?"

With each accusation, I felt a shard of ice embedding itself deeper into my chest. I wanted to scream that it wasn't just about me or Michael. It was about all of us. But instead, silence stretched between us, taut and unforgiving. I took a moment to gather my thoughts, searching for the right words that might bridge the chasm between our hearts.

"Emily," I began softly, "what if I told you that I was just as lost as you are? That I didn't choose this confusion? I'm trying to figure it all out, and I don't want to lose you."

Her expression softened momentarily, the anger flickering like a candle in the wind. But the hurt was still there, etched into her features. "What's the point if you're going to let him keep you away from me?"

As her words hung in the air, I felt the sharp edges of our friendship fraying, the threads of trust unraveling under the weight of unspoken fears and unresolved feelings. I could sense the walls closing in, not just around Emily but around my own heart. Every secret that spilled into the light felt like a nail in the coffin of our once unshakeable bond, and I knew I had to fight for us, even as I struggled to understand the tangled web of emotions binding us all together.

I watched as Emily pushed her chair back, the sound sharp and jarring in the midst of the café's buzz. She stood up, her posture rigid, as if bracing herself for a battle. I could almost hear the gears in her mind turning, calculating her next move, and it sent a pang of despair through me. I wanted to reach out, to somehow pull her back into our shared history, the laughter, the late-night confidences, but instead, I felt like I was watching her walk away from me, from us, into an uncharted territory filled with anger and misunderstanding.

"Emily, wait!" I called after her, the urgency in my voice causing a few heads to turn. A couple of patrons glanced up from their steaming mugs, their eyes flicking between us like spectators at a tennis match. I hated being the center of attention in moments like this, but there was no avoiding it. This was bigger than my embarrassment; it was about the very foundation of our friendship.

"I'm not waiting around for you to sort out your mess," she snapped, turning on her heel. Her eyes were fierce, a storm brewing behind them. "I can't believe you thought I wouldn't find out. You both acted like I wouldn't care, like I was just some piece of furniture in your little romance."

With every word she uttered, the knot in my stomach twisted tighter. I had never seen her so furious, and it was terrifying. She was usually the one with the quick smile and easy laugh, the girl who made even the dullest moments feel vibrant and alive. Now, she stood before me like a stranger, a warrior ready to defend her heart, and I felt every ounce of the love I had for her battling against the guilt suffocating me.

"It's not like that! It was never supposed to be like this!" I pleaded, desperation leaking into my voice as I stood, following her as she moved towards the door.

"Then how is it?" she shot back, her hands clenched into fists at her sides. "How is it supposed to be? Because from where I'm standing, it looks like you two have made your choices."

"Don't say that! You're my best friend. You have to believe that!" I said, reaching for her arm, but she flinched away, as if I had struck her.

"Believe what? That I'm just supposed to sit back and let this happen?" She glanced around the café, her expression shifting, and for a moment, I thought I saw a flicker of vulnerability. "I've spent so much time trying to support you both. I never asked for this chaos."

The café felt impossibly small, the noise of the patrons fading into the background as the reality of our conversation engulfed us. I took a breath, grounding myself in the moment, and tried to find the right words. "What do you want from me? I never meant to keep anything from you, but I—"

"I want honesty," she interrupted, her voice unwavering. "I want to know where I stand. Am I your friend, or just the girl left behind when the drama kicks in?"

"You are everything to me," I said, my heart racing, the truth bursting from my lips before I could stop it. "This isn't a soap opera,

Emily. I'm not trying to write you out of my life. I'm just... I'm trying to figure out how to make sense of all this."

"Figure out what?" she challenged, her gaze fierce. "How to play both sides? Because if that's the case, I can't be part of it. I deserve better than to be a pawn in your romantic games."

The accusation cut deeper than any knife, and the shame washed over me like a tide, pulling me under. My hands trembled slightly, and I could feel the weight of the café's attention on us, the hushed whispers swirling around like a cyclone of judgment. "This is not a game to me, Emily. You mean too much."

She paused, a flash of something softer crossing her face before the wall came crashing down again. "Then show me," she said, her voice barely above a whisper. "Show me that I matter more than whatever this... whatever this mess is."

"I can't lose you, not like this," I replied, the desperation spilling from my heart as I reached out again, this time with my words. "I never wanted to hurt you. Michael and I... it just happened, and now we're stuck in this weird space where I don't know what to do. But I need you, Em. I need you to help me navigate this."

Her gaze faltered for just a moment, and I seized the chance. "What if we take a step back? Just you and me, like we used to. We can talk about everything, figure out the messy parts together, but I can't do this without you."

"Talking isn't going to fix this," she said, her voice wavering, the fire in her eyes dimming slightly. "You both made choices that put me here. You want to fix it? Show me that you're not just going to run back to him as soon as I'm not looking."

"I won't," I insisted, feeling the heat of sincerity build in my chest. "You're not just a friend to me. You're my family, and I won't let anything come between us if I can help it."

"I don't want to be a consolation prize," she said, crossing her arms tightly across her chest, as if to shield herself from my words.

"You're making me feel like I should just be grateful to be part of the story again. But it's my story too, and I want to be the main character."

"Then let's make it our story," I replied, and as the words tumbled out, I felt a spark of hope. "We can rewrite this. I promise I'll be honest, and I'll make sure you're never sidelined again. We'll navigate this together."

Emily hesitated, her brow furrowing as she considered my words. "And what about Michael?"

The mention of his name was like ice water splashed across my face, chilling my resolve. "I care about him, but you're right. I've let it cloud my judgment, and that's not fair to either of you. I'll figure it out, I promise."

She sighed, the tension easing just a fraction, but the hurt still lingered like smoke in the air. "It's going to take time to trust again, you know. You can't just say the words and expect everything to be fine."

"I know," I admitted, the weight of her words heavy on my heart. "But I'll do whatever it takes to earn back that trust. Just give me a chance."

Emily studied me, her expression softening like the morning light breaking through the clouds. "Fine. But I want to be involved, every step of the way. I'm not just going to stand by and watch."

"Deal," I said, relief flooding through me. We may have been standing on shaky ground, but at least we were standing together. "Let's meet here tomorrow. I'll bring coffee and the truth. No secrets."

As we shared a tentative smile, the atmosphere shifted. The café around us resumed its rhythm, the laughter and chatter blending into a symphony of normalcy, and for the first time since this whirlwind had begun, I felt a flicker of hope. We had begun to untangle the threads of our shared story, and maybe—just maybe—we could weave something beautiful from the chaos.

The café's ambience hummed around us, but the air between Emily and me felt charged, an electric current that could either spark something new or set everything ablaze. As we settled back into our seats, the tension was palpable. I could feel the eyes of curious onlookers lingering, and I wished I could retreat into the shadows. Instead, I steeled myself, knowing that confronting the truth was the only way forward.

"Let's start fresh," I suggested, trying to infuse some lightness into the suffocating atmosphere. "What about a coffee and a plan? I'll order us something ridiculously sweet to mask the bitterness of this moment." I offered a smile that I hoped would break the ice, but Emily remained stony, arms still crossed.

"Fine, but don't think sugary drinks can cover up what's been happening," she replied, her lips twitching slightly. It was a hint of the playful banter we once shared, a glimmer that made my heart swell with hope.

"Okay, no sugar-coating it, I promise," I said, grateful for the slightest easing of her defenses. "I'll start by owning my mistakes. I've been an idiot, and I let myself get swept away in everything. I should have told you about Michael sooner."

Emily's eyes softened, if only marginally. "It's not just about him, you know. You've been keeping secrets too. I thought we were better than that."

"I thought so too," I admitted, feeling the heat rise to my cheeks. "But I let fear win. I didn't want to ruin what we had, and it seemed easier to bury my head in the sand."

"Easier until the sandstorm blows up, right?" she quipped, raising an eyebrow. "You're lucky I didn't bring a shovel."

I chuckled, grateful for her attempt at humor, even as the weight of our situation lingered. "Okay, so I deserve the shovel. I can see that now. But I'm here, and I'm ready to dig. Let's get to the bottom of this mess together."

Emily leaned back in her chair, considering my words, and for a moment, I felt a flicker of the camaraderie we once shared. "I want to believe you," she finally said, her voice softening. "But you need to know that I can't just jump back into this without some clarity."

"Agreed. Let's set some ground rules then," I proposed, feeling emboldened. "No secrets, no running. If something's bothering us, we talk about it. Deal?"

"Deal," she replied, nodding. "But that includes you and Michael too. No more hiding behind the 'it's complicated' excuse. I want to know what's really going on."

"Okay, but it's a bit messy. I care about him, but he's not... he's not you. I never wanted it to be a competition." The words spilled out, unfiltered, and the honesty tasted both refreshing and terrifying.

She looked thoughtful, her fingers tapping against the table. "So what does that mean for you? For us?"

"I don't know yet," I confessed. "I'm still trying to figure out what I want. But I know I can't lose you. You're the one who gets me, who knows all my quirks and still sticks around."

A soft smile broke across her face, the kind that brought warmth to the cold café air. "Okay, but if you're going to be honest, I need you to be all in. I don't want half-measures. I want the full package—messy, complicated, and all."

"Then let's make a pact. We'll both be all in," I proposed, my heart racing as the weight of my words settled around us. "We can figure this out as we go, together."

"Together," she echoed, and for a moment, the world outside faded away. I felt like we had carved out a small haven amidst the chaos, a fragile peace.

As we settled into a conversation about our favorite childhood memories, the tension slowly dissipated. I felt lighter, as if a great weight had been lifted from my shoulders. We laughed about the time she'd tried to bake cookies and nearly set her kitchen on fire, a moment that had solidified our friendship years ago. Her laughter rang out, bright and infectious, and I couldn't help but join in, grateful for the return of this familiar connection.

Yet, just as we were reaching a comfortable rhythm, my phone buzzed on the table, jolting me back to reality. The screen lit up with Michael's name, and a knot tightened in my stomach. "I need to take this," I said, the urgency of his message evident even before I answered.

"Yeah, go ahead," Emily said, her expression guarded. "I'll just sit here and be a third wheel while you two sort out your 'complicated' situation."

"Stop it. You know I don't want to keep you out of anything," I said, picking up the phone, but a flicker of worry crossed her face. I pressed answer, and the moment I heard Michael's voice, I felt the ground beneath me shift.

"Hey, where are you?" he asked, sounding breathless and panicked. "I need to talk to you—now."

"What's wrong?" I asked, concern creeping into my voice. "I'm with Emily. Can it wait?"

"No, it can't wait. It's about... everything. You need to come to the park. It's important," he urged, the gravity of his tone cutting through my resolve.

"Okay, just give me a minute." I hung up, my heart racing. The urgency in his voice sent alarm bells ringing in my head.

"Michael wants to meet me," I said, my voice barely above a whisper. "He said it's important."

Emily's expression darkened, a storm brewing behind her eyes. "Great. Just what we need—more complications."

"Wait, Em, it might be something serious. I need to find out what's going on," I explained, guilt flooding my chest.

"Right, because running back to him is exactly what I asked for," she retorted, her frustration palpable. "You said you'd be honest, but now it feels like you're just going to abandon our conversation. Is that how this works?"

"No! I don't want to abandon you," I insisted, desperation lacing my words. "But if he's in trouble, I can't ignore that."

"Fine," she said, standing abruptly. "Go then. But don't expect me to be waiting for you when you decide to return."

"Emily, please—"

"Just go!" she snapped, her voice echoing off the café walls as she turned away, arms crossed tightly against her body.

I hesitated, torn between the urgent pull of Michael's call and the delicate thread of connection I was trying to repair with Emily. "I'll be back. I promise."

But as I stepped out into the bustling street, the weight of uncertainty settled heavily on my shoulders. The café faded behind me, and the world outside felt impossibly vast and uncertain. I made my way toward the park, my mind racing with thoughts of what Michael might have to say, a mix of dread and curiosity swirling within me.

As I reached the park, the sun hung low in the sky, casting long shadows that stretched like fingers across the ground. I spotted Michael sitting on a bench, his face drawn and serious. The usual spark in his eyes was dimmed, replaced by a heaviness that sent a chill down my spine.

"What's going on?" I asked, trying to gauge his mood as I approached.

"I didn't know who else to turn to," he admitted, rubbing the back of his neck, a sign of stress that set my heart racing. "I've been digging into things I shouldn't have, and now... I think I've stirred up a lot more trouble than I bargained for."

"What do you mean?" I pressed, the unease swelling within me.

"Someone's watching us. Someone knows about you and me... and about Emily," he said, his voice dropping to a whisper, and the weight of his words settled like a stone in my gut.

Before I could respond, a movement caught my eye—a figure lurking behind a tree, watching us intently. My breath hitched as a wave of panic washed over me.

"Michael, we're not alone," I whispered, my heart racing as the figure stepped forward, revealing a familiar face—one I never expected to see again.

Chapter 27: The Choice

The air was thick with tension, a silence so heavy it pressed down on my shoulders, making each breath feel like a chore. I stood in the heart of the old library, surrounded by towering shelves brimming with dusty tomes, the faint scent of aged paper mingling with the lingering warmth of the afternoon sun that filtered through the tall, stained-glass windows. Each vibrant hue splashed against the oak floor, casting playful patterns like a broken kaleidoscope, yet inside me, everything felt achingly monochrome.

Michael's voice echoed in my head, a haunting melody of warmth and promise intertwined with the stinging notes of regret. Just hours ago, we had exchanged words that felt like a confession, raw and electric. The very air had crackled between us as he laid bare his dreams of a future, a future I had once envisioned alongside him. But that dream had turned treacherous, tinged with doubt and the shadow of Emily's fragile heart. A part of me craved the thrill of it—the midnight escapades, the stolen glances, the daring leap into the unknown. Yet, another part of me, the one that held Emily's laughter like a cherished secret, warned me that such desires might come at a cost too steep to pay.

I could almost feel the weight of Emily's trust pressing against my back, her unspoken words a tangible presence in the library. I thought of her: the way she tucked her hair behind her ear when she was nervous, the way her smile brightened even the dreariest days. The thought of betraying that trust made my stomach twist with a sense of betrayal sharper than any knife. How could I stand by and watch her heart break while I danced around my own desires? But the pull toward Michael was magnetic, an enticing gravity I struggled to resist. Each moment spent with him was a tangled web of laughter and longing, igniting a spark inside me that felt dangerously alive.

"Lily?" The voice was soft yet heavy with concern, jolting me from my reverie. I turned to see Jess, her brow furrowed in worry. She leaned against the doorframe, arms crossed, the sunlight behind her casting her in a golden halo. "You look like you've seen a ghost. Or worse, you're contemplating whether to adopt a family of ferrets."

I managed a weak smile, knowing all too well that my best friend could see through my carefully crafted façade. "Just... thinking." The admission felt weak, floundering like a fish out of water.

"Thinking about Michael, I assume?" she prompted, stepping further into the room. Her eyes sparkled with mischief, yet there was a seriousness to her tone, a silent plea for me to confide in her.

"Yeah." I sighed, running a hand through my hair. "It's just... everything feels so complicated right now. I don't know what to do." The words hung in the air between us, heavy with unexpressed emotions.

"Complicated? That's an understatement. Are you seriously considering going down that path with him?" Jess's voice held a note of incredulity, her arms dropping to her sides as she studied me intently.

I wanted to explain, to articulate the turmoil inside me, but it felt as if the words were stuck in my throat. "He's different with me, Jess. It's not like it was before." I could feel the truth of my statement reverberating within me. Michael had always been charming, the golden boy with an infectious smile, but there was something deeper that flickered between us—a shared understanding that had grown in the shadows, away from prying eyes.

Jess raised an eyebrow, skepticism dancing across her features. "And you think this new Michael is worth the risk of losing Emily? Because, let's be honest, if things go south, you're the one who'll end up hurt. And so will she."

I couldn't bear the thought of Emily's heart breaking, of her gaze filled with confusion and betrayal. "I know. But it's like he's pulled me into this whirlwind. I can't help but feel alive when I'm with him." I glanced down at the wooden floor, tracing the grain with my fingers, the conflicting emotions boiling beneath my skin.

"Alive? Or is it just adrenaline?" Jess countered, her voice softer now, as if she was stepping carefully through a minefield of my emotions. "You need to decide what matters more. A fleeting high or a solid friendship."

The choice loomed over me like a thundercloud, dark and oppressive. The library felt too small, the walls closing in as the realization crashed over me. I had to make a decision, and the stakes had never felt higher. If I chose Michael, would I be closing the door on something beautiful with Emily? But if I let Michael slip away, would I always wonder about the possibilities?

"Do you think I should just tell Emily everything?" The question slipped out before I could stop myself, a desperate grasp at clarity.

Jess bit her lip, her eyes thoughtful. "I think you should at least consider how it will affect her. She deserves to know the truth, but the timing matters too. You need to figure out what you truly want first. If you don't, it'll only lead to more heartache for everyone involved."

The suggestion hung in the air, a bittersweet truth. I wanted to scream, to run, to hide away from the mess I'd created. Instead, I took a deep breath, trying to steady the wild rhythm of my heart. The library, once a refuge, felt like a prison. I needed to break free, to explore the world beyond the confines of indecision and fear.

"Maybe I'll talk to her," I said, determination creeping into my voice. "Maybe it's time to face the music." Jess nodded, a flicker of approval lighting her features, but I knew the road ahead would be anything but simple. The layers of tension wrapped tightly around my heart, and I had a sinking feeling that this decision would change everything.

I stepped out of the library, the shadows lingering behind me like a hesitant ghost, clinging to my heart as I ventured into the crisp afternoon air. The world outside was alive with color—golden leaves pirouetted from the trees, a kaleidoscope of autumn hues, their crunch beneath my feet a bittersweet reminder of the inevitable changes looming in my life. The sun cast its warm embrace over the campus, yet inside, a chill of uncertainty wrapped around me tighter than any sweater could.

As I wandered toward the café, the familiar hum of laughter and chatter enveloped me, but it felt distant, as if I were watching life unfold through a glass wall. I needed to gather my thoughts, to clear the fog clouding my mind. It was a strange sensation, this disconnect. My friends were right there, yet I felt miles away, suspended in an emotional limbo that left me gasping for clarity.

"Hey, you! Earth to Lily!" Hailey's cheerful voice broke through my reverie, and I turned to see her bouncing toward me, arms waving with exaggerated enthusiasm. "What's with the daze? You look like you just time-traveled from a Victorian novel. Did you finally decide to embrace the tragic heroine vibe?"

I forced a smile, but the weight of my internal struggle was still heavy. "More like I'm caught in a plot twist that I didn't see coming. You know, the classic love triangle turned into a horror story."

Hailey tilted her head, mischief sparkling in her eyes. "Ooh, drama! Spill the tea. I need some juicy gossip to fuel my Instagram feed."

"Not so much gossip as a moral quandary." I sighed, sinking onto a bench outside the café, my shoulders slumping as if carrying the weight of the world. "It's about Michael and Emily. Things got... complicated."

"Complicated how? Did you two share a steamy kiss in the library, or did someone accidentally set fire to their love letters?" She leaned in closer, eager for details, her expression a mix of concern and playful curiosity.

"It's not that simple. It's more like a battle between what I want and what's right," I admitted, looking out at the students milling about, lost in their own worlds of carefree laughter and excitement. "I like Michael, but I can't shake the feeling that I'd be betraying Emily if I go for it. I can't help but feel torn between what my heart wants and what my loyalty demands."

Hailey's brow furrowed, her demeanor shifting from playful to earnest. "You care about her, and that's admirable. But you also deserve happiness. What's the point of sacrificing your own feelings for someone else? It sounds like a recipe for resentment."

"Maybe. But it's not just my happiness at stake. Emily's been through so much; I don't want to add to her pain." The thought of Emily's expression if she found out I was involved with Michael sent a fresh wave of dread crashing over me.

"Life is messy, Lily. Sometimes you have to be a little selfish to protect your own heart. It's not like you're plotting her downfall; you're just living your life." Her voice was gentle but firm, and I could see the sincerity in her gaze.

Before I could respond, the café door swung open, and Michael stepped outside, his presence illuminating the space with an effortless charm. He looked over, caught my eye, and a smile spread across his face, bright and genuine, igniting a spark of warmth in my chest. My heart stuttered, caught in the crossfire of conflicting emotions.

"There you are! I've been looking everywhere." He approached, his tone light yet laced with something deeper that sent my heart racing. "I thought I might find you daydreaming somewhere. Planning to leave the country and start a goat farm?"

DIANA LOCKHART

"Only if it comes with a villa and a side of 'no more love triangles,'" I replied, attempting to keep my tone light even as my insides twisted with unease.

Hailey discreetly backed away, leaving us alone, her eyes flickering with understanding. I could feel the air shift as Michael leaned against the bench, his proximity sending an exhilarating shiver up my spine. "So, what are you really thinking about? I can see the wheels turning in your head. Are you contemplating existentialism again, or is it something a little more personal?" His playful grin was infectious, yet my thoughts were tangled in a web of doubt.

"I was just—" I began, but the words felt inadequate. How could I explain the turmoil without sounding melodramatic? "You know, just thinking about choices. They can be really... complicated."

Michael's expression softened, his gaze searching mine. "Well, I'd say life is mostly about choices. Like choosing whether to face an unexpected challenge head-on or run screaming into the night. Which one are you leaning toward?"

I could almost hear the internal monologue screaming "run!" But I wasn't a coward. "Facing it, I suppose. But it's not that simple. There's more at stake than just me, Michael."

His brow knitted in concern, and I felt the gravity of the moment settle between us. "What do you mean? Is this about Emily?"

The moment hung in the air, fragile and loaded with tension. I hated myself for bringing her into our conversation, but it felt like a necessary burden. "Yeah, it is. I just can't help but feel like I'm stepping on her toes by even considering us. She's been through enough."

Michael shifted, his demeanor shifting from playful to serious, and I could see the frustration flicker in his eyes. "Lily, you can't just walk on eggshells forever. You deserve to explore what you feel without worrying about how it impacts everyone else. Emily is strong; she'll figure it out. But you? You deserve your own happiness."

The conviction in his voice sent a thrill through me, yet a part of me still clung to the chains of responsibility. "What if my happiness costs me her friendship? Can I live with that?"

"Can you live with pretending you don't care about me?" He challenged, his eyes burning with an intensity that made my heart race. The question hung there, electric and charged, as if it had the power to unravel everything I'd been so afraid to confront.

I opened my mouth to respond, but the words caught in my throat. Could I? The answer felt elusive, a ghost dancing just out of reach, teasing me with its possibilities while mocking my hesitation. I had a choice to make, and the moment felt ripe for change, but would I have the courage to take the leap?

The tension wrapped around me like an unwelcome shroud, each heartbeat echoing in the silence that stretched between Michael and me. His gaze held mine, a collision of uncertainty and desire that made my stomach flip. It was as if the universe had narrowed to this single moment, the bustling café and the chatter of our friends fading into a dull hum. I could sense the weight of our words hanging in the air, ready to tip the balance of everything I knew.

"What if I told you that I want to take that leap?" Michael broke the silence, his voice low and steady, yet laced with a hint of vulnerability that made my heart skip. "What if I want to figure this out with you, whatever it may be?"

The world outside continued its lively dance, but I felt frozen in place, the implications of his words crashing over me like an unexpected wave. The thought of pursuing something with him was intoxicating, but the idea of hurting Emily loomed like a dark cloud, ready to unleash a storm. "And what if it doesn't work?" I countered, my voice barely a whisper. "What if we're just setting ourselves up for failure?"

"Failure is part of life, right? It's not like we'd be the first to stumble." He shrugged, a grin breaking through the serious air that surrounded us. "I mean, look at every rom-com ever made. It's practically a requirement to have a dramatic misunderstanding before the grand love confession."

I couldn't help but chuckle, the tension easing just a fraction as a small smile tugged at my lips. "You're saying we should embrace our inner rom-com clichés? Because I'm pretty sure that leads to an epic public disaster or someone slipping on a banana peel."

"Hey, if it's good enough for Hollywood, it's good enough for us," he said, his tone teasing but his eyes earnest. "But seriously, Lily, I'm not here to push you into anything. I just want you to think about what you really want. Don't let fear dictate your choices."

His words struck a chord deep within me, resonating with the nagging doubts that had festered since my confrontation with Emily. The truth was, I had spent so long worrying about everyone else that I had almost forgotten what I wanted. What did I want? The answer was shrouded in fog, a distant light I struggled to see clearly.

"Maybe I'm just scared," I admitted, the honesty spilling out before I could rein it in. "Scared of ruining everything with Emily, scared of what might happen if I let myself feel something for you."

He stepped closer, the air between us charged with an undeniable energy. "You don't have to have everything figured out right now. But I'd like to be part of the journey, however messy it might be."

A part of me wanted to reach for that promise, to embrace the adventure of uncertainty, but another part of me screamed to hold back, to preserve the fragile connection I had with Emily. "It's complicated," I murmured, the weight of my words heavy.

Michael studied me for a moment, and I could see the wheels turning in his mind. "How about this? Why don't we take a step back for a second? Instead of focusing on where we're headed, let's just enjoy where we are right now."

"Right now?" I echoed, my mind racing at the implications.

"Yeah, just us. No pressure. We can grab some coffee, share a couple of laughs, and figure things out from there. No expectations." His eyes sparkled with mischief, the boyish charm that had initially drawn me in resurfacing.

A small smile crept onto my face, the thought of a carefree moment together tempting me like a warm blanket on a chilly day. "That sounds... nice," I replied cautiously, allowing myself to savor the idea without getting lost in the complexities of the future.

We walked toward the café counter, the familiar smell of freshly brewed coffee wrapping around us like an inviting embrace. Michael ordered for both of us, his easy banter with the barista filling the space with a warmth that felt comforting. I watched him, struck by how naturally he navigated the world, how at ease he seemed even in the midst of uncertainty.

"Two lattes, extra foam for the lady," he quipped as he turned back to me, a playful wink in his eye. "You have to live your best life, and that includes extra foam."

"Extra foam, huh? You really know the way to a girl's heart," I teased back, allowing myself to enjoy this light-hearted moment. But just as the warmth settled in, my phone buzzed insistently in my pocket, slicing through the bubble of our interaction like a cold gust of wind.

Pulling it out, I glanced at the screen. My heart sank as I read the message from Emily, the words stark and urgent. "Can we talk? I need to see you. It's important."

My stomach dropped as dread washed over me, a wave of anxiety tightening my chest. "It's Emily," I said, the lightness of the moment evaporating like morning mist. "She wants to talk."

Michael's expression shifted, concern creasing his brow. "What does she want?"

"I don't know, but it feels... serious," I replied, panic rising like a tide. "I can't ignore her. Not now." The reality of the situation hit me hard. My heart was caught between two worlds, and suddenly, it felt like I was on the brink of a storm.

"I get it," he said, his voice steady, though the tension in the air thickened. "Just remember, you don't have to face this alone."

With a nod, I slipped my phone back into my pocket, the weight of Michael's words swirling in my mind. I took a deep breath, grounding myself in the present as I stepped away from the café, the door swinging shut behind us with a finality that echoed in my heart.

As I made my way toward the designated meeting spot, my thoughts raced. What could Emily want to discuss? Did she sense something was off between us? The prospect of confronting the truth about my feelings made my palms sweaty, and I cursed the whirlwind of emotions threatening to unravel everything I had been trying to hold together.

I reached the corner of the park where we often met, the leaves rustling softly in the breeze, whispering secrets that felt just out of reach. Emily was already there, her back to me as she stared out at the pond, the surface glimmering like broken glass in the sunlight. She turned slightly as I approached, her expression unreadable, and my heart lurched at the sight of her furrowed brow.

"Lily," she began, her voice low, almost trembling. "We need to talk about Michael."

My breath caught in my throat, the air suddenly feeling too thick to swallow. I stood there, torn between the weight of her words and the thundering chaos of my heart, knowing that whatever came next would forever change the landscape of our friendship.

Chapter 28: The Heart's Resolution

The sun hung high in the cerulean sky, casting a warm glow over the bustling streets of Los Angeles, where palm trees swayed like sentinels guarding the vibrant chaos below. As I walked, the intoxicating aroma of street tacos wafted through the air, mingling with the sweet scent of blooming jasmine from nearby gardens. Each step echoed the rhythm of my racing heart, and the familiar sounds of honking horns, laughter, and distant music filled me with an exhilarating sense of possibility. Today felt different. Today felt like the first brushstroke of a new chapter, one I had longed for but had been too afraid to embrace.

I adjusted my sunglasses, their reflective lenses hiding the whirlpool of emotions swirling beneath the surface. The summer heat enveloped me like a warm blanket, a gentle reminder that life kept moving forward, even when my heart felt stuck in the past. As I strolled past cafés and boutiques, I spotted a couple sitting at a small table, their fingers entwined, laughter spilling from their lips like a melody. It struck me then—the effortless joy of love, the way it wrapped around you like a favorite song. I longed for that feeling, the kind of connection that sent shivers down your spine and left you breathless.

But love, as I had come to learn, was rarely simple. The shadows of my recent heartbreak loomed large, threatening to dim the brightness I had found in my renewed determination. Michael, with his dark curls and soulful brown eyes, haunted my thoughts like a ghost, a beautiful reminder of what I could lose if I didn't act. I needed to confront the swirling mess of feelings between us, to sift through the confusion that had clouded my heart since we had first crossed paths. As I navigated the streets, my mind replayed our last conversation—the hurt in his voice, the way he had pulled away as if I were a flame and he the moth, terrified of getting burned.

But today, I wasn't going to be the girl who backed down. Today, I was ready to fight. I ducked into a quaint coffee shop, its walls adorned with local art, each piece telling a story I yearned to unravel. The barista greeted me with a warm smile, and I ordered my usual: an iced caramel macchiato, sweet and rich, just like the hope blooming inside me. As I waited, I could almost hear the whispers of destiny encouraging me forward. It was time to seize my future, to embrace the chaos that came with love and the uncertainty of what lay ahead.

The bell above the door jingled, and in walked a familiar figure—Michael. My heart did an unexpected somersault, a mix of excitement and trepidation flooding my veins. He looked effortlessly handsome in a fitted navy shirt that accentuated his athletic build, his expression a mixture of surprise and something unreadable. Our eyes locked, and the air crackled with an intensity that pulled me closer, despite the space between us. For a moment, the world around us faded, and it felt as though we were the only two souls in existence.

"Fancy seeing you here," he said, a hint of a smirk playing on his lips, but there was a vulnerability in his gaze that cut straight through the bravado.

"Just grabbing some coffee," I replied, my voice steady despite the flurry of emotions dancing in my chest. "Thought I'd enjoy a little caffeine before tackling the day."

He raised an eyebrow, his amusement evident. "Tackling the day, huh? Sounds ambitious. What's on the agenda? World domination?"

I chuckled, the tension easing just a bit. "Something like that. I've decided it's time to take charge of my life, starting with the things that scare me."

"Scary things can be good," he said, stepping closer. "They push you out of your comfort zone."

The truth in his words resonated within me, a reminder of the countless times I had played it safe, unwilling to leap into the unknown. My heart pounded, and I took a deep breath, feeling the weight of our unspoken history hanging in the air like a fragile promise. I needed to be brave, to shed the layers of doubt and fear that had held me back for too long.

"Michael," I began, the name slipping from my lips like a prayer, "I know things have been... complicated between us." His expression shifted, the warmth of our banter replaced by a seriousness that sent a shiver down my spine. "But I don't want to keep pretending everything is fine. I miss you, and I don't want to lose what we have."

He hesitated, the vulnerability in his eyes making my heart ache. "I miss you too," he admitted, his voice barely above a whisper. "But I'm scared. Scared of what we could become and what could happen if it doesn't work out."

I stepped closer, narrowing the space between us. "Isn't that the point of taking risks? To embrace the messy, unpredictable journey?" I held his gaze, searching for the flicker of hope I desperately wanted to see. "I believe we're worth it. I believe we can figure it out together."

For a moment, the silence was deafening, a tension that pulled at the corners of our hearts. I could see the conflict warring within him, the battle between fear and desire. And just as I feared he might pull away again, he reached for my hand, his touch igniting a spark that surged through me.

"Okay," he said, the resolve in his voice soft but unwavering. "Let's figure it out. Together."

A surge of warmth washed over me, and suddenly the chaos of Los Angeles felt like the perfect backdrop for this moment—our moment. I smiled, the weight on my heart lifting just a little, knowing that whatever lay ahead, we were finally willing to face it together.

With Michael's hand in mine, a current of electricity flowed between us, invigorating my spirit. The world around us felt alive, pulsing with the vibrant energy of the city. We stood outside the café, the laughter and chatter of patrons creating a cozy backdrop for this pivotal moment in our lives. I looked up at him, and the corners of his mouth curled into that signature grin that made my heart flutter, a mixture of mischief and something deeper—a promise of understanding.

"Are we really doing this?" he asked, his voice a mix of disbelief and hope.

"Are we?" I countered, feeling the rush of adrenaline as I searched his eyes for reassurance. "I mean, you just held my hand. That's practically an engagement in coffee shop terms."

He laughed, a sound that sent a shiver of delight down my spine. "I'm pretty sure it's only a prelude to something more serious, like coffee for two. How about we take this further and grab some food?"

"Food sounds great," I agreed, feeling my stomach growl in enthusiastic support. "I could use some fuel for whatever this next chapter is going to be."

We wandered down the sun-kissed sidewalk, the golden rays warming our skin as we passed vibrant murals splashed across brick walls, telling stories of hope, love, and resilience. The lively atmosphere of Los Angeles embraced us like an old friend, and for the first time in what felt like ages, I allowed myself to be swept up in the thrill of the moment.

"Where's the best place to eat around here?" I asked, scanning the myriad of options. A taco stand caught my eye, its neon sign flickering enticingly.

"Ah, the taco truck. A classic," he declared, pointing to the bright blue food truck adorned with playful illustrations. "Best carne asada in the city. And a solid choice for a romantic outing, if I do say so myself."

I raised an eyebrow, playful skepticism creeping into my tone. "Romantic? Is that how you define a taco truck? I'd expect something more... extravagant, like a rooftop dinner with twinkling lights."

"Listen," he said, leaning in with a conspiratorial grin, "the magic of tacos cannot be overstated. They're like a culinary hug. Plus, who needs fancy when you have grease and good company?"

He had a point. We approached the truck, the sizzle of meat on the grill mingling with the inviting aroma that wafted through the air, awakening my senses. We ordered a feast of tacos, loaded with toppings and salsa that threatened to spill over, the perfect blend of flavors that reflected our tumultuous but deliciously exciting connection.

As we found a spot on a nearby bench, I took a moment to appreciate the way the sunlight danced through the trees, creating dappled patterns on the pavement. "So, what's the plan? Are we diving straight into the deep end of this emotional pool?" I asked, my curiosity piqued.

Michael chuckled, shaking his head as he took a bite of his taco. "You make it sound so dramatic. I was thinking more like a leisurely float. You know, dip our toes in first."

"A float, huh? That sounds nice," I replied, my heart racing at the thought. "But let's be real—our toes are already soaked. Maybe we should cannonball into the deep end and see what happens."

He swallowed his bite, a thoughtful expression crossing his face. "Cannonballing might just lead us to disaster."

"Disaster can be fun," I teased, nudging his shoulder playfully. "It's all about the thrill, isn't it? Plus, who doesn't love a good story?"

His eyes sparkled with intrigue, and a slow smile spread across his face. "All right, Miss Adventure-Seeker. Let's do this. But if we end up in the deep end and floundering, you're the one who has to save us both."

"Deal," I said, feeling the weight of our conversation shift from uncertainty to possibility. With each bite of our tacos, I could feel the barriers we had erected begin to crumble. We shared stories, laughter, and the unfiltered joy of just being in each other's company, the tension from before melting away like ice in the sun.

As our plates emptied, I felt the need to address the looming questions that had been swirling in my mind. "So, where do we go from here?" I asked, my tone serious yet hopeful. "Are we going to let the messiness of our lives define us, or can we carve out our own path?"

He paused, his expression thoughtful. "I think it's about learning to embrace the mess. Life is going to throw curveballs—trust me, I know a thing or two about that. But if we can navigate it together, we might just discover something beautiful."

"Beautiful," I echoed, savoring the word. It felt like a promise, one I wanted to hold onto tightly. "I like the sound of that."

But before he could respond, a commotion erupted nearby. A group of skateboarders zoomed past, their laughter ringing out like the music of youth, followed by a startled yelp. One of the skaters lost control, crashing spectacularly into a trash can, sending its contents tumbling to the ground in a cascade of half-eaten burritos and soda cans.

"See? Messy," I laughed, pointing at the chaos. "If that's not an omen, I don't know what is."

Michael chuckled, shaking his head. "Maybe it's a sign we should stick to tacos."

"Or that we need to be ready for anything." I smirked, watching as the skateboarders helped their friend up, the initial embarrassment quickly replaced by fits of laughter. "Sometimes, it's the unexpected moments that lead to the best stories."

"True," he agreed, his eyes bright with a spark of realization. "And it's also about how we respond to those moments. We can either crumble like that trash can or rise above it."

"Sounds like a life lesson in the making," I said, feeling a rush of warmth at how easily our conversation flowed, intertwining our thoughts and dreams. "So, are you ready to rise above?"

He leaned closer, our knees brushing against each other. "I'm ready to face whatever life throws at us. With you."

My heart soared at his words, an unexpected wave of optimism washing over me. The warmth of the sun on my skin felt like the universe giving us its blessing, urging us forward into uncharted territory. I reached for his hand again, and this time, the gesture felt like a promise—one that would anchor us amid the chaos, grounding us in the bond we were beginning to forge anew.

As we sat on that bench, sharing laughter and tacos, the world felt like it had conspired in our favor, a colorful backdrop to our unfolding story. The initial butterflies of uncertainty began to settle, replaced by a warm familiarity that enveloped us. Michael was talking about a band he loved, his voice animated and infectious. "They have this one song that's basically a soundtrack for falling in love in the middle of a taco truck frenzy," he quipped, his eyes sparkling with mischief. "You know, the kind of song that makes you want to dance like no one's watching, preferably in front of a food truck."

I chuckled, leaning back against the bench, savoring the moment. "Dancing in front of a food truck sounds like a solid plan. We'd definitely be the talk of the block."

"Talk of the block?" He raised an eyebrow, a teasing smirk playing at the corners of his mouth. "You're aiming for celebrity status in taco-town, I see. Just promise me you won't let the fame go to your head."

"Oh, absolutely," I replied, feigning seriousness. "Just a little taco truck royalty, that's all I aspire to. Nothing too extravagant."

The banter flowed effortlessly, a lifeline pulling us closer, and with each shared story, I felt the pieces of us falling back into place.

But beneath the surface, a thread of tension lingered, a whisper of doubt that reminded me our road wasn't paved with sunshine alone.

Suddenly, Michael's expression shifted, his brows knitting together as if he were wrestling with a thought too big for his mouth. "You know," he said slowly, "as great as this is, I can't shake the feeling that we're ignoring the elephant in the room."

I swallowed hard, the laughter fading as the weight of his words settled in. "Right, the elephant. The unresolved... stuff."

"Exactly. I think we both know that just because we're having tacos doesn't mean we've magically solved our issues."

"Touché." I took a sip of my drink, searching for the right words. "But I don't want to dive into the heavy stuff just yet. Can't we bask in this moment a little longer? It's nice to just enjoy being together."

Michael nodded, but I could see the flicker of concern behind his eyes. "I get that. But I don't want to lose you again to the shadows of our past. We need to confront it. I need to know if you're truly in this, or if it's just the tacos talking."

"Okay, Mr. Philosophical," I teased, trying to lighten the mood. "How about this: we finish our tacos and then we tackle the elephant. It'll make for a better story anyway, right?"

He chuckled, clearly relieved that I was willing to dance around the subject instead of shying away completely. "Fine, but I'm holding you to that. Once these tacos are gone, we'll have to get real."

With that agreement hanging in the air, we returned to our meal, the tension easing again as we exchanged bites of food and silly stories. I watched him laugh, his head thrown back, and my heart swelled. How could someone so seemingly carefree carry the weight of a complicated relationship like ours?

After we polished off the last of the tacos, I leaned back, satisfied but aware that the moment of truth was looming. Michael glanced at me, a serious look now resting on his features. "Okay, here we go. What are we?"

The question hung in the air, heavy with expectation. "Well, that's a loaded question," I replied, fighting the urge to deflect. "We're definitely more than just friends, but calling us soulmates might be jumping the gun a bit."

"Agreed." He leaned closer, his voice dropping to a hushed tone. "But I want to know if you're willing to give this a real shot, to see where it goes. Because I'm all in, if you are."

My heart raced as his words settled in, warmth blooming in my chest. "I'm willing to try," I said, my voice steady but soft. "But we have to be honest about our fears and uncertainties. No more running away."

"Deal," he said, his expression earnest. "But there's something else you need to know about me—something I've kept hidden. And it's not easy to talk about."

"Michael," I urged, concern creeping into my tone. "What is it?"

He hesitated, running a hand through his curls, a nervous habit I'd come to recognize. "It's about my past... there's a reason I've kept my distance. It's complicated."

Before he could elaborate, a sudden commotion erupted from the nearby sidewalk, drawing our attention. A crowd had gathered, and I could hear snippets of conversation laced with excitement and disbelief. "Did you see that?" someone exclaimed. "They're right over there!"

Curiosity piqued, I glanced at Michael. "What's happening?"

"Let's go check it out," he suggested, standing up and extending his hand to pull me along.

We weaved through the throng, my heart racing for a different reason now. As we neared the crowd, I caught sight of a dazzling spectacle—street performers showcasing a breathtaking display of acrobatics and dance. Colorful banners waved in the breeze, and the air was electric with the sound of drums and laughter. But amidst the artistry, something unusual caught my eye.

At the center of the performance, a girl in a flowing red dress seemed to glow, her movements almost ethereal. She twirled, and with each spin, the crowd erupted in cheers, but my gaze remained fixed on the strange energy surrounding her. It felt familiar, almost magnetic, as if I were being drawn into something far beyond the realm of mere entertainment.

"What is going on here?" I murmured, feeling a shiver run down my spine.

"I don't know, but it's mesmerizing," Michael replied, his eyes wide with intrigue. "Look at the way she moves."

Just then, the girl locked eyes with me, her expression shifting from joyful to intense, as if she recognized me from somewhere—somewhere I couldn't place. My heart skipped a beat, and I felt an overwhelming urge to reach out, to understand what was happening.

And then, without warning, the performance took an unexpected turn. The girl's graceful movements transformed into something more erratic, the energy around her shifting dramatically. The crowd gasped as a sudden gust of wind swept through, the world around us seeming to warp and twist.

"Do you feel that?" Michael asked, his voice laced with uncertainty.

"Yeah," I replied, my pulse quickening. "Something's not right."

Just as the tension reached its peak, the girl pointed directly at me, her eyes burning with urgency. "You have to leave!" she shouted, her voice cutting through the chaos. "It's not safe!"

Before I could react, the ground beneath us trembled, and the air crackled with an energy that sent my heart racing. The vibrant world around us began to blur, and the crowd erupted into chaos, panic washing over everyone.

"Run!" Michael shouted, grabbing my hand and pulling me away from the fray as the street began to warp, the reality around us twisting into something unrecognizable.

The adrenaline surged through me as I followed him, my mind racing with questions. What was happening? What had I just witnessed? And why did that girl feel so familiar?

We dashed through the crowd, but even as we fled, I could feel the pull of whatever chaos had just erupted behind us, like a tide threatening to drag me back into its depths. I glanced over my shoulder one last time, the girl still staring at me, her expression a mix of fear and determination.

And then, just like that, everything went dark.

Chapter 29: Collision Course

The cool night air wrapped around me like a whispered promise as I stepped onto the rooftop of Michael's estate. It felt like entering a sanctuary suspended above the chaos of Los Angeles. The city sprawled below, an ocean of lights flickering against the dark velvet sky, each one a heartbeat in a rhythm I could almost dance to. Yet, the excitement coursing through me was tangled with an underlying tension, a current that surged and crackled every time I caught a glimpse of Michael's silhouette against the skyline.

He stood near the edge, gazing out over the glittering expanse, his profile etched sharply against the backdrop of twinkling stars. I paused, allowing myself a moment to drink him in—the way his hair caught the wind, tousling gently, the way his broad shoulders seemed to bear the weight of the world but still carried an undeniable grace. There was a warmth to him that drew me closer, and as I stepped forward, the soft click of my heels broke the spell of silence between us.

"Beautiful night, isn't it?" I ventured, my voice barely more than a breath against the cool air.

He turned to me, a smile breaking across his face that felt like sunshine slicing through a heavy fog. "You have no idea. I've been waiting for you."

His words sent a shiver down my spine, a mixture of thrill and apprehension. There was something electric in the air, a charge that seemed to pulse between us, as palpable as the distant hum of traffic below. We had both danced around our feelings for too long, avoiding the deeper conversations like two wary dancers sidestepping each other in a crowded room.

"I hope it was worth the wait," I said, a teasing lilt in my voice that belied my own nerves.

Michael took a step closer, his gaze intensifying, and in that moment, I felt the world fade away—the city lights dimmed, the distant sounds of nightlife vanished, and all that existed was the space between us, charged with unspoken words. "It is," he murmured, his voice low and earnest. "I've thought a lot about us... about everything."

"I have too." My heart raced, pounding a desperate rhythm against my ribcage as if it wanted to escape. "We need to talk about what happened, about us."

The playful banter evaporated, replaced by a seriousness that hung heavy in the air. Michael's expression shifted, shadows flickering across his features as he stepped back, the distance suddenly feeling like an abyss. "There's something you need to know," he said, his voice trembling slightly, as if he were wrestling with the weight of his own confession.

My breath caught in my throat. "What is it?" I asked, heart in my throat, a premonition swirling around me like fog.

He looked out over the city again, the lights reflecting in his eyes, creating a kaleidoscope of emotions—fear, regret, and something else that I couldn't quite place. "It's about my family," he began, each word hesitant, like a tightrope walker taking cautious steps. "There's a reason I've kept you at arm's length. A reason I thought it was best to keep my past hidden."

I felt a pang of panic rise within me, a heavy stone settling in my stomach. "Michael, what are you talking about?"

He turned to face me, the light from the city casting a glow around him that made him appear almost ethereal, like he was caught between two worlds. "I come from a long line of people who... who have made mistakes. Serious mistakes. My father—he was involved in things that I'm not proud of. Dangerous things. And it's affected everything about my life."

A chill raced down my spine as I processed his words. "What do you mean? What kind of things?"

He hesitated, running a hand through his hair, a gesture of frustration and turmoil. "I can't go into all the details, but let's just say my family has a reputation. It's why I moved here, why I tried to distance myself. I wanted to escape it, but I can't run from who I am."

The implications of his confession weighed heavily in the air. My mind raced, trying to piece together the fragments of his past and how they intertwined with our present. "And you thought keeping this from me was the best option?" I asked, my voice barely above a whisper, a mixture of hurt and anger boiling beneath the surface.

"I thought I was protecting you," he replied, stepping forward again, his eyes earnest. "But the more I've gotten to know you, the more I realize how foolish that was. You deserve the truth, even if it means losing you."

The air around us felt thick with unspoken fears, and I could see the conflict raging within him. My heart ached, torn between the desire to understand and the instinct to protect myself from whatever shadows lurked in his past. "So, what does this mean for us?" I asked, each word heavy with implication.

"It means that I'm scared," he admitted, the vulnerability in his voice disarming. "Scared that I'll drag you into a life you never wanted. Scared that if you see who I truly am, you'll run the other way."

The raw honesty in his words hung between us, a fragile thread woven through our shared fears. I felt a wave of sympathy wash over me, realizing the burden he carried, the isolation that came with living in the shadows of his family's legacy. "You're not defined by your past, Michael. You're your own person."

He shook his head, a bittersweet smile on his lips. "Maybe, but that past is still a part of me. I can't just pretend it doesn't exist."

My heart thudded painfully against my ribs as I stepped closer, the urge to bridge the gap between us overwhelming. "We can face it together, whatever it is. But you have to trust me enough to let me in."

His gaze softened, and for a moment, I thought I saw the flicker of hope igniting in his eyes. But before he could respond, the night sky crackled with an unexpected sound—a distant thunderclap that rolled across the horizon, echoing the turmoil within me. A storm was coming, both in the skies and in our hearts.

The thunder rumbled again, louder this time, as if the heavens were echoing the chaos swirling between us. I took a step back, suddenly aware of the weight of the moment. The city below sparkled with a false calm, an unknowing witness to the tempest brewing above us. I needed to make sense of what Michael had just shared—his family's shadowy past, the mistakes that still clung to him like a heavy fog.

"Michael, I understand that your past is complicated," I said, my voice steady but laced with urgency. "But it's not a death sentence. You're not trapped in it."

He ran a hand through his hair, the moonlight catching the dark strands. "It's not that simple. You don't know what I've had to do to keep it from affecting my life. Or yours."

"And what exactly does that mean? What have you done?" I pressed, feeling the tension stretch taut like a wire about to snap.

"I've made choices—bad ones. People got hurt. I thought I could outrun it, but it's all caught up with me." His eyes bore into mine, filled with a blend of regret and fear that twisted my heart. "I don't want you to pay for my mistakes."

"I'm not afraid of your past, Michael. I'm afraid of losing you to it." The weight of those words hung in the air, thick and suffocating.

Just then, a sudden gust of wind swept across the rooftop, sending a chill racing down my spine. It felt like nature's way of reminding us that everything we were discussing was larger than us—unruly and uncontrollable. I wrapped my arms around myself, feeling exposed beneath the harsh glow of the city lights.

"Can we at least try to figure this out together?" I offered, my voice breaking slightly. "You don't have to face it alone."

He stepped closer, his eyes softening with what I hoped was the flicker of understanding. "I want to believe that. I really do. But if I can't get a grip on my own life, how can I expect to pull you into it?"

"I'm already in it, whether you like it or not," I replied, a playful smirk breaking through my concern. "I've spent the last few months trying to get through your emotional barricade. I'm not going anywhere."

For a moment, I thought I saw the corner of his mouth twitch upwards, a spark of amusement breaking through his turmoil. But then the moment passed, and he looked away, as if the weight of his family's legacy was once again pulling him into the depths of despair.

"I should have told you sooner," he admitted, the fight draining from his posture. "But the truth is, I've spent so long trying to be someone else, I forgot who I really am. And now... I'm scared you'll see me as that person."

"Maybe it's time to stop pretending," I suggested gently. "You're not your family's mistakes, Michael. You're a good person. You've helped me through so much. You deserve to be happy, and so do I."

"Happy?" He scoffed lightly, the sound both bitter and wistful. "I don't even know what that looks like for me anymore."

"Well, it's definitely not standing on a rooftop having an existential crisis," I teased, trying to lighten the mood. "Maybe it involves some tacos and a movie marathon. You know, the essentials."

He chuckled softly, the sound like a sweet balm to my nerves. "You think tacos can cure all problems?"

"Absolutely. They're like tiny edible hugs. And who doesn't need a hug right now?" I stepped closer, trying to bridge the emotional chasm that had formed between us.

His gaze lingered on me, and for a fleeting moment, I thought I saw a glimmer of hope in his eyes. But just as quickly, that flicker vanished, replaced by an expression of deep contemplation. "I wish it were that simple."

The silence that followed was heavy, thickening the air until it felt almost suffocating. Just when I thought I could finally break through his walls, I realized they were reinforced by fear—fear of what I might think, fear of bringing me into a world he believed to be tainted.

"I can't keep doing this," I finally said, my frustration bubbling to the surface. "You're overthinking everything. You think your past is a shackle, but it's just part of your story. You don't have to carry it like a burden."

His brow furrowed, and the tension in his jaw tightened. "You don't know what I've faced, the people I've had to deal with. It's not just a bad family reputation; it's more like a spider's web, and I'm stuck in it."

The image was striking, the very essence of what he was describing woven into a reality I could barely grasp. "Then let's break the web together," I urged. "What if we face it head-on? You don't have to hide from me. I'm already tangled in this with you."

For a moment, his defenses wavered. I could see the internal battle raging behind his eyes—a struggle between the man he wanted to be and the ghost of his past that loomed like a specter. But just as I thought he might yield, the clouds overhead rolled ominously, the thunder rumbling again, a warning of the storm approaching.

"We're standing in the middle of a storm, and I can't let you get caught in it," he said, his voice low and urgent.

"But I want to be here," I insisted, taking a bold step forward, my resolve hardening like steel. "If this is what it takes to keep you from spiraling back into that darkness, then let's confront it together. I refuse to let you push me away."

As I spoke, the city lights flickered, a myriad of colors reflecting the chaotic emotions swirling within me. The tension felt almost electric, pulsating with a desperate need for connection. I searched his eyes, hoping to find a flicker of agreement, a hint that he was willing to let me in.

And just like that, a fierce determination took hold of him. "Okay," he breathed, his voice barely above a whisper. "Let's do this. But I need you to promise me something."

"Anything," I replied, my heart racing in anticipation.

"Promise me you'll run if it gets too dangerous. I don't want you to get hurt because of my past."

A smile spread across my face, fueled by the adrenaline of our connection and the promise of what was to come. "Only if you promise to chase after me."

For the first time that night, the tension shifted, the air around us humming with possibilities. The storm might have been closing in, but together, we could face whatever came our way.

The moment hung between us, suspended like a thread ready to snap. I could see the resolve in Michael's eyes shifting, battling against the tides of uncertainty and the weight of his family's past. The city lights glimmered beneath us, a beautiful distraction from the storm brewing within our hearts.

"Okay, so we're going to confront your past," I said, injecting a hint of playful bravado into my tone. "But just so you know, I'm only doing this if we can make it a group project. I've always been better at surviving chaos with a partner."

Michael's lips curled into a reluctant smile, the tension in his shoulders easing just slightly. "Great, because I wasn't looking forward to this little adventure alone."

"Adventure?" I echoed, raising an eyebrow. "I was thinking more along the lines of emotional excavation. But I guess it could have its thrills."

"Just promise me we won't end up in handcuffs," he quipped, his eyes sparkling with mischief for the first time that night.

"Only if they're the fuzzy kind," I shot back, laughing despite the seriousness of the moment. But as our laughter echoed against the vast backdrop of the city, I felt a shift in the atmosphere. It was as if the very air had thickened, coiling around us with unspoken warnings.

"I need to tell you about my father," Michael said, his tone sobering as he shifted back into the weight of reality. "He's not just a distant memory. He's involved with people who don't just have a bad reputation—they're dangerous."

I nodded, my heart racing. "You mentioned he was involved in things. What does that mean? Are we talking about bad investments or something darker?"

"Darker," he confirmed, his voice low. "He's mixed up with a crime syndicate. They've done things—horrible things. And I've spent my whole life trying to distance myself from it, trying to prove I'm not him. But they don't just let go of family ties."

A chill raced through me, tightening my chest. "So, are they after you? Is that why you've been so secretive?"

"Maybe not after me specifically, but I've seen what happens to people who cross them. I can't let that happen to you," he replied, his expression turning grave. "It's not just my life on the line anymore."

The weight of his words settled heavily in the air between us, and I felt a surge of fierce determination. "You're not going to lose me. I can handle this, whatever it is. But you have to let me in. You can't push me away when things get tough."

Just then, the wind picked up, swirling around us, a mischievous breeze that teased the edges of our resolve. It howled like a distant siren, adding an eerie note to our heart-to-heart.

"What if they come after us?" he asked, his brow furrowed with genuine concern. "What if they target you to get to me? I can't let that happen."

"Then we'll fight back together," I said, my voice steady. "This isn't a fairy tale; it's our reality. If they want a fight, we'll give them one. But I refuse to stand on the sidelines."

Michael took a deep breath, the storm clouds gathering overhead reflecting the tempest of emotions within him. "You're either the bravest person I've ever met or the most reckless," he murmured, admiration and anxiety mingling in his voice.

"Probably a bit of both," I replied, a playful grin breaking through the tension. "But if we're doing this, we might as well embrace the chaos. And who knows? Maybe we'll find a way to turn it into a romantic comedy."

Before he could respond, the first drops of rain began to fall, tentative at first, like nature testing its limits. They splattered on the rooftop, creating a rhythmic patter that matched the frantic beating of my heart.

"Great," Michael said, rolling his eyes in mock exasperation. "Just what we need—a dramatic rain scene. Should we start quoting Shakespeare?"

"Only if you promise not to make me recite 'The Merchant of Venice.' That one's a slog," I joked, stepping closer as the rain began to fall more heavily, soaking us in an instant.

"Fine, but if I start quoting it, you have to join in. It's part of the deal," he shot back, laughter dancing in his eyes even as the rain drenched us.

Suddenly, the laughter faded, replaced by an unsettling quiet as a shadow fell across the rooftop. My heart lurched as I turned to see a figure emerging from the stairwell, a menacing presence silhouetted against the city lights.

"Michael," the figure called, a voice smooth yet laced with menace. "I see you've been busy."

I felt Michael tense beside me, the playful banter evaporating as if it had never existed. The figure stepped closer, revealing a man dressed in dark clothing, his features obscured by the shadows but his intent unmistakable.

"Who are you?" I demanded, instinctively moving closer to Michael, seeking his strength even as uncertainty gripped me.

"Just someone looking to have a conversation," the man replied, his eyes glinting in the rain-soaked darkness. "You've been stirring up trouble, Michael. And trouble has a way of finding you."

"Get lost," Michael snapped, the protective instinct surging within him. "You have no business here."

The stranger laughed, a sound devoid of warmth, echoing off the rooftop. "Ah, but I think we have a lot to discuss. Especially about your little friend here."

I swallowed hard, the threat lacing his words sending chills racing down my spine.

"Let's just say I'm here to remind you that running doesn't always work," the man continued, stepping closer. "Your father's choices have consequences, and they tend to spill over, don't they?"

Michael shifted protectively in front of me, his jaw clenched tight. "You don't know what you're talking about."

"Oh, but I do," the man replied, his smirk chilling. "And soon, you'll understand just how small your world really is."

The air crackled with tension, the rain falling in torrents around us, the storm growing more ferocious by the second. I glanced up at Michael, searching for reassurance, but found only a deep-rooted fear reflected in his eyes.

"Let's go," he said suddenly, grabbing my hand and pulling me toward the stairwell. "We can't stay here."

But as we turned to run, the man laughed again, a sound that sent shivers racing down my spine. "You think you can escape? I'll find you, wherever you go. The past always catches up, Michael. Always."

We dashed for the door, the sound of the man's laughter trailing behind us like a dark omen. The storm raged above, and as we descended into the shadows, I felt the weight of his words pressing down on me.

With every step, I sensed the walls closing in, the truth of Michael's past looming ever larger. And as we plunged into the darkness below, I knew this was only the beginning of a fight that would test our bond and our very will to survive.

Milton Keynes UK
Ingram Content Group UK Ltd.
UKHW041821201024
449814UK00001B/41

9 798227 072009